Praise for Dead Sleep

'Greg Iles is a phenomenal writer'
Independent on Sunday

'A potent thriller'
New York Times Book Review

'A stunning opening to a complex thriller.
Bottom line: Cancel Bedtime'
People Magazine

'Another top notch tale of suspense'
Kirkus Reviews

'Gripping, suspenseful, exciting . . .
a complex, fast-paced story'
Library Journal

'Atmospheric, sexy and provocative'
Booklist

Also by Greg Iles

Turning Angel

Blood Memory

Dark Matter / The Footprints of God

Sleep No More

24 Hours

The Quiet Game

Mortal Fear

Black Cross

Spandau Phoenix

About the Author

Greg Iles lives with his family in Natchez, Mississippi. He is the bestselling author of ten internationally acclaimed thrillers, including *Blood Memory* and *Turning Angel*, which were both *New York Times* bestsellers, and *24 Hours* (released by Sony Pictures as *Trapped*).

GREG ILES

Dead Sleep

HODDER

First published in Great Britain in 2001 by Hodder & Stoughton
A division of Hodder Headline

A Hodder paperback

12

A CIP catalogue record for this title is
available from the British Library

ISBN 978-0-340-77008-5
ISBN 0-340-77008-2

Typeset in Plantin Light by Palimpsest Book Production Limited,
Grangemouth, Stirlingshire

Printed and bound by Clays Ltd, St Ives plc

Hodder Headline's policy is to use papers that are natural, renewable
and recyclable products and made from wood grown in sustainable forests.
The logging and manufacturing processes are expected to conform
to the environmental regulations of the country of origin.

Hodder & Stoughton Ltd
A division of Hodder Headline
338 Euston Road
London NW1 3BH

In memory of
Silous Marty Kemp

ACKNOWLEDGMENTS

Thanks to Aaron Priest, Phyllis Grann, David Highfill, and Louise Burke.

Special thanks to Special Agent-in-Charge Charles Matthews, FBI, New Orleans District; Special Agent Sheila Thorne; Special Agent Bob Tucker; Ernie Porter, FBI, Washington, D.C.

Medical expertise: Jerry Iles, M.D.; Donald Barraza, M.D., Michael Bourland, M.D.; and Noah Archer, M.D.

Partners in crime: Ed Stackler, Courtney Aldridge, Michael Henry.

Miscellaneous: Geoff Iles, Carrie Iles, Madeline Iles, Mark Iles, Betty Iles, Rich Hasselberger, Caroline Trefler, Jim Easterling, Fraser Smith, Christie Iles, Kim Barker.

Many thanks to all the reps from Penguin Putnam who have worked so hard from the beginning.

To anyone omitted through oversight, my sincere apologies. All mistakes are mine.

I

I stopped shooting people six months ago, just after I won the Pulitzer Prize. People were always my gift, but they were wearing me down long before I won the prize. Still, I kept shooting them, in some blind quest that I didn't even know I was on. It's hard to admit that, but the Pulitzer was a different milestone for me than it is for most photographers. You see, my father won it twice. The first time in 1966, for a series in McComb, Mississippi. The second in 1972, for a shot on the Cambodian border. He never really got that one. The prizewinning film was pulled from his camera by American marines on the wrong side of the Mekong River. The camera was all they found. Twenty frames of Tri-X made the sequence of events clear. Shooting his motor-drive Nikon F2 at five frames per second, my dad recorded the brutal execution of a female prisoner by a Khmer Rouge soldier, then captured the face of her executioner as the pistol was turned toward the brave but foolish man pointing the camera at him. I was twelve years old and ten thousand miles away, but that bullet struck me in the heart.

Jonathan Glass was a legend long before that day, but fame is no comfort to a lonely child. I didn't see my father nearly enough when I was young, so following in his footsteps has been one way for me to get to know him. I still carry his battle-scarred Nikon in my bag. It's a dinosaur by today's standards, but I won my Pulitzer with it. He'd probably joke about the sentimentality of my using his old camera, but I know what he'd say about my winning the prize: *Not bad, for a girl.*

And then he'd hug me. God, I miss that hug. Like the embrace of a great bear, it swallowed me completely, sheltered me from the world. I haven't felt those arms in twenty-eight years, but they're as familiar as the smell of the sweet olive tree he planted outside my window when I turned eight. I didn't think a tree was much of a birthday present back then, but later, after he was gone, that hypnotic fragrance drifting through my open window at night was like his spirit watching over me. It's been a long time since I slept under that window.

For most photographers, winning the Pulitzer is a triumph of validation, a momentous beginning, the point at which your telephone starts ringing with the job offers of your dreams. For me it was a stopping point. I'd already won the Capa Award twice, which is the one that matters to people who know. In 1936, Robert Capa shot the immortal photo of a Spanish soldier at the instant a fatal bullet struck him, and his name is synonymous with bravery under fire. Capa befriended my father as a young man in Europe, shortly after Capa and Cartier-Bresson and two friends founded Magnum Photos. Three years later, in 1954, Capa stepped on a land mine in what was then called French Indochina, and set a tragic precedent that my father, Sean Flynn (Errol's reckless son), and about thirty other American photographers would follow in one way or another during the three decades of conflict known to the American public as the Vietnam War. But the public doesn't know or care about the Capa Award. It's the Pulitzer they know, and that's what makes the winners marketable.

After I won, new assignments poured in. I declined them all. I was thirty-nine years old, unmarried (though not without offers), and I'd passed the mental state known as "burned out" five years before I put that Pulitzer on my shelf. The reason was simple. My job, reduced to its essentials, has been to chronicle death's grisly passage through the world. Death can be natural, but I see it most often as a manifestation of evil. And like other professionals who see this face of death – cops, soldiers, doctors, priests – war photographers age more rapidly than normal people. The extra years don't always show, but you feel them in the deep places, in the marrow and the heart. They weigh you down in ways that few outside our small fraternity can understand. I say fraternity, because few women do this job. It's not hard to guess why. As Dickey Chappelle, a woman who photographed combat from World War II to Vietnam, once said: *This is no place for the feminine.*

And yet it was none of this that finally made me stop. You can walk through a corpse-littered battlefield and come upon an orphaned infant lying atop its dead mother and not feel a fraction of what you will when you lose someone you love. Death has punctuated my life with almost unbearable loss, and I hate it. Death is my mortal enemy. Hubris, perhaps, but I come by that honestly. When my father turned his camera on that murderous Khmer Rouge soldier, he must have known his life was forfeit. He shot the picture anyway. He didn't make it out of Cambodia, but his picture did, and it went a long way toward changing the mind of America about that war. All my life I lived by that example, by my father's unwritten code. So no one was more shocked than I that, when death crashed into my family yet again, the encounter shattered me.

I limped through seven months of work, had one spasm of creativity that won me the Pulitzer, then collapsed in an airport. I was hospitalized for six days. The doctors called it post-traumatic stress disorder. I asked them if they expected to be paid for that diagnosis. My closest friends – and even my agent – told me point-blank that I had to stop working for a while. I agreed. The problem was, I didn't know how. Put me on a beach in Tahiti, and I am framing shots in my mind, probing the eyes of waiters or passersby, looking for the life behind life. Sometimes I think I've actually become a camera, an instrument for recording reality, that the exquisite machines I carry when I work are but extensions of my mind and eye. For me there is no vacation. If my eyes are open, I'm working.

Thankfully, a solution presented itself. Several New York editors had been after me for years to do a book. They all wanted the same one: my war photographs. Backed into a corner by my breakdown, I made a devil's bargain. In exchange for letting an editor at Viking do an anthology of my war work, I accepted a double advance: one for that book, and one for the book of my dreams. The book of my dreams has no people in it. No faces, anyway. Not one pair of stunned or haunted eyes. Its working title is "Weather."

"Weather" was what took me to Hong Kong this week. I was there a few months ago to shoot the monsoon as it rolled over one of the most tightly packed cities in the world. I shot Victoria Harbor from the Peak and the Peak from Central, marveling at the different ways rich and poor endured rains so heavy and unrelenting that they've driven many a roundeye to drunkenness or worse. This time Hong Kong was only a way station to China proper, though I scheduled two days there to round out my portfolio on the city. But on the second day, my entire book project imploded. I had no warning, not one prescient moment. That's the way the big things happen in your life.

A friend from Reuters had convinced me that I had to

visit the Hong Kong Museum of Art, to see some Chinese watercolors. He said the ancient Chinese painters had achieved an almost perfect purity in their images of nature. I know nothing about art, but I figured the paintings were worth a look, if only for some perspective. Boarding the venerable Star Ferry in the late afternoon, I crossed the harbor to the Kowloon side and made my way on foot to the museum. After twenty minutes inside, perspective was the last thing on my mind.

The guard at the entrance was the first signpost, but I misread him completely. As I walked through the door, his lips parted slightly, and the whites of his eyes grew in an expression not unlike lust. I still cause that reaction in men on occasion, but I should have paid more attention. In Hong Kong I am *kwailo,* a foreign devil, and my hair is not blond, the color so prized by Chinese men.

Next was the tiny Chinese matron who rented me a Walkman, headphones, and the English-language version of the museum's audio tour. She looked up smiling to hand me the equipment; then her teeth disappeared and her face lost two shades of color. I instinctively turned to see if some thug was standing behind me, but there was only me – all five-feet-eight of me – thin and reasonably muscular but not much of a threat. When I asked what was the matter, she shook her head and busied herself beneath her counter. I felt like someone had just walked over my grave. I shook it off, put on the Walkman, and headed for the exhibition rooms with a voice like Jeremy Irons's speaking sonorous yet precise English in my headphones.

My Reuters friend was right. The watercolors floored me. Some were almost a thousand years old, and hardly faded by the passage of time. The delicately brushed images some-how communicated the smallness of human beings without alienating them from their environment. The backgrounds weren't separated from the subjects, or perhaps there *was* no background; maybe that was the lesson. As I moved among them, the internal darkness that is my constant companion began to ease, the way it does when I listen to certain music. But the respite was brief. While studying one particular painting – a man poling along a river in a boat not unlike a Cajun pirogue – I noticed a Chinese woman standing to my left. Assuming she was trying to view the painting, I slid a step to my right.

She didn't move. In my peripheral vision, I saw that she was not a visitor but a uniformed cleaning woman with a feather dust mop. And it wasn't the painting she was staring at as though frozen in space, but me. When I turned to face her, she blinked twice, then scurried into the dark recesses of the adjoining room.

I moved on to the next watercolor, wondering why I should transfix her that way. I hadn't spent much time on hair or makeup, but after checking my reflection in a display case, I decided that nothing about my appearance justified a stare. I walked on to the next room, this one containing works from the nineteenth century, but before I could absorb anything about them, I found myself being stared at by another blue-uniformed museum guard. I felt strangely sure that I'd been pointed out to him by the guard from the main entrance. His eyes conveyed something between fascination and fear, and when he realized that I was returning his gaze, he retreated behind the arch.

Fifteen years ago, I took this sort of attention for granted. Furtive stares and strange approaches were standard fare in Eastern Europe and the old Soviet Union. But this was post-handover Hong Kong, the twenty-first century. Thoroughly unsettled, I hurried through the next few exhibition rooms with hardly a glance at the paintings. If I got lucky with a cab, I could get back to the ferry and over to Happy Valley for some sunset shots before my plane departed for Beijing. I turned down a short corridor lined with statuary, hoping to find a shortcut back to the entrance. What I found instead was an exhibition room filled with people.

Hesitating before the arched entrance, I wondered what had brought them there. The rest of the museum was virtually deserted. Were the paintings in this room that much better than the rest? Was there a social function going on? It didn't appear so. The visitors stood silent and apart from one another, studying the paintings with eerie intensity. Posted above the arch was a Lucite plaque with both Chinese pictographs and English letters. It read:

NUDE WOMEN IN REPOSE
Artist Unknown

When I looked back into the room, I realized it wasn't filled with "people" – it was filled with men. Why men only? I'd stayed a week in Hong Kong on my last visit, and I hadn't noticed a shortage of nudity, if that was what they were looking for. Every man in the room was Chinese, and every one wore a business suit. I had the impression that each had been compelled to jump up from his desk at work, run down to his car, and race over to the museum to look at these paintings. Reaching down to the Walkman on the waistband of my jeans, I fast-forwarded until I came to a description of the room before me.

"*Nude Women in Repose*," announced the voice in my headset. "*This provocative exhibit contains seven canvases by the unknown artist responsible for the group of paintings known popularly as the 'Sleeping Women' series. The Sleeping Women are a mystery in the world of modern art. Nineteen paintings are known to exist, all oil on canvas, the first coming onto the market in 1999. Over the course of the nineteen paintings, a progression from vague Impressionism to startling Realism occurs, with the most recent works almost photographic in their accuracy. Though all the paintings were originally believed to depict sleeping women in the nude, this theory is now in question. The early paintings are so abstract that the question cannot be settled with certainty, but it is the later canvases that have created a sensation among Asian collectors, who believe the paintings depict women not in sleep but in death. For this reason, the curator has titled the exhibit 'Nude Women in Repose' rather than 'Sleeping Women.' The four paintings that have come onto the market in the past six months have commanded record prices. The last offering, titled simply* Number Nineteen, *sold to Japanese businessman Hodai Takagi for one point two million pounds sterling. The Museum is deeply indebted to Mr. Takagi for lending three canvases to the current exhibit. As for the artist, his identity remains unknown. His work is available exclusively through Christopher Wingate, LLC, of New York City, USA."*

I felt a surprising amount of anxiety standing on the threshold of that roomful of men, silent Asians posed like statues before images I could not yet see. Nude women sleeping, possibly dead. I've seen more dead women than most coroners, many of them naked, their clothes blasted away by artillery shells, burned off by fire, or torn away by soldiers. I've shot hundreds of pictures of their corpses, methodically creating my own images of death. Yet the idea of the paintings in the next room disturbed me. I had created my death images to expose atrocities, to try to stop senseless slaughter. The artist behind the paintings in the next room, I sensed, had some other agenda.

I took a deep breath and went in.

My arrival caused a ripple among the men, like a new species of fish swimming into a school. A woman – especially a roundeye woman – clearly made them uncomfortable, as though they were ashamed of their presence in this room. I met their fugitive glances with a level gaze and walked up to the painting with the fewest men in front of it.

After the soothing Chinese watercolors, it was a shock. The painting was quintessentially Western, a portrait of a nude woman in a bathtub. A roundeye woman like me, but ten years younger. Maybe thirty. Her pose – one arm hanging languidly over the edge of the tub – reminded me of the *Death of Marat,* which I knew only from the Masterpiece board game I'd played as a child. But the view was from a higher angle, so that her breasts and pubis were visible. Her eyes were closed, and though they communicated an undeniable peace, I couldn't tell whether it was the peace of sleep or of death. The skin color was not quite natural, more like marble, giving me the chilling feeling that if I could reach into the painting and turn her over, I would find her back purple with pooled blood.

Sensing the men close behind me edging closer, I moved to the next painting. In it, the female subject lay on a bed of brown straw spread on planks, as though on a threshing floor. Her eyes were open and had the dull sheen I had seen in too many makeshift morgues and hastily dug graves. There was no question about this one; she was supposed to look dead. That didn't mean she *was* dead, but whoever had painted her knew what death looked like.

Again I heard men behind me. Shuffling feet, hissing silk, irregular respiration. Were they trying to gauge my reaction to this Occidental woman in the most vulnerable state a woman can be in? Although if she was dead, she was technically *in*vulnerable. Yet this gawking at her corpse by strangers seemed somehow a final insult, an ultimate humiliation. We cover corpses for the same reason we go behind walls to carry out our bodily functions; some human states cry out for privacy, and being dead is one of them. Respect above all is called for, not for the body, but for the person who recently departed it.

Someone paid two million dollars for a painting like this one. Maybe even for this one. A man paid that, of course. A woman would have bought this painting only to destroy it. Ninety-nine out of a hundred women, anyway. I closed my eyes and said a prayer for the woman in the picture, on the chance that she was real. Then I moved on.

The next painting hung beyond a small bench set against the wall. It was smaller than the others, perhaps two feet by three, with the long axis vertical. Two men stood before it, but they weren't looking at the canvas. They gaped like clubbed mackerel as I approached, and I imagined that if I pulled down their starched white collars, I would find gills. No taller than I, they backed quickly out of my way and cleared the space before the painting. As I turned toward it, a premonitory wave of heat flashed across my neck and shoulders, and I felt the dry itch of the past rubbing against the present.

This woman was naked as well. She sat in a window seat, her head and one shoulder leaned against the casement, her skin lighted by the violet glow of dawn or dusk. Her eyes were half open, but they looked more like the glass eyes of a doll than those of a living woman. Her body was thin and muscular, her hands lay in her lap, and her Victorian-style hair fell upon her shoulders like a dark veil. Though she had been sitting face-on to me from the moment I looked at the canvas, I suddenly had the terrifying sensation that she had turned to me and spoken aloud. The taste of old metal filled my mouth, and my heart ballooned in my chest. This was not a painting but a mirror. The face looking back at me from the wall was my own. The body, too, mine: my feet, hips, breasts, my shoulders and neck. But the eyes were what held me, the dead eyes – held me and then dropped me through the floor into a nightmare I had traveled ten thousand miles to escape. A harsh burst of Chinese echoed through the room, but it was gibberish to me. My throat spasmed shut, and I could not scream or even breathe.

2

Thirteen months ago, on a hot summer morning, my twin sister Jane stepped out of her town house on St. Charles Avenue in New Orleans to run her daily three-mile round of the Garden District. Her two young children waited inside with the maid, first contentedly, then anxiously as their mother's usual absence stretched beyond any they remembered. Jane's husband Marc was working in blissful ignorance at his downtown law firm. After ninety minutes, the maid called him.

Knowing you could walk one block out of the Garden District and be in a free-fire zone, Marc Lacour immediately left work and drove the streets of their neighborhood in search of his wife. He cut the Garden District into one-block grids from Jackson Avenue to Louisiana and methodically drove them a dozen times. Then he walked them. He left the Garden District and questioned every porch-sitter, shade-tree mechanic, can-kicker, crack dealer, and homeless person he could find on the adjoining streets. No one had heard or seen anything of Jane. A prominent attorney, Marc immediately called the police and used his influence to mount a massive search. The police found nothing.

I was in Sarajevo when Jane disappeared, shooting a series on the aftermath of the war. It took me seventy-two hours to get to New Orleans. By that time, the FBI had entered the picture and subsumed my sister's disappearance into a much larger case, designated NOKIDS in FBI-speak, for New Orleans Kidnappings. It turned out that Jane was fifth in a rapidly growing group of missing women, all from the New Orleans area. Not one corpse had been found, so all the women were classified as victims of what the FBI called a "serial kidnapper." This was the worst sort of euphemism. Not one relative had received a ransom note, and in the eyes of every cop I spoke to, I saw the grim unspoken truth: every one of those women was presumed dead. With no crime-scene evidence, witnesses, or corpses to work with, even the Bureau's vaunted Investigative Support Unit was stumped by the cold trail. Though women continued to disappear and still do, neither the Bureau nor the New Orleans police have come close to discovering the fate of my sister or any of the others.

I should clarify something. Not once since my father vanished in Cambodia have I sensed that he was truly dead, gone from this world. Not even with the last frame of film he shot showing an executioner's pistol pointed at his face. Miracles happen, especially in war. For this reason I've spent thousands of dollars over the past twenty years trying to find him, piggybacking my money with that of the relatives of Vietnam-era MIAs, giving what would have been my retirement money to scam artists and outright thieves, all in the slender hope that one lead among the hundreds will turn out to be legitimate. On some level, my decision to take the advance for my book was probably a way to be paid to hunt for my father in person, to tramp across Asia with an eye to my camera and an ear to the ground.

With Jane it's different. By the time my agency tracked me down on a CNN satellite phone in Sarajevo, something had already changed irrevocably within me. As I crossed a street once infested with snipers, a nimbus of dread welled up in my chest – not the familiar dread of a bullet with my name on it, but something much deeper. Whatever energy animates my soul simply stopped flowing as I ran, and the street vanished. I kept running blindly into the dark tunnel before me, as though it were nine years before, during the worst of it, when the snipers shot anything that moved. A CNN cameraman yanked me behind a wall, thinking I'd seen the impact of a silenced bullet on the concrete. I hadn't, but a moment later, when the street returned, I felt as though a bullet *had* punched through me, taking with it something no doctor could ever put back or put right.

Quantum physics describes "twinned particles," photons of energy that, even though separated by miles, behave identically when confronted with a choice of paths. It is now thought that some unseen connection binds them, defying known physical laws, acting instantaneously without reference to the speed of light or any other limit. Jane and I were joined in this way. And from the moment that dark current of dread pulsed through my heart, I felt that *my* twin was dead. Twelve hours later, I got the call.

Thirteen months after that – two hours ago – I walked into the museum in Hong Kong and saw her painted image, naked in death. I'm not sure what happened immediately after. The earth did not stop turning. The cesium atoms in the atomic clock at Boulder did not stop vibrating. But time in the subjective sense – *the time that is me* – simply ceased. I became a hole in the world.

The next thing I remember is sitting in this first-class seat on a Cathay Pacific 747 bound for New York, a Pacific Rim sunset flaring in my window as the four great engines thrum, their vibration causing a steady ripple in the scotch on the tray before me. That was two whiskeys ago, and I still have another nineteen hours in the air. My eyes are dry and grainy, stinging. I am cried out. My mind gropes backward toward the museum, but there is something in the way. A shadow. I know better than to try to force the memory. I was shot once in Africa, and from the moment the bullet ripped through my shoulder till the moment I came to my senses in the Colonial Hotel and found myself being patched up by an Australian reporter whose father was a doctor, everything was blank. The missing events – a hectic jeep ride down an embattled road, the bribing of a checkpoint guard (in which I participated) – only returned to me later. They had not disappeared, but merely fallen out of sequence.

So it was at the museum. But here, in the familiar environment of the plane, in the warm wake of my third scotch, things begin to return. Brief flashing images at first, then jerky sequences, like bad streaming video. I'm standing before the painting of a naked woman whose face is mine to the last detail, and my feet are rooted to the floor with the permanence of nightmares. The men crowding me from behind believe I'm the woman who modeled for the painting on the wall. They chatter incessantly and race around like ants after kerosene has been poured on their hill. They are puzzled that I am alive, angry that their fantasy of "Sleeping Women" seems to be a hoax. But I know things they don't. I see my sister stepping out onto St. Charles Avenue, the humidity condensing on her skin even before she begins to run. Three miles is her goal, but somewhere in the junglelike Garden District, she puts a foot wrong and falls into the hole my father fell into in 1972.

Now she stares back at me with vacant eyes, from a canvas as deep as a window into Hell. Having accepted her death in my bones, having mourned and buried her in my mind, this unexpected resurrection triggers a storm of emotions. But somewhere in the chemical chaos of my brain, in the storm's dark eye, my rational mind continues to work. Whoever painted this picture has knowledge of my sister *beyond* the moment she vanished from the Garden District. He knows what no one else could: the story of Jane's last hours, or minutes, or seconds. He heard her last words. He – *He* . . . ? Why do I assume the painter is a man?

Because he almost certainly is. I have no patience with the Naomi Wolfs of the world, but there's no denying statistical fact. It is men who commit these obscene crimes: rape; stranger murder; and the *pièce de résistance,* serial murder. It's an exclusively male pathology: the hunting, the planning, the obsessively tended rage working itself out in complex rituals of violence. A man hovers like a specter behind these strange paintings, and he has knowledge that I need. He alone in the world can give me what has eluded me for the past year. Peace.

As I stare into my sister's painted eyes, a wild hope is born in my chest. Jane *looks* dead in the picture. And the audio tour announcer suggested that all the women in this series are. But there must be some chance, despite my premonition in Sarajevo, that she was merely unconscious while this work was done. Drugged maybe, or playing possum, as my mother called it when we were kids. How long would it take to paint something like this? A few hours? A day? A week?

A particularly loud burst of Chinese snaps the spell of the picture, waking me to the tears growing cold on my cheeks, the hand grasping my shoulder. That hand belongs to one of the bastards who came here today to ogle dead women. I have a wild urge to reach up and snatch the canvas from the wall, to cover my sister's nakedness from these prying eyes. But if I pull down a painting worth millions of dollars, I will find myself in the custody of the Chinese police – a disagreeable circumstance at best.

I run instead.

I run like hell, and I don't stop until I reach a dark room filled with documents under glass. It's ancient Chinese poetry, hand-painted on paper as fragile as moths' wings. The only light comes from the display cases, and they fluoresce only when I come near. My hands are shaking in the dark, and when I hug myself, I realize the rest of me is shaking too. In the blackness I see my mother, slowly drinking herself to death in Oxford, Mississippi. I see Jane's husband and children in New Orleans, trying their best to live without her and not doing terribly well at it. I see the FBI agents I met thirteen months ago, sober men with good intentions but no idea how to help.

I shot hundreds of crime-scene photos when I was starting my career, but I never quite realized how important a dead body is to a murder investigation. The corpse is ground zero. Without one, investigators face a wall as blank as unexposed film. The painting back in the exhibition room is not Jane's corpse, but it may be the closest thing anyone will ever find to it. It's a starting point. With this realization comes another: there are other paintings like Jane's. According to the audio tour, nineteen. Nineteen naked women posed in images of sleep or death. As far as I know, only eleven women have disappeared from New Orleans. Who are the other eight? Or are there only eleven, with some appearing in more than one painting? And what in God's name are they doing in Hong Kong, halfway around the world?

Stop! snaps a voice in my head. My father's voice. *Forget your questions! What should you do NOW?*

The audio tour said the paintings are sold through a

U.S. dealer named Christopher something in New York. Windham? Winwood? Win*gate*. To be sure, I pull the Walkman off my belt and jam it into my crowded fanny pack. The movement triggers a display case light, and my eyes ache from the quick pupillary contraction. As I slide back into the shadows, the obvious comes clear: if Christopher Wingate is based in New York, that's where the answers are. Not in this museum. In the curator's office I will find only suspicious curiosity. I don't need police for this, especially communist Chinese police. I need the FBI. Specifically, the Investigative Support Unit. But they're ten thousand miles away. What would the boy geniuses of Behavioral Science want from this place? The paintings, obviously. I can't take those with me. But the next-best thing is not impossible. In my fanny pack is a small, inexpensive point-and-shoot camera. It's the photojournalist's equivalent of a cop's throwdown gun, the tool you simply can't be without. The one day you're sure you won't need a camera, a world-class tragedy will explode right in front of you.

Move! orders my father's voice. *While they're still confused.*

Retracing my steps to the exhibition room is easy; I simply follow the babble of conversation echoing through the empty halls. The men are still milling around, talking about me, no doubt, the Sleeping Woman who isn't sleeping and certainly isn't dead. I feel no fear as I approach them. Somewhere between the document room and this place labeled "Nude Women in Repose," I shoved my sister into a dark memory hole and became the woman who has covered wars on four continents – my father's daughter.

With my sudden reappearance, the Chinese draw together in excited knots. A museum guard is questioning two of them, trying to find out what happened. I walk brazenly past him and shoot two pictures of the woman in the bathtub. The flash of the little Canon sets off a blast of irate Chinese. Moving quickly through the room, I shoot two more paintings before the guard gets a hand on my arm. I turn to him and nod as though I understand, then break away toward the painting of Jane. I get off one shot before he blows his whistle for help and locks onto my arm again, this time with both hands.

Sometimes you can b.s. your way out of situations like this. This is not one of those times. If I'm still standing here when Someone In Authority arrives, I'll never get out of the museum with my film. I double the guard over with a well-placed knee and run like hell for the second time.

The police whistle sounds again, though this time with a faint bleat. I skid to a stop on the waxed floor, backpedal to a fire door, and crash through to the outside, leaving a wake of alarms behind me. For the first time I'm glad for the teeming crowds of Hong Kong; even a roundeye woman can disappear in less than a minute. Three hundred yards from the museum, I hail a taxi and order him not to the Star Ferry, which someone might remember me boarding, but through the tunnel that crosses beneath the harbor.

Back on the Hong Kong side, we race to my hotel. I'm staying at the Mandarin, which is too expensive for me but has great sentimental value. As a child, I received several letters from my father on its stationery. Inside my room, I throw my clothes into my suitcase, pack my cameras into their aluminum flight cases, and take a different cab to the new airport. I intend to be out of Chinese airspace before some enterprising cop figures out that, while they may not have my name, they have a perfect likeness of my face on their museum wall. They could have flyers at the airport and the hotels in less than an hour. I'm not sure why they would

– I've committed no crime, other than stealing a Walkman – but I've been arrested for less before, and in the paranoid world of the Hong Kong Chinese, my behavior around multimillion-dollar paintings would make me an excellent candidate for "temporary detention."

Hong Kong International Airport is a babel of Asian languages and rushing travelers. I have a reservation on an Air China flight to Beijing, but that plane doesn't leave for three hours. The departure screens show a Cathay Pacific flight leaving for New York in thirty-five minutes, with a two-hour layover at Narita in Tokyo. Presenting my worn passport at the Cathay counter, I let the ticket agent gut me for full fare on a first-class ticket. The money would buy a decent used car in the States, but after what happened in the museum, I can't sit shoulder-to-shoulder with some computer salesman from Raleigh for twenty hours. That potential reality brings another to mind, and I ask the female agent if she can seat me next to a woman. On this day of all days, I cannot deal with being hit on, and twenty hours gives a guy a long time to strategize. Last year, on a flight from Seoul to Los Angeles, some drunk jerk actually asked if I wanted to go to the rest room with him and join the Mile High Club. I told him I was already a member, which was true. I'd joined nine years earlier, with my fiancé, in the cargo hold of a DC-3 somewhere over Namibia. Three days later, he was captured with some SWAPO guerrillas and beaten to death, which put me in an even more exclusive club: the Unofficial Widows. Now, at forty, I'm still single and still a member. The Cathay Pacific agent smiles knowingly and obliges my request.

Which puts me where I am now: three scotches down and my short-term memory back in gear. The alcohol is serving several functions, one of them being to damp the embers of grief stirring at the bottom of my soul. But nineteen hours is a long time to hide from yourself. I have a supply of Xanax in my fanny pack, for the nights when the open wound of my sister's unknown fate throbs too acutely for sleep. It's throbbing now, and it's not even full dark yet. Before I can second-guess myself, I pop three pills with a swallow of scotch and take the Airfone out of my armrest.

There's really only one useful thing I can do from the plane. After a few swipes of my Visa and some haggling with directory assistance, I'm speaking to the operator at the FBI Academy in Quantico, Virginia, who transfers me to the offices of the Investigative Support Unit. The ISU has more impressive digs than it once did, but Daniel Baxter, the chief of the unit, likes the bunker atmosphere of the old days, the era before Hollywood overexposure turned his unit into a myth that draws eager young college grads by the thousands. Baxter must be fifty now, but he's a lean and hungry fifty, with a combat soldier's eyes. That's what I thought when I first saw him. A guy from the ranks who found himself an officer by default, the result of a battlefield promotion. But no one will ever question that promotion. His record of success is legendary in a war where victories are few and the defeats almost unbearable. To wit, my sister and her ten sisters in purgatory. Baxter's unit scored a big zero on that one. But the grim fact is, when a certain kind of shit hits the fan, there's no one else to call.

"Baxter," says a sharp baritone voice.

"This is Jordan Glass," I tell him, trying to hide the slur in my voice and not doing well at all. "Do you remember me?"

"You're hard to forget, Ms. Glass."

I take a quick swallow of scotch. "A little over an hour ago, I saw my sister in Hong Kong."

There's a brief silence. "Are you drinking, Ms. Glass?"

"Absolutely. But I know what I saw."

"You saw your sister."

"In Hong Kong. And now I'm in a 747, bound for New York."

"You're saying you saw your sister alive?"

"No."

"I'm not sure I understand."

I give Baxter as lucid a summary as I can manage of my experiences at the museum, then wait for his response. I expect some expression of astonishment – maybe not a Gomer Pyle "Shazam," but something – but I should have known better.

"Did you recognize any other New Orleans victims?" he asks.

"No. But I never studied the photos of those beyond number six."

"You're one hundred percent sure it was your sister's face in that painting?"

"Are you kidding? It's *my* face, Baxter. My *body,* naked to the world."

"Okay . . . I believe you."

"Have you ever heard of these paintings?"

"No. I'll talk to our fine arts people in D.C. as soon as we get off. And we'll start taking this Christopher Wingate's life apart. When will you be in New York?"

"Nineteen hours. Around five p.m. New York time."

"Try to get some sleep on the plane. I'm going to book you a flight here from JFK. American Airlines. It'll be an e-ticket, just show your license or passport. I'll drive up to Washington and meet you at the Hoover Building. I have to be up there tomorrow anyway, and that's more convenient for you than Quantico. In fact, I'll have an agent pick you up at Reagan Airport. Do you have any problem with that?"

"Yes. I think they should have left it Washington National."

"Ms. Glass, are you all right?"

"I'm great."

"You sound upset."

"Nothing pharmacological therapy won't cure. Mixed with a little of Scotland's finest." A hysterical laugh escapes my lips. "I need to take the edge off. It's been a tough day."

"I understand. But leave a little edge in place, okay? I need you sharp and thinking."

"It's nice to be needed." I terminate the connection and replace the Airfone in the armrest.

You didn't need me thirteen months ago, I say silently. But that was then. Now things have changed. Now they'll want me around until they get a handle on the significance of the paintings. Then they'll cut me off again. Exclusion is the worst fate for a journalist, and a living hell for a victim's family. Better not to think about that right now. Better to sleep. I've practically lived in the air for twenty years, and sleeping on planes was effortless until Jane disappeared. Now it takes a little help from my friends.

As the chemical fog descends over my eyes, a last cogent spark flashes in my brain, and I take out the phone again. I'm in no state to hassle with directory assistance, so I plug into an entirely different connection. Ron Epstein works Page Six at the New York *Post;* he's a human who's who of the city. Like Daniel Baxter, he's addicted to his work, which means he's probably there now, despite the early hour in New York. When the *Post* operator puts me through to his section, he answers.

"Ron? It's Jordan Glass."

"Jordan! Where are you?"

"On my way to New York."

He responds with a giggle. "I thought you were off in the hinterlands, taking pictures of clouds or something."

"I was."

"You must need something. You never call just to kibitz."

"Christopher Wingate. Ever heard of him?"

"*Naturellement*. Very chic, very cool. He's made Fifteenth Street the envy of SoHo. The old dealers kiss his ass now, and the more they do, the more he treats them like shit. Everyone wants Wingate to handle their stuff, but he's very picky."

"What about the Sleeping Women?"

A coo of admiration. "Aren't *you* in the circle. Not many American collectors know about them yet."

"I want to see him. Wingate, I mean."

"To photograph him?"

"I just want to talk to him."

"I'd say you have to stand in line, but he might just be intrigued enough to talk to you."

"Can you get me his phone number?"

"If I can't, no one can. But it may take a while. I know he's not listed. He lives above his gallery, but I don't think the gallery's listed either. It's that exclusive. This guy will skip a sale just because he doesn't like the buyer. Are you somewhere I can call you?"

"No. Can I call you tomorrow? I'm going to sleep for a while."

"I'll have it for you then."

"Thanks, Ron. I owe you dinner at Lutèce."

"Let me choose the place, honey, and you're on. I hope

you're not sleeping alone. No one I know needs love more than you."

I glance around the first-class cabin at a rumpled platoon of businessmen. "No, I'm not alone."

"Good. Tomorrow, then."

The fog is descending so fast now that I can barely get the Airfone back in the armrest. Thank God for drugs. I couldn't bear to be alert right now. When I wake, the museum will seem like a bad dream. Of course, it wasn't. It was a door. A door to a world I have no choice but to reenter. Am I ready for that? "Sure," I say aloud. "I was born ready." But deep down, beneath the brittle old bravado, I know it's a lie.

3

Two hours before the Cathay Pacific jet landed in New York, I surfaced from my drug-induced dive, stumbled to the rest room and back, and asked the flight attendant for a hot towel. Then I called Ron Epstein and got Christopher Wingate's number. It took an hour of steady calling to get the art dealer on the phone. I had worried that I might have to mention the Sleeping Women to get Wingate's attention, but Epstein's hunch proved correct: Wingate was intrigued enough by my modest celebrity to see me at his gallery after hours without explanation. I couldn't tell much about him from his voice, which had an affected accent I couldn't place. He did mention my book-in-progress, so my guess is that he hopes I'm looking for a dealer to sell my photographs to the fine art market.

Meeting Wingate alone is a risk, but my work has always involved calculations of risk. Photographing wars is like commercial fishing off Alaska: you know going out that you might not come back. But on an Alaskan boat, it's you against the ocean and the weather. In a war zone there are *people* trying to kill you. Going to see Christopher Wingate could be like that. I have to assume he's heard about the scene at the museum by now. He won't have my name, but he will know that the woman who caused the disturbance in Hong Kong looked exactly like one of the Sleeping Women. Does he know that one of the Sleeping Women looks like the photographer Jordan Glass? He knows my reputation, but it's unlikely that he's seen a photo of me. I haven't lived in New York for twelve years, and my work wasn't nearly so well known then. The real danger depends on how involved Wingate is with the painter of the Sleeping Women. Does he know that the subjects in the paintings are real? That they're missing and probably dead? If so, then he's willing to turn a blind eye to murder in order to earn a fortune in commissions. How dangerous does that make him? I won't know until I talk to him. But one thing is certain: If I go on to Washington now and meet the FBI, they'll never let me close to him. Every piece of information I get will be secondhand, just like it was after Jane disappeared.

After I clear customs at JFK, I roll my bags to the American Airlines gate, collect my e-ticket to Washington, and check my bags on that flight. Then I walk out of the airport and hire a cab. I don't like letting my cameras go to Washington without me, but later tonight, when I tell Daniel Baxter I got sick and missed my plane, he'll be more likely to believe me.

Before going to Lower Manhattan, I have the cabbie take me to a pawnshop on Ninety-eighth Street. There, for $50, I buy a can of Fortified Mace to carry in my pocket. I'd prefer a gun, but I don't want to risk it. The NYPD takes weapons violations very seriously.

When the cab pulls up to Wingate's Fifteenth Street gallery in the failing light of dusk, I find a simple three-story brownstone like a thousand others in the city, with a bar on one side and a video rental store on the other. The tony atmosphere of the Chelsea art district stays in another part of Chelsea, I guess.

After paying the cabbie to wait, I get out and study the doorway from the curb. There's a buzzer by the front door, which looks normal enough but probably hides all sorts of security devices. I slip on sunglasses as I approach, in case there's a videocam.

There is. I push the buzzer and wait.

"Who are you?" asks the stateless voice I recognize from my earlier call.

"Jordan Glass."

"Just a moment."

The buzzer burps, the lock disengages, and I pull the door open. The ground floor of the gallery is half-illuminated by fluorescent light from the second floor, spilling down an iron staircase. With my sunglasses, it's hard to see, but the decor seems spare for a trendy New York art gallery. The floor is bleached hardwood, the walls white. The paintings look modern for the most part, or what my idea of modern is, anyway. A lot of stark color arranged in asymmetrical patterns, but it means little to me. I've been called an artist – often during attacks by purist photo-journalists – but that doesn't qualify me as a judge of art. I'm not even sure I know it when I see it.

"Do you like that Lucian Freud?" asks the voice I heard on the speaker outside.

There's a man standing on the landing, where the iron staircase turns back on itself. Fixed squarely in a shaft of light, he looks as though he simply materialized there. He is wiry and balding, but he compensates for the baldness with a shadow of trimmed black stubble. In his black jeans, T-shirt, and leather jacket, he looks like the midlevel mafia thugs I saw in Moscow a few years back: slightly underfed but fiercely predatory, particularly around the eyes and mouth.

"Not really," I confess, with a quick look at the painting hanging nearest me. "Should I?"

"*Should* doesn't come into it. Though it would have a better chance of impressing you if you took off those sunglasses."

"I wouldn't like it any better. I'm not here to see this."

"What are you here to see?"

"You, if you're Christopher Wingate."

He beckons me forward with his hand, then turns and starts back up the stairs. I follow.

"You always wear sunglasses in the evening?" he asks over his shoulder.

"Something wrong with that?"

"It's just so Julia Roberts."

"That'll be the one thing we have in common, then."

Wingate chuckles. He's barefoot, and his pale dirty heels seem to float up the steps. He passes the second floor, which houses sculpture, and continues up to the third. This is clearly where he lives. It has a Danish feel, all spare lines and Scandinavian wood, and it smells of fresh coffee. Standing in the middle of the room is a large, unsealed wooden crate with packing material spilling out of its open end. There's a claw hammer lying atop the crate, a scattering of nails around it. Wingate brushes a proprietary hand against the wood as he passes the crate, which comes to his shoulder.

"What's in the box?"

"A painting. Please, sit down."

I gesture at the crate. "You work up here? This looks like your apartment."

"It's a special painting. It may be the last time I see it in person. I want to enjoy it while I can. Would you like an espresso? Cappuccino? I was about to have one."

"Cappuccino."

"Good." He walks to a blue enameled machine on a counter behind him and starts to fill a small mug. While his back is to me, I move to the open crate. There's a heavy gold frame inside. Peeking between the box and the frame, I can't see much, but it's enough: the upper torso and head of a nude woman, her eyes open and fixed in a strangely peaceful stare. Wingate is dispensing the cup as I back away.

"So, to what do I owe this pleasure?" he asks the wall.

"I've heard good things about you. They say you're a very selective seller."

"I don't sell to fools." He sprays out some steamed milk with a flourish. "Unless they know they're fools. That's different. If someone comes to me and says, 'My friend, I know nothing about art, but I wish to begin collecting. Would you advise me?' This person I will help." Another hissing jet of steamed milk. "But these pretentious WASP millionaires make me puke. They took art criticism at Yale, or their wife majored in Renaissance masters at Vassar. They know so much, what do they need me for? For cachet, yes? So fuck them. My cachet is not for sale."

"Not to them, anyway."

He turns with a grin and offers me a steaming cup. "I love your accent. You're from South Carolina?"

"Not even close," I reply, stepping forward to take the mug.

"But the South. Where?"

"The Magnolia State."

He looks perplexed. "Louisiana?"

"That's the Sportsman's Paradise. I'm from the home of William Faulkner and Elvis Presley."

"Georgia?"

I'm definitely in New York. "Mississippi, Mr. Wingate."

"Learn something every day, right? Call me Christopher, okay?"

"Okay." After Ron Epstein's characterization of

Wingate, I half expected the man to make some crack about Mississippi being the home of the lynching. "Call me Jordan."

"I'm a huge fan of your work," he says with apparent sincerity. "You have a pitiless eye."

"Is that a compliment?"

"Of course. You don't shy away from horror. Or absurdity. But there's compassion there, too. That's why people connect with your work. I think there would be quite a demand, if you were inclined to market it as fine art. Not much photography really qualifies, but yours . . . no doubt about it."

"You're not living up to your advance billing. I heard you were a son of a bitch."

He grins again and sips his cappuccino. The pure blackness of his eyes is startling. "I am, to most people. But with artists I like, I'm a shameless flatterer."

I want to ask him about the painting in the crate, but something tells me to wait. "It's been said that a photograph can be journalism or art, but not both."

"Such crap. The gifted always break the rules. Look at Martin Parr's book. He turned photojournalism upside down with *The Last Resort*. Look at Nachtwey's stuff. That's art, no question. You're every bit as good. Better in some ways."

Now I know he's bullshitting me. James Nachtwey is the preeminent war photographer at Magnum; he's won the Capa five times. "Such as?"

"*Commercial* ways." A glint of mischief in the black eyes. "You're a star, Jordan."

"Am I?"

"People look at your photos – stark, terrible, unflinching – and they think, 'A woman was standing here looking at this, recording it. With a woman's sensitivity. A woman has stood this, so I must stand this.' It floors them. And it changes their perspective. That's what art does."

I've heard all this before, and while largely true, it bugs me. It smacks of *Not bad, for a girl.*

"And then there's you," Wingate goes on. "Look at you. Hardly any makeup, and still beautiful at – what? – forty?"

"Forty."

"You're marketable. If you'll suffer through a few interviews and an opening, I can make you a star. An icon for women."

"You said I'm already a star."

He barely skips a beat. "In your field, sure. But what's that? I'm talking pop culture. Look at Eve Arnold. *You* know who she is. But if I walk downstairs and ask a hundred people on the street, not one will know. Dickey Chappelle wanted to be a household name. That was her dream. She schlepped all over the world, from Iwo Jima to Saigon, but she never became what she most wanted to be – a star."

"I haven't schlepped all over the world to become a star, whatever that means."

A feral gleam in the eyes betrays a new level of interest. "No, I believe that. So, why? Why do you traipse from pillar to post, cataloguing atrocities that would shock Goya?"

"You haven't earned the answer to that question."

He claps his hands together. "But I already know it! It's your father, isn't it? Dear old daddy. Jonathan Glass, the legend of Vietnam. The shooter's shooter."

"Maybe you are a son of a bitch after all."

The smile widens. "I can't help it, as the scorpion said to the frog. It's my nature."

Some of the biggest bastards I ever met were charismatic, and Wingate is no exception. My gaze settles on the crate between us.

"And the way he died," Wingate exults, "shooting a Pulitzer-winning roll of film. That's *mythic*. Then his daughter follows in his footsteps? It's a legitimate phenomenon, no hype required. We could do a double show. Talk about free publicity. Who controls the rights to your father's images?"

"I don't believe my father died in Cambodia," I say in a flat voice.

Wingate looks as though I just told him I don't believe Neil Armstrong walked on the moon. "You don't?"

"No."

"Okay . . . so . . . that's even better. We could—"

"And I'm not interested in exploiting his work for money."

He shakes his head, his hands imploring. "You're looking at it all wrong—"

"What painting is so wonderful that you have to keep it this close to you?" I interrupt, pointing at the packing crate with my free hand.

Momentarily off balance, he answers without thinking. "It's a painting by an anonymous artist. His work fascinates me."

"You like looking at pictures of dead women?"

Wingate freezes, his eyes locked onto mine.

"Are you going to answer my question?"

He gives a philosophical shrug. "I'm not here to answer your questions. But I'll answer that one. No one knows if the subjects are dead or not."

"Do you know the identity of the artist?"

Wingate sips his cappuccino, then sets his mug on the

counter behind him. I slip my hand into my pocket to feel the cold, reassuring metal of the Mace can.

"Are you asking as a journalist?" he asks. "Or as a collector?"

"All I can afford to collect is experiences and passport stamps. I figured you could tell that with one look at my shoes."

He shrugs again. Shrugs are a major part of this guy's vocabulary. "One never knows who has money these days."

"I want to meet the artist."

"Impossible."

"May I see the painting?"

He purses his lips. "I don't see why not, since you already have." He walks around to the open side of the crate, braces his feet against the bottom, and reaches in for the frame. "Could you give me a hand?"

I hesitate, thinking about the claw hammer, but he doesn't look like he wants to bludgeon me to death. Having been in situations where people wanted to do just that, I trust my instincts more than some people might.

"Hold the other side while I pull," he says.

I set my cappuccino on the floor, then take hold of the other side of the crate while he slides out a padded metal frame that holds the gilt frame inside it.

"There," he says. "You can see it now."

I'm torn between wanting to step around the crate and wanting to stay right where I am. But I have to look. I might recognize one of the victims who was taken before Jane.

The instant I see the woman's face, I know she's a stranger to me. But I could easily have known her. She looks like ten thousand women in New Orleans, a mixture of French blood with some fraction of African, resulting in a degree of natural beauty rarely seen elsewhere in America.

But this woman is not in her natural state. Her skin should be café au lait; here it's the color of bone china. And her eyes are fully open and fixed. Of course, the eyes in any painting are fixed; it's the talent of the artist that brings life to them. But in these eyes there is no life. Not even a hint of it.

"Sleeping Woman Number Twenty," says Wingate. "Do you like it better than the paintings downstairs?"

Only now do I see the rest of the painting. The artist has posed his subject against a wall, knees drawn up to her chest as though she's sitting. But she is not sitting. She is merely leaning there, her head lolling on her marbled shoulder, while around her swirls a storm of color. Brightly printed curtains, a blue carpet, a shaft of light from an unseen window. Even the wall she leans on is the product of thousands of tiny strokes of different colors. Only the woman is presented with startling realism. She could have been cut from a Rembrandt and set in this whirlwind of color.

"I don't *like* it. But I feel . . . I feel whoever painted it is very talented."

"Enormously." Genuine excitement lights Wingate's black eyes. "He's capturing something that no one else working today is even close to. All the arrogant kids that come in here, trying to be edgy, painting with blood and making sculpture with gun parts . . . they're a fucking joke. *This* is the edge. You're looking over it right now."

"Is he an important artist?"

"We won't know that for fifty years."

"What do you call this style?"

Wingate sighs thoughtfully. "Hard to say. He's not static. He began with almost pure Impressionism, which is *dead*. Anyone can do it. But the vision was there. Between the fifth and twelfth paintings, he began to evolve something much more fascinating. Are you familiar with the Nabis?"

"The what?"

"Nabis. It means 'prophets.' Bonnard, Denis, Vuillard?"

"What I know about art wouldn't fill a postcard."

"Don't blame yourself. That's the American educational system. They simply don't teach it. Not unless you beg for it. Not even in university."

"I didn't go to college."

"How refreshing. And why would you? American institutions worship technology. Technology and money."

"Are you American?"

A bemused smile. "What do you think?"

"I can't tell. Where are you from?"

"I usually lie when someone asks that question. I don't want to insult your intelligence, so we'll skip the biography."

"Hiding a dark secret?"

"A little mystery keeps me interesting. Collectors like to buy from interesting dealers. People think I'm a big bad wolf. They think I have mob connections, criminal clients all over."

"Do you?"

"I'm a businessman. But doing business in New York, that kind of reputation doesn't hurt."

"Do you have prints of other Sleeping Women I can see?"

"There are no prints. I guarantee that to the purchaser."

"What about photographs? You must have photos."

He shakes his head. "No photos. No copies of any kind."

"Why?"

"Rarity is the rarest commodity."

"How long have you had this one?"

Wingate looks down at the canvas, then at me from the corner of his eye. "Not long."

"How long will you have it?"

44

"It ships tomorrow. I have a standing bid from Takagi on anything by this artist. One point five million pounds. But I have other plans for this one."

He takes hold of the metal frame and motions for me to brace the crate while he pushes the painting back inside. To keep him talking, I help.

"For a series of about eight paintings," Wingate says, "he could have been one of the Nabis. But he changed again. The women became more and more real, their bodies less alive, their surroundings more so. Now he paints like one of the old masters. His technique is unbelievable."

"Do you really not know if they're alive or dead?"

"Give me a break," he grunts, straining to apply adequate force without damaging the frame. "They're models. If some horny Japanese wants to think they're dead and pay millions for them, that's great. I'm not complaining."

"Do you really believe that?"

He doesn't look at me. "What I believe doesn't matter. What matters is what I know for sure, which is nothing."

If Wingate doesn't know the women are real, he's about to find out. As he straightens up and wipes his brow, I turn squarely to him and take off my sunglasses.

"What do you think now?"

His facial muscles hardly move, but he's freaked, all right. There's a lot more white showing in his eyes now. "I think maybe you're running some kind of scam on me."

"Why?"

"Because I sold a picture of you. You're one of them. One of the Sleeping Women."

He must not have heard about what happened in Hong Kong. Could the curator there have been afraid to risk losing his exhibit?

45

"No," I say softly. "That was my sister."

"But the face . . . it was the same."

"We're twins. Identical twins."

He shakes his head in amazement.

"You understand now?"

"I think you know more than I do about all this. Is your sister okay?"

I can't tell if he's sincere or not. "I don't know. But if I had to guess, I'd say no. She disappeared thirteen months ago. When did you sell the painting of her?"

"Maybe a year ago."

"To a Japanese industrialist?"

"Sure. Takagi. He outbid everybody."

"There were other bidders for that particular painting?"

"Sure. Always. But I'm not about to give you their names."

"Look, I want you to understand something. I don't give a damn about the police or the law. All I care about is my sister. Anything you know that can help me find her, I'll pay for."

"I don't know anything. Your sister's been gone a year, and you think she's still alive?"

"No. I think she's dead. I think all the women in these paintings are dead. And so do you. But I can't move on with my life until I *know*. I've got to find out what happened to my sister. I owe her that."

Wingate looks at the crate. "Hey, I can sympathize. But I can't help you, okay? I really don't know anything."

"How is that possible? You're the exclusive dealer for this artist."

"Sure. But I've never met the guy."

"But you know he's a man?"

"I'm not positive, to tell you the truth. I've never seen

46

him. Everything goes through the mail. Notes left in the gallery, money in train station lockers, like that."

"I don't see a woman painting these pictures. Do you?"

Wingate cocks one eyebrow. "I've met some pretty strange women in this town. I could tell you some stories, man. You wouldn't believe what I've seen."

"You get the paintings through the mail?"

"Sometimes. Other times they're left downstairs, in the gallery. It's like spy novels – what do they call that? A blind drop?"

"What legitimate reason could there be for that kind of arrangement?"

"Well, I thought it might be the Helga syndrome."

"The what?"

"The Helga syndrome. You know Andrew Wyeth, surely?"

"Of course."

"While everyone thought all he could do was rural American realism, Wyeth was secretly painting this woman from a neighboring farm. In the nude. Helga. Wyeth kept the paintings secret, and they were only revealed years later. The first Sleeping Woman I got was simply left here. It wasn't one of the early ones. It was from his Nabi period. As soon as I saw it, I recognized the talent. I thought it might be by an established artist, one who didn't want it known that he was experimenting in that way. Not until it was successful, at least."

"How do you pay him? You can't leave millions in train station lockers. Do you wire the money to a bank account somewhere?"

A languid expression comes over Wingate's features. "Look, I sympathize with you. But I don't see how this part of my business is your business, okay? If what you say is true, the police will be asking me all this soon enough. Maybe you'd better talk to them. And I better talk to my lawyer."

"Forget I asked that, okay? I'm not trying to hurt you. All I care about is my sister. All these women disappeared from New Orleans. Not one has been found, alive or dead. Now suddenly I discover these paintings in Hong Kong. Everyone assumes the women are dead. But what if they're not? I *have* to find the man who painted these pictures."

He shrugs. "Like I said, we'll just have to wait for the police to sort it out."

A buzz of alarm begins in the back of my brain. Christopher Wingate does not look like a man who would welcome the attention of police. Yet he is stalling me by claiming he wants to wait until they become involved. It's time to get out of here.

"Who knows about all this?" he asks suddenly. "Who else have you told?"

I'm wishing my hand was in my pocket, wrapped around the Mace can, but he's watching me closely, and the hammer is within his reach. "A few people."

"Such as?"

"The FBI."

Wingate bites his bottom lip like a man weighing options. Then a half-smile appears. "Is that supposed to scare me?"

He picks up the claw hammer, and I jump back. He laughs at my skittishness, then grabs a handful of nails, puts a few in his mouth, and begins hammering the side panel back onto the crate, like a man taking maximum precautions to protect his treasure.

"Every cloud has a silver lining, right?" The nails between his lips make him answer out of one side of his mouth. "The FBI starts investigating these paintings in a murder case, they become worldwide news. Like the guy in Spain who murdered women and posed them like Salvador Dali paintings. That means money, lady."

"You *are* a bastard, aren't you?"

"It's not illegal, is it? Yes, I'm going to make a *lot* more money on this painting than I thought. Maybe double the bid."

"What's your commission?" I ask, stepping out of range of the hammer and sliding my hand into my pocket.

"That's my business."

"What's a standard commission?"

"Fifty percent."

"So this one painting could land you a million dollars."

"You're quick at math. You should work for me."

The crate is nearly sealed. When he's finished, he'll tell me to leave, then get on the phone and start promoting his newly appreciated asset.

"Why are you selling these paintings in Asia rather than America? Were you trying to delay the connection to the missing women?"

He laughs again. "It just happened that way. A Frenchman from the Cayman Islands bought the first five, but I found out he'd spent most of his life in Vietnam. Then a Japanese collector stepped in. A Malaysian. Also a Chinese. There's something in these images that appeals to the Eastern sensibility."

"And it's not very subtle, is it? Dead naked white women?"

Wingate turns to me long enough to wrinkle his lips. "That's crude, and it's an oversimplification.

"Where is the painting in the crate going?"

"An auction house in Tokyo."

"Why go to that trouble, Christopher? Why not auction

them here in New York? At Sotheby's or wherever?"

Pure smugness now. "It's like Brian Epstein with the Beatles. You're number one in England, but at some point you have to take them to America. Maybe the time has come."

Wingate's arrogance finally triggers something deep within me, a well of outrage I try to keep capped, but which sometimes explodes despite my best efforts or interests.

"I was lying about the FBI," I say in a cold voice. "I haven't told them about the paintings yet. I wanted to talk to you first. But since you're being such a prick, and you haven't told me anything helpful, I *am* going to tell them. Do you know what will happen then? This canvas you're drooling over will become evidence in a serial murder case, and it'll be confiscated. And you won't make jack*shit* off it, because it won't be sellable. Not for a very long time, Christopher. It's like assets being stuck in probate, only worse."

Wingate straightens up with the hammer and turns to face me. He still has a couple of nails in his mouth; I'd like to shove them down his throat.

"What do you want to know?" he asks.

"I want a name. I want to know who paints these pictures."

He hefts the hammer and drops its head into the palm of his other hand with a slap. "If you haven't told the FBI yet, you're not in a very good position to make that kind of demand."

"One phone call."

Now he smiles. "A phone call requires access to a phone. Do you think you can get to that one?"

He points the hammer at a cordless phone on the counter behind him. I could probably Mace him and get to it, but that's not really the point. The point is that he's willing to hurt me – maybe to kill me – to protect his little art monopoly. Which means he probably knows a lot more than he's saying about the origin of the Sleeping Women.

"Well?" he says, almost playfully.

I back toward the iron staircase, finding the spray nozzle with my finger as I go.

"Where are you going, Jordan?" He takes three quick steps toward me, the hammer held waist high. As he does, a new scenario hits me with chilling force. What if the painter isn't the killer at all? What if Wingate masterminded the whole thing to earn millions in commissions? What if *he* kills the women and merely commissions the paintings from some starving artist? His dark eyes flash as he moves forward, and the violence in them unnerves me.

In one movement I whip out the Mace can and blast his face from six feet, the powerful stream filling his eyes, nose, and mouth with enough chemical irritant to set his mucous membranes on fire. He screams like a child, drops the hammer, and starts clawing his eyes. I almost want to steer him to the sink, so pitiful are his cries, but I'm not that crazy. As I whirl toward the stairs, my heart beating wildly, a giant hand swats me back into the room and a fusillade of distant cannon hammers my eardrums.

When I open my eyes, I see gray smoke and a screaming man. Wingate is shrieking so loudly that I can't think. You don't hear men scream like that except in war zones, when they're lying on the ground holding their guts or genitals in a bowl some medic gave them. Now Wingate is running around the room like a blind rat in a sinking ship; he might just go out a window. I scrabble to my knees and crawl toward the staircase, but the smoke only gets thicker. The lower floors of the gallery are on fire.

"Is there a fire escape?" I shout, but he doesn't hear me. He's still trying to claw his eyes out.

To my left I see a faint blue glow, a streetlight. That means a window. I crawl quickly to it and raise my head above the sill, hoping for a fire escape. I find a thirty-foot drop instead. Crabbing back toward the stairs, I stop halfway and wait for Wingate to rush by. A couple of seconds later he does, and I tackle him.

"SHUT UP!" I shout. "IF YOU DON'T SHUT UP, YOU'RE GOING TO DIE!"

"My eyes!" he wails. *"I'm blind!"*

"YOU'RE NOT BLIND! I MACED YOU! STAY HERE!"

Standing erect in the thickening smoke, I rush to the sink and fill a coffee decanter with water. Then I stagger back to him and flush out his eyes. He screams some more, but the water seems to do him some good.

"More," he coughs.

"No time. We have to get out. Where's the fire escape?"

"Bed . . . bedroom."

"Where is it?"

"Bl – Back wall . . . door."

"Get up!"

He doesn't move until I yank his arm hard enough to tear a ligament. Then he rolls over and starts crawling beside me. As we move, a roar like the voice of some satanic creature bellows from the staircase. The fire's voice. I've heard it in lots of places, and the sound turns my insides to jelly. There's a reason human beings will jump ten floors onto concrete to escape being burned alive. That roar is part of it.

I go through the bedroom door first. The smoke here is not as bad. There's only one window. As I crawl toward it, Wingate grabs my ankle.

"Wait!" he rasps. "The painting!"

"Screw the painting!"

"I can't leave it! My sprinklers aren't working!"

The pressure of his hand on my ankle is gone. When I turn back, I see no sign of him. The fool is willing to die for money. I've seen people die for worse reasons, but not many. I stand in the door and try to see through the smoke, but it's useless.

"Forget the goddamn painting!" I shout into the gray wall.

"Help me!" he calls back. "I can't move the crate alone!"

"Leave it!"

No reply. After a few seconds, I hear something whacking the crate. Probably the hammer. Then a creaking sound like tearing wood.

"It's stuck!" he yells. Then a series of racking coughs cuts through the roar of the advancing fire. *"I need a knife! I can cut the canvas loose!"*

I don't much care if Wingate wants to commit suicide, but it suddenly strikes me that the painting in that frame is worth more than money. Women's lives may depend on it. Dropping to my knees, I take a deep breath and crawl toward the coughing.

My head soon bumps something soft. It's Wingate, gagging as he tries to draw oxygen from the smoke. The flames have reached the top of the stairs, and in their orange glow I see the painting, half out of the crate but stuck against the side panel Wingate only partially removed. Unzipping my fanny pack, I take out my Canon, pop off three shots, then zip it back up and grab Wingate's shoulder.

"YOU'RE GOING TO DIE IF YOU DON'T MOVE!"

His face is gray, his eyes nearly swollen shut. I grab his legs and try to drag him to the bedroom, but the exertion makes me dizzy, and for an instant my eyes go black. I'm near to fainting, and fainting here would mean death. Dropping his feet, I rush to the window, flip the catch, and shove it upward.

The outside air hits my face like a bucketful of cold water, filling my lungs with rich oxygen and clearing my head. I have a momentary fantasy of going back for Wingate, but survival instinct overrides that impulse. Below me is the iron framework of a fire escape. It's the classic New York model; one floor down, a latched ladder awaits only my weight to send it to the pavement below. But when I crawl down to the platform and pull the latch, the ladder stays where it is. A wave of smoke billows from the window behind me. I pull down on a rung with all my strength, but nothing moves.

I lived in New York long enough to know how to work one of these things, and this one isn't functioning. It's fifteen feet to the cracked cement of the alley below, my best target a space between some garbage cans and a steam grate. A distant siren echoes up the chasm, but I don't think the fire department will start their rescue work in this alley. I've got to get down, and there's only one way to do it.

Crawling over the railing, I lower myself until I'm hanging by my hands from the edge of the platform. I'm five feet eight, which shortens the drop to about ten feet. No great shakes for a paratrooper, but I don't happen to be one. I did drop from a helicopter once in North Carolina, photographing an Army training mission. It felt like fifty feet, though it was supposedly twelve.

What the hell. A broken ankle is nothing compared with Wingate's fate. I open my hands and drop through the dark. My heels strike a glancing blow on the pavement and fly out from under me, leaving my right buttock and wrist to absorb the main force of the impact. I yell in pain, but the exhilaration of escape is a powerful anesthetic. Rolling to my left,

I get to my feet and look back up at the platform. The window I crawled through moments ago is spouting fire.

Jesus.

My next instinct is to look down the alley, and what I see there sends a cold ripple along my flesh. There's a man standing at the far end, watching me. I see him only in silhouette, because all the light is behind him. He looks big, though. Big enough to really mess me up. As I stare, he moves toward me, first uncertainly, then with a determined gait. He does not look like a fireman. My hand goes to my pocket, but the Mace is not there. I lost it upstairs. All I have is a camera, which is less than useless in this situation. I whirl and run toward the other end of the alley, toward the banshee wail of sirens.

4

Careening out of the mouth of the alley, I come face-to-face with a spectacle I covered dozens of times early in my career. The classic fire scene: engines with red lights flashing and hoses spraying; squad cars and EMS vehicles arriving; cops yelling; a crowd of spectators, the eternal crowd, spilling out of the bar and the video store, gaping, drinking, and shouting into cell phones. Most of them poured out of the bar after hearing "an explosion," and the smell of liquor spices the air. The police are trying to herd them back behind a taped perimeter, to protect them from falling brick and flying glass, but they're slow to move. I walk right past the biggest cop and point my camera at the fire.

"Hey!" he yells. "Get back behind this tape!"

"The *Post*," I tell him, holding up my camera.

"Let me see your card."

"I don't have it. I was having a drink in the bar with some friends. That's why all I have is this crappy point-and-shoot. Give me a break, man, I'm the first one here. I can scoop everybody."

As the cop deliberates, I turn back to the mouth of the alley, forty meters away, but no one comes running out of it. The corner wall blurs for a moment, though, the vertical line of brick seeming to wrinkle in the dark. Was that him? Is he trying to figure a way to get to me even now? A deep crack rumbles from the bowels of Wingate's building, and masonry cascades into the street. The crowd gives its obligatory gasp.

"Come on, man! I'm missing the show!"

The cop jerks his head toward the building, and I'm past him in a flash, moving along the perimeter of the crowd, shooting as I go. No one seems to notice that I'm shooting the crowd and not the fire. Every now and then I point the camera up at the burning building, but I don't waste any exposures on it.

The expressions on the faces are all the same: primitive fascination bordering on glee. A couple of female faces show empathy, a sense that this destruction is a tragedy, but with no shrieking mothers with infants leaping from windows, no teenagers trying to climb down burning bedsheets, the mood is more like a party.

If the guy in the alley didn't set this fire, the person who did is probably in this crowd. Arsonists love to watch their fires burn, they almost have to do it. But what are the odds that this blaze was set by a firebug? Twenty-four hours after I discover a link between the Sleeping Women and the New Orleans victims, the only human connection to the artist is burned alive? The timing is too perfect. This fire was set to silence Christopher Wingate. And the man who did it could be standing within yards of me right now. I may already have his face on film.

From the reading I did after Jane was taken, I learned that serial killers often return to the scenes of their crimes, to revel in their success, to relive their dreadful acts, even to masturbate where they listened to their victims' pleas. Killing Wingate would be nothing like killing the women in the paintings; it would be a utilitarian crime, an act of survival. But the murderer might well wait to be sure he accomplished his goal.

57

And who knows what twisted history the two men might have shared? What did Wingate say to me? *You wouldn't believe some of the things I've seen.*

As I turn back from the burning building, a furtive move-ment registers in my peripheral vision. Wide eyes dropping below the back edge of the crowd, off to my right. People are standing five deep at the tape now, and I can't see the eyes anymore. But as I watch, a sock cap begins to move along the back of the crowd, coming in my direction. Throwing up my camera arm, I pop off a shot over the heads of the crowd. The head disappears, then reappears still closer. I squeeze the shutter release again, but it won't depress, and then I feel the vibration of the rewind motor in my hand; the crowd noise prevented my hearing it.

I'm out of film.

The sock cap moves forward now, pushing slowly toward me through the crowd. I'm tempted to wait for a good look at his face, but what if he's carrying a gun? Close enough to see is close enough to shoot, and I don't want to die here. "Jordan Glass, Noted War Photographer, Shot Dead on Fifteenth Street in Chelsea." That headline has the ironic ring of truth, and I'm not waiting for it to be borne out by events. Glancing around, I rush up to the fire captain, who's standing by the one of the engines, talking to a cop.

"Captain!"

He gives me an annoyed look.

"Jane Adams, from the *Post*. I was shooting the crowd back there, and I passed a guy who smelled like gasoline. When I said something about it, he started following me through the crowd. He was wearing a sock cap."

The fireman's eyes go wide. "Where?"

I turn and point back to the spot I left moments ago. There, for an instant, I see a pale bearded face and blazing eyes beneath the sock cap. It vanishes so quickly, I wonder if it was there at all.

"*There! Did you see him?*"

The fire captain races toward the tape, followed by the cop who was standing beside him.

"What was that?" asks another cop who suddenly appears at my side.

"I smelled gas on a guy over there. They went to check it out."

"No shit? Good work. You with the *Times*?"

"The *Post*. I just hope they get him." *And what do I tell them if they do?*

"Yeah. This is one fucked-up crime scene. He could be the guy, though."

The cop is young and Italian, with a five-o'clock shadow that looks more like midnight. "What do you mean?"

"They just found a guy in a car across the street. Dead as a hammer."

"What?" I whirl and try to see, but the crowd obscures my view. "How did he die?"

"Somebody cut his throat. You believe that? Wearing a suit and tie. Looks like he hasn't been dead an hour. Something strange going on here."

"Who was he?"

"No wallet. Like a slaughterhouse in that car."

The fire captain is already pushing back toward us, the cop in tow.

"See anything?" the Italian cop calls to them.

The other cop shakes his head. "Crowd's too big. Guy could be two feet away, we wouldn't know except by the smell."

"I'll make a pass," says the Italian, tipping his cap to me as he walks toward the tape.

The guy *could* be two feet away. And there isn't any gasoline smell. He could kill me before I know he's there. It's time to go. But how? My cab is long gone, and walking isn't an option. Neither is the subway.

As I ponder my options, a yellow taxi pulls to the end of the block and disgorges a kid with two cameras hanging from his neck. The official press. Knowing he'll ask for a receipt, I start running, and I'm at full sprint before he has it in his hand.

"Taxi!" I yell. *"Don't let him go!"*

For some reason – maybe because he's seen my camera – the photographer holds the cab.

"Thanks!" I tell him, jumping into the backseat.

"Hey, are you with a paper?"

"No." I thump the plastic partition. "JFK! Move it!"

"Wait. Don't I know you?"

"Go!" I shout at the back of the cabbie's head.

"Hey, aren't you—"

With a screech of rubber, the cab is rolling toward the Queens-Midtown Tunnel.

My flight lands at Reagan National at 10:15 p.m., and when I deplane, there's a man in a suit waiting for me at the gate. He's holding a white cardboard sign that says "J. GLASS," but he doesn't look like a limo driver. He looks like a buffed-up accountant.

"I'm Jordan Glass."

"Special Agent Sims," he says with a frown. "You're late. Follow me."

He sets off down the concourse at a rapid clip and walks right past the down escalator marked "Baggage and Ground Transportation."

"I have some bags down there," I call after him. "My

cameras. They were on the earlier flight, so they're probably in storage."

"We have your camera cases, Ms. Glass. The airline lost your suitcase."

Great. Agent Sims leads me through a door marked "Airport Personnel Only," and a blast of cold air hits my face. It's fall in Washington too, but unlike New York, the humidity here adds a taste of home to the air. Home as in Mississippi. My present residence is in San Francisco, but no place I've ever lived has replaced the fecund, subtropical garden of creeks, cotton fields, oak, and pine forests where I grew up.

The concrete is slick with rain, reflecting the bright lights of the terminal and the dimmer blue ones of the runway. Sims helps me onto a baggage truck and signals its jump-suited driver, who takes off across the airfield. My aluminum camera cases are stacked in luggage that is well behind us.

"I thought we were going into the city," I shout over the engine noise. "To the Hoover Building."

"The chief had to get back to Quantico," Sims yells back. "That's where the meeting is now."

"How are we getting there?"

"On that."

As he points into the darkness, I see the sleek lines of a Bell 260 helicopter on skids. The baggage truck squeals to a stop. Agent Sims loads my cases into the chopper, then returns for me. He's a tall man, and the Bell is cramped quarters for him. Still, he doesn't look unhappy. Most of his fellow agents probably make the twenty-mile drive to Quantico in a Ford Taurus.

In less than a minute we are lifting into the night sky over the capital, the Pentagon receding behind us as we rotor southward over the lights of Alexandria, roughly parallel to I-95. In less than ten we're descending over the Quantico marine base, arrowing down to the FBI Academy helipad. There's an agent waiting to handle my baggage, but Sims leads me straight into the maze of the Academy building. After a short elevator ride and a walk along a darkened hall, I'm escorted into an empty room, sterile and white, like some convention hotel meeting space.

"Wait here," says Sims.

The door shuts, then locks from the outside. Do they think I'm going to prowl the halls, looking for something to steal? If someone doesn't show in the next two minutes I might just sack out on the table. The last thing I want to do is sit down; my behind feels like a massive hematoma. Despite my exhaustion, I'm still nervy from the fire and the knowledge that Wingate is dead. The investigation will be severely handicapped without him. One thing is sure, though. It's not going to be like last year. Nobody's shutting me out this time.

The doorknob clicks. Then the door opens and two men walk in. The first is Daniel Baxter, looking scarcely changed from thirteen months ago when I first met him. He's dark-haired and compact, about five-ten, and corded with muscle. His eyes are brown and compassionate but steady as gunsights. The man behind him is taller – over six feet – and at least ten years older, with silver hair, an expensive suit, and a bluff Yalie look. But his grayish-blue eyes, hooded by flesh, suggest a sinister George Plimpton. Baxter doesn't move to shake my hand, and he speaks as he takes his seat.

"Ms. Glass, this is Doctor Arthur Lenz. He's a forensic psychiatrist who consults for the Bureau."

Lenz extends his hand, but I only nod in return. Shaking

hands with men is always awkward for me, so I don't do it. There's no way to equalize the size difference, and I don't like them to feel they have an edge. The men I know well, I hug. The rest can make do.

"Please sit down," says Baxter.

"No, thanks."

"I suppose you have an explanation for missing the plane I booked for you?"

"Well—"

"Before you go any further, let me advise you that Christopher Wingate has been under Bureau surveillance since you called me from the airplane."

I wasn't sure whether I was going to admit being at the fire. Now there's no way to deny it. "You had people outside his gallery?"

Baxter nods, his face coloring with anger. "We've got some nice shots of you entering the building about forty minutes before it went up." He opens a file labeled "NOKIDS" and slides a photo across the table. There I am, in low-res digital splendor.

"I knew Wingate probably had information about my sister."

"Did he?"

"Yes and no."

Baxter's anger boils over at last. "What the hell did you think you were going to accomplish in there?"

"I did accomplish something in there! And it's a good thing I did, because he would have been dead by the time you guys decided to question him."

This sets them back a little.

"And if you had people outside the gallery," I push on, "why didn't they bust in there and try to save us?"

"We had one agent at the scene, Ms. Glass, doing

63

surveillance from his car. The fire started on the first floor, and it was explosive in nature. An incendiary device made of gasoline and liquid soap."

"Homemade napalm." I know it well from the "little wars" that don't make the evening news.

"Yes. The sprinkler system was disabled prior to the device being detonated, the fire alarm as well. We've since determined that the fire escape ladders were also wired in the up position. All inoperative."

"You think you're telling me something? I had to jump to save myself. Your guy couldn't do anything to help?"

"Our guy did do something. He died there."

A wave of heat tells me my face is red.

Baxter's eyes are merciless. "Special Agent Fred Coates, twenty-eight years old, married with three kids. When the bomb went off, he called the fire department. He got out of his car and shot pictures of the building and the first people on the scene, in case the perp stuck around. Then he got back into his car and called the New York field office on his cell phone. He was talking to his Special Agent in Charge when somebody reached through the window and slit his throat. The SAC heard him coughing up blood for twenty seconds. Then nothing. The killer stole his credentials and camera. He missed one flash memory card that had fallen between the console and Agent Coates's seat. That's where we got the shot of you. We lost his pictures of the crowd."

"Jesus. I'm sorry."

Baxter spears me with an accusing look. "You think that helps anything? I told you to come straight here."

"Don't try to put this on me! I didn't put that guy there, okay? You did. Whoever killed him would have set that fire whether I was there or not. And I *do* have pictures of the crowd."

Both men lean forward, their mouths open.

"Where?" asks Dr. Lenz.

"We'll talk about that in a minute. I want to clarify something right up front. This isn't going to be a one-way conversation."

"Do you realize how important every minute is?" Baxter asks. "By withholding that film—"

"My sister's been missing for over a year, okay? I think she can wait another twenty minutes."

"You don't have all the facts."

"And that's exactly what I want."

Baxter shows Lenz his exasperation.

"Could someone have killed Coates for his wallet and camera?" I ask. "Could his murder be unrelated to the fire?"

"Why leave the cell phone behind?" Baxter counters. "And the car? His keys were found in the ignition."

"What are the odds that a garden-variety arsonist would murder someone watching a fire?"

"Million to one against. Ms. Glass, that firebomb was planted to do exactly what it did. Kill Wingate and destroy his records. You're lucky you didn't go up with the rest."

"It was Wingate who almost killed me. He could have saved himself, but he tried to save the stupid painting, and like a fool I tried to save him."

"What painting?" asks Lenz.

"*Sleeping Woman Number Twenty*. It was the only one of the series he had in the place, and he killed himself trying to save it."

"I wonder why," Lenz says softly. "Surely it would have been insured."

"The insurance wouldn't have been enough."

"Why not?"

"When I told Wingate I was going to the FBI, that the women in the pictures were almost certainly the victims from New Orleans, he was ecstatic. He said the new canvas would probably sell for double the standing bid on it, and that was one point five million pounds sterling."

"Did he mention the bidder's name?"

"Takagi."

"What did the painting look like?" Lenz asks. "Like the ones you saw in Hong Kong?"

"Yes and no. I don't know anything about art, but this one was more realistic than the ones I saw. Almost photographically realistic."

"The woman appeared to be dead?"

"Absolutely."

Baxter reaches into the file, removes a photograph, and pushes it across the table at me. It's a head shot of a young dark-haired woman, a candid shot, probably taken by a family member. It's well off horizontal, which makes me think it was taken by a child. But that's not what sends a shiver through me.

"That's her. *Damn* it. Who is she?"

"Last known victim," Baxter replies.

"How long ago was she taken?"

"Four and a half weeks."

"What was the interval between her and the one before her?"

"Six weeks."

"And before that?"

"Fifty-four days. Seven and a half weeks."

This decreasing time span bears out my reading, as well. One theory says that as serial offenders get a taste for their work, their confidence grows, and they try to fulfill their fantasies more and more frequently. Another speculates that they begin to "decompensate," that the neuroses driving them begin to fracture their minds, pushing them toward capture or even death, and the path they choose is accelerated murder.

"So you figure he's due for another soon."

The two men share a look I cannot interpret. Then the psychiatrist gives a slight nod, and Baxter turns to me.

"Ms. Glass, approximately one hour ago, a young Caucasian woman disappeared from the parking lot of a New Orleans grocery store."

I close my eyes against the fearful impact of this statement. Jane has another sister in the black hole of her current existence. "You think it was him?"

Lenz answers first. "Almost surely."

"Where was she taken from?"

"A suburb of New Orleans, actually. Metairie."

He actually got the pronunciation right: *Met*-a-ree. He's picked it up from a year and a half of working the case.

"What store in Metairie?"

"It's called Dorignac's. On Veterans Boulevard."

This time he missed it. "*Dorn*-yaks," I correct him. "I used to shop there all the time. It's a family-owned store, like the old Schwegmann chain."

Baxter makes a note. "The victim left her house a few minutes before the store closed – eight-fifty p.m. central time – to get some andouille sausage. She was making dip for a birthday party at her job tomorrow. She worked in a dental office, as a receptionist. By nine-fifteen, her husband started to worry. He tried her car phone and got no answer. He knew the store was closed, so he got the kids out of bed and drove down to see if his wife had a dead battery."

"He found her empty car with the door open?"

Baxter gives a somber nod.

This happened to two victims before Jane. "It sounds like him."

"Yes. But it could be a couple of other things. This woman could have been seeing a guy on the side. She meets him at the store to talk something over, maybe even for a quickie in the car. Suddenly, she decides to split for good."

"Leaving her kids behind?"

"It happens." Baxter's voice is freighted with experience. "But talking to the detective, this doesn't sound like that type of situation. The other alternative is conventional rape. A guy on the prowl with a van and a rape kit, looking for a target of opportunity. He sees her going to her car alone and snatches her."

"Has anybody like that been operating in the area over the past few weeks?"

"No."

"Did any other victims shop at Dorignac's? Jane must have gone there sometimes."

"Several shopped there occasionally. The store stocks some regional foods other stores don't. The Jefferson Parish detectives are grilling the staff right now, and our New Orleans field office is already taking their lives apart. With help from the Quantico computers. It's a full-court press, but if it's like the others . . . none of that will come to anything."

I'm about to speak, when shock steals my breath. "Wait a minute. By what you've told me, the man who took the woman from Dorignac's couldn't have killed Wingate."

Baxter nods slowly. "Nine-one-one in New York got the call about the Wingate fire at seven fifty-one p.m. eastern time. The Dorignac's victim disappeared from Metairie between eight fifty-five p.m. and nine-fifteen central time.

That's a maximum difference of two hours and twenty-four minutes."

"So there's no way the same person could have done both. Not even with a Learjet at his disposal."

"There's one way," says Baxter. "The incendiary device used to ignite the gallery had a timer on it. If it was set long enough in advance, the same person could have gotten back to New Orleans in time to take the woman from Dorignac's."

"But it wasn't," I think aloud. "*He* wasn't."

"How do you know?"

"Because I saw him."

"What?"

As quickly as I can, I describe the drama of the man from the alley, shooting the blind photo over the crowd, and sending the fireman and cop after him.

"Where's your film?" asks Baxter, his eyes burning with excitement.

"Not here, if that's what you're thinking. Are you positive Wingate's murder was related to my sister's case?"

"Virtually certain," says Lenz.

"So you're saying there's more than one person behind the disappearances."

"I'm not saying it. The evidence is. Two UNSUBs, not one."

UNSUB is FBI-speak for Unknown Subject. "Two killers operating as a team?"

"It happens," says Baxter. "But teams usually work side by side. Two ex-cons in a van, snatching and torturing women, that kind of thing. What I'm postulating would be something far more sophisticated."

"Have you ever seen anything like that before? People cooperating over a long distance to facilitate serial murder or kidnapping?"

"Only in child pornography," says Baxter, "and that's a different thing."

"It's unprecedented in the literature," says Dr. Lenz. "Which does nothing to rule out the possibility. Harvesting women's skins was unknown until Ed Gein was caught doing it in the fifties. Then Tom Harris used it in a book and made it part of the national consciousness. In our business, you proceed from a very simple given: everything imaginable is possible, and may well be happening as we ponder it."

"How would it work?" I ask. "How do you see it?"

"Division of labor," says Lenz. "The killer's in New Orleans, the painter in New York."

"But Wingate was killed in New York."

"Different motive. That was self-preservation."

"I had the same thought up there. So the New Orleans guy kidnaps the women. How does the New York guy do the paintings? He works from photographs? Or he flies to New Orleans to paint corpses?"

"If that scenario is the answer," says Baxter, "I pray to God he flies. We can take backbearings from airline computers and work out a list of potential suspects."

"Could it really be that easy?"

"It just might be. It's been a long eighteen months, Ms. Glass. Nobody knows that better than you. We're due for a break."

I nod hopefully, but inside I know better. "If Wingate was killed to silence him, how do you think it happened? The logic of it?"

Baxter leans back and steeples his fingers. "I think Wingate himself told the UNSUB in New York about the Hong Kong incident. Wingate's phone records show a call from the curator of the Hong Kong exhibit to his gallery

70

within an hour of your making the disturbance in Hong Kong."

"Wingate knew about Hong Kong while I was talking to him?"

"Undoubtedly. Though I doubt he knew it was you who caused the disturbance."

"If he did, he was a hell of an actor."

"Did he try to get information from you?" asks Lenz.

"Not really." A hot flash brings sweat to my face. "What if he was setting me up for the killer and got caught in his own trap?"

"Quite possible," says Baxter. "If Wingate somehow knew it was you in Hong Kong, then he knew your sister was in one of the paintings. Maybe he knew everything about the crimes. He calls the UNSUB and tells him you're coming to the gallery, but he doesn't want any violence there. He also wants to know who you've talked to before you die. Wingate thinks you're going to be murdered after you leave his place, but the UNSUB has a better idea. He sees his chance to take you both out."

"That's it," I murmur. "Jesus. Wingate ensured his own death."

"Almost certainly," says Lenz. "And Wingate could have been the key to this whole case. Goddamn it."

"I'm not sure he knew that much."

"You believe what he told you?"

"To a point. I don't think he knew the killer's name. He said he wasn't even sure if it was a man or a woman."

"What?" both men ask in unison.

"He said he'd never seen the artist's face. It was all done with blind drops or something."

"He used that term?" asks Baxter. "Blind drops?"

"He said he got it from spy movies." I quickly summarize

71

Wingate's explanation of how he received the first painting, and the subsequent drops of cash in train station lockers.

"I suppose it could have happened that way," Baxter concedes. "But from what I've got on Wingate so far, he was no font of truth."

"What do you have on him?"

"For one thing, his name wasn't Christopher Wingate. It was Zjelko Krnich. He was born in Brooklyn in 1956, to Yugoslavian immigrants. Ethnic Serbs."

"You're kidding."

"Krnich's father abandoned his wife and kids when Zjelko was seven. The boy scrapped in the streets, then moved on to small-time drug dealing, then pimping. He hopped a freighter to Europe when he was twenty and kicked around there for a few years, selling grass and coke to feed himself. He hung out in resort areas, and his drug business put him in contact with some trendy people. He fell in with a Parisian woman who dealt in paintings, some genuine, others not. He picked up the trade from her. She gave him his Anglo name. After a couple of years, they fell out over money she claimed he stole. Krnich suddenly reappeared in New York, legally changed his name to Wingate, and started working at a small gallery in Manhattan. Twenty years later, he's one of the hottest dealers in the world."

"He was hot, all right. About three hundred and fifty degrees when I last saw him."

"Residential fires burn at over a thousand degrees Fahrenheit, Ms. Glass." Baxter is not up for humor tonight, not even the gallows variety. His eyes are flint hard; his patience has come to an end. "I want the film you shot tonight."

72

"Once I give you that, you're going to cut me out."

"That's not true," says Lenz. "You're a relative of a victim."

"Which counts for zero, in my experience. You weren't around last year, Doctor. Back then it was like pulling teeth to get substantive information out of this guy."

"I can assure you that won't be the case this time," Lenz says smoothly.

Baxter starts to speak, but the psychiatrist cuts him off with a wave of his hand. Arthur Lenz obviously pulls a lot of weight in the ISU.

"Ms. Glass, I have a proposal for you. One I think will interest you."

"I'm listening."

"Fate has handed us a unique opportunity. Your appearance in Hong Kong caused a disturbance not because of the connection between the paintings and the kidnappings; the people in the gallery knew nothing about that. They were upset because you looked exactly like a woman in one of the paintings."

"So?"

"Imagine the reaction you might cause in the killer if you came face-to-face with him."

"I may have done that tonight, right?"

Lenz shakes his head. "I'm far from convinced that the man who attacked you tonight is the man who painted this remarkable series."

"Go on."

"Forensic art analysis has come a very long way in the past twenty years. Not only is there X-ray analysis, spectrography, infrared, and all the rest. There may be fingerprints preserved in the oil paint itself. We may find hairs or skin flakes. Now that we know about the paintings,

73

I believe they will lead us in short order to a suspect, or perhaps a group of them. Style analysis alone could produce a list of likely candidates. And once we have those suspects, Ms. Glass, *you* are the weapon I would most like to use against them."

Lenz wasn't kidding before. They do need me. They cooked all this up long before I got here.

"How would you feel about that?" asks the psychiatrist. "Posing as a special agent at suspect interviews? Casually walking into a room while Daniel and I observe suspects?"

"She'd kill to do it," says Baxter. "I know that much about her."

Lenz fires a harsh look at him. "Ms. Glass?"

"I'll do it."

"What did I tell you?" says Baxter.

"On one condition," I add.

"Shit," mutters Baxter. "Here it comes."

"What condition?" asks Lenz.

"I'm in the loop from now till the day you get the guy. I want access to everything."

Baxter rolls his eyes. "What do you mean by 'everything'?"

"I want to know everything you know. You have my word that I won't reveal anything you tell me. But I can't be excluded like last year. That almost killed me."

I expect Baxter to argue, but he just looks at the table and says, "Done. Where's your film?"

"I dropped it in a mailbox at JFK."

"A U.S. Postal Service box?"

"Yes."

"Do you remember which one?"

"It was near the American Airlines gates. It's addressed to my house in San Francisco. I'll give you the address. I bought the stamps and envelope near a newsstand. It was close to the mailbox as well."

"We'll get it. We can develop it at the lab right here."

"I figured you guys had mastered mail theft."

Baxter stifles an obscene reply and takes out a cell phone.

"One other thing," I add. "I shot three photos of *Sleeping Woman Number Twenty* before I escaped the building. It was in bad light, but I bracketed the exposures. I think they'll come out."

With a look of grudging admiration, Baxter dials a number and tells someone to find out who the postmaster general is and get him out of bed. When he hangs up, I say, "I want digital copies of those pictures e-mailed to the New Orleans field office and a set printed for me. I'll pick them up in the morning."

"You're going to New Orleans?" asks Lenz.

"That's right."

"It's too late to get a flight tonight."

"Then I expect you guys to get me a plane. I only came here at your request. I need to tell my sister's husband what's happened, and I want to tell him face-to-face. My mother, too. Before they hear about it some other way."

"They won't hear anything," says Baxter.

"Why not?"

"What's happened, really? You upset a few art lovers in Hong Kong. Nothing that would hit the papers."

"What about the fire in New York? Your dead agent?"

"Wingate was reputed to have mob ties. FBI surveillance would be expected. One reporter has already speculated that Wingate torched the place for the insurance and killed himself in the process."

"Are you saying you intend to keep this investigation secret?"

"As far as possible."

"But you must be trying to gather all the paintings, right? For forensic analysis? Won't that get out?"

"Maybe yes, maybe no. Look, Arthur is going to New Orleans in the morning, to speak to some art dealers there. Why don't you fly down with him then?"

"I'd be happy to fly down tonight," Lenz says, "if Ms. Glass feels such urgency. Can the plane be made ready?"

Baxter considers this. "I suppose. But Ms. Glass, please urge your brother-in-law to be discreet. And as for telling your mother . . . perhaps you should wait a bit on that."

"Why?"

"We've had some contact with her in the past year. She's not in the best shape."

"She never was."

"She's drinking heavily. I don't think we could rely upon her discretion."

"It's her daughter, Mr. Baxter. She deserves to know what's going on."

"But what do you really have to tell her? Nothing encouraging. Don't you think it might be better to wait?"

"I'll make that decision."

"Fine," he says wearily. "But your mother and brother-in-law are the limit of the circle. I know you worked for the *Times-Picayune* in New Orleans years ago. I'm sure you have friends down there. If you're going to be effective in our investigation, no one can know you're in town. No drinks with old friends, no human-interest story about the Pulitzer Prize-winning photographer back on her old beat. We'll be glad to put you up in a hotel."

"I'll probably stay with my brother-in-law. I haven't seen my sister's kids in a long time."

"All right. But you agree about the isolation? Until we

have suspects and you've confronted them, you talk to nobody who knows you, and you stay out of sight."

"Agreed. But I want a full update on the plane. That's our deal, right?"

Baxter sighs and looks at Lenz as if the psychiatrist has named his own poison. "Arthur can handle that."

Dr. Lenz stands and rubs his hands together, and I notice again how tall he is. "Why don't we get some coffee and doughnuts?" he says. "There's no in-flight service."

"Just a minute, Arthur," Baxter says. He looks at me, his eyes glacier cold. "Ms. Glass, I want you to listen to me. Nothing about this case fits known parameters. Our New Orleans UNSUB is not some low-self-image maintenance man with a gimp leg and a collection of mutilated Barbie dolls. We're dealing with at *least* one highly organized personality. A man who has kidnapped and probably killed twelve women without a trace. You may be on his radar. We don't know. We *do* know you're about to enter his territory. Be very careful, Ms. Glass. Don't let your mind wander for a moment. Or you could join your sister a lot sooner than God ever intended."

Despite the melodramatic tone, Baxter's warning gives me pause. This man does not speak lightly of danger. "Do you think I need protection?"

"I'm inclined to say yes. I'll make a final decision on that before you land in New Orleans. Just remember: Secrecy is the best protection."

"I hear you."

He stands and gives me a curt nod. "I appreciate your willingness to help us."

"You knew I would. It's personal for me."

Baxter reaches into the NOKIDS file and tosses out a photo of a brown-haired man in his late twenties, an

All-American boy smiling like it's his first job interview. Special Agent Fred Coates, no doubt. It's hard to picture him with his throat cut, spitting blood into a cell phone.

"It's personal for us too," says Baxter.

He speaks softly, but behind his eyes burns a volcanic fury. Daniel Baxter has tracked and caged some of the deadliest monsters of our time. Until tonight, the one that took my sister was merely one among others still at large. But now Special Agent Fred Coates lies on a cold morgue slab somewhere. FBI blood has been spilled. And the situation has most definitely changed.

5

The FBI Learjet hurtles into the Virginia sky at three a.m., after a long wait for mechanical checks, refueling, and a fresh flight crew. I should have waited for morning, but I couldn't. I learned unflappable patience during twenty years of globetrotting and thousands of hours behind my camera, but Jane's disappearance robbed me of that. I can no longer bear waiting. If I'm standing still, I have too much time to think. Motion is my salvation.

The interior of the jet is strangely comforting to me. I've done a fair amount of corporate work in my career, mostly shooting glossy annual reports, and corporate-jet travel is one of the perks. Some of my purist colleagues have criticized me for this, but when all is said and done, they have to worry about paying their bills, and I don't. I grew up poor; I can't afford to be a snob. The interior of this Lear is configured for work. Two seats face each other over a collapsible desktop, and Dr. Lenz has chosen these for us. He seems accustomed to the cramped quarters of the cabin, despite his heavy frame. I imagine he once shuttled between murder scenes the way I shuttled between wars.

Lenz looks at least sixty, and his face has begun to sag with a look of permanent weariness that I recognize from certain men I know – men who have seen too much and run out of emotional energy to deal with the burdens they already carry, much less those of the future. He looks, in short, like a man who has surrendered. I don't judge him for it. I'm twenty years younger, and I've come near to cracking myself.

"Ms. Glass," he says, "we have a little over two hours together. I'd like to spend that time as profitably as we can."

"I agree."

"Interviewing you – particularly since you're an identical twin – is almost like being able to interview your sister before the fact. I'd like to ask you some questions, some of them very personal."

"I'll answer what I think is relevant."

He blinks once, slowly, like an owl. "I hope you'll try to answer them all. By withholding information, you may prevent my learning something which could advance our efforts to find the killer."

"You've been using the word 'killer' since I arrived. You believe all the women are dead?"

His eyes don't waver. "I do. Daniel holds out some hope, but I do not. Does that bother you?"

"No. I feel the same way. I wish I didn't, but I can't imagine where they could possibly be. Eleven women – maybe twelve now – all held prisoner somewhere for up to eighteen months? Without one escaping? I can't see it. And the women in the later paintings look dead to me."

"And you have seen much death."

"Yes. I do have one question, though. Are you aware of the phone call I received eight months ago?"

"The one in the middle of the night? That you thought might be from your sister?"

"Yes. The Bureau traced it to a train station in Thailand."

Lenz grants me a smile of condolence. "I'm familiar with the incident. It's my opinion that the guess you made the following morning was correct. That it was someone you'd met during your efforts to locate your father, someone from an MIA family."

"I just thought maybe . . . me finding the paintings in Asia—"

"We're certainly looking into it. Rest assured. But I'd like to move on now, if we could."

"What do you want to know?"

"I understand you weren't that close to your sister as an adult, so I'd like you to tell me how you grew up. What shaped Jane's personality. And yours."

It's times like now I wish I smoked. "Okay. You know who my father was, right?"

"Jonathan Glass, the renowned war photographer."

"Yes. And there was only one war in Mississippi. The one for civil rights. He won his first Pulitzer for that. Then he went off to the other wars, which meant he was almost never home."

"How did the family react to that?"

"I handled it better than my sister or mother did. I understood why he went, even as a child. Why would you hang around the Mississippi backwoods if you could be roaming the world, going the places in his pictures?"

"You wanted to travel to war zones as a child?"

"Dad shot all kinds of pictures in those places. I didn't see any of his war stuff until I was old enough to go down to the public library and read *Look* and *Life* for myself. Mom wouldn't keep those shots in the house."

"Why did your mother marry a man who would never be home?"

"She didn't know that when she married him. He was just a big handsome Scots-English guy who looked like he could handle anything that came along. And he could, pretty much. He could survive in the jungle with nothing but a pocketknife. What he couldn't survive was married life in Mississippi. A nine-to-five job. That was hell for him.

"He tried to do right by her, to keep her with him as his career took off. He even moved her to New York. She lasted until she got pregnant. During her eighth month, he went on assignment to Kenya. She went down to Grand Central Station with six dollars in her purse and rode a train all the way to Memphis. Then the bus from Memphis to Oxford, Mississippi. If she hadn't been pregnant when she left, Dad probably never would have come back home. But he did. Not that often, but when he did, it was paradise for me. There were some glorious summers."

"What about Jane?"

"Not so much for her. We were twins, but emotionally we were different from early on. Some of it was just bad luck."

"How so?"

"Jane was mauled by a dog when she was four. It really tore up her arm." I close my eyes against that memory, a vicious attack I watched from forty yards away. By the time my mother reached her, the damage had been done. "She had to go through rabies shots, the whole thing. It made her fearful for the rest of her life."

"Did your mother dress the two of you identically, all that?"

"She tried. My father always resisted it when he was home, so I did too. He wanted us to be individuals. That's the photojournalist ethos in a nutshell. Rugged individualism. He taught me that, and a lot more."

"Photography?"

"Not so much that. He taught me to hunt and to fish. A little about the stars, trees, wild plants you could eat. He told

82

me stories about all the far-off places he'd visited. Strange customs, things you'd never read in *National Geographic*."

"Did he teach Jane those things?"

"He tried, but she wasn't open to much. She was like my mother that way. I think his stories reminded them that he was only home for a little while, that one day they'd wake up and he'd be gone."

"You were his favorite."

"Yes. And Jane was Mom's. But somehow that didn't count for as much. Because Dad was the dominant personality, even when he wasn't home. He was a doer. My mother just tried to cope, and didn't succeed very well at that."

"Jane resented his absences more as time passed?"

"Yes. I think she got to hate him before he disappeared, because of how sad Mom was, and because money was so tight."

"Your father didn't earn much money?"

"I don't really know. Some of the leading photojournalists of the Vietnam era worked for almost nothing. Whether my father did or not, he never sent much money back to us. He was big on bringing presents, though. I'm not saying he was a great guy, okay? I'm just saying he and I had a bond."

"Did your mother work?"

"For a while. Waitressing, a laundry, menial stuff. After she started drinking, not even that."

"Why did your father marry her?"

"I honestly think he did it because it was the only way she would have sex with him."

Lenz smiles wistfully. "That was common in my generation. Your mother was beautiful?"

"Yes. That was the irony that crippled the marriage. She looked exotic, but she wasn't. That was her Alsatian blood, I guess, the exotic part. Outside, a mysterious princess

– inside, plain as pabulum. All she wanted was a man to build her a house and come home from work every day at five-thirty."

"And Jane wanted the same thing?"

"Absolutely. From her father and her husband, when she found one. Dad never gave it to her, but she found a husband who did."

Lenz holds up his forefinger. "A few moments ago you used the word 'disappeared' about your father. Isn't it generally accepted that he died in Vietnam?"

"Yes. Cambodia, actually. But I've never accepted that. I never felt that he was dead, and over the years there've been occasional sightings of him in Asia by former colleagues. I've spent a lot of money through the years trying to find him."

"What sort of scenario do you envision? If your father survived, that might mean that he chose not to return to America. That he chose to abandon you, your sister, and your mother."

"Probably so."

"Do you think he was capable of that?"

I pull back my hair, digging my fingernails into my scalp as I go. "I don't know. I always suspected that he had a woman there. In Vietnam. Maybe another whole family. Lots of servicemen did. Why should photographers be any different?"

Lenz's blue-gray eyes flicker with cold light. "Could you forgive him that?"

The central question of my life. "I've spent a lot of time in distant countries photographing wars, just as he did. I know how lonely it can be. You're cut off from the world, some-times from any friendly contact. You might be the only person for a hundred miles who understands English, living in a hell no one else will ever really see. It's a loneliness that's almost despair."

"But Vietnam wasn't like that. It was bursting with Americans."

"Dad worked a lot of other places. If I find out he's alive – or that he did survive for a while – I'll deal with it then."

"You said you never *felt* your father was dead. What about Jane? Do you feel she's dead?"

"I felt it twelve hours before I got the call."

"So you two shared the sort of intuitive bond that many twins speak of?"

"Despite our differences, we had that. It's a very real thing, in my opinion."

"I don't dispute it. You're being very forthcoming with me, Jordan, and I appreciate that. I think we could save a lot of time if you would just describe what you consider the seminal events in your lives as siblings."

"I don't recall any particularly seminal events."

Lenz's eyes appear soft, but there is a hardness beneath them, a cruelty even, and it shows now. Perhaps that's a requirement for his type of work.

"This is not psychotherapy, Jordan. We don't have weeks to labor through your defense mechanisms. I'm sure if you think about it, certain events will come to mind."

I say nothing.

"For example, I noticed in your file that you never graduated high school. Jane graduated with honors, participated in all sorts of extracurricular activities. Cheerleading, debate, et cetera. You did none of that."

"You guys really dig, don't you?"

"I also discovered that you had the highest ACT score in your school. So." He folds his arms and raises his eyebrows. "Why would such a student drop out?"

85

The small jet suddenly seems smaller. "Look, I don't see how questions about my high school life are going to help you understand Jane."

"What happens to one child happens to the other. Think back. The two of you are twelve years old. Your father has died, your mother can't cope, there's no money to buy necessities. You're twins, you have the same teachers, yet you turn out opposites. What's the story?"

"You just summed it up, Doctor. Let's move on to something that might actually help you find Jane's killer. That's the goal here, right?"

Lenz only watches me. "You're a photographer. You use filters to produce certain visual effects, yes? To modify light before it reaches the film?"

"Yes."

"Human beings use similar filters. Emotional filters. They're put in place by our parents, our siblings, our friends and enemies. Will you concede that?"

"I guess."

"Daniel and I intend to use you for a critical purpose in this case. But before we bring you into contact with any suspects, I must understand you. I need to be able to correct for your particular filter."

I look at the porthole window to my left. There's not enough moonlight to show clouds. We could be at five thousand feet or thirty-five thousand. That's how I feel in relation to my past and future, unanchored, floating between the unknown and the known-too-well. Lenz wants my secrets. Why? Psychiatrists, like photographers, are essentially voyeurs. But some things are between me and my conscience, no one else. Not even God, if I can help it. Still, I feel some obligation to cooperate. Lenz is the professional in this sphere, not me. And he is trusting me not to screw up his investigation. I suppose I have to trust him a little.

"The years after my father disappeared were difficult. The truth is, Jane had been living as though he were dead for several years before that. Her strategy was assimilation. Conformity. She studied hard, became cheerleader, then head cheerleader, and kept the same boyfriend for three years. I give her a lot of credit. Being popular isn't easy without money."

"Money seems to be a recurring theme with Jane."

"Not only with her. Before Dad was gone, I didn't realize how poor we were. But by thirteen, you start to notice. Material things are part of high school snobbery. Clothes and shoes, what kind of car you have, your house. Mom wrecked our car, and after that we didn't have one. She drank more and more, and it seemed like the power company cut our electricity every other month. It was embarrassing. One day, prowling through the attic, I discovered three footlockers filled with old camera equipment. Mom told me that when she got pregnant with us, she persuaded Dad to open a portrait studio, to try to make their lives more stable. I don't know why he went along with her. It never came to anything, of course. But he kept the equipment. A Mamiya large-format camera, floodlights, a background sheet, darkroom equipment, the works. Mom wanted to sell it all, but I threw a fit and she let me keep it. Over the next few months, I taught myself to use the stuff. A year later, I was running a portrait studio out of our house and shooting snaps for the Oxford *Eagle* in whatever spare time I had. Our lives improved. I was paying the light bill and buying the groceries, and because of that, I could pretty much do what I wanted."

Lenz nods encouragement. "And what did you want?"

"My own life. Oxford's a college town, and I rode all over

87

it on my ten-speed bicycle, watching people, shooting pictures. Sony introduced the Walkman in my junior year of high school, and from the moment I got one, I lived with a soundtrack pouring into my ears and a camera around my neck. While Jane and her friends were dancing to the Bee Gees, I listened to homemade tapes of my father's records: Joni Mitchell, Motown, Neil Young, the Beatles, and the Stones."

"It sounds like an idyllic childhood," Lenz says with a knowing smile. "Is that what it was?"

"Not exactly. While other girls my age were riding out to Sardis Reservoir to fumble around in backseats with guys from the football team, I was doing something a little different."

A deep stillness settles over Lenz's body. Like a priest, he has heard so many confessions that nothing could surprise him, yet he waits with a receptivity that seems to pull the words from my mouth.

"The first week of my senior year, our history teacher died. He was about seventy. To fill his shoes, the school board hired a young alumnus named David Gresham, who was teaching night classes at Ole Miss. Gresham had been drafted in 1970, and served one tour in Vietnam. He came back to Oxford wounded, but his wounds weren't visible, so the school board didn't notice them. After a few days in his class, I did. Sometimes he would stop speaking in midsentence, and it was clear that his mind was ten thousand miles away. His brain had skipped off track, jumped from our reality to one my classmates couldn't even guess at. But I could. I watched Mr. Gresham very closely, because he'd been to the place where my father vanished. One day after school, I stayed to ask him what he knew about Cambodia. He knew a lot – none of it good, except the beauty of Phnom Penh and Angkor Wat. When he asked why I was interested, I told him about my father. I hadn't meant to, but when I looked into his eyes, my pain and grief poured out like a river through a broken dam. A month later, we became lovers."

"How old was he?" asks Lenz.

"Twenty-six. I was seventeen and a half. A virgin. We both knew it was dangerous, but there was never any question of him seducing an innocent child. Yes, there was a void in my life because of my father's death; yes, he was a sympathetic older man. But I knew exactly what I was doing. He taught me a lot about the world. I discovered a lot about myself, about my body and what it could do. For me and for someone else. And I gave some peace to a boy who had been broken in some fundamental way that could never be corrected, only made less painful."

"It's amazing that you found each other," Lenz says without a trace of judgment in his eyes. "This did not end well, of course."

"We managed to keep our relationship secret for most of the year. During that time, he opened up about Vietnam, and through his eyes I experienced things my father must have seen as well. Seen, but kept out of his letters. Even out of his photographs. In April, one of David's neighbors saw us kissing at the creek behind his house – with my flannel shirt open to the waist, no less – and took it on himself to report it to the school board. The board called a special meeting, and during something called 'executive session' gave David the option of resigning and leaving town before they opened an investigation that would destroy both our futures. To protect him, I denied everything, but it didn't help. I offered to leave town with him, but he told me that wouldn't be fair to me. Ultimately, we were incompatible, he said. When I asked why, he said, 'Because you have something I don't.' 'What?' I asked.''

"A future?" Lenz finishes.

"Right. Two nights later, he went down to the creek and managed to drown himself. The coroner called it an accident, but David had enough scotch in him to sedate a bull.''

"I'm sorry.''

My eyes seek out the porthole again, a round well of night. "I like to think he was unconscious when he went under the water. He probably thought his death would end the scandal, but it only got worse. Jane had a breakdown brought on by social embarrassment. My mother just drank more. There was talk of putting us in foster homes. I went back to school with my head high, but it didn't last. My Star Student award was revoked. Then my appointment book went blank. No one wanted me shooting their family portraits. I'd done a lot of the senior pictures, but people didn't even pick them up. They had them reshot elsewhere. When I refused to abase myself in contrition, various mothers told the school board that they didn't want their daughters exposed to a 'teenage Jezebel.' They really called me that. Before long, the ostracism bled over onto Jane. She was cut dead a hundred times on the street by parents who thought she was me. At that point, I did what David should have done. I had three thousand dollars in the bank. I took two thousand, packed my clothes and cameras, rode the bus to New Orleans, got a judge to emancipate me, and scratched up a job developing prints for the staff photographers at the *Times-Picayune*. A year later, I was a staff photographer myself.''

"Did you continue to support your family financially?''

"Yes. But things between Jane and me only got worse.''

"Why?"

"She was obsessed with being a Chi-O. She thought—"

"Excuse me? A what?"

"A Chi-Omega. It's a sorority. The apogee of southern womanhood at Ole Miss. Blue-eyed blondes raised with silver spoons in their mouths. Like that song, 'Summertime'? 'Your daddy's rich, and your mama's good-lookin' . . .'"

"Ah."

"Several of her cheerleaders friends were going to pledge Chi-O. Their sisters were already in, or their mothers. Like that."

"Legacies," says Lenz.

"Whatever. Jane really thought she had a chance. She thought I was the only obstacle to her getting it. She claimed active Chi-Os had seen me around Oxford on my bike, looking ratty and saying whatever I felt like, and thought I was her. That probably did happen. But the truth was, she never had a chance. Those bitches wouldn't have given her that. They got their self-esteem from *excluding* girls like Jane, who wanted it terribly but had some flaw. And Jane had several. She had no money – therefore no high-end clothes, car, or any of the other trappings; her father had been a celebrity, but not the right kind; and then there was me. Jane was prettier than all of them, too. You hear beauty is its own aristocracy, but that's not always true. A lot of attractive women fear beauty."

"Interesting, isn't it?" Lenz's eyes play over my body in a strange way, not lustfully, but in a coldly appraising manner. "Jane broke down after the scandal over you and the teacher?"

"She wouldn't leave the house. But when they started talking about making us wards of the state, she went back to school. She graduated salutatorian, but she never got to be a Chi-O. She pledged Delta Gamma, which was considered decent but definitely second tier."

"You've asserted how beautiful Jane was. You're her identical twin. How do you feel about your own looks?"

"I know I'm attractive. But Jane cultivated her looks in a way I never have. Toward the ideals of southern beauty, you know? That's a weird thing that extends from your appearance right into your personality. For me looks are secondary. I've used them to gain advantage in my work – I'd be a fool not to – but it makes me uncomfortable. Beauty is an accident of genetics for which I deserve no credit."

"That's disingenuous, to say the least."

This makes me laugh. "You're a man, okay? You don't know how many times I've listened to my mother whine about how much 'potential' I have, that if I'd just *do* something with it, fix myself up a little – like Jane, is the subtext – I'd find a wonderful provider who'd marry me and take care of me for the rest of my life. Well, wake up, Mom. I don't need a goddamn provider, okay? I *am* one."

"For whom do you provide, Jordan?"

"Myself."

"I see." Lenz looks at his watch, then taps his knees. "Jane married a wealthy attorney?"

"That's right."

"Jump to her disappearance. You didn't handle it well? The file says you interfered with the investigation."

"I don't take exclusion well, okay? I'm a journalist. This was my sister. And the FBI was getting exactly nowhere with the case. I badgered them for the victims' families, walked the streets, worked my old contacts at the *Times-Picayune*. But none of it did any good."

"So what did you finally do?"

"Took off and tried to bury myself in work. Literally. I

went to Sierra Leone. I took crazy risks, had some close calls. Word got back to my agency. They begged me to slow down, so I did. I slowed down so much that I couldn't get out of bed. I was sleeping around the clock. When I finally came out of that, I couldn't sleep at all. I had to have prescription drugs just to close my eyes without seeing Jane being raped, tied hand and foot in some dark room."

"Was rape a particular fear of hers?"

"It's a particular fear for every woman."

"What about you? You must have placed yourself in some very dangerous situations vis-à-vis rape. War zones full of men. Teenagers with guns."

"I can take care of myself. Jane's a lot softer."

Lenz nods slowly. "If we found Jane tomorrow – alive – what would you say to her? In other words, what have you most regretted not saying to her?"

"That's none of your business."

"I've explained why—"

"Some things are too personal, Doctor. Let's leave it at that."

Lenz rubs his face with his hands, then inclines his head to me. "Some years ago, I worked a very difficult murder case. I lost my wife during that investigation. She was murdered. Violently. Viciously. And I felt responsible. Perhaps I was. We had grown apart in our marriage, but that hardly lessened the agony. We've all done terrible things to the people we love, Jordan. It's our nature as humans. If there's something like that between you and your sister, it would help me to know. To see her as she really was."

The pain in Lenz's eyes looks genuine, but he's an old hand at this game. He could have a stock of stories like this one, barter beads he uses to elicit intimacies.

"There's nothing like that."

He takes a frustrated breath through his nose, and I'm reminded of a surgeon working to remove a bullet, his gloved thumb and finger in forceps, trying first one angle and then another, probing for a route to the heart of the wound.

"Certain types of people become targets for predators," Lenz says. "The same way that injured or weak animals are chosen as prey by leopards. Certain types of children tend to be molested, for example: the shy ones, those who don't fit in, who play at the edge of the group, who separate themselves for various reasons. The same holds true for adults. I'm currently profiling every known victim in this case. Some had very low self-image, but others were super-achievers. Some had siblings, others none. Some were housewives, others career women. I must find—"

"I've told you all I know, Doctor."

"You haven't begun to tell me what you know." He shifts in his seat, and the cruelty reappears in his eyes. "Why have you never married, Jordan?"

"I was engaged. He was killed. End of story."

"Killed how?"

"He was an ITN reporter. He was shot down in a helicopter over Namibia and tortured to death."

"You've lost your father, your fiancé, and your sister to violent death?"

"Bad things come in threes, right?"

"You're forty years old. There must be more to your romantic life than one engagement."

"I've had lovers. Does that make you happy?"

"Did Jane have lovers?"

"One boyfriend through high school, like I said. She never had sex with him."

"How do you know?"

"I just *know*. Okay? After him, she dated around, but nothing serious. Then in college she met a guy from a wealthy family in New Orleans. Married him his senior year of law school. She found the handsomest, most reliable provider she could, married him, had two kids, and lived happily ever after."

For some reason this inaccurate summary brings a wave of tears to my eyes. "I need a drink. Do you think they have any of those little airplane bottles stowed on this plane?"

"No. Jordan, I want you to—"

"Get off it! Okay? You wanted our story, you've got it. We're poster girls for nurture in the nature-versus-nurture debate. We're identical right down to our mitochondria, but emotionally we're opposites. Jane acted like she despised me, but she was so jealous of me it made her sick. She was jealous of my *name*. She thought 'Jordan' was exotic, while hers was literally plain Jane. I called her that when I was angry. She hated having to depend on me for money, for her cheerleading outfits and expenses. She wanted Izod shirts and Bass Weejuns, and I made her wear J.C. fucking Penney! That's how petty it was, okay? But to girls in our situation, that was a big deal. Was she weak or frail in some way? Yes. But weaker people can't help being weak, you know? I tried to protect her. Until she stopped wanting me to, and even then I tried. Jane became a southern belle because it was the only choice she was capable of making. She had to feel safe."

"We're all defined by the choices we make to survive," Lenz says in a fatherly voice. "The Walter Mittys and the monsters."

His paternalistic bit finally snaps my patience. "Is that supposed to be profound? Doctor, you may have lost your

95

wife to a killer, but I suspect that most of the trauma you've encountered was vicarious. Told to you by patients or prisoners. It can be tough to hear things, I know. I've heard some bad things myself. But I have also *endured* some bad things. I have descended into the pit of hell, if you want to know. I have *seen some shit.* And all this talk we're doing means nothing. Jane is alive or she's dead. Either way, I have to know. That's the way I'm built. But your games aren't taking us any closer to an answer. I don't think anything connects all these victims, except the fact that they're women."

"Jordan, don't you want to—"

"What I *want* is what Baxter promised me. A complete breakdown of the FBI's investigation so far. I want it clear and concise, and I want it now."

Lenz splays his age-spotted hands on the desktop and leans back. "Did that outburst make you feel better?"

"Start talking, damn it!"

"There's not much to tell. We're now gathering every known painting that belongs to the Sleeping Women series."

"Where?"

"The National Gallery in Washington."

"How many do you have so far?"

"None. Four will arrive by plane tomorrow, several more the next day. Some collectors have refused to ship their paintings but agreed to allow Bureau forensic teams and art consultants to travel to their collections. First we'll try to match the paintings to the known victims in New Orleans. In some cases it should be easy. Harder with the more abstract canvases, but we have some ideas about that. Then we'll establish the order in which the canvases were painted, if we can; it may differ from the order in which they were sold. While this is being done, we'll be searching the canvases for fingerprints, hairs, skin flakes, other biological artifacts. The paint itself will be analyzed and lot numbers traced, if possible. Brush fibers may be found and traced. Connoisseurs will make studies of the painter's style and try to draw comparisons with known artists. And that's only the beginning of what the paintings will go through."

"Who's in charge of the case for the Bureau?"

"Overall responsibility will be held by the Director. Tactically, there are different tracks to the investigation. Daniel will run the Washington track; he'll be in charge of all profiling, with me consulting. The New Orleans SAC will run that end of the case."

"Who's the SAC? Same one as last year?"

"No. Patrick Bowles. He's a competent man." Lenz looks as though he's about to continue, but he stops himself.

"What is it?"

"Another man in New Orleans may be playing the primary role in the investigation at this point. That's one of the things I'm going down there to address."

"Who?"

Lenz sighs. "His name is John Kaiser. He's a journeyman agent now, but two years ago he was a member of the Investigative Support Unit."

"In Quantico? With Baxter?"

"Yes."

"Why is he in New Orleans?"

"He transferred out of the Unit at his own request. Daniel tried to get him to take a leave of absence and come back, but Kaiser refused. He said if he didn't get journeyman duty, he'd resign from the Bureau."

"Why? What happened to him?"

"I'll let him tell you. If he will."

97

"Why would Kaiser have the primary role in this case?"

"The atmosphere in New Orleans has become highly charged over the past year. You can imagine: Victim after victim being taken, no progress by the police. Not even a lead. The NOPD is under tremendous pressure. Complicating the issue is the multijurisdictional nature of the investigation. What people think of as New Orleans is actually a group of communities—"

"I know all about it. Jefferson Parish, Slidell, Kenner, Harahan. Sheriff's departments and cops all mixed together."

"Yes. And the only man in the area with any real experience in cases like this – full time, on the ground – is John Kaiser. It's my understanding that he resisted involvement when he arrived, but as more victims were taken, he began to work the case. Now he's obsessed with it."

"Has he made any headway?"

"No one had, until you found those paintings. But I've no doubt that John Kaiser knows more about the victims and attacks than any man alive. Except the killer, of course. And perhaps the painter, depending on the degree to which they interact."

"You really believe this is some sort of team? A conspiracy?"

"I do. It helps explain the extreme professionalism of the kidnappings in New Orleans. The fact that we have no witnesses and no corpses. I'm starting to think the painter in New York is masterminding the operation, and merely paying a pro to snatch the women for him."

"Who's a professional at kidnapping?"

Lenz shrugs. "Perhaps the painter spent some time in prison. He might know a convict from New Orleans. Or perhaps he's originally from New Orleans himself. He may have many contacts there. That would explain the selection of the city in the first place."

The psychiatrist's theory makes logical sense, yet I feel that it's wrong somehow. "Was this Kaiser good when he was at Quantico?"

Lenz looks over at the porthole. "He had a very high success rate."

"But you don't like him."

"We disagree about fundamental issues of methodology."

"That's psychobabble to me, Doctor. I've learned one thing in my business, like it or not."

"What's that?"

"You don't argue with results."

Lenz keeps looking out his window.

"What do you think about Baxter's theory? Catching one of the guys by using airline computers? Tracing passengers on New York flights?"

"I'm not hopeful."

I lean back in my seat and rub my eyes. "How much longer to New Orleans?"

"About an hour."

"It's too late to call my brother-in-law. I think I'll get a room at the airport hotel, call him tomorrow."

"I'm staying at the Windsor Court. Why don't you sleep there?"

I hope I've misunderstood his tone. "In your room?"

He wrinkles his mouth as though the idea were absurd. "For God's sake. At the hotel."

"As I recall, the Windsor Court is about five hundred dollars per night. I'm not going to pay that, and I know the FBI won't."

"No. But I'll treat you."

"Are you rich?"

"My wife's insurance policy has made a certain standard of living possible, one I never enjoyed before."

"Thanks, but I'll stay at the airport."

Lenz studies me with a strange detachment in the dim light, like an anthropologist studying some new primate. "You know, I used to ask everyone I interviewed three questions."

"What were they?"

"The first was, 'What is the worst thing you've ever done?'"

"Did people answer that?"

"A surprising number did."

"What was the second?"

"'What moment are you proudest of in your life?'"

"And the third?"

"'What's the worst thing that ever happened to you?'"

I force a casual smile, but something slips in my soul at his words. "Why didn't you ask me those things?"

"I don't ask anyone anymore."

"Why not?"

"I got tired of hearing the answers." He shifts in his seat, but his eyes never leave my face. "But in your case, I think I'd like to know."

"You're old enough to be accustomed to disappointment."

He waves his hand. "Something tells me that before all this is done, I'm going to find out anyway."

A high beeping sounds in the cabin. Lenz reaches into his jacket, removes a cell phone, and presses a button. "Yes?" As he listens, he seems to shrink in his seat. "When?" he says at length. "Yes. . . . Yes. . . . Right."

"What is it?" I ask as he drops the phone in his lap. "What's happened?"

"Twenty minutes ago, two teenagers found the body of the woman taken from Dorignac's grocery store."

"Her *body*?"

Lenz wears an expression of deep concentration. "She was lying on the bank of a drainage canal, nude. The kids climbed a wall behind some apartments to drink beer and heard noises by the water. She was lying in the weeds. A nutria was feeding on her, whatever that is. The police sealed the crime scene for a Bureau forensic team. Her husband just identified the body."

"It's a big water rat."

"What? Ah," Lenz says, his mind a thousand miles away.

This news nauseates me, but not because of its ugliness. "It wasn't him," I say quietly. "If they found a body, it's unrelated."

"Not necessarily. It could still be him." Lenz nods with a strange intensity. "Think about it. It's been four and a half weeks since the last victim. The New Orleans UNSUB was on the prowl tonight – maybe all afternoon. He may have known what happened in Hong Kong, but he didn't know what his partner did: that Wingate was about to be silenced, along with you. He snatches the woman from Dorignac's and takes her back to his house. When he arrives, he finds an urgent message on his machine from his partner. Or maybe he gets a call. The victim was found, what" – Lenz checks his watch – "seven hours after he took her? Plenty of time. His New York partner tells him Wingate is no longer a problem, and also that Jordan Glass got away. The investigation is about to get very hot. So, instead of painting this woman, he kills her and dumps her in a canal. Sometime in the last seven hours." Lenz slaps his knee with excitement. "Seven *hours,* by God. I won't be surprised if there's staging. Not at all."

"What's staging?" I ask, searching my memory for remnants of the crime-classification manuals I read in the month after Jane vanished.

Lenz's eyes are glowing. Like all of Baxter's team, he's a hunter at heart. "Staging is an attempt to mislead investigators by altering the crime scene or the corpus. The UNSUB may mutilate the body in an attempt to create the impression of a violent rape, a satanic murder, any number of things. No, we can't discount this victim just because we found her body."

I want to believe him, but for some reason I don't. "But we know he's smart enough to dump the body without it being found."

"That's the point!" Lenz snaps. "He's *letting* us find her, in order to confuse the trail."

"But isn't that risky, if he's actually had her in his possession? I mean, with all the forensics at your disposal?"

The psychiatrist smiles for the first time in a long while. "Yes, it is. We can establish a baseline of hair and fiber evidence. Perhaps there's even semen for DNA. And if we're very damned lucky, some biological artifact from one of the paintings will match something we find on or in the body. That's a long shot if the painter and kidnapper are two different men, but it's possible. It would be one hell of a start."

"God forgive me, I hope it was him that took her."

Lenz squeezes his left hand into a fist. "If it was, this is the turning point of the case."

"Because you have a body?"

"No. Because he's no longer calling the tune. He's reacting to us."

"To me," I remind Lenz. "Finding the paintings." Images of the canvases I saw in Hong Kong float through my mind with eerie clarity. "What makes this guy tick, Doctor? He's trying to re-create some fantasy, right? What is it?"

An odd serenity eases the lines of Lenz's face. "If I knew that, he'd be in custody right now." The psychiatrist closes his eyes and lays his hands on the armrest of his seat. "Please don't speak. I need to think."

Shit. I reach into my fanny pack, open my trusty pill bottle, and swallow three Xanax. By the time I hit the airport hotel, I'll be like a zombie, and glad for it. The last thing in the world I want to do right now is think.

6

This morning I slept in, and I'm glad. Except for my right flank, which feels like a mule kicked it, my muscles have that deliciously liquid feeling that only sex or too much sleep can give. It's been a while since I had the former, so I owe my thanks to a quiet hotel room in America, which can be quite a luxury for me. I ate breakfast in the lobby, then called Budget and rented a Mustang convertible. After traveling in the East for months, riding in underpowered taxis, cyclos, and even rickshaws, an American muscle car feels exactly right. It's late October in New Orleans, but I have the convertible top down. The leaves are green and still on the trees, and the morning sun tells me the temperature could hit eighty by lunchtime. That's the way this city is: heat and rain, rain and heat. When winter finally comes, the humidity makes it cold, but winter doesn't last long.

I'm late for my meeting with the FBI, because nobody bothered to tell me they moved the field office from downtown – where they were forever – to a brand-new building on the south shore of Lake Pontchartrain, between Lakefront Airport and the University of New Orleans. It's a massive four-story brick structure designed to look like a college campus building, but the closer I get, the more it looks like a fortress in disguise. Set far back from the main road, the building is surrounded by a heavy iron fence topped with sharp fleur-de-lis and fronted by a guardhouse with antiterrorist barriers embedded in the concrete road. The armed gate guard checks my driver's license, radios upstairs, then raises the barrier and waves me into the parking lot.

As I lock the Mustang and walk toward the entrance, I sense that I'm being watched on screens inside. I won't win any fashion awards today: jeans, a silk blouse, espadrilles, and my fanny pack. No purses for Jordan Glass, unless I'm doing a formal party. I know how to dress up, but I don't do it for the FBI. The entrance is also built on the heroic scale, with flags and black marble inscribed with the FBI motto: "Fidelity, Bravery, Integrity." Other law-enforcement agencies have come up with more derogatory words for the acronym, but I'll reserve my opinion today.

A metal detector at the door leads me into a small vestibule not unlike a doctor's office, where a female receptionist waits behind glass. When I give her my name, she pushes a sheet through a slot for me to sign, and assures me someone will be down for me in a minute. Thirty seconds later, the door opens and a tall man with deep-set eyes and a day's growth of beard steps through the door by her window.

"Jordan Glass?"

"Yes. Sorry I'm late. I went to the federal building downtown."

"That's our fault, then. I'm John Kaiser."

This guy does not look like the FBI agents I've known. He's six feet two, lanky, and looks as comfortable in his white button-down shirt and sport jacket as a cowboy in a tuxedo. His dark brown hair is past the unwritten regulation length, and his aura is about as unofficial as anything I can imagine. He looks like a law student who's been studying for three days without sleep. A forty-five-year-old law student.

As if reading my mind, he pulls out his wallet and flips it open to reveal his FBI credentials. His bona fides are there in black and white: "Special Agent John Kaiser." His photo looks much neater than the man standing before me, but it's him all right. He cleans up well.

"You don't look like an FBI agent."

A lopsided grin. "My SAC is fond of telling me that."

"Why did they move the field office?"

"After the bombing in Oklahoma City, the government mandated a hundred-foot setback from the road. This office has twice as much space as downtown, and a hell of a lot better view. They moved last September, a month before I got here."

"Are we going upstairs?"

He lowers his voice. "To tell you the truth, I'd rather talk to you alone first. Do you like Chinese food? I haven't eaten since last night, so I ordered some. I ordered for two."

"I like Chinese. But why don't you want to eat it in your office?"

Kaiser has hazel eyes, and they focus on mine with subdued urgency. "Because I'd rather talk without any interference."

"From whom?"

"You met him last night."

"Doctor Lenz?"

He nods.

"So the dislike is mutual?"

"Afraid so."

"You can't keep Lenz out of your office?"

"I'm not sure. But I can definitely keep him off a picnic

table on Lakeshore Drive, especially if he doesn't know I'm going there."

"I'll go if we take my car."

"You read my mind, Ms. Glass."

Kaiser collects his sacks and follows me through the main doors. He tries to match his stride to mine, but with the height differential it's a struggle.

"We got your film from the fire scene," he says.

"What did it show?"

"You got some good crowd shots. New York is busting its collective ass trying to trace every face in them. It's a big job. The good news is, the video store had a list of members, and the bartender says a lot of his patrons that evening were regulars."

"I thought maybe I got a shot of the guy who set the fire. It would have been a downward shot, forty-five degrees toward the back of a crowd."

Kaiser gives me a strange look. "You're not going to believe this."

"What?"

"You got the top of some heads, and a Caucasian hand flipping you the bird."

"Flipping . . . ? You're kidding me."

"My sense of humor doesn't extend to cases like this one."

"Do you think it was him? Or just some kid?"

"Photo analysts say it's an adult hand, likely but not positively male. You think the UNSUB saw what you were doing in time to duck down and flip you off?"

"He saw what I was doing, all right. He was moving along the back of the crowd, following me. I think he was trying to get close enough to kill me. That's why I got the firefighters after him."

"That was smart."

"I thought I got that camera up quick enough. Damn."

"It's in the past," he says. "You can't change it, so forget it."

"You make it sound easy. Is that what you do when you screw up?"

"Do as I say, not as I do."

"This is it."

He stops beside the red Mustang and flashes a broad smile of pleasure. "Pony car."

I unlock the Mustang with the remote, climb in, and put the top down. Kaiser drops his takeout sacks on the tiny backseat and folds his long frame into the passenger seat beside me. In seconds we're roaring down Lakeshore Drive, headed for the green expanses beside Lake Pontchartrain. He leans his head back and looks up at the sky.

"Damn, this feels good."

"What?"

"Riding in a ragtop with a pretty girl. It's been a long time."

Despite the strangeness of the situation, I feel a little flush of pleasure. Being noticed by John Kaiser is a lot different from objectively discussing my looks with Dr. Lenz. "A long time since you've been in a ragtop? Or close to a pretty girl?"

He laughs. "I plead the fifth."

Kaiser looks a few years older than I, but he's aged well. And though I hate to admit it, he reminds me a little of David Gresham, the history teacher I told Lenz about. Something about the way he carries himself, more than physical similarity. There's a wariness in his motion, as though he's always aware of exactly where he is, and of his immediate surroundings. I wonder how much Lenz told him about last night's "interview" on the plane.

Braking to a near stop, I nose the Mustang into a cement semicircle by a wooden bench on the lake side of the road. While I put up the top to keep the gulls from trashing the interior, Kaiser carries the food to the bench, straddles one end, and lays out the cardboard containers and drinks in front of him. As he sits, his pant legs ride up his ankles, revealing a black holster with the butt of an automatic pistol protruding from it.

"I got Peking Chicken and Spicy Beef," he says. "Also some shrimp fried rice, egg rolls, and two iced teas, unsweetened. Take whatever you want."

"Peking Chicken." I straddle the other end of the bench and reach for one of the cups.

"Go for it," he says.

I spread some white rice onto a tiny plate, top it with the spicy chicken and zucchini, and dig in.

"Do you want to start?" he asks. "Or do you want me to?"

"I will. I want you to know this is a strange situation for me. I didn't handle Jane's disappearance well, but in the past year I've managed to deal with it. On some level, I accepted that I'd never see her again, and that the case would never be solved. Now all that certitude has been taken away. And I'm glad it has. It's just . . . disturbing. I feel vulnerable again."

"I understand, believe it or not. I've seen similar things happen before. Missing-person cases that have lain dormant for years, then suddenly the child or husband turns up. It's disorienting to people. *Homo sapiens* survived by adapting rapidly to change, even terrible change. Being forced to reverse an adaptation you've made to survive can cause a lot of strange feelings. A lot of resentment."

"I don't feel any resentment."

He watches me, his eyes full of kindness. "I wasn't saying you did. I've just seen it in other cases."

I take a long sip of tea, and I feel the caffeine in my skin and heart. "I'd like to know where you are on the case. And what you think the odds are of solving it."

Kaiser has already polished off an egg roll; now he's exploring the spicy beef. "I don't like giving odds. I've been disappointed too many times."

"Do you believe the death of Christopher Wingate is part of my sister's case?"

"Yes."

"You believe there's more than one person behind all this."

Kaiser cocks his head to the side. "Yes and no."

"What do you mean? You don't share Lenz's theory? The kidnapper in New Orleans and the painter in New York?"

"No, I don't."

"Why not?"

"Instinct, mostly. It's an elegant theory, and it explains a lot. The reason we can't find any common factors among the victims, for example. Lenz would say that since the New Orleans UNSUB is being paid to kidnap the women, he simply chooses them at random. But that's not how this kind of thing is done. Predators will take targets of opportunity, yes, but there's always an underlying pattern beneath the victims' selection. Even if it's just geographic."

"You think something links all the victims?"

"Something always does. Serial murder is sexual murder; that's axiomatic. It may appear otherwise, but always at bottom lies serious sexual maladjustment. And the criterion for victim selection usually arises from this. The victims are from New Orleans. My gut tells me the selections are being made here. And not randomly, either. We just don't understand them yet."

"Have you formed some picture of this guy, then? Of what drives him?"

"I've tried, but there's not much to go on. The normal rules are out the window. Organized versus disorganized personality? Comparing this guy to Ted Bundy – who was classified as organized – is like comparing Stephen Hawking to Mister Rogers. No corpses. No witnesses. No evidence. The victims might as well have been kidnapped by aliens. And that frightens me more than anything."

"Why?"

"Because it's hard to hide a body well. Especially in an urban environment. Corpses stink. Dogs and cats root them out. Homeless people discover them. Passersby report suspicious actions more often than you'd think. And nosy neighbors see everything."

"There's a lot of swamp around New Orleans," I point out. "I have nightmares about that. Jane wedged under a cypress stump somewhere."

Kaiser shakes his head. "We've been dragging the swamps for months with no results. Lake Pontchartrain, too. And those swamps aren't empty. There are hunters, fishermen, oil people. Game wardens, families living in shacks on the water. Think about it. If the UNSUB dumps a woman off a causeway, she's going to float within sight of somebody. Eleven bodies in a row? Forget it. And if he goes deep into the swamp – carrying a dead body in a boat – he almost has to do it at night. Do you see an artist talented enough to paint these pictures striking out into a swamp full of snakes and alligators in the dead of night? I don't. If they're dead, I think he's burying them. And the safest place to do that is beneath a house. A house he's living in. A basement or a crawl space."

"New Orleans houses don't have basements. The water table's too high. That's why they bury people above ground."

"That was always more out of custom than necessity," he says. "And the water table has fallen considerably in recent years. He could be burying them under a house, and they would stay buried. And dry. Toss in a little lime every now and then, they wouldn't even stink."

A beeping sound comes from Kaiser's pocket. He takes out a cell phone and looks at its LED screen. "That's Lenz, trying to find me. We'll let him keep looking."

"Excuse me . . . you just said *if* they're dead."

Kaiser carefully formulates his reply. "That's right."

"Doctor Lenz is positive they're dead."

"The doctor and I disagree about a lot of things."

"You're the first law-enforcement officer who's expressed any real doubt. Baxter says he'll hold out hope until he sees an actual body, but he's just being courteous."

"Baxter's a nice guy." Kaiser's eyes bore into mine. "But he thinks they're dead."

"And you don't?"

"I've never seen a case like this. Eleven women vanish into thin air? Absolutely no word from the UNSUB? Normally, a guy who snatched that many women and got away with it would be taunting us some way."

"But what makes you think they might be alive? Where could they possibly be?"

"It's a big world, Ms. Glass. There's something else, though. The autopsy on the Dorignac's victim is mostly complete. Externally, the body was clean, but we took some skin from beneath her fingernails. There's nothing to compare that to right now, but later it could be very important. Toxicology will take a little longer."

"All that's great. But why does that make you think the victims could be alive?"

"It doesn't. But we also found a strange burn on her neck. The kind of contact burn consistent with an electrical stun device, like a taser."

My pulse quickens. "What does that tell you?"

"That while the snatches were previously thought to have been blitz attacks, the force used was not necessarily deadly force. That means the UNSUB may not have wanted to risk killing his victims, even by mistake."

"Oh, God. Please let that be it."

"I don't want to create false hope, but it's a good sign in my book. By the way, we're telling the media that we don't think the Dorignac's victim is part of this case. We're playing it as a random rape-murder. The dumping of the body supports that story."

"I hope that fairy tale doesn't come back to haunt you."

Kaiser takes another bite of spicy beef and gives me a measuring look. "A couple of other things make this UNSUB very interesting to me."

"Like what?"

"One, he's the only serial offender I know of to earn enormous profit from his crimes. Most serials don't profit in any way from what they do. Money isn't part of the equation for them. But for this guy, it is."

"Okay."

"Two, he's not after publicity. Not the usual kind, anyway. If the victims *are* dead, he's not leaving the bodies where they'll be found and cause big news. And if they're not dead, he's not sending severed fingers to relatives or the TV stations. So for him, the women are simply part of the process of creating the paintings. That's what the murders are about. The paintings."

"But aren't the paintings a kind of publicity in themselves?"

"Yes, but a very specialized kind. Publicity and profit are linked here. If the artist were painting these images solely to fulfill his private needs, he wouldn't need to sell them. Think of the risk he's taking by putting them on the market. That's the only way we've learned anything about him. If he hadn't sold any paintings, we'd be as lost today as we were after the first kidnapping."

"How are profit and publicity linked?"

"He wants the art world to see what he's doing. Maybe critics, maybe other painters, I don't know. The money might not be important in and of itself. It wouldn't surprise me if he hasn't spent a dime of it. He probably knows that in our society, the value of art is determined by what people pay for it. Therefore, if the world is to pay attention to his work, it must sell for a great deal of money. That's why he took the risk of dealing with Christopher Wingate. Or dealing with whoever killed Wingate for him. I'm only speculating, of course."

"It makes more sense than what I've heard so far. What does he want people to get from his work? Why paint the women dead? And why start with almost abstract faces, then paint women who look asleep, and only later get to explicit views of death?"

"I'd just as soon not speculate about that yet." Kaiser looks at his watch. "I'd like to ask you about something personal, if you don't mind."

"What?"

"The phone call."

"Phone call?"

"The one you got from Thailand."

"Today I woke up thinking about that call. It was the most unsettling experience of my life."

"I'm not surprised. I know you gave us a statement when it happened, but would you mind telling me about it?"

"Not if you think it might help you."

"It might."

"It was five months after Jane disappeared. A bad time for me. I was having to sedate myself to sleep. I don't remember if I told them that in my statement."

"You said you were exhausted."

"That's one word for it. I wasn't too happy with the Bureau then. Anyway, the phone rang in the middle of the night. It must have rung a long time to wake me up, and when I finally got to it, the connection was terrible."

"What was the first thing you heard?"

"A woman crying."

"Did you recognize the voice? Right at that moment?"

"No. It made me more alert, but it didn't zing straight to my gut. You know?"

"Yeah. What then?"

"The woman sobbed, 'Jordan.' Then there was static. Then: 'I need your help. I can't – ' Then there was more static, like a bad cell phone connection. Then she said, 'Daddy's alive, but he can't help me.' Then: 'Please,' like she was begging, at her wits' end. At that point I felt that it was Jane, and I was about to ask where she was when a man in the background said something in French that I didn't understand and don't remember." Even now, in seventy-degree sunlight, a chill goes through my body at the memory. "And I thought for a second—"

"What?"

"I thought he sounded like my father." I look defiantly at

Kaiser, daring him to call me a fool. But he doesn't. Part of me is glad, yet another part wonders if *he's* a fool.

"Go on," he says.

"Then in English the man said, 'No, *chérie,* it's just a dream.' And then the phone went dead."

My appetite is gone. A clammy sweat has broken out under my blouse, sending a cold rivulet down my ribs. I press the silk against my skin to stop it.

"Do you have a clear memory of your father's voice?"

"Not really. More an impression, I guess. I think the voice on the phone reminded me of his because Dad spoke a little French sometimes. He learned it in Vietnam, I think. He called me *chérie* sometimes."

"Did he? What happened next?"

"To be honest, my brain was barely functioning. I thought the whole thing was probably a delusion. But the next day, I reported it to Baxter, and he told me they had found a record of the call and traced its origin to a train station in Bangkok."

"When you found that out, what did your gut tell you?"

"I hoped it was my sister. But the more I thought about it, the less I believed it. I know a lot of MIA families, from searching for my father for so long. What if it was a female relative of an MIA in the middle of a search? They go over there all the time. You know, a wife or daughter of an MIA, in trouble and needing help? Maybe she's drunk and depressed. She pulls my card out of her purse. The conversation fits, if you fill in the blanks a certain way. 'Jordan . . . I need your help. *My* daddy's alive, but he' – referring to *her* father – 'can't help me.'"

"But MIA relatives go over to try to help the missing soldier, right? Not the other way around."

"Yes."

116

"Did you check with the MIA families you knew?"

"Yes. The FBI did too. We never found anyone who would admit to calling me. But there are more than two thousand MIAs still unaccounted for. That's a lot of families. And at the meetings, they all talk to me, because I'm well known and because I've traveled in the East so much."

"If that were the case, who would the man's voice have belonged to?"

"A husband. A stepfather. Who knows? But I thought of another possibility. What if it was the killer playing a trick on me? Using some woman he knows to upset me."

Kaiser shakes his head. "No other relatives of victims received such calls. I checked."

"So, what do you think?"

He idly pokes a leftover slice of beef. "I think it might have been your sister."

I take a deep breath and try to steady my nerves.

"I'm telling you this," he says soberly, "because Baxter told me you were tough."

"I don't know if I'm that tough."

He waits, letting me work through it.

"This is why you didn't want Lenz here, isn't it?"

"Partly."

"When I asked Lenz what he thought about the phone call, he brushed it off."

Kaiser looks at the ground. "The consensus in the Unit is that your mystery caller was a member of an MIA family, just as you guessed. Lenz didn't ask you about it because he'd seen the statement you made at the time, and he'd consider that a more reliable description of the event than what you remember now."

"That sounds like an official reply. What's your personal opinion?"

"If your sister is alive, it throws Lenz's present theory – whatever that might be – into question. Lenz talks a lot about how everything is possible, how there are no rules, but deep down he's wearing blinders. I don't think he always did. But these days he's prejudiced toward the tragic ending. I'm open to something else. That's it in a nutshell."

"Why are you open to something else?"

A wistful smile touches the corners of Kaiser's lips and eyes. "Because I know the world obeys no laws. I learned that the hard way." He picks up a plastic-wrapped fortune cookie, then discards it. "Lenz probably asked you about all sorts of family stuff. Right? Intimate stuff?"

"Yes."

"That's the way he works. He likes to know all the underlying relationships. He's upset a lot of the victims' families doing that. I'm not criticizing him for it. He did some groundbreaking work early in his career."

"That's pretty much what he said about you."

"Really? Well, I won't kid you, I don't think he should be involved in this investigation."

"Why not?"

"I don't trust his instincts or his judgment. He was involved in a case a while back that turned into a real clusterfuck. And Baxter places too much weight on what he says, because of their history."

"Lenz told me his wife was killed during a case. Is that what you're talking about?"

"Yes. Did he tell you why?"

"No. He just said it was a vicious killing."

"It was that, all right. And it happened because Lenz did something supremely arrogant and stupid. He got there five minutes after she died on her own kitchen table."

"God."

"He retired after that. He's done some consulting for Baxter since, but I don't think he learned the right lesson from what happened. He still has too much faith in his own abilities."

"What do you think about his plan to use me to rattle any suspects you dig up?"

"It could work, but it's not as simple or safe as it sounds. The results could be inconclusive, and the strategy could put you right in the killer's sights."

Kaiser's cell phone beeps again. He lifts it from the detritus of the meal and scans the LCD. "Lenz again."

"Are you going to answer?"

"No."

Since Kaiser took the conversation into personal territory, I feel justified in doing the same. "You've told me Lenz's dirty laundry. What about yours? Why did you leave Quantico?"

"What did Lenz tell you?"

"Nothing. He said he'd leave it for you to tell me, if you would."

Kaiser looks off toward a stand of palm trees, where two lovers and a dog lie on a blanket, an ice chest beside them. "It's pretty simple, really. I burned out. It happens to everyone in that job, sooner or later. I just snapped a little more spectacularly than most."

"What happened?"

"After four years at Quantico, I was pretty much Baxter's right hand. I was handling far too heavy a load. Over a hundred and twenty active cases. Child murders, serial rapes, bombers, kidnappings, the whole sick spectrum. You can't assign priorities in a situation like that. Behind every single case, every photo, is a desperate family. Distraught parents, husbands, siblings. Frustrated cops aching to help them. It got to where I was actually living at the Academy. When my personal life fell apart, I hardly noticed. Then one day the inevitable happened."

This vague reference to his personal life makes me check his left hand. There's no wedding band there.

"What was that?" I ask. "The inevitable?"

"Baxter and I were out at the Montana State Prison, interviewing a death-row inmate. He'd raped and murdered seven little boys. Tortured most of them before they died. It was no different from interviews I'd done a dozen times before, but this guy was really enjoying telling us what he'd done. A lot of them do, of course, but this time . . . I just couldn't detach myself. I couldn't stop thinking about this one little boy. Six years old, screaming for his mother while this guy shoved power tools up his rectum." Kaiser swallows hard, like his mouth is dry. "And I lost control."

"What did you do?"

"I went over the table. I tried to kill him."

"How close did you come?"

"I broke his jaw, his nose, and assorted other facial bones. I damaged his larynx and put out one of his eyes. Baxter couldn't pull me off. He finally clubbed the base of my skull with a coffee mug. Stunned me long enough for him to drag me out. The guy was hospitalized for twenty-six days."

"Jesus. How did you keep your job?"

Kaiser slowly shakes his head, as if gauging how much to tell me. "Baxter covered for me. He told the warden the con jumped me and I defended myself." Kaiser's eyes search out the lovers again. "I guess you're going to go all liberal on me now, tell me I violated his civil rights?"

"Well, you did. You know that. But I understand why. I've made myself part of the story before, instead of covering it. It sounds to me like you had a delayed reaction to something else."

He looks back at me as though surprised. "That's what it was, all right. I'd lost a little girl a week before. Working a rape-murder case in Minnesota. I was advising Minneapolis Homicide, and we were close to getting the UNSUB. Really close. But he strangled one more little girl before we did. If I'd been one day faster . . . well, you know."

"It's in the past. Isn't that what you told me? You can't change it, so forget it."

"Glib bullshit."

His honesty brings a smile to my face. "A while ago you said 'clusterfuck.' That's a Vietnam term, isn't it?"

He nods distractedly. "Yeah."

"Were you there?"

"Yeah."

"You look too young for it."

"I was there at the end. Seventy-one and -two."

Which makes him forty-six or forty-seven, if he went over when he was eighteen. "The end was seventy-three," I remind him. "Seventy-five, really. There was still a lot of ground fighting in seventy-one."

"That's what I meant. The end of the fighting."

"What branch of service?"

"Army."

"Were you drafted?"

"I wish I could tell you I was. But I volunteered. Every civilian was trying like hell to stay out of the military, every soldier was trying to get out of Vietnam, and I was trying to get in. What did I know? I was a kid from rural Idaho. I went to Ranger School, the whole nine yards."

"How did you feel about journalists over there? Photographers?"

"They had a job to do, like I did."

"A different job."

"True. I met a couple who were okay. But some of them just stayed in the hotels and sent Vietnamese out to get their combat shots. I didn't care much for them."

"That still happens in some places."

"I've seen your name under some pretty rough pictures. Are you a lot like your father?"

"I don't know, to tell you the truth. All I know is what people have told me about him. Guys who worked with him in the field. I think we're different as photographers."

"How so?"

"Wars attract different kinds. There are the hotel guys you talked about, who don't even count. There are the Hemingway wanna-bes, out there to test themselves. Then you have the ones who get off on the danger, who live for the rush. They're the crazy ones, like Sean Flynn, riding hell-for-leather through fire fights on a motorcycle, with a camera in his hand. And then there are the good ones. The ones who do it because they feel it's the right thing to do. They know the danger, they're scared shitless, but they do it anyway. They crawl right into the middle of it, where the mortar rounds are dropping and the machine guns are churning up the mud."

"That's the kind of courage I respected over there," Kaiser says quietly. "I knew some soldiers like that."

His face is lined with silent grief; I wonder if he knows it. "Something tells me you were a soldier like that."

He doesn't respond.

"That's the kind of courage my father had," I tell him. "He wasn't that gifted a photographer, when you get down to it. His composition was never that great. But he would get so close to the elephant that the crazies wouldn't even go there. And when you're that close, composition doesn't matter. Just the shot. And that made his pictures unique. He went into Laos and Cambodia. He spent twelve days underground at Khe Sanh, during the worst of the siege. I have a photo a marine shot of him peeing in the middle of the Ho Chi Minh Trail."

Kaiser's eyes flick toward me at last. "Who told you that? About the elephant?"

"My dad. When I was a kid, I asked him why he did such a dangerous job, and he tried to make out like it wasn't dangerous at all. He said the soldiers called combat 'seeing the elephant,' that it was like a big circus."

"It was, in a lot of ways."

"Later, when I got a taste of it myself, I understood better."

"If you're not like him, what kind of photographer are you? Why do you do it?"

"Because I have to. I don't even remember making a conscious choice."

"Are you trying to change the world?"

I laugh again. "In the beginning I was. I'm not that naive now."

"You've probably changed it more than most people ever will. You change people's minds, make them see things in a new way. That's the hardest thing to do in this world, if you ask me."

"Will you marry me?"

He laughs and hits me on the shoulder. "Are you that starved for affirmation?"

"This past year has really sucked."

"The past two have sucked for me. Welcome to the club."

Kaiser's cell phone rings again. He ignores it, but this

time it does not relent, and he finally picks it up and looks at the LCD. "That's Baxter at Quantico." He presses Send.

"Kaiser." His face grows tight as he listens. "Okay, I will." He hangs up and gathers the leftovers into the bags.

"What happened?"

"Baxter wants me back at the field office."

"Why?"

"I don't know, but he said to bring you with me. They're setting up a video link to Quantico, and he wants you there."

My heart stutters. "Oh, God. Do you think they've found out something about Jane?"

"No point in guessing." He tosses the bags one after another at a metal trash can ten feet away. They bang in without touching the rim. "Baxter's voice was on edge, though. Something's popped somewhere."

7

The FBI field office is run from the fourth floor, which was designed so that you see nothing but hallways and doors unless you walk through one of the doors. A few of the doors are open, and as I walk past them, I sense people watching me. At a door marked "Patrick Bowles, Special Agent in Charge," Kaiser gives me a look of encouragement.

"Don't be shy. Just say what you think."

"I usually do."

He nods and ushers me into a large L-shaped room with a broad window overlooking Lake Pontchartrain. There's a desk in the dogleg of the L, and sitting behind it is a florid man with quick green eyes and silver hair. On the way over, Kaiser told me that SAC Bowles is the senior FBI official in the state of Louisiana, in charge of 150 field agents and 100 support personnel. Trained as an attorney, Bowles has served in six other field offices and has supervised several major investigations. Fashion-wise, the SAC is the antithesis of John Kaiser: he's wearing a three-piece suit that never hung on any department store rack, silver links on his French cuffs, and a silk tie. When he gets up to greet me, I see that his shoes are Johnston & Murphy, at the least.

"Ms. Glass?" he says, offering his hand. "Patrick Bowles."

A little Irish in his voice. It makes me think of the Irish

Channel, but of course the Channel is now home to black and Cuban families, not Irish immigrants. To avoid awkwardness I shake his hand and give him a guarded smile.

"Take a seat here," he says, motioning toward a leather chair in a group.

Glancing to my left, I see Arthur Lenz on a sofa in a private seating area in the deep leg of the L. The good doctor doesn't look happy, but he stands and walks over to us. He and Kaiser do not exchange greetings. Kaiser sits in a chair opposite mine, and Lenz claims the sofa against the wall to my right. SAC Bowles retakes his place behind his desk. He looks like a no-nonsense kind of guy, which is fine with me.

"Have you learned something about my sister?" I ask.

"You've met Daniel Baxter?" asks the SAC, ignoring my question. "Of the Investigative Support Unit?"

"You know I have."

He glances at his watch. "Mr. Baxter wants to discuss something with the four of us. We'll have a satellite video link in about thirty seconds."

Bowles pushes a button on his desk, and a three-foot section of wall above Dr. Lenz slides back, revealing a large flat-panel LCD screen.

"Just like James Bond," I say softly.

Lenz gets up with an irritated sigh and leans against the long window to the right of Bowles's desk. I glance over at Kaiser, who gives no indication of his feelings. I guess there's a lot of hurry-up-and-wait in the FBI. There's a lot of it in photojournalism, too. After a moment, the LCD screen goes blue and numbers begin flickering in the bottom right corner.

"There's a camera above the screen," says Bowles. "Baxter can see us all in a wide-angle shot."

Suddenly, Daniel Baxter's face fills the screen, and his voice emanates from hidden speakers.

"Hello, Patrick. Hello, Ms. Glass. John. Arthur."

The video feed isn't jerky like some home-computer hookup. It has the seamless resolution of corporate America's tête-à-têtes. The ISU chief looks directly at me as he speaks, which gives me the feeling that he's actually standing in the room.

"Ms. Glass, from the moment you called me from your return flight from Hong Kong, we've been using the combined weight of the Departments of Justice and State to gather the Sleeping Women paintings for forensic analysis. Negotiations like these usually take weeks, but the exigencies of this situation allowed us to apply unprecedented pressure. We now have six paintings in our possession. We've already begun our analysis, using both our own technicians and outside consultants. The bad news is, we've found no fingerprints preserved in the paint."

"Damn," curses Bowles.

"There are hundreds of prints on the frames, of course, but they're probably meaningless. We *have* found traces of talc in the paint, which suggests that the artist wore surgical gloves while doing his work. We have what we believe to be the first painting, and it tests positive for talc, which means the UNSUB was intent on protecting his identity from the start. This guy doesn't learn as he goes. He's a savant. We're X-raying the paintings to find out if there are any hidden messages or ghosts, but we—"

"What's that?" asks Bowles. "A ghost?"

"A painting beneath a painting," says Lenz, speaking for the first time.

"X rays might also detect fingerprints on the canvas beneath the paint," Baxter continues. "Our UNSUB may not have been so careful as he made sketches, knowing that the surface would soon be covered with paint."

"I wouldn't count on that," Kaiser says. "Artists know about X-ray analysis."

"I'm glad you're letting me in on all this," I say to the screen. "But what's it leading to? What's the urgency?"

"Bear with me," says Baxter. "We've made arrangements for eight paintings to be shipped to us in Washington. The owners of six more – all in Asia – have given us permission to send forensic teams to their homes or galleries to make the necessary studies. Those teams are en route now."

"That leaves five," says Kaiser. "Nineteen total, right?"

Baxter nods. "The remaining five are owned by a man named Marcel de Becque."

"A Frenchman?" asks Bowles.

Something ticks in my brain, something Christopher Wingate said.

"It's more complicated than that," says Baxter. "De Becque was born in Algeria in 1930, but reared in Vietnam. His father was a French colonial businessman who put his money into tea plantations."

"And he lives in the Cayman Islands," I finish.

"How did you know that?" Baxter asks sharply.

"Wingate mentioned him."

"De Becque won't send us his paintings?"asks Kaiser.

"He's not only refused to ship his paintings to us, but also refused to allow our forensic teams to go to his estate on Grand Cayman to study them."

Kaiser and Lenz share a look.

"What reason did he give?" asks the psychiatrist.

"He said it was inconvenient."

"Frog son of a bitch," growls Bowles. "What's he doing in the Caymans? Probably running from something."

"He is," Baxter confirms. "In 1975, while we scraped the last Americans off the Saigon Embassy roof by helicopter, de Becque was slipping out in a private plane. He'd sold his plantations just before the Tet offensive, which is suspicious in and of itself. He was tied to intelligence people on both sides, and he undoubtedly played both ends against the middle when he could. Word is, he was heavily involved in the unofficial war economy throughout the conflict."

"Black marketeer," Kaiser says with obvious distaste.

"Four years ago," says Baxter, "Marcel de Becque was implicated in a stock-fraud scheme on the Paris Bourse. The scam involved a fraudulent platinum discovery in Africa. He had to flee, but he netted close to fifty million from the deal."

Bowles whistles from his desk.

"The French can't extradite him from Cayman, because at some point he established residency in Quebec and obtained Canadian citizenship. Canada and the Caymans have no extradition treaty. *We* can extradite from Cayman, but de Becque has committed no crime on U.S. soil. He's immune to pressure from us."

"As far as we know," says Bowles, "if we got enough evidence to issue an arrest warrant on conspiracy, we could go in and bring him back under the new laws."

"That's not an option at this time, Pat," says Baxter.

Kaiser unexpectedly voices my thought for me. "What does all this have to do with Jordan Glass?"

Baxter turns to me again. "Monsieur de Becque has made a very unusual proposition. He personally told me that he would allow his Sleeping Women – that's how he refers to them, as though they're real women – he would allow them to be photographed – not forensically examined,

129

mind you – but only if the photographer was Jordan Glass."

The room goes silent, and cold apprehension climbs my spine.

"Why in the world would he ask for me?"

"I was hoping you could shed some light on that," says Baxter.

"Maybe de Becque is the killer," suggests Bowles. "He killed Jane Lacour, and now he's discovered she has a twin sister. He wants to do her as well. Make a set."

In a voice dripping with disdain, Lenz says, "Please confine your theories to subjects with which you're familiar. Like bank robbery."

"Arthur," Baxter warns.

Bowles is so red he looks ready to pop a blood vessel.

"De Becque is seventy years old," says Baxter. "He falls well outside all profiles for serial murder."

"This may not be serial murder," says Kaiser, earning odd looks from the other men. "And de Becque could easily be behind the selections. We need to find out if he's come to New Orleans in the past eighteen months, and if so, how often."

"De Becque owns his own jet," says Baxter. "A Cessna Citation."

Kaiser's eyebrows go up.

"We're trying to trace its movements now."

Lenz focuses on Kaiser. "Do you really think a murderer – or a kidnapper – who's been so careful up to this point would invite his next victim to his lair through the medium of the FBI?"

"He might," says Kaiser, "as a joke. A final joke. He's getting old. He knows we've discovered the link between his victims and the paintings. He killed Wingate, or ordered his death, so his marketing conduit's shut down. One way or another, he knows he hasn't got much time. So he decides to immortalize himself by the way he goes out. Murder-suicide with a celebrity."

Despite the antipathy between Kaiser and Lenz, the psychiatrist seems to be weighing this theory. "If he's the suicidal type, why bother to kill Wingate at all?"

"Knee-jerk response. Like people who kill every snake they see. He perceived a threat and neutralized it before fully exploring how it would affect his situation."

Lenz purses his lips in thought. "Did de Becque's jet fly to New York yesterday?"

"No," says Baxter. "It was on Grand Cayman for the past twenty-four hours. We've confirmed that. We are checking commercial carriers."

"You can forget that," mutters Lenz.

"De Becque says he'll send his jet to pick up Ms. Glass and her equipment," says Baxter. "The catch is, she has to go alone."

Kaiser looks incredulous. "You're not actually considering this."

"John, we have to look at—"

Kaiser whirls on Lenz. "How long have you known about de Becque?"

"I heard what you did, when you did," Lenz says quietly. Which is not exactly a denial.

"I'll do it," I tell them.

The room goes quiet again.

"If you do," says Baxter, "it won't be under de Becque's conditions."

"Under no conditions," says Kaiser. "We have no control down there."

"We have to see those paintings, John."

"If she took one of our planes," says Bowles, "we could

131

put the Hostage Rescue Team inside. She goes in wired, and if it starts going south, they can bust in and bring them both out – Glass *and* de Becque."

"If it starts going south?" echoes Kaiser. "You mean like if de Becque shoots her in the head? Then HRT, which is at the airport, starts for the estate?"

"Don't waste your breath," scoffs Lenz. "He's talking about invading a foreign country."

"We'd talk to the Brits first," says Bowles. "Cayman is still a British colony."

"Good God," mutters Lenz, as though rendered speechless by the ignorance around him. Either the psychiatrist has forgotten whose territory he's on, or he feels that Baxter's patronage makes him bulletproof.

"Let me get this straight," I say to Kaiser. "You think a seventy-year-old man is going around New Orleans kidnapping women in their twenties and thirties? Without leaving a trace? My sister ran three miles a day and worked out with weights. She could kick the crap out of most seventy-year-old men, pardon my French."

"Seventy isn't that old," says Lenz, playing devil's advocate. "There are seventy-year-old men in excellent health."

"And you're forgetting the taser wound on the Dorignac's victim," says Kaiser. "But if de Becque is behind it, I see him commissioning the paintings. Paying one or more men to take the women for him, and one artist to paint them. A guy like that? A wanted expatriate? He probably has all kinds of bodyguards on his property. Retired Israeli commandos. Ex-Paras or -Foreign Legion. Maybe even GIGN."

"An elegant scenario," says Lenz.

"You think de Becque could paint them himself?" asks Bowles.

"He's a collector, not a painter." Lenz sighs dismissively. "But if he commissions them, why does he only own five paintings? Why wouldn't he have them all?"

"He could be selling them," says Baxter.

"A guy worth fifty million?" asks Bowles.

"An elaborate hoax," suggests Kaiser. "Turning the art world upside down. For kicks. For some twisted fantasy we don't yet understand."

I can't tell who's arguing for what. Though Lenz and Kaiser dislike each other, they clearly respect each other's opinions, and Baxter respects them both, because he's letting them run with the ball. As they bat it back and forth, something occurs to me.

"Wingate told me de Becque bought the first five Sleeping Women," I tell Baxter. "So how did you test the first painting for talc?"

"The paintings didn't sell in the order they were painted," he replies. "We tested the first one *painted*. One of the more abstract ones. It was the realistic ones that sold first and started the phenomenon."

"His Nabi period," says Lenz.

"The Nabis," I echo. "Wingate mentioned them. Hebrew for 'the Prophets.'"

"Just so."

"Did de Becque know I'm already involved with you?" I ask.

"He seemed to," says Baxter.

"How the hell would he know that?" Kaiser asks.

"I don't know, John."

Kaiser turns to Bowles. "How tight have you kept this?"

The Irishman's lips tighten. He is, after all, Kaiser's boss. "If there's a leak, it's not our people."

Kaiser doesn't look convinced. Neither does Lenz.

"So, what are we going to do?" asks the SAC.

"I'm going to Grand Cayman," I tell them. "One way or another."

Lenz nods approval, but Kaiser gives me a hard look.

"This isn't some jaunt through Somalia with a press pass in your pocket."

Now my face is red. "I'm flattered by your desire to protect me, Agent Kaiser, but I don't think it's going to advance this investigation."

"She's right," says Lenz.

"What we're going to do," Baxter says in a conclusive tone, "is let Ms. Glass go about her business. We know her wishes. It's up to us to decide what strategy makes the most sense."

"She needs protection," says Kaiser. "We have no idea what's going on in this case, no idea about motive. De Becque could have people in New Orleans right now. They could snatch or kill her any time."

"Agreed," says Baxter. "Patrick, could you put one of your agents with Ms. Glass until we contact her?"

Bowles nods assent.

"Ms. Glass," Baxter says in a conclusive tone, "I appreciate your willingness to go through with this. And if Agent Kaiser knew you like I do, he'd know there's no point in arguing with you."

Bowles looks at Kaiser. "Take her outside and find her some protection, John. Somebody you'll be satisfied with."

Kaiser gets up and walks out without a glance in my direction.

I stand and say, "Gentlemen," with the panache I've developed over twenty years working in a profession dominated by men, then follow him out.

Kaiser is waiting in the hall, his jaw tight.

"Your work has dulled your ability to assess risk," he says. "You think because you've tromped through a few battlefields, a visit to the Cayman Islands is nothing. But there's a difference. In a war zone, a journalist's enemy is bad luck. You might take a stray bullet or a piece of shrapnel, but nobody's trying very hard to kill you. De Becque may have nothing else on his mind *but* killing you. Do you get that? You could walk in the front door, and he could stick a knife in your throat and laugh in your face."

"Are you through?"

"Not if you still think you're going. We can get pictures of those paintings some other way. You have no business taking that kind of risk."

"Do you have a sister, Agent Kaiser?"

"No."

"A brother?"

"Yes."

"So why are we arguing?"

He sighs and looks at the floor. I start past him, but he takes hold of my shoulder.

"What about the protection?"

"Find me somebody who's not a robot, and I'm fine with it." I touch him lightly on the elbow. "I'm not stupid, okay?"

"What do you plan on doing his afternoon?"

"Buying presents for my niece and nephew. I'm supposed to stay with them tonight. My brother-in-law's house."

"That's where your sister disappeared. The Garden District."

"Which proves no neighborhood's safe, right? Unless you move across the lake with all the white flight. Where do you live?"

"Across the lake. Most of the agents here do."

"What does that say about your crime-fighting efforts?"

Kaiser turns and starts toward the elevators, and I follow. "Homicides don't fall under our jurisdiction," he says.

"Except very special ones."

"Right."

"I don't guess you're available to guard me this afternoon?"

He chuckles. "No. I've got someone good in mind, though."

"Is he tough?"

"Why do you assume it's a man?"

"Okay, is *she* tough?"

"Her hobby's competitive pistol shooting. She's a member of our SWAT team."

"Is she going to make a pass at me?"

Kaiser frowns, but his eyes are smiling. "If you were in the Bureau, you'd be disciplined for that remark."

"But I'm not."

"Are you suggesting that aggressive career women are sometimes gay?"

"I've run across it in my time."

He pauses in the corridor and looks me up and down. "You fit that category pretty well yourself, Ms. Glass."

"I do, don't I?"

Now he's looking at my left hand. It takes men longer to wonder about the marriage state. Seeing no ring, he raises his eyebrows. I can't help but smile. "Don't worry, Agent Kaiser. I like my bread buttered on the traditional side. Now introduce me to my bodyguard."

He walks past the elevators and into the stairwell.

"We need the exercise?" I ask.

"The elevators are painfully slow."

I follow him down one floor, and we emerge into a

beehive of activity, a wide-open cube farm of glass-windowed partitions with well-dressed men and women hurrying between the workspaces. Ten seconds into the room, I realize something they managed to conceal upstairs: The New Orleans FBI office is a building under siege. The agents' faces look hunted, their smallest movements marked by frustration. The air-conditioning is running full blast, but it can't drive out the reek of desperation. For a year and a half – two sweltering summers – these men and women have labored in vain as an ever-growing string of victims generated fear and then panic in a city that in the early nineties grew inured to the highest murder rate in the nation. Outside this building, my sister is a dim memory, a blurred element of the free-floating paranoia tainting the streets of this usually laid back city. But here, in this seemingly corporate cube farm, Jane is remembered. Here the shame of impotence weighs heavily on civilian soldiers who have no idea who their enemy is. As I move through the room at Kaiser's side, the looks I get run the scale from awe to resentment. *There she is,* they say to themselves. *The one who found the paintings. The photographer. The one whose sister got it. The one who was in the fire.* . . .

In the corner of the huge room is an office with four real walls and an open door. Kaiser leads us inside, where a man in shirtsleeves sits behind a desk, talking on the phone. His office is a quarter of the size of the SAC's upstairs, but his voice carries the weight of authority. When he hangs up, he winks at Kaiser.

"What's up, John?" he says, his eyes ready for anything.

"Bill, this is Jordan Glass. Ms. Glass, Bill Granger, head of the Violent Crimes Squad."

Granger leans forward and shakes my hand. "I'm sorry

about your sister, Ms. Glass. We've been doing everything we can."

"Thank you. I understand."

"The SAC wants to put an agent with Ms. Glass for a few hours," says Kaiser. "Maybe for the night. There's no imminent threat, but we want someone armed with her. I was thinking of Wendy Travis. Can you spare her?"

Granger bites his bottom lip, then nods and picks up the phone. "I think we can spare her for a few hours." He taps his fingers on his knee, then says, "Could I see you for a moment? . . . Thanks." When he hangs up, he gives Kaiser a knowing look. "I heard we've got a Quantico shrink upstairs, and Baxter himself may be flying down. You guys have a plan?"

"Working on one."

"Anything for my people to do?"

"I sure as hell hope so."

There's a knock behind us, and I turn to see a young woman a couple of inches shorter than I, but twice as fit. She's attractive in a well-scrubbed American way, dressed in a navy skirt, cream blouse, and a matching jacket that looks like Liz Claiborne. She could be an accountant for a Big Five firm, but for the pistol I see through the opening in her jacket.

"Ms. Glass," says Granger, "this is Special Agent Wendy Travis. Agent Travis, Jordan Glass. I'd like you to spend the day with her. It's a protective detail."

Agent Wendy gives me a pert smile and offers me her hand. When I take it, she shakes with a firmness two levels above that of most female professionals.

"Let me get my purse," she says. "And I'm ready to go."

I expect her to leave, but she remains in the doorway, her eyes on John Kaiser.

Kaiser smiles and says, "Thanks, Wendy. I knew you were the one for this."

Practically glowing with pleasure, Agent Wendy nods and walks briskly toward one of the glass cubes. When I turn back to the desk, Kaiser is blushing, and Bill Granger is smiling wryly and shaking his head.

8

I'm sitting on St. Charles Avenue in my rented Mustang, trying to work up the courage to knock on my brother-in-law's door. I parked a little way up from the house in case my niece and nephew are watching through the windows. My female bodyguard is standing thirty yards away, beneath a spreading oak, her hands hanging loosely at her sides. Agent Wendy has turned out to be all right, and I feel safer than I have in years. Wendy would think Jane was a lightweight for running only three miles a day. It's not hard to imagine her standing on a shooting range next to 250-pound men annoyed that a "goddamn girl" is outshooting them. She entered the FBI Academy in 1992, which tells me she's probably one of the "Starlings" who signed up for the Bureau after seeing Jodie Foster's inspiring portrayal of a fictional agent trainee in *The Silence of the Lambs*. I'm not knocking her. After I saw *Annie Hall*, I walked around in floppy pants, a man's necktie, and a hat for three weeks. At least Wendy picked something worthwhile to emulate.

She also kindly followed me around town while I searched for presents for my niece and nephew. Henry is eight, and named after the father of my brother-in-law, Marc Lacour. Lyn is six, and named after my mother. I've only seen them once since I left New Orleans eleven months ago. I promised myself I would visit more often, but that was a hard promise to keep. The reason is simple: I look exactly like their missing mother. And no matter what their father says to prepare them for my visits, they end up confused and crying.

Wendy is staring at the Mustang, willing me to get out. She knows I'm nervous about the visit. An hour ago I persuaded her to take me to a funky little bar on Magazine. She didn't drink, but I had two gin-and-tonics. To keep my mind off what was coming, I asked her about the New Orleans field office. She started with SAC Bowles, who initially found the ambiguities of Louisiana crime and politics – at one time virtually the same industry – a bit slippery. But now he has trials pending against a former governor and assorted other luminaries. The interesting thing was the way Wendy talked about John Kaiser. She didn't volunteer information; I had to ask. And her self-conscious glances told me she was trying to gauge the nature and level of my interest.

Kaiser, it seems, is the resident hunk of the office. All the assistants and secretaries flirt shamelessly with him, but he has never asked one for a date, patted a rump, or even squeezed a shoulder, which impresses Agent Wendy to no end. Kaiser's biography is interesting, too. He was sheriff in Idaho when Daniel Baxter was called in by a neighboring sheriff to consult on a string of murders that overlapped Kaiser's county. With Baxter's help, Kaiser ultimately caught the killer, proving exceptionally adept at interrogating suspects and extracting a confession. Duly impressed, Baxter encouraged the young sheriff to apply to the FBI Academy. Against the odds, the country boy from Idaho won admission, and after serving in the Spokane, Detroit, and Baltimore field offices, Kaiser was tapped by Baxter for the Investigative Support Unit. His record there was stellar until he snapped under the pressure. When I told Wendy I knew that part of the story, she couldn't hide her suspicion. How, she wondered, had I learned something in one day that it had taken her weeks to discover?

"His wife left him," she said. "Did he tell you that?"

"No."

A satisfied smile. "She couldn't take the hours he put in. That's pretty common. We're getting more and more intra-Bureau marriages now. But he didn't even stop working then, to sort it out. He just let her go."

"Kids?" I asked.

She shook her head.

"He told me he served in Vietnam. Do you know anything about that?"

"He doesn't talk about it. But Bowles told my SWAT commander that he'd seen John's service record, and that he has a bagful of medals. Bowles thought we ought to try to get John on the SWAT team. My commander approached him, but he wasn't interested. What do you think about that?"

"It doesn't surprise me. Men who've seen a lot of combat don't have many illusions about solving problems with weapons."

Wendy bit her lip and wondered if that was an insult. "You've seen it?" she asked. "Combat, I mean? You've taken pictures of it and all?"

"Yes."

"You ever get shot?"

"Yes."

I instantly went up two notches in her estimation. "Did it hurt?"

"I don't recommend it. I took a piece of shrapnel in the rear end once, too. That hurt a lot worse than the bullet did. Talk about *hot*."

Wendy laughed, I laughed with her, and by the time we

finished talking, I knew she was more than half in love with John Kaiser and that, though she liked me, she viewed me as an interloper of the first order.

Now the gin is wearing off, and if I don't get out of the Mustang immediately, I never will.

I sense Wendy's relief as I climb out with my gift-wrapped packages and walk up the block to my brother-in-law's house. House is actually a misnomer. Jane and her husband settled in one of those massive St. Charles Avenue homes that would be called a mansion anywhere else. On this part of St. Charles, the wrought-iron fences cost more than houses in the rest of the city. I mount the porch and swing the brass knocker against the knurled oak door. The resounding bang announces the acres of space that lie behind the door. I expect the knock to be answered by Annabelle, the Lacour family maid, now inherited by the scion, but it's Marc himself who opens the door.

You'd think people would be blessed with money or looks, not both, but Marc Lacour shatters that assumption. He has sandy blond hair, blue eyes, a chiseled face, and a muscular frame that looks ten years younger than its forty-one years. After the kids were born, he put on twenty pounds, but Jane's disappearance knocked them back off, as he manically exercised to combat depression. Tonight he's wearing blue wool trousers, cordovan wing tips, and a Brooks Brothers shirt. He smiles when he sees me, then pulls me to him for a hug, which I return. He smells faintly of cologne.

"Jordan," he says as I draw back. "I'm glad you're here."

He pulls me into the huge central hall, then closes the door and leads me to a formal living room that looks like a layout from *Architectural Digest*. There's not a cast-aside toy or empty pizza box in sight. I feel almost guilty setting my presents on the floor, as though I'm disturbing some hidden plan. Jane kept things looser. I suppose the life of the house has begun to revert to the patterns Marc knew in childhood. He has no other map, of course, but the sterility of the environment makes my heart hurt for the kids.

"Are Henry and Lyn upstairs?" I ask, perching on a wing chair that looks like it should have a braided museum rope tied across its arms.

"They're at my parents' house." Marc sits opposite me on a sofa.

"Oh. When will they be back?"

"My folks bought a place down the street. They'll bring the kids as soon as I call."

Okay. "What's going on, Marc?"

"I wanted to talk to you before you see them."

"Is something wrong?"

"No. But there's something you need to know."

"What?"

He takes a lawyerly pause, then speaks in the deepest voice he can muster. "The kids know Jane is dead, Jordan."

"What?"

"I had to tell them. I had no choice."

It's amazing, really, the degree to which we deceive ourselves. For months I've been telling myself that I've mourned and buried my sister in my heart. But now, confronted with a concrete act based on that assumption, I want to scream denial. The voice that emerges from my mouth sounds like a stunned four-year-old's. "But . . . *you don't know she's dead.*"

Marc shakes his head. "How long are you going to wait before you accept it? Your father's been dead almost thirty years, and you're still looking for him. I have to raise these kids, and they can't wait that long."

"It's not right, Marc."

"What is, then? They thought Jane was out there suffering somewhere, at the mercy of some 'bad person.' That she couldn't get away or find her way back home. It was driving them crazy. They couldn't do their schoolwork, couldn't sleep, couldn't *eat*. All they did was sit at the window, waiting for Jane to come home. I finally told them that God had taken Mama to heaven to be with Him. She wasn't with any bad person, she was with God and his angels."

"How did you say she died? They must have asked."

"I told them she went to sleep and didn't wake up."

Jesus. "What did they say?"

"Did it hurt?"

I can't even respond to this.

Marc's face is resolute. "It's for the best, Jordan. And I don't want you saying anything to them about what's going on now. The paintings, the investigation, none of it. Nothing to give them some crazy hope that she might come back. Because you know she won't. Those women are dead. Every one of them."

Maybe it's that I have no kids of my own. Maybe the daily demands of raising children simply can't be handled with a giant question mark hanging over everything.

"I want you to be part of their lives," Marc says. "But you have to understand the ground rules. In this family, Jane has passed away. We had a memorial service for her."

"What? You never called me."

"You were in Asia, no one knew where."

"My agency could have found me."

"I thought it would be less confusing if their mother's mirror image didn't suddenly fly in from parts unknown to be at her funeral."

"I can't believe this." Suddenly a decision I made months ago seems like a bad one. "There's something I never told you, Marc. I got a phone call eight months ago, from Thailand. There was a lot of static, and I could have been mistaken, but I thought it might be Jane."

"What?"

"She said she needed help, but that Daddy couldn't help her. Then a man came on the phone and said something in French. Then in English he said, 'It's just a dream,' and hung up the phone."

"And you thought that was Jane? Calling from *Thailand*?"

"I wasn't sure. Not at the time. But now that I've found these paintings in Hong Kong . . . I mean, don't you think that puts it in a new light?"

"Why didn't you tell me about this call before?"

"I didn't want to upset you."

"When did the call come? Daytime? Or the middle of the night?"

"Why?"

"Because eight months ago was when you couldn't get out of bed, wasn't it? Your little prescription vacation?"

My anger flares, but I press it down. "Yes, but I had the FBI check with the phone company. I really did get a call from Thailand in the middle of the night. From a train station."

Marc looks at me a bit longer, then turns to a portrait of his parents on the wall. They look wealthy and distant. "You do what you have to, Jordan. That's what we all do. But I don't want to know about it. Not unless you get positive evidence that Jane or one of the other women is alive. Anything short of that is all pain, no gain."

"Spoken like a true lawyer."

His cheeks color. "You think I don't miss her? I've suffered more—" He stops, takes a cell phone from his pocket, and hits a speed-dial number. "It's me. . . . I'll meet you at the door." He hangs up and stands from the sofa.

"I'm surprised you're letting me see them at all."

"I told you, I want you to be part of this family. That's why I asked you to stay with us. You're a great person. And you're a terrific role model for Lyn."

"Do you really believe that?"

"Look, let's forget the other stuff and concentrate on the kids."

The "other stuff" being his missing wife. "I'll wait in here."

Marc sighs and leaves the room.

The truth is, I really don't know much about Jane and Marc's relationship. Jane liked to project an image of perfection. They married young, but Marc wanted to postpone having children until he'd put in the years of hundred-hour weeks required for making partner. That worried Jane, who wanted kids almost immediately, more to cement the relationship, I feared at the time, than for the children themselves. But when she finally got them, she proved a wonderful mother, creating the warm, secure environment that she and I had never known.

The sound of the front door opening reaches me, then subdued voices. A society matron's cigarette-parched drawl rises above the others. "I just don't think it's the *proper* thing to do. They've been through too much already." The muted drone of Marc's lawyer voice assures his mother that he knows exactly what he's doing. Then, God help me, comes the patter of small shoes on the hardwood floor, followed by the percussive clack of Marc's wing tips. I feel more acute anxiety than I have waiting to meet heads of state. The steps grow louder, then stop, but the doorway remains empty.

"Go ahead," says Marc from somewhere in the hall. "It's okay."

Nothing happens.

"She brought *pres*-ents," he says in a singsong voice.

A small face appears from behind the door post. Lyn's face. A physical echo of my own. With her large dark eyes, she looks like a fawn peeking from behind a tree. As her mouth falls open, Henry's blond hair and blue eyes appear above her. Henry blinks, then disappears. I smile as broadly as I can and hold out my arms. Lyn looks behind her – presumably at her father – then steps into the open and runs to me.

It takes a supreme effort to keep from crying as her little arms wrap around my neck like a drowning child's and she says, *"Mama, mama,"* in my ear.

I gently pull her back and look into her wet eyes. "I'm Jordan, sweetie. I'm—"

"She knows," says Marc, ushering Henry toward me with his hands on the boy's shoulders.

"She said 'Mama.'"

"Lyn, do you know who this lady is?"

She nods solemnly at me. "You're Aunt Jordan. I've seen your pictures in books."

"But you said 'Mama.'"

"You remind me of my mom. She's gone to heaven to be with God."

I put my hand over my mouth to hold my composure, and Marc helps out by pushing Henry forward. "This big guy here is Henry, Aunt Jordan."

"I know that. Hello, Henry."

"I got a first-place trophy in soccer," he announces.

"You *did*?"

"You want to see it?"

"Of course I do. But I brought you a present. Would you like to see that first?"

He looks back at his father for permission.

"Let's see it," Marc says.

I point to the wrapped package by the door. "Are you big enough to open that, Henry?"

"YEAH!"

He practically attacks the package, and in seconds exposes a hardcover book-sized box that says "Panasonic." "It's a DVD player, Dad! Look! One for the car!"

"A little extravagant, isn't it?" says Marc, arching an eyebrow at me.

"That's a maiden aunt's privilege."

"Looks that way."

Lyn is standing quietly at my knee, watching me. She doesn't even ask if I got her anything.

"And this is for you," I tell her, handing her the smaller box from the foot of the chair.

"What is it?"

"Look inside."

She carefully removes the bow and sets it aside, and by this simple act breaks my heart again. She learned that frugal habit from Jane, as Jane learned it from our mother. My sister lives on in ways large and small. At last the box becomes visible, and Lyn studies it intently.

"What is it?"

"Let's see if you can figure it out. Can you read the box?"

"Nick on? *Ni*kon? Coolpix. Nine-nine-zero."

"Perfect! Let me get it out for you." I open the box, remove the foam from the odd-shaped plastic housing, and hand it to her. "What do you think it is?"

She studies the two-piece body, then focuses on the small lens.

"Is it a camera?"

"Yes."

Her lips pucker in an unreadable expression. "Is it a kid's camera, or a grown-up camera?"

"It's a grown-up camera. A very good one. You have to be careful while you learn to use it. Wear the strap so you don't drop it. But don't be *too* careful. It's only a tool. What's important is your eyes, and what you see in your head. The camera just helps you show other people what you see. Do you understand?"

She nods slowly, her eyes bright.

"Dad!" cries Henry. "There's two DVDs in here! *Iron Giant* and *El Dorado*!"

"Are you really spending the night with us tonight?" asks Lyn.

"I am."

"Will you teach me how to use this?"

"I sure will. The pictures from this camera go into a computer before they go onto paper. I'll bet you have a computer."

"My dad has one."

"We'll just borrow his until he gets you your own. Right, Dad?"

Marc shakes his head, but he's smiling. "Right. Okay, who's ready for supper?"

"Did you actually cook?"

"Are you kidding? Annabelle!"

After thirty seconds or so, the clicking of heels comes up the hallway, followed by an elderly black woman's voice. "What you hollerin' about, Mr. Lacour?"

"How's supper coming?"

"Almost ready."

Annabelle appears in the doorway, not heavy and slow like I pictured her, but thin and tall and efficient. She has a warm smile on her face until her eyes settle on me. It fades instantly, replaced by a mix of wonder and fear.

"Annabelle, this is Jordan," says Marc.

"Lord, I see that," she says softly. "Child, you the spittin' image of . . ." She glances at the kids and trails off. As though impelled against her will, Annabelle advances across the room until she's standing over me. I reach up and take her hand, and she squeezes mine with remarkable strength. "God bless you," she says. Then she goes to Henry and Lyn, bends nearly double, gives each a hug, and walks back to the door.

"You can go on when supper's done," Marc says. "Have a good night."

"Soon as I get the biscuits out the oven," she says in a faraway voice, "I'll be gone home."

When she disappears, I say, "I didn't think they still made them like that."

"You've been out of the South too long," Marc replies. "Annabelle's the best. This family couldn't function without her. I think you gave her a shock, though."

By the time we reach the dining room, the table is laden with food. A pork loin with what smells like honey-and-brown-sugar glaze, cheese grits, cat-head biscuits, and a token salad. After months of Asian food, these smells from childhood nearly overwhelm my senses. Jane is everywhere around me. She and I were raised knowing nothing of fine china, so naturally she spent months deciding on the fine old Royal Doulton pattern that sits before me now. Same with the Waterford crystal and Reed & Barton silver.

"It looks terrific, doesn't it?" I tell Henry. "Here, come sit by me. Lyn, you sit on this side."

"But your setting's at the end of the table," she says, pointing.

"I'd rather sit by you."

Lyn's smile could split the world. She and Henry take the chairs on either side of mine, and we all dig in. It's surprising how quickly we fall into a natural rhythm of conversation, and the only awkward moments come in the silences. The children look at me as though they've lost all sense of time, and I know they are reliving hours spent at this table with their mother. Once, even Marc's eyes seem to glaze over, as he slips into the same dimension the kids visit so much more easily. I can't blame them. Thirteen months ago a divine hand reached into the Norman Rockwell painting of their life together and rubbed out the mother figure, leaving a painful, puzzling space. Now, magically, that space has been filled again, by a woman who looks exactly like the one who was erased.

"It's getting close to bedtime," Marc says.

"No!" the children cry in unison.

"How about cutting them a little slack this first night?"

Marc looks like he's getting tired of my interference, but he agrees. We retire to the living room, and I give Lyn an introductory lesson on the digital Nikon while Henry loads *El Dorado* into his portable DVD player. Lyn is deft with her hands, and a proprietary glow of pride takes me by surprise. After she shoots a few test shots, I load them into Marc's notebook computer. The results are good, and Lyn practically bursts with pleasure. Marc tries again to get the kids to bed, but they refuse, crawling into my lap for me to argue their case. I oblige, and before long Henry is zonked out and both my legs are asleep. Marc sits in a chair across the room, his legs draped over an ottoman as he half-watches a stock market report on CNBC, so he doesn't notice when I look down and see Lyn staring up at me, her chin quivering.

"What is it, honey?" I whisper.

She closes her eyes tight, squeezing out tears as she turns her face into my breast and sobs. "I miss my mama."

This time there's no stopping my tears. I have never known a protective instinct as powerful as the one that suffuses me now. Not even when I was practically raising Jane in Oxford. I would kill to protect these children. But who can I kill to protect them from the loss of their mother? All I can do is caress Lyn's forehead and reassure her about the future.

"I know you do, baby. I do, too. But I'm here for you now. Think about happy times."

"Are you going to stay with us?"

"I sure am."

"How long?" Her eyes are wide and fragile as bubbles.

"As long as you need me. As long as it takes."

Marc looks over at us, his eyes suddenly alert. "What's the matter?"

"Nothing a little hugging won't fix," I tell him, rocking Lyn as best I can with Henry weighing me down. But what I'm hearing in my mind is the voice on the telephone eight months ago. *God, let that have been Jane,* I pray silently. *These children need more than I can ever give them.*

A half hour later, Marc and I carry the kids to their beds. They've slept together since Jane disappeared, insisting on the room next to Marc's rather than the larger but more isolated ones upstairs. When we get back to the living room, he opens a second bottle of wine, and we methodically drink most of it while reminiscing about Jane. Marc wasn't lying when he said he missed her. As he drains the last of the bottle, his eyes mist over.

"I know you think I'm a bastard for telling them she's dead. I'm just trying to make things as easy on them as I can."

I give him a conciliatory nod. "Now that I see them, I understand better why you did what you did. But what will you do if it turns out you're wrong?"

He snorts. "You don't really think those women are alive, do you?"

"I honestly don't know. I had convinced myself that Jane was dead. But now I won't give up until I see her body."

"Just like with your father," he mumbles. "You never give up."

"I wish you wouldn't either. In your heart, at least."

"My heart?" He gestures toward his chest with the goblet, and wine sloshes onto his shirt. "For the last thirteen months, my life has been shit. If it weren't for those kids, I might not even be here."

"Marc—"

"I know, I know. Self-pitying slob."

"That's not what I was thinking."

He's not listening anymore. He has covered his eyes and begun sobbing. Alcohol and depression definitely don't mix. I feel a little awkward, but I get up, walk over to him, and lay my hand on his shoulder.

"I know it's hard. I've had a tough time myself."

He shakes his head violently, as though to deny the tears, then sits up and wipes his face on his shirtsleeve. "Goddamn it! I'm sorry I got like this."

I sit on the ottoman and put my hands on his shoulders. "Hey. You've been through one of the worst things anyone can go through. You're allowed."

His bloodshot eyes seek out mine. "I just can't seem to get it together."

"Maybe you need a break. Have you taken a vacation since it happened?"

"No. Work helps me deal with it."

"Maybe work helps you *not* deal with it. Have you thought of that?"

He laughs like he doesn't need or appreciate amateur psychology. Privileged men are masters of ironic distance. "I'm just glad you came," he says. "I can't believe how the kids responded to you."

"I can't believe how I responded to them. I almost feel like they're mine."

"I know." His smile vanishes. "Just . . . thanks for coming." He leans forward and embraces me. The hug does me good, too, I must admit. I haven't had many these past months. But suddenly a current of shock shoots through me. There's something moist against my neck. *He's kissing my neck.* And there's nothing brotherly about it.

I go stiff in spite of my desire not to overreact. *"Marc?"*

He takes his lips away, but before I can gather my thoughts, he's kissing my mouth. I jerk back and put my hands on his arms to restrain him.

His eyes plead silently with me. "You don't know what it's been like without her. It's not the same for you. I can't even make myself *look* at another woman. All I see is Jane. But watching you tonight, at the table, with the kids . . . you almost *are* her."

"I'm not Jane."

"I know that. But if I let my mind drift just a little, it's like you are. You even *feel* like her." He pulls his arms free and squeezes my hands. "Your hands are the same, your eyes, your breasts, everything." His blue eyes fix mine with a

155

monk's intensity. "Do you know what it would mean to me to have one night with you? Just one night. It would be like Jane had come back. It would—"

"*Stop!*" I hiss, afraid the children will wake. "Do you hear yourself? I'm not Jane, and I can't pretend to be! Not to ease your grief. Not for the kids, and especially not in your bed. In *her* bed. My God."

He looks at the floor, then back up at me, and his eyes shine with an unpleasant light. "It wouldn't be the first time you pretended to be her, would it?"

It's as though he flushed liquid nitrogen through my veins. I am speechless, unable to move. Only when he squeezes my hands do I yank them away in reflex.

"What are you talking about?"

He smirks like a little boy with a secret. "You know."

Without knowing how I got there, I find myself standing three feet away from him with my arms crossed over my breasts. "I'm leaving. I'm going to stay at a hotel. Tell the kids I'll be back during the day."

He blinks, then seems to come to his senses a bit, or at least to feel some sense of shame. "Don't do that. I didn't mean to upset you. You're just so damn beautiful." He stumbles over the ottoman as he comes toward me. My instinct is to jump forward and help him, but I don't. I don't want things to get any worse than they already are.

"I'm going upstairs to get my bags. You stay here while I do it."

"Don't be melodramatic. You don't have anything to worry about."

"I mean it, Marc."

Without waiting for a reply, I run up the stairs and grab my suitcase, thanking God I didn't unpack yet. When I go back down, he's waiting at the foot of the stairs.

"What am I supposed to tell the kids?" he asks.

"Don't you dare use them against me like that. Tell them I got called away to a photo shoot. I'll be back to see them. I just won't be spending the night."

He looks penitent now, but the sense of entitlement I heard in his voice only moments ago still haunts me. Before he sinks into drunken apologies, I push past him and leave without a word.

As I hit the sidewalk, a car door opens a few yards away and a dark figure floats onto the sidewalk.

"Jordan?" says a female voice. "What's the matter?"

"I'm fine, Wendy. I'm just staying elsewhere."

"What happened?"

My joke to Kaiser about Wendy making a pass at me comes back to me like instant karma. Someone made a pass tonight, all right. But I could never have imagined it would come from my sister's husband. "Men problems," I murmur.

"Gotcha. Where are we going?"

"A hotel, I guess."

She takes my suitcase and starts toward the Mustang, then pauses. "Um, look . . . I don't know how you feel about hotels, but I've got an extra bedroom at my apartment. I've got to stay with you no matter where you go, so, you know. It's up to you. But that way we'd have food and coffee, toiletries, whatever you need."

There have been nights I would have killed for a hotel room. I've slept in shell craters and been grateful for them. But tonight I don't want a sterile, empty place. I want real things around me, a humanly messy kitchen and CDs and a crocheted comforter on the couch. I hope Wendy isn't a compulsive cleaner. "That sounds great. Let's go."

I'm about to start the Mustang when a soft beeping sounds in it. "What's that?" I ask, looking around in confusion.

"Cell phone," she announces. "A Nokia. I recognize the ring. We use some at the office."

"Oh." I grab my fanny pack from the backseat, unzip it, and remove the phone Kaiser gave me back at the FBI office. "Hello?"

"Ms. Glass? Daniel Baxter."

"What's up?"

"I've been negotiating with Monsieur de Becque of the Cayman Islands."

"And?"

"He says you can go on our plane, and you can bring one assistant to help with lighting, et cetera."

"Great. When do I leave?"

"Tomorrow. A few of us have spent the last half hour arguing over who your assistant should be. I'm backing a member of the Hostage Rescue Team. If things take a nasty turn, he'd have the best chance of getting you out of there alive."

"Is someone arguing with your choice?"

"Agent Kaiser has a different opinion."

I smile to myself. "Who does the sheriff want to send?"

Baxter's hand covers the mouthpiece, but despite his effort I hear him say, "She just called you 'the sheriff.'" When the ISU chief removes his hand, he says, "The sheriff doesn't want to send anybody. He wants to go himself."

"You should let him go, then."

"Is that who you want?"

"Absolutely. I feel safer already."

"Okay. You'll probably leave tomorrow afternoon. I'll call you in the morning to give you the travel details."

"I'll talk to you then. And Wendy's taking good care of me."

"Good. See you tomorrow."

"What's happening?" Wendy asks after I hang up.

"I'm going to the Cayman Islands."

"Oh." She shifts in her seat. "What was that about a sheriff?"

"A joke. I was talking about Kaiser."

She guessed as much. "He's going with you?"

"It looks that way. For security."

She looks out her window. "Lucky you," she says finally.

The eternal plight of women. A minute ago we were fast friends. Now she'd like to revoke her offer to share her apartment. But her manners are far too good for that. I'd like to reassure Agent Wendy that she has nothing to worry about, but I don't want to insult her intelligence. I start the engine and pull into St. Charles Avenue.

"Give me some directions. It's time to get some sleep."

"Straight," she says. "I'll tell you where to turn."

I start down the tree-lined avenue, the streetcar tracks gleaming silver under the lights as the Mustang swallows them. The leaves on the trees look gray, but only a small part of my brain registers this. The rest is rerunning Marc Lacour's remark again and again: *It wouldn't be the first time you pretended to be her, would it?* And then Dr. Lenz's voice, out of the dark: *What's the worst thing you've ever done?*

If only you could plead the fifth with your conscience.

9

Most flights to the Cayman Islands stage out of Houston or Miami, but with the FBI Lear, things are simpler. It's Kaiser, me, and two pilots up front for the two-hour run from New Orleans to Grand Cayman, largest of the three islands that make up the British colony. The last time I made this flight, my knuckles were white for half the journey. I was covering the air convoy that American pilots take to the Caymans for the annual air show there, one "highlight" of which is the provocative overflight of communist Cuba. Fifteen years ago, this was no joke, and I'm happy to be cruising along with nothing more to worry about than a seventy-year-old Frenchman who for some unknown reason has requested my presence.

We've been in the air for an hour, and Kaiser is un-characteristically quiet. I don't suppose there's much to say. Or perhaps I'm radiating enough hostility to discourage conversation. I can still feel my brother-in-law's lips against my neck, and the emotional fallout is hard to shake. Most difficult of all is the remark Marc made as I rebuffed him: *It wouldn't be the first time you pretended to be her, would it?* I'd hoped that particular chapter of my life was shared only by my sister, but apparently I hoped for too much. The fact that Jane told her husband about it reveals a piercing truth: she never really believed my side of the story.

What's the worst thing you've ever done? Dr. Lenz used to

ask his patients. A simple but devastating question. And the other one – what was it? *What's the worst thing that ever happened to you?* Several terrible things have happened to me, none of which I want to dwell on now, but in making choices about my behavior, I haven't often gone against the dictates of my conscience. On the most painful occasion when I did, I was eighteen years old. It's almost embarrassing that twenty-two years of post–high school living haven't given me some greater claim to infamy, but the journey through adolescence is one of the hardest we ever make, and the wounds sustained along the way last a lifetime.

Years of simmering tension between my sister and me came to a boiling point during our senior year, just weeks before my affair with David Gresham became the sensation of the school. Jane was riding her high horse, chattering endlessly about how she was going to be a Chi-Omega the next year and asking why I didn't get my act together, "fix up" a little, and try to be "halfway normal," whatever that meant to her. When I wasn't worrying about how I was going to pay her expenses at Ole Miss, I was shooting portraits in my tiny studio or sneaking through the woods to my history teacher's house. Looking back on it, I was like a ghost. Silent during classes, vanishing after school, skipping pep rallies and ball games, never going to high school hangouts.

Jane suspected I was involved with someone, but I had no idea of the shape of her suspicions. One day, during an argument over something stupid, I realized she thought I was gay. That I was slipping off at all hours to meet a woman. It was funny, really, but when I treated it as such, she started screaming about how strange I was, how I was ruining her chance to become a Chi-O and have a normal life. I told her that her idea of a normal life wasn't anything to aspire to. I also told her I wasn't gay, and that I knew more about men than she ever would. She smirked in a superior way that dismissed me completely. I said if circumstances had been slightly different, it could be me dating Bobby Evans, her wealthy boyfriend of three years, and her doing the work that paid the light bill. She looked at me incredulously and said, "Bobby and *you*? Together? You've got to be kidding." And then she laughed. For some reason, that really cut me to the quick. "Why not?" I asked. "Because you're so *weird*," she said, looking at me with pity. I understood then that she saw me exactly as others did, as some sort of self-exiled outcast. All I'd done to keep our family together, she simply took as her due.

Two days later, I got home from school and found a note taped to Jane's window. It was from her boyfriend, and it said to meet him that afternoon in the woods behind the coliseum. I threw away the note, put my hair up in a ponytail, slipped on a pair of Jane's earrings and one of her precious Lacoste sweaters, and rode her bike down to the woods. Bobby Evans was waiting there in his letter jacket. He looked a like a young Robert Redford standing there, though his IQ left a bit to be desired.

I played Jane to perfection. We'd been impersonating each other since we were babies; it was easy. Why did I do it? I wanted to know what lay behind that smirk she'd given me. And I suppose I was jealous of her in my own way. The road of the nonconformist is a lonely one, and I'd been walking it for a long time. Bobby Evans was one of the rewards for being a "good girl," which meant following every hypocritical southern folkway and more with the rigidity of a Victorian virgin. As we talked, Bobby steered us over into the trees, and I realized this was a ritual of theirs. He kissed me in the shadows, first delicately, then with passion. It was typical high school stuff – or what I imagined that to be, anyway – all rushed and breathless and intense, him crushing my breasts from outside my sweater and pressing his pelvis against mine. Very different from my experiences with David Gresham. When I let him put his hand inside her sweater, I could tell that was as far as they ever went. The way he slowly lowered his hand toward my waistband told me that. He was waiting for a "No," a "Not yet," or an "I want to, but we just can't."

I didn't say any of those things.

A few minutes of touching me there was more than he could handle. Afterward, he sat down at my feet, too embarrassed to look at me, and stared down at the ground. It was like someone had finally given him the keys to paradise. He asked why I had let him do that, and I said I'd just decided that today was the day. It was getting dark by then. He looked up like a puppy and said, "Do you have to go back now?" I said the only person who would notice I was late was Jordan, and who cared about her? He laughed.

This time when he touched me, I touched back. I'm not sure why. I'd already gotten whatever petty revenge I wanted against Jane. It was a hormonal thing by that point, I think. I was eighteen and experienced, he was eighteen and good-looking, and things took their natural course. When we were half undressed, I almost stopped pretending. There didn't seem much point anymore, and I didn't want him thinking he had deflowered Jane. But I couldn't bring myself to tell him the truth. I kept my blouse on to hide the arm where Jane had her scars, and kept my mouth over his to keep from talking.

Once he was inside me, he did the opposite of what I expected. He didn't close his eyes and flail away. He went very slowly and looked right into my eyes, pure rapture on

163

his face. Part of that, I realized, was his belief that the girl he had put on a pedestal for three years was finally giving herself totally to him. I wanted to stop then, but there was no graceful way to do it. Instead, I tried to make it end faster. As I did, he looked down with a strange light in his eyes and said, "You're not Jane, are you?"

It was the most chilling moment of my life. He *knew*. If he hadn't, he wouldn't have risked saying that.

"No," I said, terrified that he would jump up and start screaming to the trees that I was a slut. I should have known better. I learned a lesson about men that day. There was hardly a hitch in his rhythm. His eyes got bigger, he groaned in ecstasy, and enjoyed it twice as much. It was the biggest ego trip of his young life, and I was a fool to think for an instant that he would be able to keep quiet about it. He didn't tell his friends, which would have been bad enough. He did something infinitely worse.

The next time he was with Jane, he acted as though she had made love with him the last time they were together, and insisted that she do it again. She flew into a rage and demanded an explanation, and he let her figure it out for herself. She didn't speak more than ten words a month to me for three years afterward. I tried to explain why I'd done it, and what had really happened, but it was useless. For Jane to accept the truth about Bobby's actions would have made the betrayal complete, and thus unbearable. Two months later, my relationship with David Gresham went public, and I left for New Orleans.

The obvious rancor slowly faded. Bobby Evans was consigned to the past with the other trappings of high school. (He now sells residential real estate in Oxford.) I continued to help Jane financially until her junior year of college, when she found some other source of money. I next saw her at her wedding, though I was not invited to be maid of honor (that office went to Marc Lacour's sister). But in the twenty years since, we slowly but surely made overtures that bridged the chasm that once divided us. In the three years before she disappeared, we were closer than at any time in our lives, thanks to Jane's efforts more than mine, and I came to believe that the bond we shared – formed in the face of paternal abandonment and maternal incapacity – was stronger than a break over any man. And perhaps it was. Perhaps she revealed my betrayal in the early days of her marriage to Marc.

Looking back now, it's easy to see Jane's entire life as a flight from the family fate had handed her. All her efforts to reach out, to join, to belong – to the cheerleaders, school clubs, church groups, sororities – all seemed part of a desperate attempt to find a surrogate family, to become part of the Brady Bunch perfection so prevalent on the television of our youth, which our home environment resembled not at all. In that context, my one-day fling with Bobby Evans was no simple sexual betrayal; it was an arrow in the heart of Jane's illusions of progress. And since our illusions are always our most precious possessions, how could she ever forgive me?

But the final, terrible irony of her life was worse. Having succeeded in her impossible quest, having attained a rich and handsome husband, a mansion, and two beautiful children – all the hallmarks of gentility and security – she was plucked from the heart of her fantasy by some tortured soul undoubtedly born into a family even more dysfunctional than ours. If Jane is dead, I cannot imagine what her last thoughts must have been. If she's alive –

"Are you sleeping?"

I blink from my trance and look across the narrow aisle at

John Kaiser, who is studying me with a worried gaze. He's wearing navy slacks, a polo shirt, and a tan suede jacket that perfectly fits his shoulders. I dressed for this trip myself, in tailored black silk pants and a matching jacket, with a linen blouse cut low enough to reveal a swell of cleavage. A kinky old Frenchman might just respond to some tasteful décolletage.

"Hey," he says. "You in a trance?"

"No. Just thinking."

"What about?"

"We don't know each other well enough for you to ask that question."

He gives me a tight smile. "You're right. Sorry."

I straighten up in my seat. "You probably have some grand plan for this meeting, right? A strategy?"

"Nope. Doctor Lenz would have one. But I go on instinct a lot of the time. We're going to play it by ear."

"You must have some idea about what de Becque wants with me."

"Either de Becque's been behind this whole thing from day one – every disappearance – or it's some sort of diversion for him. A rich man's game. If it's a game, I figure he knows you're a double for one of the Sleeping Women. Maybe he saw Jane's portrait when Wingate put it up for sale. Then when he heard about what happened in Hong Kong – a twin of one of the Sleeping Women showing up – he put two and two together."

"But how? Unless he had prior knowledge, how could he make the leap from one of the faces on the paintings in Hong Kong to me? To knowing my name?"

"You're a celebrity of sorts. If he had a print of Jane's painting, he could have scanned it and e-mailed it around. Asked if anyone recognized you."

"There are no prints of the Sleeping Women. Wingate told me. No photos, nothing."

"Then maybe someone in Hong Kong recognized you. Knew you were in town."

"I wasn't there on assignment. I'm doing a book. I go where I want, and only a few friends ever know where I am."

"Then maybe he did have prior knowledge. If that's the case, we're walking into something complicated."

"Like?"

Kaiser bites his lip and looks at the seat back ahead of him.

"What is it?"

"I wasn't going to say anything before the meeting, but this might help prepare you for what we could encounter."

"What?"

"The Vietnam connections are starting to bother me."

"How so?"

"Your father disappeared in Vietnam in 1972, right?"

"On the Cambodian border."

"Same thing. And de Becque lived in Vietnam for years."

"And?"

"The Sleeping Women are sold exclusively in the East. And your mystery call came from Thailand, which is practically next door to Vietnam. I did R-and-R there myself in 1970."

"Catch any embarrassing diseases?"

"No, but not for lack of trying."

"How could Vietnam play into this?"

"I don't know. But the coincidences are starting to build. You thought you might have heard your father's voice during that Thailand phone call, right?"

A strange and disturbing buzz has started in the back of my head. "What are you saying, Agent Kaiser?"

167

"I'm just pulling threads together."

"Are you suggesting my father could have taken Jane? And the others too?"

"You believe he's still alive, right?"

"I'm the only person who does. But even if he is, he wouldn't . . ."

"Wouldn't what? Go on, say it. If he's still alive, he wouldn't take Jane to be with him. Right? He would take you."

"I guess that's what I was thinking. Hoping. But how could that even be possible? He'd have to be in the U.S."

"There's a plane every day. If he is alive, you have to accept two things. One, he's chosen not to contact you for almost thirty years. Two, you know nothing about him, other than what a twelve-year-old girl knew about her young father."

"I can't believe what you're suggesting. My father was an award-winning photojournalist. What motive could he possibly have to get involved in some sick situation like this?"

Kaiser sighs and lays his hands on his knees. "Look, all this is speculation. It's almost certain that your father's dead."

"I know that." Though I feel an irrational anger toward Kaiser in this moment, I can't dismiss his ideas. "But I'm sitting here trying to remember if my father ever painted anything."

He watches me for a few moments. "Did he?"

"No. Only photography."

"Good. Because the connoisseurs studying the Sleeping Women say they were painted by someone with enormous ability and classical training."

Thank God.

"How old was your father when he disappeared?"

"Thirty-six."

"And he'd never painted anything. I'd say that lets him off the hook right there."

I nod agreement, but new fears aren't so easily banished. The Vietnam coincidences are indeed starting to build, and the image of a conspiracy has been taking shape almost from the beginning. *What ties the Sleeping Women to Asia?* There's really no use trying to puzzle it out now. But perhaps Marcel de Becque, the colonial French tea planter and black market trader, can shed some light on the question.

Grand Cayman lies 150 miles south of Cuba. Fifteen years ago, it was an unspoiled paradise. Now it's not much different from Cancún – heavily commercialized and functionally Americanized – though it is more upscale. Parts of the island are still undeveloped, but to get the flavor of the old Caymans, you have to fly a puddle-jumper east to the smaller, more primitive island of Cayman Brac.

Our FBI pilot swings once around North Bay to show us de Becque's estate, a gated compound that stands on a jutting point of land near the marina. The Frenchman is aparently unconcerned with keeping a low profile, or he would have settled in the more discreet community of Cayman Kai, near Rum Point. Looking down at the emerald water, white beaches, and stunning homes, I expect to hear the voice of Robin Leach in my ear, but instead I hear our pilot instructing us to belt in for landing at the airport near Georgetown.

A white Range Rover awaits us on the runway, and the small matter of customs has been taken care of in advance by the Justice Department. The British governor of the islands knows we are here, and should anything questionable happen during our stay, there will be no doubt as to who was at fault. A Caucasian driver and his Caymanian associate load my camera and lighting equipment into the back of the Rover, and after leaving the airport, we swing northward.

"How far to Monsieur de Becque's estate?" I ask.

"A few minutes," the driver replies in a French accent.

Kaiser says nothing.

In the Caymans, as in the United Kingdom, all traffic proceeds on the left. Every few seconds, our driver wheels into the right lane to pass colorful jeeps, vans, and scooters, all driving at a leisurely vacation speed. Mixed with the tourist vehicles is a healthy contingent of Mercedeses and BMWs. The Cayman Islands have been wealthy ever since King George III absolved their citizens from taxation, for their heroism during the tragic Wreck of the Ten Sails. This status – along with airtight banking secrecy laws – has made the Caymans an international tax haven, and the fifth-largest financial center in the world. Unlike the rest of the Caribbean, where beggars can be a nuisance, the Caymans boast natives richer than many tourists.

A high wall surrounds de Becque's estate, but when our driver opens an iron gate with a coded remote, I see a larger version of what I saw from the air: a British colonial mansion that, like some embassies, gives the impression of a fortress. The driver pulls the Rover into a crescent drive and stops before wide marble steps. His assistant gets out, opens our doors, then motions us upward.

The massive door opens before we ring the bell, and I find myself facing one of the most beautiful women I have ever seen. With fine black hair, light-brown skin, and almond eyes, she possesses that rare combination of Asian and European features that makes it impossible for me to guess her age. She could be thirty or fifty, and her self-possession is remarkable. She stands utterly still, and gives the impression that she could remain so for an hour or a day. It's almost a surprise when she speaks.

"*Bonjour,* Mademoiselle Glass."

"Hello."

"I am Li. Please come in."

I step inside, followed by Kaiser, who with the driver brings in the aluminum flight cases. After they set them down in the granite-floored foyer, Li says, "I must ask that you leave any weapons with these gentlemen."

She says this as easily as another hostess would ask for our coats.

"I'm not armed," says Kaiser.

"Me either."

"Please forgive this imposition."

The driver's Caymanian assistant walks in with a black wand and sweeps it over the length of Kaiser's body. Then he scans mine and nods to Li, who smiles at us.

"If you will follow me, *s'il vous plaît?* Your equipment will be taken to the proper room."

Kaiser shrugs and follows the soft-spoken apparition.

Our journey through de Becque's mansion is an education in understated elegance. There's a Zen-like simplicity to the spaces and to the furniture that adorns them. All lighting is indirect, and the few visible beams fall upon paintings spaced at tasteful intervals. I don't know enough about art to recognize the works, but I have a feeling that someone who knew what she was looking at would be suitably shocked.

Our destination is a large, high-ceilinged room with a massive wall of glass facing the harbor. It's furnished with pieces of Southeast Asian provenance, but the theme isn't overdone. Beyond the glass wall lies an infinity lap pool, one of those indigo things, which seems to bleed right into the sea beyond it. In the distance, a dozen boats ply the waters of North Bay, and as I watch them I realize a man is standing at the lower right edge of the glass, watching me. I didn't notice him at first because he stands with the same stillness and self-possession exhibited by the woman who met us at the door. Of medium height and deeply tanned, he has piercing blue eyes and a full head of close-cropped silver hair.

"Bonjour," he says in a soft but masculine voice. "I am Marcel de Becque. I was just recalling happier days. I trust your trip was not too bumpy?"

"It was fine."

He walks forward and, before I know what he's doing, takes my hand, bends, and kisses it with courtly grace. "You are far more beautiful in person, *ma chérie*. I thank you for coming."

Despite the strangeness of the situation, I feel my face flush. "This is my assistant, John Kaiser."

De Becque smiles in a way that lets us know he will play along with this fiction, but also that he recognizes it as such. Then he waves his hand toward the wall to my right, which holds a large display of black-and-white photographs. Most of them appear to date from various phases of the Vietnam War, and each is clearly the work of a master photographer.

"Do you like them?" de Becque asks.

"They're remarkable. Where did you get them?"

"I knew many journalists during the war. Many photographers as well. They were kind enough to give me prints from time to time."

Not all the photos are of military subjects. Several are studies of Vietnamese men, women, or children; others show temples and statuary; still others groups of khaki-clad men with the stateless look of war correspondents. On closer inspection, I recognize several photographers: Sean Flynn, Dixie Reese, Dana Stone, Larry Burrows. The best of the best. Capa is there too, the archetype of them all, his rakish grin giving him a youthful glow even in middle age. As I move to the next photo, my blood goes cold in my veins. Standing alone by a stone Buddha is my father. Jonathan Glass.

10

Unable to find my voice, I lean closer to the photograph on the French expatriate's wall. My father is wearing a Leica on a neck strap and carrying a Nikon F2 in his hand, the same camera I own today. That means the photo was shot in 1972, the year that camera was released and also the year he supposedly died.

"Where did you get this?" I finally whisper, pointing with a shaking finger.

"Terry Reynolds shot that in seventy-two," says de Becque. "Before he himself disappeared in Cambodia. I knew your father well, Jordan."

He says my name with a soft "J." I straighten up and try to maintain my composure as I speak. "You did?"

De Becque takes me by the elbow and leads me to a table, where a bottle of wine and three glasses have been placed. He pours a glass of white wine, which I drink in two swallows, then offers one to Kaiser, who declines. De Becque pours for himself and takes a small sip.

"Only in moderation," he says. "My liver is trying to tell me something."

"Monsieur—"

He stops me with an upraised hand. "I'm sure you have a thousand questions. Why don't you photograph my paintings first? Then you may return here and satisfy your curiosity."

My face feels hot, my throat unable to open.

"Please," says de Becque. "There is time."

"Tell me one thing first. Is my sister alive or dead?"

He shakes his head. "*Je ne sais pas, ma chérie.* That I do not know."

Photographing de Becque's paintings is a simple exercise, technically speaking. Before we left New Orleans, I made a list of equipment, which Baxter sent FBI agents out to procure. The main piece was a Mamiya medium-format camera shooting 5 × 5 film negatives, which gives superior image quality without compromising portability. The difficulty is the human factor. Kaiser does his best to follow my orders in setting up the lighting, but it's clear to Li – whom de Becque sent along to make sure we don't get too close to the canvases – that my "assistant" has never handled a softbox or barn door in his life.

I'm not in top form myself. The prospect of picking de Becque's brain about my father is so tantalizing that it pushes my concern for Jane almost out of my mind, and makes the simplest tasks – like attaching strobe heads to poles – difficult. Kaiser is soon distracted by other things. The bulk of de Becque's art collection is displayed in three large museum-style rooms, and his Sleeping Women are merely part of it. The rest date from several different periods, according to Kaiser, who has apparently given himself a crash course in art history over the past two days. The majority date from about 1870 to the present, and include several pieces by the Nabis. Kaiser moves methodically through the rooms, memorizing what he can, once returning to me to whisper that some of the paintings might have been stolen by the Nazis during the Second World War. He asks Li if we can photograph the entire collection, but she demurs, saying that de Becque specifically restricted our activities to the Sleeping Women.

I shoot the paintings with a thoroughness bordering on compulsion, but I try not to look too hard at them. In one sense, each of these women is Jane to me. Yet there's no denying their remarkable power. Unlike the painting I saw in Wingate's gallery, the women in these canvases are saturated in color rather than surrounded by it: vivid blues and oranges highlighted with whites and yellows. Two are lying in bathtubs, posed much like the woman in the first painting I saw in Hong Kong, but their faces are less defined than hers. If I didn't know these women might be dead, I would believe them asleep, for their skin fairly hums with light.

But I do know.

The man who painted these images sat or stood before petrified human beings, absorbing the hard metallic odor unique to sweat produced by terror. Unless the women were already dead when he painted them. How long could he have stood that? Staying in the room with dead women while they decomposed? I've photographed a lot of corpses, and close proximity with them isn't something easily endured. But perhaps for some people it's no hardship. Perhaps for some it's actually pleasurable, though after a while, even a necrophiliac would have to be driven off by the smell alone. Or is even that a naive assumption?

"How long would it take to paint these?" I ask Kaiser, sotto voce.

"Experts say two to six days. I don't know what they're basing that on. I read in a book last night that the Impressionists believed you should start and finish a painting at one sitting."

"If the women are dead, do you think he could be

preserving them somehow before painting them? Embalming them?"

"It's possible."

I fire off two more shots of the last painting. "Look at this picture. What do you see? Is this woman dead or alive?"

He walks closer to the canvas and studies the woman.

"I can't tell," he says at length. "There's nothing obvious that says death to me. Her eyes are closed, but that's not conclusive." He turns back to me, his face thoughtful. "I mean, where's the line between sleep and death? How far apart are they, really?"

"Ask the dead."

"I can't."

"There's your answer." I cap the Mamiya's lens and remove the last exposed film. "I'm done. Let's go see de Becque."

Li appears silently in the archway to my left, like an escort to some other world.

The old Frenchman is waiting in the glass-walled room. He stands with his back to us, a wineglass in his hand, and watches a yacht sail out of the bay into the Caribbean.

"Hello?" I call.

He turns slowly, then gestures toward a matched pair of sofas that face each other before the great window. Li pours wine for us, then vanishes without even a sound of slippers on the granite floor.

"You wish your 'assistant' to join us?" de Becque asks, one eyebrow arched.

I turn to Kaiser, who sighs and says, "I'm Special Agent John Kaiser, FBI."

De Becque walks forward and gives Kaiser's hand a light shake. "Isn't that a relief? Deception is a wearying art, and foolish deception the most wearying of all. Please, sit."

Kaiser and I take one sofa, de Becque the one facing us.

"Why have I brought you here?" the Frenchman says to me. "That is question number one?"

"That's a good place to start."

"You're here because I wanted to see you in the flesh, as they say. It's that simple. I knew your father in Vietnam. When I learned you were involved in this case, I took steps to meet you."

"How did you learn Ms. Glass was involved?" asks Kaiser.

De Becque makes a very French gesture with his opened hands, which I translate as *Some things we must accept without explanation.* Kaiser doesn't like it, but there's not much he can do about it.

"How did you meet my father?"

"I collect art, and I consider photography an art. At least when performed by certain people. I owned a tea plantation in a strategic part of Vietnam. It provided a good base for those journalists whom I allowed to use it. My table was famed throughout the country, and I enjoy good conversation."

"And access to information?" Kaiser asks bluntly.

De Becque shrugs. "Information is a commodity, Agent Kaiser, like any other. And I am a businessman."

"What do you know about my father's death?"

"I'm not at all sure he died when and where the world believes he did."

There it is. Spoken by a man in a position to know.

"How could he have survived?"

"First, he disappeared in a very embarrassing place. Embarrassing for the American government, I mean. Second, while the Khmer Rouge generally killed journalists

178

out of hand, not all Cambodians did. I believe Jonathan was shot, yes. But he could well have been nursed back to health. And like you, I've heard reports over the years that he has been sighted."

"If he survived," says Kaiser, "and he considered you a friend, why wouldn't he seek you out?"

"He may have. But I had sold my plantation by the time he went missing. If he went there in search of me, he would not have found me. But there's a simpler answer. By late 1972, Vietnam was not a place anyone would want to return to."

"Neither was Cambodia," I point out. "If he didn't get out before Pol Pot started his genocide, he couldn't possibly have survived."

Another shrug. "It is a mystery. But I've heard Jonathan was twice sighted in Thailand, and by reliable sources."

"Do you think he could still be alive?"

A smile of condolence. "That would be too much to hope for, I think."

"How recent were the sightings you mentioned?"

"The first around 1976. The last in 1980."

More than twenty years ago. "We're here for another reason, of course. But would it be all right for me to telephone you later for specifics?"

"I'll make sure you have my numbers before you go."

Kaiser leans forward, his wineglass between his knees. "I'd like to ask you a few questions."

"Of course. But I may be selective about my answers."

"Do you know the identity of the artist who paints the Sleeping Women?"

"I do not."

"How did his paintings first come to your attention?"

"I was acquainted with Christopher Wingate, the art

dealer. I'm in the habit of buying new artists whose work catches my eye. It's a risk, but all life entails risk, no?"

"Is this purely a business endeavor?"

De Becque's eyes shine with humor. "It has no connection whatever to business. If I wanted to make money, there are much surer ways."

"So Wingate introduced you to the Sleeping Women, and—"

"I told him I would buy all he could get me."

"And he got you five?"

"Yes. I made the mistake of letting certain Asian acquaintances see my paintings. The price skyrocketed overnight. After the fifth, Wingate betrayed me and began selling to the Japanese. But" – de Becque turns up his hands – "who expects honor from a Serb?"

"What initially attracted you to the paintings?"

The Frenchman purses his lips. "Hard to say."

"Did you have any idea that the subjects might be real women?"

"I assumed they were. Models, of course."

"Did you have any idea that they might be dead?"

"Not at first. I assumed the poses were of sleep, as everyone else did. But after I saw the fourth, I began to get a feeling. Then I saw the genius of these paintings. They were paintings of death, but not in any way that had been done before."

"How do you mean?"

"In the West, the attitude toward death is denial. The West worships youth, lives in terror of age and disease. Most of all in terror of death. In the East it's different. You know. You were there."

This statement throws Kaiser off his rhythm. "How do you know that?"

"You're a soldier. I saw it when you first came in."

"I haven't been a soldier for twenty-five years."

De Becque smiles and waves his hand. "I see it in your walk, your way of watching. And since you're American, your age tells me Vietnam."

"I was there."

"So. You know how it is. In America, someone gets bitten by a rattlesnake, they move heaven and earth to race to the hospital. In Vietnam, a man gets bitten by a krait, he sits down and waits to die. Death is part of life in the East. For many it's a sweet release. That is part of what I see in the Sleeping Women. Only, the subjects aren't Asian. They're Occidental."

"That's interesting," says Kaiser. "No one's mentioned that interpretation before."

De Becque touches the corner of his eye. "Everyone has eyes, young man. Not everyone can see."

"You know that at least one of the subjects in the paintings is missing and probably dead?"

"Yes. This poor girl's sister."

"How do you feel about that?"

"I'm not sure I understand the question."

"Morally, I mean. How do you feel about the fact that young women may be dying to produce these paintings?"

De Becque gives Kaiser a look of distaste. "Is that a serious question, *mon ami?*"

"Yes."

"Such an American question. You fought in a war that cost fifty-eight thousand of your countrymen's lives. A million Asian lives beyond that. What did those deaths buy, other than misery?"

"That's a separate discussion."

"You're wrong. If nineteen women die to produce

181

eternal art, then in the historical sense, the price was cheap. Laughable, really."

"Unless you loved one of those women," I say quietly.

"Quite so," concedes de Becque. "That's another matter entirely. I merely point out to Monsieur Kaiser that many human endeavors are begun with the knowledge that they will cost human lives. Bridges, tunnels, pharmaceutical trials, geographic exploration, and of course wars. None of these goals even approaches the importance of art."

Kaiser's face is reddening. "If you knew for a fact that women were being murdered to produce these paintings, and you knew the identity of the murderer, would you report him to the authorities?"

"Happily, I do not find myself in that dilemma."

Kaiser sighs and puts down his wine. "Why wouldn't you send your paintings to Washington for study?"

"I am a fugitive. I don't trust governments, particularly the American government. I had many dealings with it in Indochina, and I was always disappointed. I found American officials naive, sentimental, hypocritical, and stupid."

"That's something, coming from a black marketeer."

De Becque laughs. "You hate me, young soldier? For the black market? You might as well hate rainfall or cockroaches."

"I'm no fan of the French, that's for sure. I saw what you did in Vietnam. You were a lot worse there than we ever were."

"We were brutal, yes, but on a small scale. The American infantry handed out chocolate bars while their air force killed civilians by the tens of thousands."

"You were glad enough when we did it in Germany."

"This isn't getting us anywhere," I cut in, giving Kaiser

a sharp look. After years of traveling the world, I've learned to avoid conversations like this one. Most Europeans will never understand the American point of view, and even when they do, they'll loudly condemn it. At the bottom of their fervor, I believe, lies jealousy, but there's nothing to be gained by arguing with them. I would have thought Kaiser knew that.

"You've seen me in the flesh now," I tell de Becque. "What do you think?"

His blue eyes twinkle like Maurice Chevalier's. "I would love to see you au naturel, *chérie*. You're a work of art."

"Would naked be enough? Or would naked and dead be better?"

"Don't be ridiculous. I am a libertine. I celebrate life. But" – he holds up his glass in a silent toast – "death is always with us."

"Did you commission the painting of my sister?"

His humor vanishes. "No."

"Did you try to buy it?"

"I never had the chance. I never saw it."

"Would you have known who she was?"

"I would have thought she was you."

Kaiser says, "When did you first become aware of Ms. Glass's existence?"

"When I saw her name beneath a photo in the *International Herald Tribune*. The early 1980s, it would have been." De Becque chuckles. "I nearly jumped out of my skin. The credit read 'J. Glass,' same as her father's."

"I did that as an homage to him."

"And a fine one it was. But a bit of a shock to those who knew him."

"That happened to a lot of people. After a few years, I started using my full name." Unable to focus on the task at hand, I steel myself and ask de Becque the question foremost in my mind. "What kind of man was my father?"

"In the beginning? A wide-eyed American, like a thousand others. But he had eyes to see. You only had to tell him a thing once. He had tasted little of Asia, but he was open to it all. And the Vietnamese loved him."

"I presume that included women."

Another Gallic gesture, this one I translate as *Men will be men*.

"Was there one woman in particular?"

"Isn't there always? But in Jon's case, I don't really know."

"Don't you? Did he have a family over there, Monsieur de Becque? A Vietnamese family?"

"How would you feel if he did?"

"I'm not sure. I just want to know the truth."

"You saw Li?"

"Yes."

"She's French-Vietnamese. They're the most beautiful women in the world."

"Did my father have a woman like her?"

"He was certainly exposed to them."

"At your plantation?"

"Of course."

De Becque is a man who speaks between the lines. I'm normally good at reading such men, but in this case I'm lost. If my father had a Vietnamese family there, why not tell me outright?

"Have you considered this?" asks de Becque. "The year your father disappeared, *Look* and *Life* folded."

"And?"

"They were the great picture magazines. That was the end of an era. Jonathan never had to live through shrinking markets, the dominance of television, the humiliating transformation of the industry in which he made his name."

"Are you saying he had nothing to come back to?"

"I merely point out that, professionally speaking, the best years of photojournalism were in the past. Jon had won all the awards there were to win. He had experienced life on the razor's edge, with a rebel band of brothers. They photographed the horrors of the century, then moved on to the next before the last could crush their spirits. They were glorious in their way. They owned nothing, yet they owned the world. They were a cross between young Hemingways and rock-and-roll stars."

"But their day was over. That's what you're telling me?"

"The world changed after Vietnam. America changed. France, too."

Kaiser puts down his wine and says, "I'd like to return to Ms. Glass's sister."

"I would, as well," says de Becque, his eyes on me. "What exactly do you hope to gain by being part of this investigation, Jordan? Do you have some fantasy of justice?"

"I don't think justice is a fantasy."

"What would justice be in this case? To punish the man who has painted these women? The man who stole them from their homes to immortalize them?"

"Is he one and the same?" I ask. "Is the kidnapper the painter?"

"I have no idea. But is that your desire, to punish him?"

"I'd rather stop him than punish him."

De Becque nods thoughtfully. "And your sister? What are your hopes along that line?"

"I'm not sure."

"Do you think she might be alive somewhere?"

"I didn't until I saw her painting in Hong Kong. Now . . . I'm not sure."

When de Becque makes no comment, I ask, "Do *you* think the women are alive or dead?"

The Frenchman sighs. "Dead, I would say."

For some reason, his opinion depresses me far more than that of someone like Lenz.

"But," he adds, "I would not assume all these women share the same fate."

"Why not?" asks Kaiser.

"Things happen. No plan is perfect. I wouldn't think it absurd to hope one or more out of nineteen is alive somewhere."

"Is it nineteen women?" Kaiser asks. "We've been trying to match the paintings to the victims, but we're having trouble. There are only eleven victims in New Orleans. If each painting is of a different woman, then there are eight victims we don't know about."

"Perhaps those seven are simply common models?" de Becque suggests. "Paid off long ago and forgotten. Have you thought of that?"

"We'd like that to be true, of course. But the abstract nature of the early paintings has made it impossible for us to match the faces to victims. We haven't even matched them to the eleven known victims yet."

"The early paintings aren't abstract," says de Becque. "They were done in the Impressionist or Postimpressionist style. This involves using small drops of primary colors in close proximity to produce certain hues, rather than blending colors. It produces an effect much closer to the way the human eye actually perceives light. He probably painted them very quickly, and merely meant to suggest their faces, rather than to clearly depict them."

"Or he may have meant to conceal their faces," says Kaiser.

"This also is possible."

"If any of these women are still alive," I ask, "where could they possibly be? Why wouldn't they have come forward by now?"

"The world is very wide, *chérie*. And full of people with strange appetites. I'm more concerned with you. I think this is an unstable time for the man painting these pictures." De Becque's eyes burn into mine. "I also think your involvement with the FBI may bring you to his attention. I would not have anything happen to you."

"She'll be protected," says Kaiser.

"Good intentions aren't enough, Monsieur. She should consider staying here with me until this thing is over."

"What?" I ask.

"You would be free to come and go, of course. But here I can protect you. I haven't much confidence in the FBI, to be frank."

"I appreciate your concern, Monsieur, but I want to remain part of the effort to stop this man."

"Then take a word of advice. Be very careful. These paintings show an artist in search of himself. His early work is confused and derivative, important only for what it led to. The recent paintings give us a certain view of death. Where is this man going? No one knows. But I would not like to see you come up for auction anytime soon."

"If I do, buy me. I'd rather hang here than in Hong Kong."

A white smile cracks the Frenchman's tanned face. "I would top any price, *chérie*. You have my word upon it."

De Becque stands suddenly and looks through his great glass window at the bay. I have photographed several prominent prisoners in my life, and something in the Frenchman's stance throws me back to those occasions. Here in his multimillion-dollar mansion, with a fortune in art hanging on his walls, this expatriate shares something with the poorest convict pacing out a cell in Angola or Parchman.

"I think it's time to go," I tell Kaiser.

I wait for de Becque to turn back to me, but he doesn't. As I walk to the door, he says in a melancholy voice: "Despite what your friend says, Jordan, remember this. The French know the meaning of loyalty."

"I'll remember."

"Li will show you out."

"Merci."

At last de Becque turns to me and raises a hand in farewell. In his eyes I see genuine affection, and I'm suddenly sure he knew my father far better than he claimed.

"Your numbers!" I call. "I never got them."

"They're waiting in your plane."

Of course they are.

The Range Rover hums steadily toward the airport. Bright sunlight glints off the hood and the road signs, chasing a blue iguana beneath a green roadside bush. As the reptile vanishes, the Sleeping Women I saw in de Becque's gallery flash through my mind, and a minor epiphany sends a chill along my skin.

"I just realized something important." Before I can continue, Kaiser grips my thigh behind the knee and nearly cuts off the circulation to my lower leg. I remain silent until we reach the plane, where our escorts load the equipment cases for us, then vanish without a word.

"What is it?" asks Kaiser. "What did you think of?"

"The paintings. I know where they're being done."

"What?"

"Not exactly where, but how. I told you, I don't know anything about art. But I do know about light."

"Light?"

"Those women are being painted in natural light. It's so obvious that I didn't notice it in Hong Kong. Not even today, not at first. But a minute ago it registered."

"Why? How can you tell?"

"Twenty-five years of experience. Light is very important to color. To the natural look of things. Photographic lights are color-balanced to mimic natural light. I'll bet artists are even pickier about it. I don't know how important that is to the case, but doesn't it tell us something?"

"If you're right, it could help a lot. Is light shining through a window natural light?"

"That depends on the glass."

"If he's painting the women outdoors, that would mean a really secluded place. There's lots of woods and swamp, but getting there with a prisoner or body could be tough."

"A courtyard," I tell him. "New Orleans is full of walled gardens and courtyards. I think that's what we're looking for."

Kaiser squeezes my upper arm. "You'd have done well at Quantico. Let's get on board."

I don't move. "You know, you weren't very helpful back there. What was all that crap about France?"

He shrugs. "You don't learn anything about a man in a short time by having a polite conversation with him. You push buttons and see what pops out."

"De Becque just wanted to stroll down memory lane."

"No. It was more than that."

"Tell me."

"Let's get on board first."

He hustles me onto the Lear, then goes forward to confer with the pilots. After a moment, he walks back to my seat.

"I've got to call Baxter. It may take a while."

"Tell me about de Becque first."

"He was making some kind of decision about you."

"What kind of decision?"

"I don't know. He was trying to read you, to understand you."

"He knows a lot about my father, I know that."

"He knows a lot about more than that. He's in this thing up to his neck. I can feel it."

"Maybe the women really *aren't* being killed. Maybe they're being held somewhere in Asia."

"Moved there on de Becque's jet, you mean?"

"Maybe. Have you traced its movements over the past year?"

"We're having some trouble with that. But Baxter will stay on it. He's a bulldog with that kind of thing."

Kaiser walks forward, takes the seat by the bulkhead, and in moments is holding a special scrambled phone to his ear. I can't make out his exact words, but as the conversation progresses, I see a certain tension developing in his neck and arm. The jet begins to roll, and soon we're hurtling north toward Cuba again. After about ten minutes, Kaiser hangs up and comes back to the seat facing me. There's an excitement in his eyes that he can't conceal.

"What's happened? It's something good, isn't it?"

"We hit the jackpot. The D.C. lab traced those two brush hairs they took from the paintings. They're unique, the best you can buy. They come from a rare type of Kolinsky sable, and the brushes are handmade in one small factory in Manchuria. There's only one American importer, based in New York. He buys two lots a year, and they're sold before he gets them. He has specific customers. Repeat customers. Most are in New York, but there are several sprinkled around the country."

"Any in New Orleans?"

Kaiser smiles. "The biggest order outside New York went to New Orleans. The art department of Tulane University."

"My God."

"It's the third order that's gone there in the past year and a half. Baxter's meeting with the president of the university right now. By the time we land, he'll have a list of everyone who's had access to those brushes in the past eighteen months."

"Wasn't one of the victims kidnapped on the Tulane campus?"

"Two. Another from Audubon park, near the zoo. Which is very close to Tulane."

"*Jesus.*"

"That's only three out of eleven. The grid analysis alone didn't point to Tulane. But this definitely changes things."

"Where was the next closest order of these brushes to New Orleans?"

"Taos, New Mexico. After that, San Francisco."

My stomach feels hollow. "This might really be it."

Kaiser nods. "Lenz told us the paintings would lead us to suspects. I was skeptical, but the son of a bitch was right."

"You were more right than he was. You told me yesterday you thought the killer or kidnapper was based in New Orleans. That the selections were being made there, and that the killer might be the painter. Lenz had the painter in New York."

Kaiser sighs like a man whose premonitions are often

borne out but bring little pleasure when they are. "You know something?"

"What?"

"De Becque lied to us in there."

"How?"

"He told us he never saw the painting of Jane. This is a guy who can get on his private jet and fly to Asia anytime he wants. He's pissed at Wingate for selling the later Sleeping Women out from under him, to Asian collectors. Even if he didn't see those paintings when they were offered for sale, you think he didn't fly to Hong Kong the minute they went on exhibition there?"

"It's hard to imagine him not doing that."

"And did you notice that he sent Li with us to see the paintings? He didn't come himself?"

"Yes. You'd think he would have wanted to show off his collection."

"And to watch your reaction. He's got a thing about those paintings. And a thing about *you.* De Becque is a different breed of cat. I'll bet he's got a streak of kinkiness that's off the chart. And he may have watched your reactions. I didn't see any obvious surveillance cameras, but that doesn't mean anything these days."

"So, what are you saying?"

Kaiser looks out the porthole window, his face blue in the thickly filtered sunlight. "This is like digging up a huge statue buried in sand. You uncover a shoulder, then a knee. You think you know what's down there, but you don't. Not until it's all out of the ground." He cuts his eyes at me. "You know what feeling this gives me? The conspiracy angle, I mean. What it makes me think of?"

"What?"

"White slavery. Women kidnapped from their hometowns, sent far away, and forced into prostitution. It still happens in various ways, even in America. But it's big business in Asia, especially Thailand. Crime syndicates steal young girls from the mountain villages and take them down to the cities. They lock them in small rooms, advertise them as virgins, and force them to service dozens of clients a day."

I close my eyes and press down a wave of nausea. The mere mention of this horror forces me to accept that it is one of Jane's possible fates. But even if it isn't, the image created by Kaiser's words makes me shiver with fear and outrage. I can walk through a corpse-littered battlefield and hold in my lunch, but the thought of a terrified young girl locked in some cubicle of hell until she contracts AIDS is too much for me.

"I'm sorry," Kaiser says, lightly touching my knee. "My head is full of stuff like that, and sometimes I forget."

"It's all right. It's just . . . of all the bad things, that's the toughest for me."

Though he tries to conceal it, the question in his mind shines through his eyes.

"Don't ask. Okay?"

"Okay. Look, we're a lot closer to finding him. Closer to stopping him. Focus on that."

"Okay."

"Can I get you some water or something?"

"Yes . . . please."

He gets up and goes forward, and I snatch up a copy of the jet's safety card from the seat back across the aisle. Anything to focus on, to keep my mind from following its own dark course. *What's the worst thing that ever happened to you?* Lenz asked his patients. *What's the worst thing . . .*

I I

In the main conference room of the New Orleans field office, a strategy meeting is deciding what direction the NOKIDS case will take from here. I am not at that meeting. I've been banished to SAC Bowles's office. Once again, exclusion defines my status as an outsider. The meeting is being chaired by a deputy director of the FBI, and includes the U.S. Attorney for New Orleans, the New Orleans chief of police, the sheriff of Jefferson Parish, and various other big shots. It's amazing how they come out of the woodwork when there's a whiff of success in the air.

While I wait, my mind whirls with memories of Marcel de Becque, his paintings, his beautiful Vietnamese servant, and the photo of my father on his wall. But these memories are only static crackling around the electric knowledge that, if Daniel Baxter's plan is not overruled, I will soon be facing suspects – men who may have killed my sister – in the hope of rattling them into betraying themselves. This prospect does more to settle my soul than anything I've tried in the past year.

Agent Wendy, my bodyguard, has walked in twice and tried to make small talk, but I couldn't concentrate, and she took the hint. This time when Bowles's door opens, John Kaiser walks in, his face all business. As the door closes behind him, I catch sight of Wendy looking in from the hall.

"You ready?" he asks.

"What's happened so far?"

"Lots of nothing. The bureaucrats had to weigh in. Beaucoup jurisdictional asses to kiss on this one. The Deputy Director and the U.S. Attorney are gone. They wanted to meet you, but I told them you weren't a big fan of the Justice Department."

"There are certain elements I like better than others."

Kaiser smiles. "The big news is, we have four suspects. And all of them were here in town the day Wingate died in New York. We'll both hear the details in there. When we get done, I'd like to talk to you alone. We never got dinner. Maybe we can have a late meal, if you're up for it."

"Sure. Wendy, too?"

He blows air from his cheeks. "I'll handle that. Let's go."

It's a quick walk to the conference room, which is stunning in size and decor. I expected a ten-foot table and some doctor's office chairs. What I find is a forty-foot-long room with a window running the length of it, giving a panoramic view of Lake Pontchartrain, recognizable in the dark by the receding lights of the causeway. The conference table is thirty feet long and surrounded by massive blue plush executive chairs with the FBI crest embroidered in the upholstery, where a tall man's head would rest. At the near end of the table sit the usual suspects: Daniel Baxter, SAC Bowles, Dr. Lenz, and Bill Granger, the head of the Violent Crimes Squad. Piles of paper and files are spread out between Styrofoam coffee cups, half-empty water bottles, and a triangular speaker phone. Kaiser takes a seat beside Granger, opposite Bowles and Lenz, and I sit beside him.

Baxter looks tired but resolute at the head of the table, like a sea captain who has spent days riding out a hurricane but has now come within sight of his home port. When he speaks, his voice is hoarse.

"Ms. Glass, we've made phenomenal progress in the past eight hours. The sable brush hairs led us to the Tulane University art department. With the help of the president of the university, we've determined that this particular order was placed by one Roger Wheaton, the artist-in-residence at Newcomb College, which is part of Tulane."

"The name sounds familiar."

"Wheaton is one of the most highly regarded artists in America. He's fifty-eight years old, and he came to Tulane just two years ago."

"About the time the disappearances started," says Bill Granger.

"Wheaton was raised in Vermont," Baxter continues, "and except for four years spent in the marine corps, lived his life between Vermont and New York City. For the past ten years he's been besieged by offers like the one that brought him to Tulane, but he's something of a recluse, and he always rejected such offers before. But two years ago, he accepted the position at Tulane."

"Why?"

"We'll get to that in a minute. The main point is that Wheaton didn't order the special sable brushes only for himself. He has three graduate students taking studio classes for full credit, and they've been studying under him since he arrived. Two are male, and followed him down from New York. The other is a woman, a Louisiana native."

"One of your suspects is a woman?"

"She has access to the sable brushes, and the taser used in the snatch of the Dorignac's victim makes a female perpetrator possible."

As unlikely as this sounds to me, I go right to my next question. "Wheaton brought his own students with him?"

"Tulane hired Roger Wheaton for his reputation. It's a

feather in their cap to have him, and he was given absolute discretion over whom he would select for his program. Wheaton also teaches a lecture class – fifty-one students – and any of them could conceivably have got hold of these brushes. But we're not going to use you in that phase of the investigation. Wheaton and the three graduate students will be our targets."

"When are we talking to them?"

"Tomorrow. All of them, no matter how long it takes. I want to minimize any chance of interaction between them prior to questioning. Before we go into details, though, you should understand our position in the present climate. The Investigative Support Unit normally works in an advisory capacity for state or local police agencies. We provide expertise relating to serial offenders, but the police do the legwork. They conduct the interviews, make the arrests, and get the credit. However, in a long-running case like this one, where we have knowledge that crimes will likely be committed in the future, we become heavily involved in all aspects of the investigation."

"I understand."

"We have a unique situation here in New Orleans. The spread-out nature of the city has created a jurisdictional nightmare. There are seven separate police departments involved in these disappearances. And though not all of them have homicide detectives, there are over two dozen detectives working this case. We're presently leading the joint task force, but all these police detectives would like to interview Wheaton and his students. However, the most potent weapon anyone could have in such an interview, Ms. Glass, is you. And to put it bluntly, you're on our team."

"For the moment."

Baxter gives Kaiser a quick glance, but Kaiser remains

expressionless. "We've also managed to gather many of the Sleeping Women at the National Gallery in Washington, something metropolitan police agencies could never have managed. Because of this, and because of jurisdictional rivalry, we're going to be given the first shot at these suspects. All four have been under surveillance from the time they were identified, but they won't be approached until after we go in tomorrow. The pressure on this investigation is enormous. The victims in this case come from affluent families. One of the Tulane students was – *is* – the daughter of a federal judge in New York. So, while we interview Roger Wheaton at the university, NOPD will be searching his residence from top to bottom. We're already turning his life inside out, insofar as it exists on paper. His three students get the same treatment, though I'm not optimistic in two cases. Investigating art students is like investigating waiters; they almost don't exist on paper. Right now none of the four has a paper alibi for the Dorignac's snatch. All four were at an opening at the New Orleans Museum of Art until seven-thirty p.m. The chancellor verified that. Beyond that we know nothing." Baxter's dark eyes burn into mine. "Tomorrow, Ms. Glass, we are the point of a very bulky spear. We have to hit our target. If we miss, we lose the best chance we'll ever have to surprise our UNSUB into a confession."

"I get it. Let's have the details."

Baxter shuffles a stack of papers. "I'm going to give you a quick sketch of each," says Baxter. "This is for John's benefit, too."

SAC Bowles gets up and kills the lights, and a large screen hanging from the ceiling at the end of the room comes alive with white light.

"I want you to see all four first," Baxter says. "See if any look familiar. Then we'll break them down. These images are being relayed from our Emergency Operations Center, which is also on this floor." Baxter leans forward and addresses the speakerphone on the desk. "Give us the composite, Tom."

Four photos appear simultaneously on the screen. None looks familiar, or even like what I expected, but why would they? My mental picture of artists comes from books and films, mostly images from other centuries. When I hear the word "students," I think of people in their twenties. The oldest here – Roger Wheaton, I presume – is wearing bifocal glasses and reminds me of Max von Sydow, the actor. Severe and Scandinavian-looking, with shoulder-length gray hair. Beside his photo is a fortyish guy who looks like an ex-convict: hollow-eyed, unshaven, tough. Then I realize he's actually wearing prison garb.

"Is that guy a convict?"

"He's done two stretches in Sing Sing," says Baxter. "We'll get to that. We've got a real grab-bag of weirdos, here, I kid you not."

"Is that a scientific description?" asks Kaiser.

Bowles belly-laughs.

"These faces ring any bells?" asks Baxter, cutting his eyes at me.

"Not so far."

The other man in the composite is stunningly handsome, and my sixth sense tells me he's gay. I generally make this judgment based on physical appearance, speech, and behavior. All I have here is a photograph, but I've spent most of my life studying photographs, and this guy I feel certain about. The woman is also attractive, with long black hair, light skin, and black eyes. But despite her skin tone, something about her features suggests African blood.

"The older man is Roger Wheaton," says Baxter. "The convict is Leon Isaac Gaines, age forty-two. Raised in Queens, New York. The third man is Frank Smith. He's thirty-five, and also a New York native. The woman is Thalia Laveau, thirty-nine, a native of Terrebonne Parish here in Louisiana."

Now I've got it. Thalia Laveau is a Sabine, a racial group the FBI has probably never even heard of.

"All four suspects lived in New York for a time," says Baxter, "so all could have ties to whoever killed Wingate." He leans toward the speakerphone. "Put up Wheaton alone."

The composite vanishes, replaced by a candid shot of Roger Wheaton. The artist has deep-set eyes behind his bifocals, and a long, strong face. He looks more like a craftsman than a painter, a genius with metal or wood.

"Before we do his bio," says Baxter, "let's deal with why Wheaton came to New Orleans. Three years ago, this reclusive artist of international reputation was diagnosed with scleroderma, a potentially fatal disease." Baxter turns to Dr. Lenz. "Arthur?"

Lenz sniffs and inclines his head toward me as he speaks. "Scleroderma is commonly thought of as a woman's disease, but it does affect men, and usually with more severity. The external symptoms, such as hardening of the facial skin, et cetera, are not always obvious or even present in men, but the internal damage is accelerated. Scleroderma is vascular in nature, and causes scarring and eventual failure of the internal organs, including the lungs. One particularly important symptom in Wheaton's case is called Raynaud's phenomenon. This is a spasm and constriction of the blood vessels of the extremities – usually the fingers, but sometimes the nose or the penis – which is caused by contact with cold temperature, usually air or water. These attacks completely cut off circulation to the digits, sometimes for long enough to cause irreversible tissue damage. Amputations aren't uncommon. Sufferers frequently wear gloves for most of the day."

"Wheaton moved south to avoid this?" I ask.

"Apparently, though that kind of move isn't advised by physicians. It's pointless, in a way. There's more air-conditioning in the South, and even opening a refrigerator can bring on an attack. But the university has taken great pains to accommodate Wheaton's special needs. The artist Paul Klee suffered from scleroderma later in life. It greatly affected his work. His paintings became very dark in content, and the damage to his fingers forced him to change his painting style completely. He—"

Baxter has raised his hand. "We need to stay macro here, Arthur. There's a lot to cover."

Lenz likes to hear himself talk, and does not take kindly to interruptions. But Daniel Baxter doesn't hesitate to cut him off.

"Roger Wheaton," Baxter says in the tone of a man reading from a cue card. "Born 1943, in rural Vermont. Youngest of three brothers. His brothers joined the service upon graduating high school – one army, one navy. Wheaton had no formal training as a child, but in interviews – of which he's done damned few – he says his mother was a great lover of classical art. She bought him supplies and encouraged him to imitate the old masters, copying color plates from a book she bought him. He showed phenomenal talent, and at seventeen he left home for New York. We don't have a lot of information on this period of his life, but in interviews he's said he supported himself doing odd jobs and painting portraits on the street. He was unsuccessful as an artist, and in 1966 he joined the Marine Corps. He did two tours in Vietnam, earning a Bronze Star and a Purple Heart. . . ."

I glance at Kaiser, who steps on my foot beneath the table.

"Wheaton also instituted a disciplinary action against two members of his platoon for raping a twelve-year-old Vietnamese girl. He pushed it to a court-martial, and the men did time in Leavenworth. Any thoughts, John?"

Kaiser nods in the half-dark. "That would have made Wheaton about as popular as trench foot in his platoon. It tells us something about him, but what, I'm not sure. Either what he saw was really bad, and he felt morally compelled to push it, or the guy has some kind of hero compulsion."

This remark rankles me. "What rape wouldn't be really bad to see?" I ask, trying to keep my voice under control. "Why couldn't Wheaton simply have been doing the right thing by pushing it?"

Baxter answers for Kaiser. "I served in Vietnam myself, Ms. Glass. Most soldiers coming upon the situation I've described would have been offended and outraged, but they would have looked the other way. A few would have participated. But very few would have bucked the chain of command and forced disciplinary action. It's not pretty in hindsight, but at that time, no one was inclined to discipline our own troops for anything short of a massacre. Wheaton transferred out of his unit after that, and it's not hard to guess why. Still, he had a spotless record, with several commendations from his commanders."

"We should track down the names of men he served with," says Kaiser. "Not just his officers."

"We're on it," Baxter replies. "You should also note that Wheaton lost one brother in Vietnam. Killed in a Saigon bar by a terrorist bomb. The other died in 1974, from a stroke."

Baxter shuffles some papers. "After Vietnam, Wheaton returned to New York, enrolled in the art program at NYU, and slowly made a name for himself painting portraits. He supported himself this way for years, while he worked on his private obsession, which is landscapes. For the past twenty years, he's painted the same subject over and over again. It's a forest clearing, and every painting in the series is called The Clearing. He began in a very realistic style, but over the years he's gone more abstract. The paintings are still called The Clearing, but they're not recognizable as such. The early, more realistic ones showed a Vermont-style forest clearing, but also jungle foliage typical of Vietnam – and sometimes the two mixed – so there's no telling about the real origin of the image, or its significance. When asked about it in interviews, Wheaton says the paintings speak for themselves."

"A progression from realistic to abstract," says Kaiser. "The exact opposite of the Sleeping Women."

"Wheaton's progression is much more marked," says Lenz. "His style is so defined now that it's spawned a genre or school in the worldwide art community. They call it 'Dark Impressionism.' Not because the paintings themselves are necessarily dark – though most of his recent work is – but because of their content. He uses Impressionist techniques, but the original Impressionists tended to paint what you might call happy subjects. Pastoral, tranquil themes. Think of Manet, Renoir, Monet, Pissarro. Wheaton's work is very different."

"De Becque said the Sleeping Women artist uses Impressionist techniques," I tell Lenz. "In the way he lays down color, anyway."

"That's true," says Lenz. "But he abandoned the pure

style very quickly. Many beginning artists emulate the Impressionists, just as young composers imitate the popular composers of the past. But Impressionism in the pure sense is passé. Wheaton succeeds because he's brought something new to the style. As for him painting the Sleeping Women, though, two connoisseurs have already told us that the Sleeping Women share no similarities whatever with the paintings of Roger Wheaton."

"Could one man paint two radically different styles and an expert not be able to tell he did both?" asks Baxter.

"If he did it to prove a point, probably."

"What about to avoid detection?" says Baxter.

"Probably. But over the course of a body of work, certain idiosyncrasies reveal themselves. We've got hold of several portraits Wheaton painted years ago, to compare his execution of skin, eyes, hair, et cetera with that of the Sleeping Women artist. It's all very technical, but the final answer is no. He couldn't hide himself that way. Of course, we'll analyze the paints, canvases, and all other materials to be sure."

"Have you found these Kolinsky sable brush hairs in Wheaton's paintings?"

"Yes. We've also found them in the paintings of Smith, Gaines, and Laveau."

"Dating how far back?"

"Two years. When they came to Tulane."

"Wheaton just started using these special brushes?"

"Apparently so. We'll have to ask him why. Let's move on. I could talk for an hour about Wheaton alone, but we have a much more viable suspect in this bunch." Baxter says to the speakerphone, "Put up Gaines, Tom."

The photo of Wheaton is replaced by a mug shot of the convict. This guy I would walk across a busy interstate to avoid. Crazed eyes, pasty skin, tangled black hair, a stubbled face, and a broken nose. The only paintbrush I can see him holding would be six inches wide.

"Leon Isaac Gaines," says Baxter. "If I had to lay odds right now, this is our man in New Orleans. His father and mother were both drunks. The father did a stretch in Sing Sing for carnal knowledge of a juvenile, paving the way for junior, I guess."

"Male or female juvenile?" asks Kaiser.

"Female."

"Age?"

"Fourteen. Leon was arrested repeatedly as a juvenile. Burglary, assault, peeping, you name it. He did juvy time for starting fires, and was in and out of reformatories until he was twenty."

Kaiser grunts, and I know why. Childhood arson is one leg of the "homicidal triangle" of indicators for serial killers as children. Bed-wetting, arson, and cruelty to animals: I remember them all from my reading last year.

"He rings the chimes on animals, too," says Baxter. "When he was twelve, he buried a neighbor's cat up to its neck in a sandpile and rolled over it with a lawn mower."

"Enuresis?" asks Kaiser.

"No record of it. Both parents are deceased, but they weren't the kind to have sought medical care for that. Still, we're trying to track down physicians working in the area at the time." More shuffling paper in the semidark. "Gaines is a two-time loser, once for aggravated battery, once for attempted rape."

"Jesus," mutters Bowles.

"No gang affiliations while incarcerated, but he was part of a bad riot at Sing Sing. We're tracking down his cellmates and sending agents to interview them. Gaines never picked up a paintbrush in his life until his first term in Sing Sing – 1975. He showed so much promise that the warden showed his stuff to some New York dealers. They apparently kept an eye on him, because during his second hitch, they made some sales for him. He attracted the attention of the New York art community, much as Jack Henry Abbott attracted the attention of Norman Mailer and those other chumps with his 'Belly of the Beast' nonsense."

"Is that when Wheaton first heard about Gaines?" asks Kaiser.

"Wheaton isn't mentioned by anyone at that time in connection with Gaines. Wheaton's always been a recluse, associates with no other artists. Since his diagnosis, he's broken off all contact with everyone but his dealer and his students. Local patrons of the arts in New Orleans have invited him for parties, dinner, like that, but he always declines. The president isn't happy about that."

"What does Gaines paint?" asks Kaiser.

"He started with prison scenes. Now he paints nothing but his girlfriend. Whatever girlfriend he has at the time. As far as we can tell, he's regularly abused every woman he's ever been with. He paints that, as well, by the way. Reviews of his stuff call it 'violent,' and that's a quote."

"How many applicants did Wheaton have to choose from when he picked this guy?"

"More than six hundred."

"Jesus. Why did he pick Gaines?"

"You can ask him that tomorrow."

Kaiser tenses beside me. "I'm doing the interview?"

"We'll get to that after we cover these bios," Baxter says quickly.

The rivalry between Kaiser and Lenz will surely come to a head over this.

"So Gaines is essentially painting a series, as well?" I ask. "The same subject again and again? Just like Wheaton and the UNSUB?"

"The others are too, in their ways," says Lenz. "Wheaton apparently used this as a criterion in his selection. He's on record as saying that only deep study of a particular subject can produce new understanding, deeper levels of truth."

"That and fifty cents'll buy you a cup of coffee," cracks Bowles.

"I'm inclined to agree," says Baxter. "But they pay Wheaton very big bucks."

"How much?" asks Kaiser.

"His last painting went for four hundred thousand dollars."

"That's not even close to the Sleeping Women prices."

"True. But Wheaton's a lot more prolific than our UNSUB. You should note that NOPD has been called to Leon Gaines's duplex several times by neighbors, but the girlfriend has yet to swear out a complaint. Gaines is usually drunk when they get there."

"I think we've got the picture on Gaines," says Kaiser.

"Not quite. He owns a Dodge utility van with tinted windows all around."

The room goes silent.

"Anybody else have that kind of transport?" asks Kaiser in a soft voice.

"No," says Lenz.

"We've got to get inside that van. If we find biological trace, we can compare it to samples from our victims' DNA bank."

"Where did you get DNA from the victims?" I ask. "You have no bodies."

"For four victims, we have locks of hair saved from

childhood," says Kaiser. "Two victims were breast cancer survivors, and have bone marrow stem cells stocked at hospitals for future transplant. Two victims have eggs stored at fertility clinics. And two stocked umbilical cord blood when their youngest children were delivered. That's not a direct match to the mother, but it could be helpful."

"I'm impressed."

"John put that together," Baxter says proudly. "All grist to the mill."

"As an identical twin," says Kaiser, "you could add to the bank for your sister. I meant to ask you before."

"Anytime."

"As soon as you conclude Gaines's interview tomorrow," says Baxter, "NOPD will confiscate the van."

"What's the deal with the utility van? Good way to move a body?"

Kaiser turns to me, his face a shadow with glinting eyes. "Rapists and serial killers favor this type of vehicle by a huge margin. It's the most important part of their equipment, a means to quickly get the victim out of sight, even in a public place. Later, it often becomes the scene of the final crime."

I try in vain to shut out images of Jane being raped and cut up inside a dark and stinking van.

"My money's on Leon Gaines," says Baxter. "But we need to cover everybody. Let's have Frank Smith, Tom."

Gaines's face is replaced by the almost angelic visage I saw earlier in the composite.

"This one's a riddle," says Baxter. "Frank Smith was born into a wealthy family in Westchester County in 1965. He focused on art from an early age, and took an MFA degree from Columbia. Smith is openly gay, and he's painted homosexual themes – usually nude men – from his college days."

"Not nude sleeping men?" asks Kaiser.

"If only," says Baxter. "By all reports, Smith is enormously talented, and paints in the style of the old masters. His paintings look like Rembrandt to me. Really unbelievable."

"More like Titian, actually," says Lenz, earning a snort from the SAC. "Frank Smith stretches his own canvases and mixes his own pigments. The mystery is what he's doing in Wheaton's program at all. He's already famous in his own right. Wheaton has far more stature, of course, but I'm not sure what Smith could learn from him."

"I'll ask Smith tomorrow," says Kaiser.

Lenz sighs and looks at Baxter, who gazes pointedly at the table. The blue light of the projector beam highlights the fatigue lines in the ISU chief's face.

"Smith's paintings now sell for upwards of thirty thousand dollars," Lenz adds.

"Oh, I forgot," says Baxter. "Wheaton's currently working on a painting that takes up a whole room over at the Woldenberg Art Center at Tulane."

"You mean a whole wall?" asks Kaiser.

"No, a whole *room*. Multiple canvases stretched over curved frames to form a perfect circle. He's painted on curved canvases for years, to create a feeling that you're walking into this clearing he's painting. Monet tried this as well. But this new thing is a complete circle. Huge. Takes up half of a thirty-five-hundred-square-foot gallery."

I know photographers who've tried this for exhibitions. It usually comes off as cheap and contrived, like some clunky diorama exhibit.

"Does Smith have a jacket?" asks Kaiser.

"He got popped a couple of times for unnatural acts in his twenties, during park sweeps. Nothing major. His parents made the sodomy charges disappear, but he's mentioned the arrests in interviews. He seems proud of them. I got the old arrest records from New York to verify them."

"What about alibis for these people?" I ask. "For all the disappearances? Is anybody checking that?"

"About two hundred cops," growls Bowles. "Plus us. That's something the police know how to do. But until they actually interrogate the suspects, they can only do so much. It's all paper trails. Credit card charges, like that. So far, all the suspects appear to have been in the city during the kidnappings. After your interviews tomorrow, the gloves come off. These people will go under the hot lights. Then they'll hire lawyers, and the whole thing will become a media nightmare."

"What about the girl?" says Kaiser. "What's her story?"

"Waste of time," Lenz says. "There's no precedent for a woman committing this type of murder."

"We don't know they *are* murders," Kaiser says with restrained anger. "Until we find some bodies – even one definite – we don't know what we're dealing with. I'm not ruling out anybody based on standard profiling techniques. Look at Roger Wheaton. The guy is well over our age limit, but based on what I've heard, I have questions."

"Thalia Laveau," says Baxter, trying to tamp down the flaring tempers. "Born on Bayou Terrebonne in 1961. Father a trapper, mother a housewife."

"What did he trap?" asks Kaiser.

"Anything that didn't trap him first," I answer.

Bowles belly-laughs again.

"You know about these people?" Baxter asks.

"We did a couple of stories down there when I was on the *Times-Picayune*. Troubles in the shrimp industry. It's another world down there. The whole place smells like drying shrimp. You never forget it."

"Chime in with anything relevant." Baxter squints down at a file. "Racially, Laveau is part French, part African-American, and part Native American."

"A redbone?" asks Bowles.

"No, that's different," I tell him.

"What's a redbone?" asks Kaiser. "Like Leon Redbone?"

"Redbones are part black, part Indian," I reply. "They're settled all over western Louisiana and East Texas. Thalia Laveau is what's called a Sabine."

"That's not right," says Baxter, misunderstanding my pronunciation.

"Yes, it is. In Lafourche and Terrebonne Parishes they say '*Sob*-een,' not *Say*-been or *Say*-bine, like the ones you learned about in Roman history. I have no idea why, that's just the way it is."

"That girl didn't look black to me," says Bowles.

"Or Indian," says Kaiser, who grew up in the West. "Put her picture back up."

"Let's have Laveau, Tom," says Baxter.

In the next photo – this one color – Thalia Laveau is not merely attractive but beautiful. Her eyes and hair are so black and shiny they seem to float off the screen, while her skin has the look of buttermilk.

"You're the expert," Baxter says to me. "Tell us about these people."

"The Sabines are trappers and fishermen," I answer, thinking back. "Shrimpers. They live in shacks along bayous that lead to the Gulf of Mexico. They're not Cajuns, but at her age she would have grown up speaking French.

They used to have to be taught English at school. They're Catholic, but they have strange superstitions. There's some voodoo in there, I think. Inbreeding, too. They range from white-skinned like this woman to very dark. They can have kinky hair, or straight like hers. They're tough people, but they love to dance and play music. They're clannish. Not likely to go to the authorities over trouble. In the eighties they had problems with Vietnamese refugees coming into their shrimping grounds to compete. There were shootings and boat-rammings. It was big news."

"That's more than I have here," says Baxter. "As far as we know, Thalia Laveau had no formal training as an artist. She just started drawing one day and showed a knack for it. Eventually she moved on to painting, mostly watercolors of the bayous and the Gulf. She quit school in the tenth grade and at seventeen went to New York."

"Just like Wheaton," I say quietly.

"Yes. And like Wheaton, she had no early success. She supported herself in various ways, from waitressing to working in art galleries. A female art professor thought she heard Laveau say something about stripping for money in New York, but later decided she'd misunderstood. Laveau *has* worked as a model for a graduate painting class at Tulane, and some of that is nude work. The most significant thing we've heard so far is that she's a lesbian."

"Is that rumor or fact?" I ask.

"Unconfirmed. We didn't want to question students at this point. We'd like these people to be totally unprepared at their interviews tomorrow."

"What does Laveau paint?" asks Kaiser. "Nude women?"

"No. She goes into the homes of strangers, lives there for a while, then starts painting their lives."

"Like the documentary photographers of the sixties," I think aloud. "Gordon Parks."

"All her paintings are finished at one sitting," Baxter goes on. "She's attracted a lot of print media attention, but her work doesn't sell for much. Not remotely in the class of Wheaton or Frank Smith."

"How much?" asks Kaiser. "A thousand bucks apiece?"

"Ahh . . . Seven hundred is the highest sum paid to date."

"Do Leon Gaines's pictures sell?" I ask.

"Somebody paid five thousand for one. He could make a living at it, if he wasn't so deep in debt. He's borrowed to the hilt on student loans, and he owes bookies as well. One former cellmate said he picked up a serious heroin habit in prison."

"I get the feeling Laveau and Gaines live pretty close to the bone," says Kaiser. "So where are the millions earned from the Sleeping Women?"

"Good question."

Dr. Lenz says, "Right now I like Wheaton or Frank Smith. They're already wealthy, so they would have the knowledge to hide the money, or know people with that knowledge. Gaines is a violent, self-absorbed punk. The attempted rape is an indicator, but he's too obvious. Too coarse for the crimes we're dealing with. And Laveau . . . is a woman."

"I'm not excluding anybody," says Kaiser. "After visiting Cayman, I'm convinced Marcel de Becque could be behind it all. He could easily be commissioning someone to paint the pictures and paying them peanuts compared to the overall take. That includes Thalia Laveau or a skell like Gaines."

"If de Becque is behind this," Lenz counters, "why draw

attention to himself by demanding that we send Glass to see him in exchange for photos of his paintings?"

"He's a ballsy guy. He's not scared of us."

"Not one bit," I confirm. "But what about Thalia Laveau? What would be her motive? Do you really think a woman's going to paint dead women for money?"

"I haven't talked to her yet," says Kaiser. "So I don't know. But the kind of people you described – Sabines – they tend to stay where they grow up, right?"

"Yes."

"So why did she leave? Was she a brilliant kid with ambition? Or was she running from something?" Kaiser looks at Baxter without waiting for an answer. "How are we going to handle the approach? Who's going in?"

Baxter walks to the wall and switches on the overhead lights. Lenz blinks against the brightness, but he looks set for battle.

"John," says Baxter, "I know you've been point man on this thing for a long time, and against your own wishes, which counts for a lot in my—"

"Damn it," Kaiser mutters.

Baxter implores Kaiser with his hands. "Listen, John. Because of Wheaton's artistic stature, and because of his medical condition, I'm inclined to let Arthur take the lead on this one. He has a broad knowledge of art, and he'll be able to question Wheaton intelligently on his disease, gauge his mental state related to it, and . . ."

Kaiser sits in silence as Baxter drones on. The decision has been made, and the medical angle makes argument pointless.

"Normally, I would be going in as well," Baxter concludes. "But because I think you should be there, John, I'm going to send you in in my place. If you feel that some path is being left unexplored, you can go down it. You'll be there. Okay? It's just that Arthur will take the lead on the questions."

"Where will you be?" Kaiser asks in a taut voice.

"Surveillance van outside. Arthur's going to wear a wire."

Kaiser's mouth falls open.

"It's a major break with Bureau policy," says Baxter, "but the Director has personally approved it. The police insisted on live transmission and tapes as a condition of letting us handle the interviews alone."

"And Glass?" Kaiser says without looking at me.

"She'll be in the van with me until Arthur cues her. The code phrase is, 'I'm sorry, our photographer was supposed to be here ten minutes ago.' That's the story for the suspects: we're not confiscating their paintings, just photographing them. Once we've finished, though, NOPD will be confiscating everything in sight. These suspects are going to be totally alienated after that, and there's nothing we can do about it. We've got one shot at each of them. Wheaton we treat with kid gloves. Gaines is second, and we go in hard. John, you'll take the lead with Gaines, because you have more experience with convicts. Smith and Laveau we play by ear. But in every case, when Ms. Glass comes in—"

"Please just call me Jordan," I cut in. "'Ms. Glass' is getting old."

Baxter nods gratefully. "When Jordan comes in, she won't look directly at the suspect. This will make someone who's shocked by her appearance have to work harder to confirm what his eyes are telling him. The innocent people won't look at her twice – though I'm sure Gaines will ogle her a little – but the guilty one should look like he's seen a ghost. Which, in a sense, he will have."

"Or she," says Kaiser.

"Or she," Baxter concedes.

"Gaines will ogle me a little?" I echo. "He looks like he'd walk up, lick my face, and dare me to slap him."

"If he does," says Bill Granger, the violent crimes supervisor, "kick him in the balls."

Baxter frowns. "If Gaines does do something like that, don't overreact. We have no idea what could happen when you walk into these situations. The painter could be the killer – if the women *are* being killed – and he could decide the game is up the moment he sees you. He could do something totally crazy. For this reason, John will be armed going in." Baxter looks hard at his former protégé. "Use your best judgment about force."

This part of the plan clearly makes Lenz nervous. Even I see a mental image of Kaiser leaping over a metal prison table and trying to strangle the death-row inmate he told me about. But Baxter is showing clear support for Kaiser, and Lenz doesn't question it. Not in front of him, anyway.

"If either of you comes out and says somebody's dirty," says Baxter, "we bring them in for interrogation before the police get in on the act." He looks around the table. "Okay. We'll have another strategy meeting tomorrow morning, here, seven a.m. From eight o'clock on, we'll have police observers with us. Everybody good to go?"

Lenz sniffs and gives Baxter an ironic smile. I try to catch Kaiser's eye, but he gives me nothing.

"I need a bite to eat and some sleep," I tell them, rising from my chair.

"Take Agent Travis with you," Baxter says, meaning Wendy.

"I will."

"The Camellia Grill is still open," Kaiser says in an offhand voice. "You know it?"

"I probably ate there a hundred times in my younger days."

"What do you keep in that waist pack?" asks Lenz.

"It's my genie's lamp. I rub it, and whatever I need comes out."

"It must weigh a lot," SAC Bowles says dryly.

"It does. But aren't you glad I had a camera in there during the gallery fire?"

"Yes, we are," says Baxter. "Get some sleep, Jordan. Tomorrow's a very big day."

"I'll see you here at seven."

Kaiser gives me a wave as I depart, but Dr. Lenz only watches, his wise eyes missing nothing.

12

The Camellia Grill stands at the intersection of Carrollton and St. Charles, with the river rolling past just beyond the levee. Like many New Orleans institutions, it's a modest place, an old-time grill with pink walls, aproned employees, and stools at the bar. Agent Wendy and I have been here long enough to get menus when John Kaiser walks through the door and scans the room. He comes straight to us and looks down at Wendy, whose expression quickly morphs from surprise to discomfort.

"Could I see you alone for a minute?" he asks.

She gets up without a word and follows him outside. Through the window, I see Kaiser speaking, Wendy listening attentively. When they come back in, Wendy goes to the far end of the bar while Kaiser takes her stool beside me.

"That didn't look very smooth," I tell him. "What did you say to her?"

"That I needed to talk to you without Lenz hearing."

"I see. She's got a terrible crush on you."

"I never encouraged it."

"You think that makes it any better for her?"

Kaiser picks up a menu. "She's a good girl, and she's tough. She can handle it." He glances up at me, and his eyes seem to hold more understanding than his words. The skin around his eyes is dark with fatigue.

"Okay," I say, looking at my own menu. "What are we doing here?"

"This is our first date, isn't it?" He says it deadpan, and I laugh in spite of myself.

"Come on. What's going on?"

"Just what I told Wendy. I want to talk to you without Lenz around. Or Baxter, for that matter. I have a certain amount of anxiety that we're behind the curve. That whoever's running this thing is ahead of us. Maybe way ahead."

I sense the disquiet in him, in the way he holds himself. "Okay. Tell me about it."

"I can't explain it. It's a feeling. I want to do something about it, though."

"What?"

"We'll get to it. Let's order."

Kaiser signals a waiter, and he comes almost immediately. We order omelets and orange juice, and I ask for café au lait as well. It's nice to be in a place where they'd look at you like an idiot if you asked for some fancy latte or exotic extras. Glancing to my left, I catch Wendy watching us over her shoulder.

"What will Baxter say about you talking to me alone?"

"I don't think Wendy will tell him. She'll give us the benefit of the doubt this time."

"But he wouldn't like it, would he?"

"He trusts me, to a point. He wouldn't like what I'm going to say."

"Which is?"

Kaiser puts his elbows on the counter and rotates his stool so that he faces me more directly. "Have you ever fired a handgun?"

"Yes."

"An automatic or a revolver?"

"Both."

"If I got you one, would you carry it?"

"What would Baxter think about that?"

"He wouldn't like it. And the Office of Professional Responsibility would probably fire me."

"So why are you suggesting it?"

"Because I think you're in danger. If the UNSUB wants you, he could shoot Wendy before either of you knew he was there. Then it would just be you and him. If you're armed, you might have a chance to react in time."

"You mean kill him?"

"Could you do it?"

"If he shot Wendy in front of me? You're damn straight."

"What if he just knocked her out and tried to pull you into a car? Would you shoot him then?"

A wave of discomfort rolls through me, flashes of memory that I thrust back into the dark. "I'll do what I have to do to save myself."

Kaiser's eyes never leave my face. "Have you ever shot anybody before?"

"I've been shot before. Let's leave it at that."

"I get the feeling your life has been exciting even by the standard of war correspondents."

"It hasn't been dull."

"Has it taken a lot out of you?"

I look away and focus on Wendy's straight back. The more I watch her, the more I like her. The path she chose is much more regimented than mine, but she brings to it the passion I brought to mine when I was younger. "Yes, it has."

"That's why you took time out to do this book you were doing?"

"Yes."

"You've been wanting to do that for a long time?"

"Yes." I look back at Kaiser, into the hazel eyes that appear to hold genuine curiosity. "But once I really started, I wasn't sure it was going to give me what I wanted out of it."

"What was that?"

"I'm not sure."

Our omelets and juice arrive, but neither of us lifts a fork.

"May I ask you a personal question?" he says.

"You can ask."

"You've never been married?"

"That's right. Does that shock you?"

"It surprises me. Not many heterosexual women who look like you make it to forty without getting married at least once."

"Is that a nice way of asking what's wrong with me?"

Kaiser laughs. "It's a nice way of being nosy."

"You'd think I'd be a prize catch, wouldn't you?"

"Yes, I would."

"A lot of guys think that. From a distance."

"What's wrong up close?"

"I'm not like most women."

"How so?"

"Well, it goes like this. I meet a guy. Good-looking, successful, independent. Doctor, journalist, investment banker, A-list actor. Whatever. He can't wait to go out with me. I'm a not-so-ugly woman in what a lot of people see as a glamour job. The first few dates, he shows me off to his friends. We like each other. We get intimate. Then, in a week or a month, I get a new assignment. Afghanistan. Brazil. Bosnia. Egypt. And not a fly-in-and-out Dan Rather junket. A month on the ground schlepping cameras. Maybe

221

this particular guy is making international partner the next week and wants me at his celebration party. Maybe the Oscars are next week. But I take the assignment. I won't even discuss turning it down. And by the time I get back, he's decided maybe the relationship isn't working out after all."

"Why do you think that is?"

"Because most guys have the one-up gene."

"The what?"

"The one-up gene. They have to be in the superior position. They love the *idea* of being with me. But the reality is far from what they envision. Some don't like that I make more money than they do. The ones who make more money than I do don't like it when their friends act like my job is more important than theirs. Some can't take the fact that I have a higher priority than them in my life. I don't mean to complain about it. I just want you to understand."

"I make sixty-eight thousand dollars a year," says Kaiser. "I know you make more than that."

"How do you know?"

"I saw your tax return."

"You *what?*"

"We had to rule you out as a suspect. That was part of it."

"Great."

"But I don't think your job is any more important than mine." He picks up a fork and takes a bite of his omelet. "Do you?"

"No."

"And I know I'm not the highest priority in your life."

"True."

"And I'm perfectly okay with that."

I watch him as he pours hot sauce on his omelet, but I

222

can't read anything in his eyes. "What are we talking about?"

"I think you know."

"Well, at least we're on the same page."

He smiles, and this time his white teeth show and his eyes sparkle. "I didn't really come here to say that, but I'm glad I did. I feel awkward because of your sister."

"That has nothing to do with my sister. What happened to Jane only confirmed something I learned a long time ago. If you wait to do things you want to do or ought to do, you may be dead before you get the chance."

"I learned that too. In Vietnam. But it's easy to lose sight of it in the rush of everyday life. To get so caught up in what you're doing, people depending on you, that you develop tunnel vision. You know that feeling?"

"For a long time, the only part of the world I saw was through a lens."

"And now?"

"Now I'm drifting. Until I found the paintings, anyway. But beneath that, I'm not really tethered to anything."

"Can you handle another personal question?"

"Might as well."

"Lenz told me you weren't close to your sister. Yet you're doing far more than any relative involved in this case. You've made it your mission to find her, or to find the truth. How do you explain that?"

How do I explain that? "I didn't tell Lenz everything. Jane and I had problems growing up, yes. Some of those problems lasted into adulthood. But about three years ago, I had a bad health scare. I'd gone to the emergency room for pain, and the next thing I knew, I was in the oncology ward. They thought I had ovarian cancer. I was lucky it happened in San Francisco, and not while I was on assignment somewhere.

223

But my friends *were* on assignment. I was alone and scared to death."

I pause and swallow, fighting the lump rising in my throat. "Sometime in the middle of the night, I woke up to find Jane standing beside my bed, holding my hand. I thought I was dreaming. She said she'd awakened from a dead sleep the night before. She felt a painful shock go through her, like a labor contraction, and her mind filled with an image of my face. She called my house and got my machine. Then she called my agency and found out I was in the hospital. She left the kids with Marc and flew straight out to be with me. She slept in that hospital room for four days. She wheeled me to the tests, handled the doctors and nurses, everything. She never left my side."

"You hadn't been close before that?"

"No. And I'm not saying the sins of the past were magically redeemed. But she told me some things. She said that as she got older, she'd begun to understand the sacrifices I'd made to take care of her when we were kids. That she knew I'd only wanted the best for her, even if I didn't always know what that was. I told her I respected the life she'd made for herself, even though I'd belittled it before. It meant a lot to her." I pick up my fork and draw imaginary circles on the countertop. "It's easy to feel independent when you're young, that you don't need anybody. But as time passes, family starts to matter. And with our mother in the shape she was in, Jane and I only had each other."

"You're speaking in the past tense."

"I don't know what I believe right now. All I know is that I have to find her. Dead, alive, whatever. She's my blood, and I love her. It's that simple. I have to find my sister."

Kaiser reaches out and gently squeezes my wrist. "You will, Jordan."

224

"Thanks."

"Have you ever wanted your own family? To settle down, have kids, the whole thing?"

"Every woman I ever knew wanted that in some form or fashion."

"And you?"

"I hear the clock ticking. I visited my nephew and niece last night, and my feelings for them overwhelmed me."

He glances down the counter. "Wendy said there might have been some trouble over there. At your brother-in-law's."

"You know, I can take you guys in my life up to a point. But there's a line you don't cross."

"She only told us because it's her job to protect you."

"I won't give up all my privacy to be protected." I take a long sip of my coffee and try to keep my temper in check. "Just what do you know about me, anyway? My medical records? Everything down to my bra size?"

"I don't know your bra size." His face is absolutely serious.

"Do you want to?"

"I think I'm up to investigating the question."

"Given adequate time, you mean."

"Naturally." He takes a sip of juice and wipes his mouth with his napkin. "How much time do you think that would be?"

"At least four hours. Uninterrupted."

"We won't get four hours tomorrow."

"And we don't have it tonight."

He looks again at Wendy, who's making a point of not looking at us. "No, we don't. The task force is meeting right now in the Emergency Operations Center. I have to get back, and I don't know when I can get out of it."

225

"Speaking of that, you told de Becque you're having trouble matching the abstract faces in the paintings to victims, right?"

Kaiser nods. "Eleven victims, nineteen paintings. Two major problems. There must be victims we don't know about. Murders or disappearances that don't match the crime signature exactly. Maybe they were hookers or runaways rather than society women, and nobody reported them missing. Maybe we've actually found their bodies, but since they match the more abstract paintings, we can't tell. But a Jefferson Parish detective and I have gone over every homicide and missing person in New Orleans for the past three years, and we only have a handful of possibles, none very likely."

"How many paintings have you matched to known victims?"

"Six definitive matches out of eleven. Two strong probables. But the faces are so vague in some of the paintings, or so distorted, that we just can't get anywhere with them."

"Who do you have working on them?"

"The University of Arizona. They've done great work for us in the past. Digital photo enhancement."

"But not this time?"

"Not so far."

"I think that's because what you want in this case isn't really photo enhancement. The distortions you want to correct aren't the result of blur or a lack of resolution that masks reality. They're distortions created in the mind of a human being, perhaps an insane one. They may have little or no correspondence with reality."

Kaiser watches me with an unblinking gaze. "What do you suggest?"

"I know some photographers who work exclusively in the

226

digital domain. I don't want to mention names, but I recall one of them talking about a system that was being developed for the government – the CIA or NSA or somebody – for satellite photo interpretation. Its purpose was to try to bring visual coherence out of chaos. He couldn't say much about it, and I wasn't that interested, but I remember that much."

"How long ago was this?"

"Two or three years."

"Did this system have a name?"

"At the time he called it Argus. You know, the mythical beast with a hundred eyes?"

"I'll ask Baxter to talk to the other acronym agencies and see what he can find out."

"Okay. There's my contribution. Is the Bureau buying this breakfast?"

"I think the Bureau can afford it." Apropos of nothing, Kaiser reaches out and touches my hand, and the thrill that races up my arm sets an alarm bell ringing in my brain. "Look," he says, with another glance at Wendy, "why don't we—"

I pull back my hand. "Let's don't push it, okay? It's there. We know it's there. Let's see what happens."

He nods slowly. "Okay. It's your call."

We eat the remainder of our meal in silence, watching each other and the gentle comedy of late diners around us. I'm grateful that he doesn't feel pressured to make small talk; it bodes well.

After he pays the check, he leads me over to Wendy and thanks her for the time she gave us. He speaks and moves with such professional detachment that Wendy seems to take heart. This is no reflection on her intelligence. All of us see what we want to see until we're forced to see otherwise.

Outside, amid a throng of partying Tulane students, Kaiser bids us farewell and leaves for the field office. Wendy doesn't talk much on the way back to her apartment, and I'm glad for it. As much as I like her, I think tomorrow would be a good day to find a hotel.

13

I'm sitting in a cramped FBI surveillance van on the campus of Tulane University, home of the Green Wave, a fitting name for teams whose campus has the verdant look of a garden, even in October. The oaks are still in leaf, the palms flourishing, and the lawns shine like freshly mown meadows in the sun. Twenty yards away from the van stands the Woldenberg Art Center, a stately old brick complex that houses the university's art departments and the Newcomb Art Gallery.

Thirty seconds ago, John Kaiser and Arthur Lenz went through the doors of the gallery to meet Roger Wheaton, the artist-in-residence at the university. Dr. Lenz is wearing a concealed microphone and transmitter, which he tests repeatedly as he walks deeper into the building.

"Arthur has no faith in technology," says Baxter, who is sitting beside me, wearing a headset mike. "By the way, I checked on that computer program you told John about. Argus. It does exist. The National Reconnaissance Office uses it for satellite photo interpretation. It's been crunching on digital photos of the unidentifiable Sleeping Women for the past two hours."

"Has it come up with anything?"

Baxter gives me a "keep your chin up" smile. "They tell me it's been spitting out faces that look like Picasso drew them. But they're going to keep running it."

"Maybe we'll get lucky."

"I also got you set up at a hotel. The Doubletree, just down the lakefront from the field office. They think you're with a corporation, so don't mention the Bureau."

"No problem. I appreciate it."

The interior of the van is uncomfortably warm, even at nine a.m. One reason is the outside temperature, another body heat, and compounding them convection from the electronic equipment lining the walls of the Econoline. There's a battery-powered fan perched on a cooler filled with dry ice to provide relief, but its rattling blades barely cut the dense atmosphere.

"Before there were female agents," says Baxter, "we stripped down to our shorts in these things."

"Don't hesitate on my account. I'll strip myself if I have to stay in here much longer."

Baxter laughs. At his request, I'm wearing a skirt suit and heels, so that I'll look more feminine to the suspects when I go in. A female field agent was dispatched to Dillard's department store this morning with a list of my sizes. Getting the store to open early was apparently no trick for SAC Bowles, but trying on the various selections caused me to miss most of this morning's strategy meeting.

"How much notice of this interview did Wheaton get?"

"An hour. The president of the university handled it. He's deep into CYA mode. If a university employee turns out to be behind the disappearance or death of a student, the legal exposure would be considerable. He told Wheaton to cooperate with us, even though the idea that he could be involved in any crime was patently absurd. He didn't mention the sable brushes or the Sleeping Women, only that we had evidence connecting the Tulane art department to a murder."

"Wheaton had no problem with being questioned?"

"Not so long as we talked to him while he's working. He's apparently obsessive about his work schedule."

"We're going in," says Lenz through a crackle of static.

Baxter checks the meters on an ADAT to make sure the psychiatrist's words are being recorded.

A knocking sound reverberates from the small monitor speaker mounted on the console before us. Then the sound of a door opening.

"What the hell?" says Kaiser.

"It's the painting," says Lenz. "Keep going. There, to your right."

Baxter says, "We want to get you in there pretty quickly, Jordan. Before Wheaton gets too comfortable."

"Are you Roger Wheaton?" asks Kaiser.

There's a pause, then a man with a deep, avuncular voice says, "Yes. Are you the gentlemen from the FBI?"

"I'm Special Agent Kaiser. This is Doctor Arthur Lenz. Doctor Lenz is a forensic psychiatrist."

"How curious. Well, good day to you both. How can I help you?"

"We have some questions for you, Mr. Wheaton. They shouldn't take too long."

"Good. I like to get the paint on quickly."

"This painting is . . . stupendous," says Lenz, his voice filled with awe. "It's your masterpiece."

"I hope so," Wheaton replies. "It's my last."

"The last Clearing, you mean?"

"Yes."

"It's a monument to your entire body of work."

"Thank you."

"But why stop now?"

There's another pause, and when Wheaton answers, his

voice is heavy with regret. "My health isn't what it once was. It's time for a new direction, I think. You have some questions, the president said? It all sounded very mysterious."

"Mr. Wheaton," says Kaiser, "over the past year, eleven women have disappeared from the New Orleans area without trace. Are you aware of that?"

"How could I not be? There are safety-awareness meetings twice a week for the female students here. Flyers on every wall."

"That's good. We're here about those disappearances. You see, several of the victims have turned up, in a manner of speaking."

"I read that the woman taken from the grocery store was found. But the paper said the FBI doesn't think she was taken by the same man."

Kaiser's voice takes on a tone of confidence. "The media has its uses. I'm sure you understand."

After a pause, Wheaton says, "I see. Well. You said several of the victims have turned up. You've discovered more bodies?"

"Not exactly. We've discovered a series of paintings that depicts these women."

"*Paintings?* Paintings of the missing women?"

"Correct. In these paintings, the women are nude, and posed in positions of sleep. Possibly in death."

"My God. And you've come to ask me about this?"

"Yes."

"Why? Were the paintings discovered nearby?"

"No. In a museum in Hong Kong."

"Hong Kong? I don't understand."

I touch Baxter's arm. "I thought Dr. Lenz was going to take the lead on the questions."

"Arthur wanted it this way. He wants John to ask the

questions that have to be asked. He'll jump in when he's ready. Arthur's a subtle guy."

"Mr. Wheaton," says Kaiser, "in examining these paintings forensically, we've recovered some hairs from them. The hairs come from a special type of paintbrush. Kolinsky sable."

"You're investigating every artist in America who uses Kolinsky sable brushes?"

"No, that would be too big a job, even for us. But these weren't ordinary Kolinsky sable. They're a very fine grade – the finest, actually – produced by one small factory in Manchuria. There's only one U.S. importer, and he sells a very limited quantity. To select customers."

"And Tulane University was one of those customers. Now I see. Of course. I placed that order. For obvious reasons, I hope."

"Could you tell us why, obvious as it may be?"

"They're the finest brushes in the world. Highly resilient. They're generally used for watercolor, but they're adaptable to any medium. I use them for fine work in my oils."

"Your students use them as well?"

"Had I not ordered them for this program, two of my students wouldn't be able to afford such tools. That's one of the benefits of an academic setting."

"That would be Ms. Laveau and Mr. Gaines?"

Wheaton chuckles. "Yes. Frank could buy a Manchurian sable ranch if he chose to."

"You're referring to Mr. Smith?" asks Kaiser.

"Yes. Frank Smith."

"Is that a Kolinsky brush you're using now?"

"No, this is hog bristle. Crude-sounding, isn't it? But a fine brush all the same."

"Have you always used the rare Kolinsky brushes?"

"No." This time the pause seems interminable. "Three years ago I was diagnosed with an autoimmune disease that affects my hands and fingers. I've had to alter the mechanics of my brush stroke to remain consistent with my own style. I experimented for a while, and finally discovered the special Kolinskys. They worked so well that I encouraged my students to try them."

"I see. How many people have access to these brushes?"

"My graduate students, of course."

"Anyone else?"

"Well . . . this isn't a high-security area, as you can see. Anyone could walk in here and take one if they really wanted to. Undergraduates frequently come through to see my work in progress. We'd have to have twenty-four-hour guards to keep them out."

"Mr. Wheaton," Kaiser says in an apologetic tone, "I hesitate to ask this, but would you have any trouble providing alibis for a group of dates over the past eighteen months?"

"I'd have to see the dates. Are you saying I'm a suspect in these terrible crimes?"

"Anyone with access to these brushes is by definition a suspect. Do you know where you were three nights ago, after the opening at the museum? Say from eight forty-five to nine-fifteen?"

"I was at home. And I foresee your next question. I was alone, as it happens. Should I contact an attorney?"

"That's your prerogative, sir. I wouldn't want to influence you either way."

"I see." Wheaton is answering more slowly now, his words preceded by careful thought.

"Would you mind telling us how you selected each of your students?" asks Kaiser.

"I suppose not. Each applicant submitted paintings for review. There were quite a lot to go through. I initially looked at photos sent through the mail. Then I flew down and examined a group of paintings by each of the finalists."

"Did you use any criteria other than the applicants' paintings?"

"None."

"Did you have biographical information on the applicants?"

"I believe I had a brief sheet on each one. A CV of sorts, though with artists that's not a very formal document. Leon Gaines's résumé made interesting reading."

"I imagine it did." Kaiser is trying to sound friendly, but there's no hiding the fact that this is an interrogation. "What was it about the work of each that impressed you?"

"I don't think I can give you a short answer to that," Wheaton replies.

"Could you give us a verbal sketch of each student?"

"I really don't know that much about them."

"Frank Smith, say."

Another long silence, but whether it's caused by reluctance to comply or by Wheaton searching for words is unknowable from the isolation of the van.

"I'm very fond of Frank," Wheaton says finally. "He's a talented boy. He's never known financial hardship, but I think his childhood was difficult. He had one of those fathers, you know. Great expectations, of the conventional kind. Frank's talent and dedication are unbounded, and he's only going to get better. He's meticulous in technique and fearless in dealing with his subject matter. I don't know what else to say. I'm not a critic. And I'm certainly no detective."

"Of course. Have you ever seen Frank Smith get violent?"

"*Violent?* He's passionate about his work. But violent? No. He hasn't much respect for other artists' work, I can tell you that. He rubs a lot of people the wrong way. Frank knows just about everything there is to know about art history, and he doesn't suffer fools gladly. You can imagine how that affects a man like Leon Gaines."

"Why don't you tell us?"

"Leon would probably have killed Frank by now if it wouldn't put him in Angola penitentiary for life. It would make him a three-time loser, you see. They'd never let him out again."

"Tell us about Gaines."

Wheaton sighs loudly enough for it to reach us over the transmitter. "Leon is a very simple man. Or very complicated. I haven't been able to decide. He's a tortured soul who'll never rid himself of his demons. Not even through his art, which is certainly violent enough to exorcize a few demons."

"Are you aware that Gaines beats his girlfriend?"

"I have no idea what Leon does in his spare time, but nothing would surprise me. And his paintings are full of that kind of thing."

"Do you think he's capable of murder?"

"We're all capable of killing, Agent Kaiser. Surely you know that."

"You served in Vietnam," Kaiser says, taking a cue from Wheaton's reply. "Is that right?"

"You must know I did."

"You had quite a distinguished record."

"I did what was asked of me."

"You did more than that. You won a Bronze Star. Do you mind telling me how you got that?"

"Surely you've got hold of the citation somehow."

Daniel Baxter shakes his head beside me. "Wheaton's getting comfortable. He's turning the questions back on John."

"Citations never quite tell the story, do they?" asks Kaiser.

"You were there, weren't you?" Wheaton replies.

"Yes. I was a Ranger. H Company, Ninth Cav. You were a Marine?"

"Third Division."

"They didn't hand out medals for digging foxholes."

"No. It was a straightforward enough action. My company was pinned down in a paddy near Quang Tri. Our sergeant had stepped on a mine that took off his leg above the knee. Two men went out after him. Both were shot dead by a sniper in the tree line. The weather was too bad to call in napalm on the sniper, but it was clear enough for him to shoot. Our artillery couldn't seem to get him either. The sergeant screamed that if anyone else came out after him, he was going to pull the pin on one of his own grenades. I thought he might actually do it, but he was bleeding to death, so I went and got him."

"Just like that?"

"That's how it is sometimes, isn't it? The sniper shot at me but missed."

"The citation said you killed the sniper as well."

"I think getting the sergeant back alive gave me delusions of invulnerability. Did you ever get that feeling over there?"

"Only once, thank God. It's a dangerous feeling."

"Yes. But I used it. I borrowed a grenade launcher from a corporal and made a dash across the paddy—"

"Which was mined?"

"Yes. But as I zigged across the paddy, the sniper kept shooting and missing. That allowed me to get a fix on his muzzle flash. When I got within range, it was too late for him to move. He was stuck up in his tree. Tied in, actually. I just planted my feet and gave it to him. I was lucky that day. He wasn't."

"That's the way it was, all right. What about the rape incident?"

More dead air as Wheaton adjusts to the shift of conversational gears; Kaiser has gone from comrade-in-arms to adversary in two seconds.

"What about it?" asks Wheaton.

"It must have cost you some friends in your company, to push it as far as you did."

"I didn't have any choice."

"What do you mean?"

"I was raised to treat women with respect, Agent Kaiser. No matter what language they speak or what color they are."

I feel like cheering aloud.

"And this wasn't a woman," he adds. "She was a child."

"Was it an attempted rape, or a fait accompli?"

"I walked in on the crime in progress. We were checking a ville for weapons caches, and I heard screams from a hootch near the back."

"I see. Two perpetrators?"

"That's right. One was sitting on her chest with his knees on her arms, holding her down. The other was . . . committing the act."

"And what did you do?"

"I told them to stop."

"But one of them was your superior, right? A corporal?"

"That's right."

"Did they stop?"

"They laughed."

238

"What did you do then?"

"I held up my weapon and threatened to shoot them."

"Your M-16?"

"I carried a Swedish K-50 at the time."

"Sounds like you knew your weapons."

"I didn't want to die because my M-16 jammed when I needed it. I bought the K off a Lurp on leave in Saigon."

"What happened next?"

"They cursed me and threatened to kill me, but they stopped."

"Would you have shot them?"

"I'd have wounded them."

"You reported the incident right then?"

"That's right."

"Did you make any attempt to comfort the girl?"

"No. I didn't want to turn my back on those two."

"Sounds like a smart decision."

"The girl's mother was in the hootch. They'd knocked her cold, but she was waking up by then. Is this relevant to your investigation?"

"I have no idea, Mr. Wheaton. But we have to ask about everything. I appreciate your being frank with us, though. That says a lot in your favor."

"Does it?"

The sound of fabric rubbing against the mike tells me Lenz is moving around the room.

"Get ready," says Baxter beside me.

"Mr. Wheaton," says Lenz. "I must tell you, I'm floored by this work-in-progress. A return to your original inspiration will turn the art world on its ear."

At this remove, it's easy to hear the culture and education in the psychiatrist's voice as compared to Kaiser's.

"That's something I wouldn't mind doing," says

239

Wheaton. "I don't think about critics much, but I don't like them. They've always been kind to me, but they have savaged work by people I admire, and I won't forgive them that."

"What did Wilde say about critics?" asks Lenz. "'Those who find ugly meanings in beautiful things are corrupt without being charming'?"

"Yes!" cries Wheaton, bright pleasure in his voice. "You sound like Frank. He's a big fan of Wilde."

"Really? I'm sure we'll get along splendidly, then." More shuffling from Lenz's clothes. "Mr. Wheaton, as a forensic psychiatrist, I'm also a medical doctor. If you don't mind, I'd like to ask about your disease, and how it's affected your work."

"That's something I'd prefer not to talk about."

Lenz doesn't immediately reply, but I can imagine the laserlike stare that must be searching Roger Wheaton's face at this moment. "I understand," the psychiatrist says finally. "But I'm afraid I must insist. Such diagnoses deeply affect human psychology, as you know too well, I'm sure. Did you know that Paul Klee also suffered from scleroderma?"

"Yes. His work suffered equally."

"I see you're wearing gloves. Has the move south relieved your Raynaud's phenomenon to any degree?"

"Somewhat. But more because the university has done so much to protect me. A prerequisite of joining my lecture class was an agreement to attend it in a hall without air-conditioning. In New Orleans that can be quite a hardship. But no one seems to mind too much."

"I wouldn't think so. You're a very famous man."

"In some circles. I still have frequent episodes of Raynaud's, to answer your question."

"Have you had permanent tissue damage to your hands?"

"Again, I'd prefer not to discuss it."

"I'll be as brief as possible. Are you being treated here in New Orleans?"

"I visited the rheumatology department at Tulane once. I was not impressed."

"Surely there were other university cities you could have gone to, where autoimmune diseases have more of a priority? Did you consider other offers?"

"Wherever I go, the treatments are essentially palliative. You must know that, Doctor. I find that I do better by simply living in denial and doing the best I can."

"I see. Have you been tested for organ function in the past year?"

"No."

"Do you have your blood pressure checked regularly, at least?"

"No."

"You realize that accelerating hypertension is a hallmark of—"

"I'm not a fool, Doctor. I'd rather move on to something else, please. My time is too short to spend it discussing what is killing me."

A wave of pity rolls through me at Lenz's relentless questioning. "Why doesn't he leave the guy alone?"

"He feels he's onto something," Baxter says in a taut voice.

"Do you think he is?"

"Diagnosis of a terminal disease is a major stressor. It could initiate homicidal behavior in a predisposed individual."

"Are you aware that there are some revolutionary new

241

treatments being tried?" Lenz asks. "In Seattle for example, they're using autologous bone marrow transplant—"

"I'm aware of all this, Doctor . . . ?"

"Lenz."

"Doctor Lenz, thank you. I fully understand my situation. I wonder if you do. I'm an artist. I have no family. My priority is my work. I shall do the work I am strong enough to do for as long as I can do it. When I die, my work will live after me. That's more satisfaction than most men will ever know."

Wheaton's voice is a knife blade of truth, and it demands respectful silence, the way a prayer does.

"Come on," Baxter says, anxiously tapping the console before him. "Get her in there."

But Lenz doesn't know when to quit. "I'd like to move on to—"

"I apologize, Mr. Wheaton," Kaiser says sharply. "Our photographer was supposed to be here ten minutes ago. If—"

"*Go!*" Baxter says, slapping my knee.

I throw open the van's rear door, and in seconds I'm clacking across the sidewalk toward the Newcomb Art Gallery, fighting to keep my balance in unfamiliar heels, my heart pounding against my sternum.

The smell of oil paint hits me as I go through the door, and grows stronger as I move toward the main gallery, guided by my memory of a floor plan Baxter showed us in the van. The entrance area is ornamented with Tiffany stained glass panels, mounted on both sides of a wide doorway. When I walk through, I find myself facing a curved white wall. Then I see wooden framing. I'm looking at the back of Wheaton's room-size canvas circle.

To my right is an opening in the curved wall. As I go

through, I concentrate on Baxter's instructions to act detached and professional, but my first sight of the painting stops me in my tracks.

The circle of joined canvas panels is eight feet high and at least thirty-five feet across. The scale alone inspires awe. But it's the image itself that takes my breath away. I feel as though I've walked into J. R. R. Tolkien's Mirkwood, a shadowy world where roots wind around the feet and gnarled limbs bind the throat, where tangled vines and deadfalls conceal things we wish would remain out of sight. Through this dark world winds a narrow black stream, occasionally rippling white over rocks or fallen branches. The scene shocks me because I expected something abstract, as all Wheaton's later work has been. This is what Lenz meant by "a return to your original inspiration." I feel I could reach into the painting, pick up a twig, and snap it in two with a loud crack. Were the smell of paint and linseed oil not so strong, I think I would smell decaying leaves. Only one curved panel is unfinished, and before it stands Wheaton himself, paintbrush and palette in his white-gloved hands.

The size of the artist is my second shock. The head shot I saw last night gave me the impression of a slight man, but that merely proves how deceptive photographs can be. Wheaton is but an inch shorter than Kaiser, who stands six-three. He has wiry arms but large hands with long fingers, and shoulders only slightly bowed by age. His face is so strong that the wire-rimmed bifocals he wears – I can see the lines on the lenses from here – seem merely an ornament rather than functional spectacles. At fifty-eight, he has a full head of silver hair that sweeps back from his forehead, some of it reaching his shoulders, and his skin is remarkably smooth. He gives the impression of a man who has reached a place of extraordinary peace, though from the little I know about his history, that is a misconception.

"Is this your photographer?" he asks, and then he smiles at me.

Wheaton's smile fades as he turns to Lenz, who like Kaiser has not even heard the artist's initial question, so intent is he on picking up signals of recognition in Wheaton's face. I could save them the trouble. This guy has never seen me before in his life.

"Yes, sir," I say loudly, trying to snap them out of it.

Wheaton turns back to me. "What are you here to photograph?"

"Your work."

"Well, fire away. As long as your pictures will be held by the FBI, that is. I don't want any reporters seeing this painting until I've completed it."

"Absolutely," Kaiser says finally. "They'll be held in the strictest confidence."

Kaiser glances at me, and I see instantly that he too shares my judgment of Wheaton. The big Vermonter has no idea who I am. After this initial moment of confusion, I realize how hot it is in the studio. Kaiser has removed his coat, revealing a pointillist abstract of sweat on his shirtfront, but Lenz still has his jacket on, probably to hide a suspicious bulge or trailing wires. With the Mamiya I used at de Becque's, I take a few flash shots of various panels of the painting, but it's all a sham. Many of Wheaton's paintings will be confiscated as soon as this interview ends, which in the true sense it already has. I feel guilty being part of this charade, knowing how the subsequent acts will affect and confuse the artist, who appears willing to do all he can to help us.

As I work, Wheaton drags a ladder to the unfinished

244

panel, laboriously climbs it, then begins painting with small strokes about seven feet up. A few times in my career, I've sensed I was in the presence of true greatness. I have that feeling now. I have a powerful desire to shoot Wheaton, to document the artist at work. After a moment's hesitation, I take a few shots of him, and he doesn't seem to mind. There's spare film in my fanny pack, and in less than a minute I'm reloading, so caught up am I in the essential act of my profession. Wheaton has a gift that many great men possess: the ability to carry on with what he's doing as if no camera were there. Even as I shoot, I know these pictures will be remarkable, and some corner of my brain hopes the FBI won't insist that the negatives remain their property.

Lenz and Kaiser have moved across the room to confer quietly, and I sense that they're ready to move on to Leon Gaines. Sure enough, Kaiser catches my eye and nods at me to wrap it up. There's more film in the van, so I finish out the roll before I walk up to the ladder and offer Wheaton my hand. I don't usually shake hands, but in this case I feel I should make some gesture of thanks for his generosity. Leaving his brush and palette atop the ladder, Wheaton climbs down and gives my hand a gentle shake. Even through the cotton gloves I can tell his hand is soft as a woman's. His disease must keep him from any sort of manual work other than painting.

"Thanks for making that easy for me," I say.

The artist smiles shyly. "It's very easy to tolerate the attentions of a pretty girl."

"Thank you."

He looks up, his eyes narrowed behind the bifocals. "Have you always worked for the FBI?"

"No. I was a photojournalist before." This is not exactly a lie.

He studies me a bit longer, then smiles again. "Please stop by and tell me about it sometime. Photography interests me. I rarely have visitors anymore, mostly due to self-imposed restrictions, I'm afraid."

"I'll try to do that."

"Mr. Wheaton," says Kaiser, "I want you to know how much we appreciate your help. The New Orleans police will probably want to talk to you as well. My advice is to co-operate as fully as you can, despite whatever inconvenience they cause. That will end the ordeal sooner than anything else."

Wheaton sighs as though he has some inkling of what is to come.

Dr. Lenz says, "We must also ask you to refrain from contacting your graduate students about this, or speaking of it in the next few days. I'm sure you understand."

The artist looks as if he understands all too well.

"Good day, gentlemen," he says, and then he turns to me. "Good day, my dear."

Kaiser turns to go, but Lenz hangs back. "There's one question I forgot to ask. Is the clearing a real place? Somewhere near your childhood home in Vermont, perhaps? Or is it a place in Vietnam?"

Wheaton hesitates, as though deciding whether to answer at all. At length, he says, "I've known several places like this in my life. They seemed a sort of nexus to me. A place where the power of nature is focused. The forest or jungle is there but held in abeyance, so that you can see sun and sky. There's water, but not an overpowering amount of it. And then there's the earth."

"You make it sound peaceful," says Lenz. "But your paintings aren't peaceful."

"Some are," says Wheaton. "Others not. Nature isn't a

kindly force. She has many faces, and none cares a thing for us or our needs."

"True enough," Lenz says. "Oh, one thing more, if you don't mind."

I want to slap him for his stupid Columbo tactics.

"Leon Gaines paints women exclusively. Sometimes nude, sometimes not. Frank Smith paints nude men. Have you ever known him to paint nude women?"

Wheaton shakes his head. "Frank adores women, but only with their clothes on."

Kaiser looks ready to drag the psychiatrist out of the room. At last Lenz offers Wheaton his hand, but the artist merely inclines his head in acknowledgment and goes back to his ladder, causing me to smile.

We are nearly to the door when Wheaton calls: "Thalia Laveau paints women. Is that important?"

Kaiser and Lenz are back to him in seconds. "What do you mean?" asks Kaiser. "Women working in their homes? Like that?"

"No. Her documentary paintings actually surprised me. Because the audition paintings she submitted were nude studies."

"Of women?" Lenz almost whispers.

"Exclusively."

Lenz looks at Kaiser, who asks, "Do you have any of those paintings?"

"No. But I'm sure she does. Are you going to talk to her?"

Kaiser and Lenz are staring at each other like hunters who have walked into a thicket after a lion and found a unicorn.

14

"Come on!" Baxter shouts from the open door of the surveillance van. "Get in!"

Kaiser and Lenz are lost in thoughts of Thalia Laveau and her nudes, but something in Baxter's voice brings them out of it. We scrunch into the cramped van and squat in the heat, our faces inches apart.

"Ten minutes ago," says Baxter, "a finance company repossessed Leon Gaines's van."

"Damn it," snaps Kaiser. "Murphy's Law."

"The repo guy had apparently tried to get it before, and Gaines ran him off. Today he just walked up to the house, popped the lock, and drove off before the NOPD surveillance team could do anything."

"Where's the van now?"

"Jefferson Parish deputies stopped it on Veterans Highway. They're going to take it to their impound lot and seal it for our evidence team."

"Does Gaines know the van is gone?" Lenz asks.

"Oh, yeah. He's fighting with his girlfriend right now. They can hear him yelling out in the street, and parabolics have picked up the sound of slaps and blows."

Lenz shakes his head. "Do we know if he has a gun in there?"

"This is Louisiana," says Kaiser. "Assume he does. What do we know about the girlfriend?"

"Name's Linda Knapp," Baxter replies. "She's twenty-nine, a barmaid. He's been with her on and off for a little over a year. So. Do we talk to him now or do we wait?"

"Now," says Kaiser. "While he's pissed. Go in hard, settle him down, then bring Jordan in."

Baxter turns to me, and when he speaks I smell coffee on his breath. "This isn't like talking to Roger Wheaton. Gaines is a violent felon."

"I signed your release this morning. Kaiser's armed, and there'll be cops outside. I'm ready."

Baxter hesitates a moment longer, then slaps the panel separating us from the van's driver. The motor roars, and we lurch backward, then forward. As we roll off of the campus, Kaiser catches my eye and gives me a nod of gratitude.

Leon Gaines lives in a shotgun house on Freret Street, beyond the terminus of St. Charles and Carrollton, very near the river. It's a mostly black neighborhood behind an old shopping center, where people mind their own business and a prison record carries no stigma. Old people sit on screened porches, some drinking from paper bags, others rocking slowly and watching the cars go past. Kids too young for school play in tiny yards or the street, and knots of school-age kids stand on the corners. Our driver circles the block once for us to get a look, then stops a couple of driveways up from Gaines's place.

Baxter opens the door. "Remember what's at stake, John. This is our only clean shot at him."

Kaiser nods, then gets out and starts up the cracked sidewalk, Dr. Lenz working hard to keep pace with him. After a few seconds, Kaiser's voice comes from the speakers.

"Don't react to anything I do. Act like you expect it, even if you're shocked."

"What are you going to do?" Lenz asks.

"Whatever feels right. And don't let me forget to ask if he knows Marcel de Becque. We forgot to ask Wheaton."

"You're right," huffs Lenz.

Beside me, Baxter says, "You missed most of the meeting this morning. We confirmed that there was bad blood between de Becque and Christopher Wingate. Most of the art community knew about it. When Wingate sold those paintings he'd promised de Becque, de Becque retaliated by spiking some big investment deal Wingate was involved in. We don't have the details yet."

"I can hear Gaines yelling from here," says Lenz, sounding nervous.

"Here we go," says Kaiser.

Their shoes bang on plank steps; then a screen door slaps against its frame and a hard knocking echoes through the van.

"Leon Gaines!" shouts Kaiser. *"Open up! FBI!"*

There's a pause, then a muffled shout of challenge.

Baxter says, "This is going to be tricky."

The unmistakable sound of a door being jerked open comes from the speakers. Then a New York accent laced with alcohol booms, "Who the fuck are you? Pencil-dicks from the finance company? If you are, I got something for you."

"I'm Special Agent John Kaiser, FBI. And I've got something for you, Leon. A search warrant. Step back from the door."

"FBI?" A puzzled silence. "Search warrant? For what?"

"Step back from the door, Leon."

"What is this, man? This is my house."

A faint female voice says something unintelligible.

"Get back in the bedroom!" Gaines yells.

"I told you twice to clear the door," says Kaiser. "Do it now or I move you out."

"Hey, no problem. But I need to see that warrant first."

A scuffling noise is drowned by a grunt of shock by Lenz, and vocal complaint by Gaines.

"What did Kaiser do?" I ask, gripping a metal rack rail.

"Moved him out of the door," says Baxter. "Like he said he would. With a con, you have to establish dominance quickly."

"We've got two choices here, Leon," Kaiser says in a voice I hardly recognize. "We can talk to you, or we can search this dump. Right now I want to talk. If I like what I hear, we might not have to search. If I *don't* like what I hear, we'll have to search, and we might conceivably stumble across some drugs. Or a gun. Either beef would put you right into Angola—"

"What do you want to talk about?"

"Art."

"Art who?"

"*Art,* Leon. Your paintings."

"Oh."

"Eleven women have disappeared from New Orleans over the past year and a half. You know about that?"

"Yeah. So?"

"What do you know about it?"

"What I see on TV."

"We found a series of paintings that show these missing women. In the paintings, the women are nude and posed like they're asleep or dead. Eyes closed, skin pale, like that."

"So?"

"The last sold for over a million bucks."

"Do I look like I just made a million bucks to you?"

"Your paintings reveal a predilection for violence," says Lenz.

"Who the hell are you?"

"This is Doctor Lenz, Leon," says Kaiser. "You speak to him with respect, or you'll be funding the Vaseline concession at Angola. That's the only real self-help program that means anything there."

Gaines says nothing.

"The artist painting these pictures doesn't sign his work. But we've found some rare sable brush hairs in the paint on some of them. Sound familiar?"

There's a pause as Gaines works it out. "It's those expensive brushes Wheaton got us. Right?"

"Right."

"You tracked brush hairs from Hong Kong to Tulane?"

"That's what we do, Leon. We can track pubic hairs from an Algiers whorehouse to your ass if we need to. I want some answers. You waste five seconds of my time, you're on your way up Highway Sixty-one."

Gaines says nothing.

"Where were you three nights ago, after the opening at the museum?"

"Right here."

"Can anybody verify that?"

"*Linda!*" Gaines yells, clipping the mike Lenz is wearing. There's a pause; then Kaiser says, "Ms. Knapp?"

"Who's asking?" says a scratchy female voice.

"I'm with the FBI. Could you tell us—"

"Tell these guys we were here after the NOMA thing," Gaines cuts in. "They don't believe me."

"Shit," mutters Baxter.

"That's right," the woman says. "We came straight

252

home. I was bored. Everybody thinks they're hot shit at those art things. We were here all night."

"Can anyone else confirm that?" asks Kaiser.

"No," says Gaines. "We were having some quality time, you know?"

"Right," Kaiser says wearily.

"That's all," Gaines says, dismissing his girlfriend as he would a waitress.

"She your steady alibi, Leon?" asks Kaiser.

"Don't know what you're talking about."

"Tell me about Roger Wheaton."

"What about him?"

"Why did you want into his program?"

"Roger's the man."

"What do you mean?"

"He does his thing and doesn't give two shits what anybody thinks about it. And because he's done that his whole life, he's now a rich and famous man."

"You want to be rich and famous too, Leon?"

"Whatever."

"Do you like Wheaton?"

"What's to like or not like? The guy paints, that's it."

"Do you respect him?"

"The guy's dying, but he keeps working and he doesn't bitch. I respect that. You see the piece he's doing now? The room thing?"

"Yes."

"It's tearing him up, doing that. He's got all kinds of joint problems. His tendons or something."

"Enthesopathies," Lenz says.

"Whatever. He has to climb that ladder and sit there for hours, holding his neck in one position. It's worse than the Sistine Chapel. Michelangelo had scaffolding, so he could

253

lay on his back, you know? And Wheaton's hands . . . Sometimes his fingers turn blue, man. *Blue*. First white, then blue, sometimes even kind of black. There's no blood going to them, and he can't paint or anything else. It's agony. But he just sits down and waits until it stops, then goes right back to work."

"You clearly respect him," says Lenz. "And I suspect you don't give respect easily."

"You got that right. I think Roger saw a lot of shit in the war. He's got wisdom, and he knows how to pass it on. By example."

"What about Frank Smith?" asks Lenz.

Gaines makes a spitting sound.

"You don't like Smith?"

"Frankie's a silver-spoon butt pirate from Westchester. He walks like he has a dildo stuck up his butt, and he preaches every time he opens his mouth."

"What about his paintings?"

Gaines laughs in derision. "The nude fag series? Very tasty. You seen any of them? He cops the old masters so the stuff looks less like porn, then pawns it off on ignorant queens from New York. It's a sweet scam, I'll give him that. I'd try it myself, but I have this aversion to anal penetration. You know? But hey, maybe that's just me."

"What about Thalia Laveau?" asks Lenz.

Another pause, as though Gaines is debating whether to answer. "She's a tasty piece, if you like dark meat. Which, on occasion, I do. She doesn't look black, but she's got the blood, all right. Darker the berry, sweeter the juice, right?"

"What about her paintings?" asks Kaiser.

"She paints the poor and downtrodden. Who wants to buy that? A few guilty liberals from New England. She ought to go back to stripping."

"She told you she stripped for money?" asks Lenz.

"A Newcomb art history chick told me. She and Thalia munch carpets together on occasion. Don't tell me you guys didn't know."

"Do you know a man named Marcel de Becque?" asks Lenz.

"Never heard of him."

"We're going to want to take some pictures," Kaiser says in a detached voice. "Our photographer was supposed to be here already, but I'm sure we can find something to talk about in the meantime."

Baxter slaps my knee. "*Go.* And if it gets rough, hit the floor."

He opens the door, and I'm on the concrete, moving up the line of shotgun houses to the sound of R. Kelly coming from a boom box. I nod to the porch-sitters who'll assume from my clothes and the camera around my neck that I'm what I used to be, a newspaper photographer sent down here for pictures of a corpse or drug activity.

The green paint is peeling from the walls of Gaines's house, and the screen on the door is a rusted patchwork of orange and black. I feel a moment's trepidation as I reach for the handle, but the knowledge that Kaiser has a gun settles me enough to knock and go through the door.

The first thing that hits me is the smell. The scents of paint and oil that made Wheaton's studio so pleasant are here smothered by the stink of mildew, stale beer, rotting food, tobacco, and marijuana. Kaiser, Lenz, and Gaines practically fill the front room, which is long and narrow and throws me back to the countless shotgun houses I visited when I worked for the *Times-Picayune*.

"Who's this?" asks Gaines.

There's a strange caesura as Kaiser and Lenz judge his

reaction to me. I force myself not to look at him by busying myself with my camera. Past the camera I see a brown sofa pitted with cigarette burns and a threadbare carpet stained with drops of oil paint. The walls are bare but for an airbrushed Elvis on one wall and a small but elegant abstract over the sofa. A large easel stands the corner nearest me, a dirty cloth thrown over it.

"She's our photographer," says Kaiser. He points at the easel. "Is that painting yours?"

"Yeah," Gaines replies, and from the sound of his voice I can tell he's still looking at me.

I give him my face, searching his eyes for signs of recognition. They're dark coals set in yellow sclera, and they look permanently wide, like a hyperthyroid patient's, the effect exaggerated by dark half-moons beneath them. A limp black perm hangs over his forehead, and three days' growth of beard stubbles his face. In person, his skin has the sickly white pallor of a snake's belly. It's not hard to imagine him rolling a lawn mower over a live cat.

"Take the sheet off the painting so she can shoot it," Kaiser orders.

"Maybe I don't want it shot till it's finished."

"Maybe somebody somewhere gives a shit what you want." Kaiser walks over to the easel and yanks off the sheet.

Because I expected so little, Gaines's painting is startlingly powerful. A lank-haired blond woman with a hard face sits at a kitchen table in the harsh light of a bare bulb. She's surrounded by dirty cereal bowls and fast-food bags, and her shirt is open to the waist, revealing small sagging breasts. Her hollow eyes look out from the canvas with the sullen resignation of an animal that has helped build its own cage. It's hard to imagine such truthful art coming from the creature standing across the room, but talent isn't handed out on a merit system.

I set the flash on the Mamiya and start shooting, doing my best to ignore Gaines, whose eyes I feel like greasy fingers on my skin. After ten shots, I turn to the small abstract on the other wall. It's different from Gaines's work, but it looks like an original. Some female art student probably gave it to him after he slept with her.

"Who painted that?" I ask, shooting a snap of the small canvas.

"Roger," Gaines replies.

"Roger Wheaton?" asks Lenz.

"Yeah." Gaines moves closer to me. "I can tell you like my picture. You ought to come back later and let me paint you."

I would laugh were the situation not so grave.

"Shut up, you cheating bastard!"

I whirl to find the blond woman from the painting charging into the room. Wild eyes flash in her pale face, and a livid red mark the size of a fist covers one cheek from eye to mouth, the center of it already turning dark.

"Get back in there!" Gaines yells, his right hand balled into a fist.

Kaiser interposes himself between Gaines and the girl, who's wearing only a thin nightgown. "Has this man assaulted you, miss?"

"He fucked me over, is what he done! He's a goddamn liar! He said I was gonna be a model!"

"Have you modeled for him without clothes?"

"Hell, yes! He hardly lets me put anything on. But he don't want to paint, he just wants to fuck. That and get stoned, all day every day. And once he gets stoned, he can't even do that!"

"Get out, goddamn it!" Gaines screams, raising his fist.

The girl looks at me with a defiant rage. "Don't let them crazy eyes get you, honey, he's a loser."

"Like you'd know?" Gaines yells. "This lady's got class."

The woman laughs. "Yeah? That means she don't lay down with trash like you."

Gaines lunges at her, but Kaiser does something with his foot and suddenly Gaines is on the floor, clutching his knee with both hands. The girl laughs hysterically and points at Gaines.

"I think you'd better come with us," Kaiser tells her.

"I got nowhere to go he can't find me."

"We can arrange a shelter. A protected place."

"For real?"

"You try it, slut," Gaines groans.

Kaiser looks over at Lenz. "You have any questions?"

The psychiatrist shakes his head.

"Maybe I will go with you," the girl says to Kaiser.

When he nods, she runs into the back of the house, and after a crash and some scuffling sounds, returns with a purse and a grocery bag filled with clothes.

"You can forget what I said before," she says. "I don't know where he was three nights ago. He was supposed to come back after the NOMA opening, but he never did."

Gaines stares up from the floor with murder in his eyes.

"Well, Leon," says Kaiser. "I think you've got a problem. The NOPD will be in touch."

"Just a second," says the girl. She reaches down beside the sofa and comes up with half a glass of what looks like flat beer. She gives Gaines a vicious look, then splats the beer against the painting on the easel. "You got all you're gettin' out of me, scumbag."

Gaines roars in fury, and she darts through the front door. Lenz follows her, and I'm close on his heels, surprised by how badly I want out of this self-created hell.

"Hey, picture lady," Gaines calls after me. "You know where to find me when you get an itch."

I turn back in time to see Kaiser crouch beside Gaines, blocking my line of sight. At first I think he's whispering something, but then Gaines screams like a woman, and the girl starts laughing on the porch. Lenz sticks his head back through the door and stares transfixed as Kaiser stands, face placid, and walks toward us.

"What the hell was that?" Lenz asks.

"I don't have the patience I used to," Kaiser mutters.

Once on the sidewalk, Kaiser signals to someone I can't see. A man in plainclothes and a shoulder holster jogs up the street, confers with Kaiser, then leads Gaines's girlfriend away. The three of us gather by the opened rear door of the van, and Baxter looks expectantly at his two emissaries.

"What do you think?"

"It's not Gaines," says Lenz.

Baxter looks at Kaiser. "John?"

"I don't know."

Lenz snorts. "We've already wasted too much time. Let's go see Frank Smith."

"He sure reacted to me," I say softly.

"Like a hound to a bitch," says Lenz. "That's all that was. You didn't spook him a bit. He'd never seen you before."

Baxter is watching me. "What did you think about him?"

"I know he seems too obvious. But there was something in him that scared me. Like all that attitude was covering up something else, something that repelled me on a whole other level. Does that make sense?"

"Yes," says Kaiser. "I felt it too."

"The quality of his painting surprised me. He really sees into the women he paints."

Baxter says, "He had a painting by Roger Wheaton on his wall?"

"He did," Kaiser replies. "I'm surprised he hasn't sold it for dope already."

"We'd better check with Wheaton to make sure he didn't steal it," adds Lenz.

"Drop all that," says Baxter. "NOPD's ready to go in now and tear the place apart. Is that what we want?"

"They're bound to find drugs or weapons," says Kaiser. "We could put him in Angola and see if the kidnappings stop."

"Do you really expect more kidnappings?" I ask. "Now that we're this close?"

"We don't know how close we are," says Lenz. "Our interest might cause a more conventional serial offender to slow down, but whoever's behind this has no reason to. For all we know, the painter is a replaceable element in the equation. If they want another woman, they'll take one. They might even do it just to show they can."

No one questions Lenz's use of the plural pronoun.

"Don't arrest Gaines," Kaiser says. "If he's involved, we'll learn more by trailing him than jailing him."

Baxter looks at Lenz, who nods.

Baxter presses a button on the console and speaks into his headset mike. "Ed? Roust Gaines, but if you can keep from arresting him, we'd like you to leave him in place. . . . Same search, everything, just leave him home. . . . Thanks. I'll see you at the four o'clock meeting."

Baxter takes off the headset and looks at me. "Ready for Frank Smith?"

"He's got to be an improvement over Gaines."

"Cleaner, anyway," says Kaiser.

Baxter knocks on the front panel, and the van screeches onto Freret Street, headed for the more agreeable ambience of the French Quarter.

15

"Roger Wheaton called Smith and warned him we're coming," Baxter says, pulling off his headset. "Wiretap just picked it up."

We're parked across the street from a beautiful Creole cottage on the downriver side of Esplanade, the eastern border of the French Quarter. For the past two years it's been the home of Frank Smith.

"Why wouldn't Wheaton warn him?" asks Kaiser.

"We asked him not to," says Lenz.

"And now they're tearing his house apart and informing him he's going to have to supply skin and blood for DNA testing to compare to the skin we took from under the Dorignac's victim's fingernails."

"The call actually makes Wheaton look less suspicious," Kaiser says. "He's not stupid. He knows he's a suspect, which probably means a wiretap, but he made the warning call anyway. That's what somebody does when they're innocent and pissed off."

"Unless they do it to *look* innocent," says Lenz.

"Why didn't he warn Gaines?" I ask.

"Maybe he doesn't like Gaines," Kaiser says with a laugh. "That's not hard to imagine."

"Did he warn Thalia Laveau?" asks Lenz.

"Not yet," Baxter replies. "Only Smith."

262

"'I'm very fond of Frank,'" says Kaiser. "Those were Wheaton's words in the interview."

"I wonder if there could be a homosexual link," Lenz says.

"Wheaton has never married," says Baxter. "Why didn't you ask him if he's gay? He's never married."

"He may be in the closet," says Lenz. "I didn't want to burn my bridges with him entirely. We can find that out elsewhere."

Kaiser moves to the rear door. "Frank Smith is openly gay. Maybe he'll tell us." He looks at me. "See you in a few minutes."

He and Lenz leave the van and slam the door.

Baxter presses his face to the van's tinted porthole window. "The house doesn't look as fancy as I pictured it."

"You're looking at the back," I tell him. "Most of these houses face inward. Some onto courtyards, others onto fantastic gardens of tropical plants."

"John told me about your natural light theory. This house does have a courtyard. Smith's the only suspect who has one. Wheaton has an outdoor garden, but no walls. Hey, look at this."

I put my cheek to his, and my eyes to the darkened port-hole.

Frank Smith stands waiting for Kaiser and Lenz on his porch. He's sleek and handsome, his dark tan set off by white tropical clothing, linen or silk. He has large vivid eyes and an ironic smile on his lips.

"Look at this guy," says Kaiser over the monitor speaker. "A smart-ass, I can tell already."

"I'll be primary," Lenz says.

Through the speakers, Frank Smith's voice has the

263

festive tone of a man greeting party guests. "Hello! Are you the gentlemen from the FBI? When do the storm troopers arrive?"

"Jesus," mutters Kaiser. "There aren't any storm troopers, Mr. Smith. Because of certain evidence, you've become a suspect in some very serious crimes. There's no way to sugarcoat that. We're here to ask you some questions."

"You're not here for a blood sample? Urine perhaps?"

"No. We're here to talk."

"Well, I don't have an alibi for the night the woman was taken from Dorignac's. I was here, alone, listening to music." Through the window, I see Smith hold out his hands as if for handcuffs. "Let's get it over with."

"We're just here to talk," Kaiser insists.

"Foreplay for the police?" Smith asks in a taunting voice.

"We don't control the police in this town."

"I thought after all the corruption scandals here, you did."

Beside me, Baxter says, "He's pretty well-informed for a recent transplant."

Not many years ago, police corruption and the city's homicide rate were at an all-time high. Two police officers actually committed murder in the execution of a robbery, and the chaos that followed almost resulted in the Justice Department federalizing the New Orleans police force.

"We can talk here, in a civil manner," says Kaiser, "or the police can haul you downtown."

Smith laughs. "My God, it's Humphrey Bogart in elevator shoes. Why don't we go into the salon? I'll have coffee brought in."

Footsteps and a closing door echo in the van, then more footsteps.

"Please, sit," Smith says.

There's a groan of springs compressing under Dr. Lenz's weight.

"Juan? Three coffees, please."

"*Si.*"

"The guy has a servant," says Baxter. "Shit. My student days were a little different."

"Mr. Smith," Lenz begins, "I'm Arthur Lenz, a forensic psychiatrist. This is Special Agent John Kaiser. He's a psychological profiler for the Bureau."

"Two Van Helsings in my salon. Should I be flattered or insulted?"

"What's he talking about?" asks Baxter.

"Van Helsing was the professor who hunted Dracula," I tell him.

"This is going to be fun, I can tell."

"Put the tray there, Juan. Thank you." There's a pause, then Smith half-whispers, "I'm still training him. He has a long way to go, but he's worth it. How do you take your coffee, Doctor?"

"Black, please."

"Same for me," says Kaiser.

There's a tinkle of china, more groaning of springs.

"I'm not sure where to begin," Lenz says. "We—"

"Let me save you both some time," Smith interrupts. "You're here because of the women who've been vanishing. You've discovered that the series of paintings known as the Sleeping Women depicts these women. Some bit of evidence has led you to Roger Wheaton's program at Tulane. You're now questioning Wheaton and the rest of us before turning the police loose on us and ripping our lives apart. Roger is very upset, and that upsets me. I'd very much like to hear the details of this supposed evidence."

"You sound as if you were already aware of the Sleeping Women," says Kaiser.

"I was."

"How did you learn about them?"

"From a friend in Asia."

"You have a lot of Asian friends?"

"I have friends all over the world. Friends, colleagues, clients, lovers. About three months ago I heard that paintings from a new series were topping a million in private sales. Then I heard some were to be exhibited in Hong Kong. I've been thinking of going to view them."

"You were aware of the subject matter?" asks Lenz.

"Nude women sleeping was what I understood in the beginning. I only recently heard the rumors about the death theory."

"How did you feel about the prospect that women might be dying to produce those paintings?"

A long pause. "I haven't seen the paintings, so that's difficult to answer."

Lenz sips from his coffee cup; we can hear it over the mike. "Do you mean the quality of the paintings would determine your view of the morality of women dying to produce them?"

"To paraphrase Wilde, Doctor, there's no such thing as a moral or immoral painting. A painting is either well done or badly done. If the paintings are beautiful, if they are indeed great art, then they justify their own existence. Any other circumstances involved in their creation are irrelevant."

"That sounds familiar," says Kaiser.

"How so?" asks Smith.

"Do you know a man named Marcel de Becque?"

"No."

266

"He's a French expatriate who lives in the Cayman Islands."

"I don't know him. But there's a certain irony in the name."

"What's that?" asks Lenz.

"Emil de Becque was the French expatriate in *South Pacific*."

"Son of a bitch," hisses Baxter.

I can feel Lenz's embarrassment through the ether. "You're right," he says. "I'd forgotten."

"Perhaps this man took the surname as an alias?"

"De Becque's father went to Southeast Asia in the 1930s," says Lenz. "Maybe Michener heard the name and gave it to one of his island characters."

"I'll tell you someone I did know," says Smith. "This should get you hot and bothered. Christopher Wingate."

This time the silence is longer. "Why would you bring up Christopher Wingate?" asks Lenz.

"Let's not play games, Doctor. I heard about Wingate's death. I knew he was the dealer for the Sleeping Women. I thought nothing of it at the time. But now that the paintings are connected with possible murders, I see his death in a different light."

"How did you know Wingate?" asks Kaiser.

"A mutual friend introduced us at a party in New York. I was considering switching from my present dealer to him."

"Why?"

"Because he was, in a word, hot."

"I'm going to ask you a sensitive question," says Lenz. "Please don't take offense. This is very important."

"I'm on pins and needles."

Lenz is probably furious at being mocked, but he soldiers on. "Is Roger Wheaton gay?"

Smith barks a little laugh that's hard to read. "Did you ask Roger that?"

"No. I wasn't sure, and I didn't want to offend him."

"I'm offended for him. Not because of anything to do with being gay, but because of the invasion of his privacy."

"When people are dying, private matters often must become public. If you won't answer the question, I will have to ask Wheaton. Is that what you want me to do?"

"No."

"Very well."

After a thoughtful pause, Smith says, "I wouldn't say Roger is gay."

"What would you say?"

"He's a complex man. I've only known him personally for two years, and all that time he's been seriously ill. I think his illness has caused him to concentrate on nonsexual areas of his life."

"Have you ever seen him out with a woman?" Lenz asks. "Or with a woman at his home?"

"Roger doesn't 'go out.' He's either home or at the university. And yes, he has female guests."

"Overnight?"

"I don't think so."

"Does he have particular male friends?"

"I flatter myself that I'm his friend."

"Have you been his lover?"

"No."

"Would you like to be?" asks Kaiser.

"Yes, I would."

"Listen to this guy," says Baxter. "Cool as they come."

"Would you have any problem giving us your whereabouts on a particular set of dates?" asks Kaiser.

"I wouldn't think so. But let me be frank about something, gentlemen. I'll cooperate with this investigation up to a point. But if the police upset my life to an inordinate degree, without direct evidence against me, I'll institute legal action against both the police and the FBI. I have the resources to vigorously pursue such an action, and with the recent history of the NOPD in this town, I'd say my chances were good. So be forewarned."

There's a silence I can only interpret as shock. I doubt that representatives of the FBI are accustomed to being talked to in this way by serial-murder suspects.

"Psychology happens to be a particular interest of mine, Doctor," Smith goes on. "I happen to know that the incidence of homosexual serial killers is zero. So I think you'd have some difficulty persuading a jury that I'm a good candidate for harassment in this case."

"We don't necessarily believe the painter is the killer in this case," Lenz says. "But we're not focusing on you as a suspect. You're simply one of four people with access to particular brush hairs taken from Sleeping Women canvases."

"Tell me about these hairs."

Kaiser quickly summarizes the link between the factory in Manchuria, the New York importer, and Wheaton's special orders. When he finishes, Smith says, "So many questions behind your eyes, Agent Kaiser. Like little worms turning. You want to know everything. How exactly does it work? Does Frank really take it up the bum? Is he promiscuous? You have images of the old bathhouse scene in your mind? I was there for it, all right, the tail end of it. I was only seventeen. I sucked till the muscles in my face cramped. Does that make me a killer?"

"*Listen* to this guy," says Baxter.

"Why do you live in the French Quarter rather than close to Tulane?" asks Kaiser.

"The lower Quarter is a haven for gays. Didn't you know? There may be more of us here than there are of you. You should come back on Gay Pride Day and see me with my entourage. I'm quite a celebrity down here."

"Tell us about your fellow students," says Lenz. "What do you think of Leon Gaines?"

"Pond scum. Roger gave him a matched pair of abstracts as a gift, small but very fine. Leon sold one of them two weeks later – for heroin, I'm sure. I didn't have the heart to tell Roger."

"And Gaines's work?"

"His *work*?" Another laugh. "The violence has a certain authenticity. But I think of Leon as a graffiti artist. A boy painting dirty words and symbols on a wall. He wants desperately to shock, but he has no real insight, so the ultimate effect is flat."

"What about Thalia Laveau?"

"Thalia's a lovely creature. Lovely and sad."

"Why sad?"

"Have you talked to her yet?"

"No."

"She suffered terribly as a child, I think. She carries a great deal of pain around."

"What about her paintings?"

"They're charming. A sort of tribute to the nobility of the lower classes – a myth to which I don't happen to subscribe, but one she somehow manages to bring to life on canvas."

"Have you seen any of her nude work?"

"I didn't know she did any."

"What do you think of her skill as an artist?"

"Thalia has a gift. She works very fast, probably because

270

she sees to the heart of things so quickly. She'll do well, if she sticks with it."

"Why wouldn't she?"

"As I said . . . she has a certain fragility. Fragility at the center of toughness. Like a nautilus hidden within a shell."

"What about Roger Wheaton's work?" asks Kaiser.

"Roger's a genius." Smith's tone is matter-of-fact, as though he'd said, "The sky is blue." "One of a handful I've met in my life."

"Why is he a genius?" asks Kaiser.

"Have you seen his work?"

"Some of it."

"You don't think he's a genius?"

"I'm not qualified to make that judgment."

"Well, I am. Roger isn't like the rest of us. He paints from within. Utterly and completely. I try to do it, and I like to think I occasionally succeed. But the external is an important part of the process for me. I plan, I use models, rigorous technique. I strive to capture beauty, to freeze and yet animate it. Roger doesn't use models or photographs or anything else. When he paints, the divine simply flows out through his brush. Every time I look at his canvases, I see something different. Particularly the abstract ones."

"Do you know anything about the clearing he supposedly paints? Is it a real place?"

"I assume it is, or was, but I really have no idea. I don't think it matters. It's just a point of departure for him, the way a cliff might be the point of departure for an eagle."

"It may well matter in relation to these crimes," says Lenz.

"Are you really looking at Roger as a suspect? That's ludicrous. He's the gentlest man I know. Also the most ethical."

"Did you know he killed several men in Vietnam?" asks Kaiser.

"I know he was in the war. He doesn't talk about it. But surely you don't consider killing in combat to be murder?"

"No. But a man who's killed once can kill again. Perhaps more easily than some others."

"Perhaps. Have you ever killed anyone, Agent Kaiser?"

"Yes."

"In war?"

"Yes."

"As a civilian? In the line of duty?"

"Yes."

"I'll bet you have. There's violence in you. I can see it. I'd like to paint you sometime."

"I'm not available."

"You've seen some terrible things, haven't you?"

"It's a tough world, Frank."

"Isn't it? Dr. Lenz has seen things, too, but they don't affect him the same way. Evil and brutality offend you. You have a strong moral streak. A compulsion to judge."

"This is a waste of time," Kaiser says testily. "Our photographer should be here any minute."

Baxter takes hold of my elbow. "Move. Go, go, go."

Outside the van, I look both ways, then cross Esplanade, my eyes on Frank Smith's cottage. It presents a simple face to the street: four windows, three dormers, and a gabled roof, with a door where the porte cochere would have been a century ago. My knock is answered by a beautiful Hispanic boy of about nineteen. Juan, I presume.

"*Jes?*" he says.

"I'm from the FBI. I'm here to take some pictures."

"*Sí.* Follow me."

As he leads me through the entrance hall, I realize that

Smith's Creole cottage has been transformed from humble nineteenth-century abode into a showplace for antiques and art. To my right is a luxurious dining room with a Regency table, Empire chandeliers, and a huge mirror over a French commode. On the wall above a hunt board hangs a life-size portrait of a nude man reclining on a chaise. He looks vaguely familiar: large-boned but not well-muscled, yet his face has a remarkable nobility. The picture is languidly erotic, with full frontal nudity, and looks as though it could have been painted in the 1500s.

"*Señora?*" Juan says. "Please?"

A few steps and a left turn take us to the salon, where the others sit drinking coffee. This room, too, is stunning, with Oriental wood screens and an Aubusson rug the size of a wading pool. Frank Smith looks up as I reach the door, and though I intended to keep my eyes on my camera, I find myself looking square into Smith's face. The young painter has sea-green eyes, an aquamarine shade I've only seen in the eyes of women. They're set in a deeply tanned face, above a Roman nose and sensual mouth. Both his face and body have a remarkable symmetry, and he looks lean and muscular under his white linen clothes. Suddenly recalling my purpose for being here, I blink and turn to Kaiser.

"I'm sorry I'm late. What do you want me to shoot?"

"Anything by Mr. Smith here."

Frank Smith hasn't taken his eyes off me, and I'm eerily certain that he has seen me before. Me or my sister. That possibility closes my throat and brings sweat to my face.

"The nude in the dining room is mine," Smith says.

I nod and manage to speak one sentence. "I won't be a minute."

"I beg your pardon," he says. "Have we met?"

I clear my throat and look at Kaiser, half hoping he'll draw his gun. "I don't think so."

"In San Francisco, perhaps? Have you been there?"

I live there when I'm not working. . . . . "Yes, but not for—"

"My God, you're Jordan Glass."

Kaiser, Lenz, and I stare at one another like fools.

"You *are*," Smith says. "I might not have recognized you, but with the camera, something just clicked. My God, what are you doing here? Don't tell me you've joined the FBI?"

"No."

"Well, what in the world are you doing here?"

The truth has a voice of its own. "My sister was one of the victims."

Smith's mouth drops open. "Oh, no. Oh, I see." He gets to his feet and looks as though he wants to hug me, as though the tragedy had just happened. "Actually, that's not true. I don't see at all."

Kaiser is glaring at me like I shouldn't have given away the game, but once Smith recognized me, there was really no point in continuing.

"We were identical twins," I explain.

The artist's eyes narrow as he tries to understand; it doesn't take him long.

"You're a stalking horse! They're using you to try to panic the killer into revealing himself."

I say nothing.

Smith shakes his head in amazement. "Well, I'm happy to meet you, despite the circumstances. I love your work. I have for years."

"Thank you."

"How did you recognize her?" asks Lenz.

Smith directs his answer to me. "Someone pointed you

out to me at a party in San Francisco. I stood within three feet of you for twenty minutes, talking to someone else. I wanted to meet you, but I didn't want to intrude."

As I look back at Smith, the portrait in his dining room clicks in my mind. "Is the man in the dining room painting Oscar Wilde?"

His eyes light with pleasure. "Yes. I used the photo on the cover of the Ellmann biography for his face, and various other photos to get an idea of the rest of his body. Wilde is a hero of mine."

"I love the cottage," I tell him, laying a hand on his arm to gauge his reaction. He clearly enjoys it. "Do you have a garden?"

Smith beams. "Of course. Follow me."

Without paying the slightest bit of attention to Kaiser or Lenz, he escorts me to the front door, which leads to a walled garden filled with citrus plants, roses, and a gnarled wisteria that's probably as old as the house. One wall of the garden is formed by an old servants' quarters, which appears to have been converted into a wing of the cottage. Rushing water from a three-tiered fountain fills the courtyard with sound, but what holds me rapt is the light – glorious sunlight falling softly through the foliage with the perfect clarity I remember from Marcel de Becque's Sleeping Women.

"It's lovely," I say softly, wondering if my sister ever lay unconscious or dead on the paving bricks before me.

"You have a standing invitation. I'd love to entertain you. Please call anytime."

My second invitation today. "I just might do that."

Footsteps sound on the porch behind us. Kaiser says, "Mr. Smith, we'd like you to keep Ms. Glass's presence in New Orleans to yourself."

"Spoilsport," Smith retorts, cutting his eyes at me. "They're no fun at all, are they?"

"And please do not contact Thalia Laveau about his visit."

Anger flares in Smith's eyes. "Stop giving me orders in my own house."

In the awkward silence that follows, I suddenly want out of this place, away from this man who could have been the last person my sister ever saw.

"We really must go," Lenz says.

"No rest for the wicked," Smith quips, his humor inexplicably back in gear. Taking my arm, he leads me back through the house to the porch facing Esplanade Avenue.

"Remember," he says. "You're always welcome."

I nod but do not speak, and without a word to Kaiser or Lenz, Smith turns and goes back into his cottage, leaving us on the small porch.

"So much for the element of surprise," Kaiser says as we cross through traffic to the van. "How about that picture of Oscar Wilde?"

"Beautifully done," says Lenz, who appears preoccupied by something.

"Smith reminds me of Dorian Gray," I think aloud. "A beautiful amoral man who will never age."

"Why amoral?" asks Kaiser. "Not because he's gay."

"No. It's something I sense about him. He's like de Becque, yet different somehow. What do you think, Doctor?"

Lenz has a strange smile on his face. "You know what no one remembers about Dorian Gray?"

"What?"

"He murdered a man, then bribed a chemist to come to his house and destroy the body. The chemist used special compounds to burn the corpse until there was nothing left."

"You're kidding," says Kaiser.

"No. Wilde was ahead of his time in many ways. Dorian Gray's theory of murder was no corpse, no evidence, no crime."

16

Thalia Laveau lives on the second floor of a three-story Victorian rooming house near Tulane University. Nine other women and two men live in the house, which is a nightmare for the NOPD surveillance team. Seven doors, twenty-one ground-level windows, and two fire escapes. Parked on the student-dominated block, we hunch inside the FBI surveillance van like J. Edgar Hoover-era G-men spying on "outside agitators."

"The plan is for John to take the lead on Laveau," Baxter says, looking at Dr. Lenz. "Does anybody want to change that before you go in?"

Kaiser and Lenz glance at each other, but neither speaks.

"I do," I tell them.

All three men look at me in confusion.

"What do you mean?" asks Baxter.

"I want to go in alone."

"*What?*" they cry in unison.

"This is a woman, guys. Maybe a gay woman. I'll get twice as much out of her as you could."

"The point isn't to get something out of her," Baxter reminds me. "It's to find out whether she's seen you before, and therefore your sister. And since no one else seemed to recognize you – except Smith, who didn't try to hide it – this interview may be critical."

I look him dead in the eye. "Do you really believe a

278

woman is behind all these disappearances? Or even involved?"

"Let her do it," says Dr. Lenz, surprising me. "The odds that Laveau is involved are low, and her nude paintings will probably tell us more than she will. But if Jordan can gain her trust, we might learn something valuable about one of the men."

"You saw how Smith responded to me," I press Baxter. "I think he would have opened up to me if I'd been alone. Wheaton, too."

"Smith was responding to your fame," says Kaiser, who looks uncomfortable with the idea. "Not your gender."

"If you went in alone, what would you say?" asks Baxter.

"I won't know that until I get there. That's the way I work."

The ISU chief looks tempted but worried. "Jesus, the liability—"

"What liability? I'm a private citizen walking up to someone's door. If she invites me in, so what?"

"What if she sees you and freaks?" asks Kaiser. "Attacks you? If she's involved, that's a real possibility."

"I wouldn't turn down a gun if you offered me one."

Baxter shakes his head. "We can't give you a gun."

"How about some Mace?"

"We don't have any."

"This is a bad idea," says Kaiser.

"It's better than sending you and Lenz in there," I insist. "Look, I'll know whether she's seen me before as soon as she answers the door. Then I'll tell her you guys are outside. I'll tell the truth. I'm the sister of one of the victims, trying to find some answers, and the FBI is kindly providing some protection for me."

"Let her go," Lenz says. "We need to know what Laveau

knows. This is the best way to find that out." He looks at Kaiser. "You disagree?"

Kaiser looks like he'd like to argue, but he doesn't. "Put the wire on her, and I'll stand just outside the house with a receiver." He watches me, his hazel eyes intense. "If you sense it going bad in any way, yell for help. And I mean yell. No codes that can be misunderstood."

"That works for me," Baxter says. "Let's move, before Laveau decides to go out and get her hair done."

"Get the T-4 off," Kaiser tells Lenz, who removes his coat and starts unbuttoning his shirt, his elbows bumping us in the tight quarters. Baxter unstraps the tape from Lenz's ribs, and Kaiser chuckles at the psychiatrist's grimaces.

"She'll see that transmitter under this blouse," I point out, holding out the thin cotton.

"You'll have to wear it under your skirt," says Lenz, cradling the transmitter, dangling antenna, and microphone in his hands.

"Do you have more tape?"

Baxter digs into a metal drawer and comes up with a roll, which he hands awkwardly to me.

"This is no time to be shy," I tell them, pulling my skirt up. "I am wearing underwear."

"And very nice underwear it is," says Dr. Lenz, looking at the cream silk bikinis.

"Come on, tape it on."

"I don't really know what I'm doing," Lenz protests.

"Give me that," snaps Baxter.

He takes the transmitter from Lenz, and under the close scrutiny of the other two leans over and tapes the transmitter and antenna securely to my inner thigh, high enough to give me goose bumps despite my bravado about modesty. When he's done, he hands me the tiny microphone, which is connected to the transmitter by a thin wire.

"Run that under your waistband and up to your bra."

"Why don't you guys shut your eyes for this part?"

They do, and I secure the mike between the cups of my Maidenform with the tiny clip attached to it. "Ready or not," I say softly. "Let's do it."

They open their eyes, and Kaiser opens the back door.

"Remember," says Baxter. "You get a weird vibe, sing out, and the cavalry will bust in there."

"Nothing's going to happen."

Laveau's rooming house needs a new roof and a coat of paint, neither of which it's likely to get in the next ten years. The door to her second-floor apartment stands at the head of some rickety wooden steps attached to the peeling clapboard exterior of the house. I cling to the handrail as I climb the steps, since I'm about as comfortable in heels as I would be in snowshoes. The door and facing are scarred from years of careless tenants. I knock loudly and wait. After a moment, I hear footsteps.

"Who is it?" calls a voice muffled by the wood.

"My name is Jordan Glass. I want to talk to you about your paintings."

Silence. Then: "I don't know you. How did you know where to find me?"

"Roger Wheaton sent me."

There's a sound of bolts sliding back; then the door opens to the length of a chain lock. One dark eye peeks out and examines me.

"Who did you say you are?"

So much for my face rattling her into a confession. "Ms. Laveau, do you know about the women who've been disappearing from New Orleans over the past eighteen months? Two were taken from Tulane."

"Do I know about them? I've been carrying a gun for three months. What about them?"

"One of them was my sister."

The dark eye blinks. "I'm sorry. But what does that have to do with me?"

"I found some paintings of the victims. The paintings were in Hong Kong, but the FBI found special sable paintbrush hairs stuck in the paint, and they traced them to Roger Wheaton's program at Tulane."

The eye widens, then blinks twice. "That's crazy. Paintings of the kidnapped women?"

"Yes. They're all nudes, and the women are posed like they're either asleep or dead. Ms. Laveau, I'm trying to find out if my sister is alive or dead, and the FBI is helping me. Or letting me help them, rather."

"Why would they do that?"

I feel odd talking to a crack in a door, but I've done it more than once in my life, and you work with what you have. "Because my sister and I were identical twins. The FBI is parading me in front of suspects, hoping I'll rattle the killer into revealing himself."

"Or *her*self?" asks Laveau. "Is that what you're telling me? That I'm a murder suspect because of some brush hairs?"

"No one really believes you're involved, but the fact that you have access to these special brushes forces the FBI to try to rule you out."

"I guess you want to come in?"

"I'd like to, if you'll talk to me."

"Is my choice you or the FBI?"

"That's pretty much it, yes."

The eye disappears, and I hear her sigh. The door closes, the chain rattles, and then the door opens again. I slip through before she can change her mind, and she shuts it behind me.

Facing Thalia Laveau at last, I realize how misleading the photograph of her was. In the pictures I saw last night, her black hair looked cornsilk fine, but it must be kinkier than that, because today it's done in long thick strings that look like dreadlocks but aren't, and that hang almost to her midriff. Her skin is as light as mine, despite her African blood, but her eyes are a piercing black. She's wearing a colorful robe that looks Caribbean, and her expression is that of a woman comfortable in her own skin and amused by the pretensions of others. The overall effect is exotic, as though she were a beautiful priestess of some obscure tribe.

"Why don't you come into the back?" she says, waving at the tiny front room. "There's not enough room in here to cuss a cat without getting fur in your mouth."

Her voice is throaty and devoid of accent, which tells me she's worked hard to get rid of the sound of her childhood. I follow her through an empty door frame into a larger room.

I half expected a den filled with beads, incense smoke, and voodoo charms, but instead I find a conventional room furnished with rather spartan taste. There's a comfortable sofa, which she motions me to, and a chair with an ottoman, which she takes. After she sits, a heavy striped cat that looks half wild creeps out from behind her chair. It gives me a suspicious glare, then leaps onto Laveau's thighs, preens, and settles into her lap. Laveau tucks her feet beneath her and strokes it between the ears. She sits with remarkable ease, watching me as though she could wait forever for me to explain myself.

283

On the wall behind her is a painting of the St. Louis Cathedral in Jackson Square. This surprises me, because the cathedral is probably the most overpainted image in New Orleans, done and redone by students and hacks who hawk them to the tourists in Jackson Square. It seems an unlikely adornment for the apartment of a serious artist, though this rendering seems several cuts above the usual.

"Did you paint that?" I ask.

Laveau chuckles softly. "Frank Smith painted it, as a joke."

"A joke?"

"I told him he wasn't a New Orleans artist until he'd painted the cathedral, so he took an easel, walked down to the square, and sat for four hours. You never saw anything like it. By noon all the artists in the square had gathered round him like the Pied Piper. They couldn't believe how good he was."

"That sounds like him."

"You've talked to Frank?"

"Yes." Suddenly self-conscious, I pull my skirt down over my knees to be sure she can't see the transmitter taped to my thigh.

"Who else?"

"Roger Wheaton. Gaines."

"So, you saved me for last. Is that good or bad?"

"The FBI suspects you the least."

She smiles, revealing white teeth with a hint of gold toward the back. "That's good to know. Did your plan work? Did any of the others freak out when they saw you?"

"It's hard to say."

Laveau nods, acknowledging the fact that I can't be completely candid about some things. "Were you close to your sister?"

The question takes me aback, but I see no reason to lie. "Not in the way most sisters would say they were. But I loved her."

"Good. What was your name again?"

"Jordan. Jordan Glass."

"I like that."

"However things were between my sister and me, I have to find out what happened to her."

"I understand. Do you think she could still be alive?"

"I don't know. Will you help me find out?"

"How can I?"

"By telling me what you know about some things."

Her lips disappear between her teeth, and for the first time she looks uncomfortable. "Talk about my friends, you mean?"

"Is Leon Gaines your friend?"

She wrinkles her lip in distaste.

"May I call you Thalia?"

"Yes."

"I won't lie to you, Thalia. After I leave, the police are going to come here and question you about your whereabouts on the nights the women disappeared. Will you have any trouble giving alibis for those nights?"

"I don't know. I spend a lot of time alone."

"What about three nights ago, after the NOMA event?"

Confusion clouds her eyes. "The papers said the woman taken that night was unrelated to the others."

"I know. The FBI has its own way of working."

"Then – oh God. He's still taking them. And you think I—"

"I don't think anything, Thalia. I was just asking a question and hoping you had an answer that could keep the police off your back."

"I came straight home and did some yoga. It was a week-night, and I wasn't feeling well."

"Did anyone see you or call you? Anyone who could confirm that?"

Lines of worry now. "I don't remember. I don't think so. Like I said, I'm alone a lot."

I nod, uncertain which way to go with her.

"You are too, aren't you?" she says.

My first instinct is to change the subject, but I don't. Sitting here facing this woman I've never met, it strikes me that I've been surrounded by men ever since I arrived from Hong Kong. There's Agent Wendy, of course, but she's fifteen years my junior, and seems almost like a kid. Thalia is close to my age, and I feel a surprising comfort with her, a kind of relief in the essentially feminine security of her home.

"I am," I concede.

"What do you do?"

"How do you know I do anything? How do you know I'm not a housewife?"

"Because you don't act like one. And you don't look like one, even in that skirt. You should pick a better disguise than heels next time, unless you have plenty of time to practice in them."

I can't help but laugh. "My sister was a housewife. Before she disappeared, I mean. I'm a photojournalist."

"Successful?"

"Yes."

She smiles. "I'll bet it feels good, doesn't it? That validation?"

"It does. You'll get there too."

"I wonder sometimes." Thalia strokes the cat's back, and with each caress it rises against the pressure of her hand. "I

286

see you want to ask me questions. Go ahead. I'll tell you if I mind."

"Some of these questions are the FBI's. But if I don't ask you, they will."

"I'd rather have you ask them."

"Why did you leave Terrebonne Parish and go to New York?"

"Have you ever been to Terrebonne Parish?"

"Yes."

Surprise flickers in her eyes. "Really?"

"I worked for the newspaper here once. A long time ago. I spent a few days down there."

"Then you know why I left."

"What I remember is people who didn't have much in the way of material things but loved the place they lived."

She sighs bitterly. "You weren't there long enough."

"Why did you want to study under Roger Wheaton?"

"Are you kidding? It was a one-in-a-million opportunity. I always loved his paintings. I couldn't believe it when he selected me."

"You submitted female nudes for your audition paintings?"

"Yes." Her hand goes to her mouth. "My nudes make me look like a suspect, don't they?"

"To some people. Why did you switch from nudes to painting people in their homes?"

"I don't know. Frustration, I guess. My nudes weren't selling, except to businessmen who wanted something for their offices. Something arty with tits, you know? I wasn't put on earth to fulfill that function."

"No."

"Have you seen any of my work?"

"No. It's just a feeling I have about you."

"That's interesting."

"Thalia, do you know a man named Marcel de Becque?" She shakes her head. "Who is he?"

"An art collector. What about Christopher Wingate?"

"No."

"He's a big art dealer in New York."

"Then I definitely don't know him. I don't know any big dealers."

"You'll never know this one. He was murdered a few days ago."

This sets her back a little. "Was he part of this? The disappearances?"

"He's the man who sold the paintings of the victims. The series is called The Sleeping Women."

"May I see one? Do you have a photo or something?"

"No. I wish I did."

"Are they good?"

"Connoisseurs say they are."

"Do they sell?"

"The last one sold for two million dollars."

"*God.*" She closes her eyes and shakes her head. "And the woman looked dead in that picture?"

"Yes."

"The buyer was a man, of course."

"Yes. A Japanese."

"Isn't that typical?"

"What do you mean?"

"A dead naked woman sells for two million dollars. Do you think another type of painting by the same artist would have sold for that? A landscape? An abstract?"

"I don't know."

"Of course it wouldn't! Roger's paintings don't sell for that."

"They sell for a lot."

"A quarter of that. And he's been working for decades."

"Now that I think about it, you're right. This artist's first paintings were more abstract, and they didn't sell. What started the phenomenon were the ones where it was clear the women were Occidental, nude, and asleep or dead."

Thalia sits with her mouth shut tight, as though she refuses to lower herself to discuss what makes her so angry.

"Tell me about Leon Gaines. What do you think about him?"

"Leon's a pig. He's always sniffing around, telling me what he'd like to do to me. He offered me five hundred dollars to model nude for him. I wouldn't do it for ten thousand."

"Would you model nude for Frank Smith for five hundred?"

"I'd model for Frank for free, but he only paints men."

"What about Roger Wheaton?"

A strange smile touches her lips, an emblem of private thoughts that will not be shared. "Roger would never ask me to model for him. He's still distant after two years. I think I intimidate him. Maybe he's attracted to me and doesn't want to cross some line, I don't know. He's a complex man, and I know he's sick. He doesn't talk about it, but I can read the pain in his face. Once I walked into his studio when he was buttoning his shirt, and his chest was covered with hemorrhages, from coughing. It's in his lungs now, whatever it is. He feels something for me, but I don't know what. He's almost embarrassed around me. I think he may have seen some grad student's paintings of me in the nude."

"Does he know you're gay?"

Thalia's body stiffens, and her eyes go on alert. "Has the FBI been spying on me?"

"No. But the police have. You didn't notice them?"

"I saw some cops watching the house. I thought they were narcs, staking out the two guys who live here."

"No. They've only been on you for one day, though."

She looks relieved.

"The FBI does want to know whether you're gay or not. They do a lot of psychological profiling in these cases, and they feel that's important."

She purses her lips and looks at the coffee table between us, then raises her eyes to mine. "Do you think I'm gay?"

"Yes."

She smiles and strokes the cat. "I'm strange. I don't really fit anywhere. I have a sex drive like anyone else, but I don't trust it. It betrays me. It makes me want to use sex to get noticed. So when I need someone, I go to women."

"What about love and tenderness?"

"I have friends. Mostly women, but men too. Do you have a lot of friends?"

"Not really. I have colleagues, people who do what I do and understand the demands of my life. We share experiences, but it's not, you know, the real thing. And I spend so much time traveling that it's hard to make new friends. I have more ex-lovers than friends."

· She smiles with empathy. "Friends are hard to find when you're forty. You really have to open yourself up to people, and that's hard to do. If you have one or two friends left from childhood, you're lucky."

"I left the place I grew up, like you did. Do you have friends left back home?"

"One. She's still down on the bayou. We talk on the phone sometimes, but I don't go back to visit. Do you have any kids?"

"No. You?"

"I got pregnant once, when I was fifteen. By my cousin. I had an abortion. That was that."

"Oh." I feel my face growing hot. "I'm sorry."

"That's why I hate the place. My father abused me from the time I was ten, my cousin later. It really messed me up. I ran away when I was old enough, but it took me a long time to come to terms with it. I've never really gotten over it. I can't have a man on top of me, no matter how much I might care for him. That's why I choose women. It's a safe harbor for me. I used to think that might change, but I don't think it ever will."

"I understand."

She looks skeptical. "Do you?"

"Yes."

"Were you sexually abused?"

"Not like that. Not by family. But . . ." I'm suddenly hyperconscious of Baxter and Lenz and Kaiser in the surveillance van, monitoring every word. I feel like a traitor, both to Thalia and to myself, and I want to yank off the transmitter I'm wearing. But if I did, Thalia couldn't possibly understand.

"Take your time," she says. "Would you like some tea?"

"I was raped," I say softly, not quite believing the words as they fall from my mouth. "It was a long time ago."

"Time doesn't mean anything when it's that."

"You're right."

"Was it a friend?"

"No. I was in Honduras, during the war in El Salvador. I was just starting out, really. I'd been photographing this refugee camp with a couple of print reporters, and we got separated. They left without me, and I had to walk back to the town. This car came along and stopped for me. There were government soldiers in the car. Four of them, one an officer. They were polite and smiling. They said they'd take me into town. I was always really careful, but it was a long way back to town. I took the ride. A mile down the road, they turned off and drove me into the jungle. So far that no one could hear me screaming. I know, because I lost my voice that night."

"It's all right," Thalia murmurs. "I'm here with you."

"I know. But it's not all right. It's never gotten all right. I'm more ashamed of that than anything I've ever done."

"You didn't *do* anything, Jordan. What did you do? You accepted a ride from men who said they'd help you."

Tears of anger and self-disgust sting my eyes. "I'm not talking about the rape. I'm talking about after. Before they started, they tied my hands behind my back. There was no way to fight, and it went on for hours. At some point during the night I passed out. At dawn I woke up with my arms numb but my hands free. I followed the tire tracks out to the road, then limped into town bleeding and crying. I didn't tell a soul what they'd done. I thought I was so tough, but I didn't have the nerve even to go to a hospital. I thought if the people I worked for found out what had happened, they'd pull me out of there before I knew what hit me. Not to protect me, but because they'd think I couldn't handle myself. You know? I *hate* myself for that fear. I've been haunted ever since by the women who might have been raped after me because I didn't report those men."

Thalia slowly shakes her head. "There were probably women before you and women after. But it's over now. You've punished yourself enough. Those soldiers are dead. If they're not physically dead, their souls are. What matters is how you are now. That's the only thing you can change."

"I know that."

"Your head knows it, but not your heart. That's where you have to know it, Jordan."

"I know. I try."

"You're afraid for your sister, aren't you? Afraid she'll have to go through something like that."

"Or worse."

"Okay, but look what you're doing. You're doing everything humanly possible to find her. More than any other relative of these women, I'll bet."

"I have to know, Thalia."

"You will, honey. You'll know." She lifts the enormous cat and sets it on the floor, then walks over and pulls me to my feet. "Come in the kitchen. I'm going to make you some green tea."

"I'm sorry I did this. You're the first person I ever told that to, and I don't know why I did. I don't even know you."

Thalia Laveau places both her hands on my shoulders and looks deep into my eyes. "You know what?"

"What?"

"You just found a friend at forty."

A strange feeling akin to religious absolution rolls through my chest.

"Now, come on in this kitchen, girl."

Thirty minutes later, I walk down the rickety stairs and hear John Kaiser whispering to me from the corner of the house.

"This way, Jordan."

I don't want to see him, but there's no avoiding it. When I go around the corner, he falls into step beside me.

"I'm sorry we heard that," he says. "I'm sorry it happened to you."

"I don't want to talk about it." I must be walking very

fast, because even with his long stride, Kaiser is having trouble staying beside me.

"I'm sorry about the way I talked about the rape Roger Wheaton stopped in Vietnam," he says.

The van comes into sight, rolling slowly toward us along the street.

"What do you want, Jordan? Just tell me."

"I want to go to my hotel and take a shower."

"You're on your way."

"And I don't want to ride in the van."

"I'll get a car here. I'll wait with you, then drop you. Okay?"

I don't look at him. I feel a powerful, irrational anger toward him, and at the knowledge that he desires me. He wants to hold me now, to comfort me, but he can't. Only a woman I foolishly believed could have been involved with my sister's disappearance could comfort me, and she has already done what she could.

The surveillance van stops, and its rear door opens. Kaiser trots over behind the door, then jogs back to me.

"A surveillance car is on the way. In one minute, you'll be on your way to your hotel. Okay?"

I fix him with a level gaze. "Thalia didn't know me. She'd never seen me before in her life. Which means she's never seen Jane. You got that, right?"

"Right."

"Good."

17

In the shower in my hotel room, my composure finally blows apart, spinning images through my head without coherence: Wingate trying to save his painting, flames licking at his feet; soldiers tying my hands and pressing my face into the jungle floor; my brother-in-law kissing my neck, trying to bed the ghost of his wife; de Becque watching me with a glint in his eye as he doles out bits of information about my father . . .

I turn the water as hot as I can stand it, my eyes closed against the spray even as I see the four strange souls I encountered today: a dying man, a violent man, a feminine man, and a wounded woman. Yesterday I had some hope of resolution. I was fooled by the confidence of men in their systems and their evidence, by the illusion of progress, by the belief that time must inevitably yield some answer. But deep down I know that time, like fate, operates under no imperative. What are those men saying now, after the failure of their grand plan? Baxter. Lenz. Kaiser. They paraded me past their suspects and saw not one flicker of panic. Not even a flinch at my face –

A telephone is ringing. At first I think it's in my head, because it's impossibly loud. Then I pull back the shower curtain and see a phone mounted on the wall, low by the commode. I press my right palm into the white towel on the rack, then pick up the receiver.

"Yes?"

"It's John."

"John?"

"Kaiser." He sounds uncomfortable.

"Oh. What is it?"

"I'm still downstairs."

"Why?"

"We're about to have a meeting. Before the official task force meeting. Baxter, Lenz, Bowles, and me. I know you're upset, but I thought you might be more angry if you missed it."

"I'm in the shower. It's basically going to be a wake, right?"

"I don't think so. I just spoke to Baxter on my cell. He says he has a couple of new things."

"What things?"

"I won't know till I get to the office."

As badly as I want to crack open the minibar and flop onto my bed wrapped in towels, I know he's right. I'll feel worse if I don't go.

"Give me five minutes."

Kaiser hangs up, undoubtedly thinking that no woman he ever knew could go from naked in the shower to ready in five minutes.

He's about to get a lesson.

This time we meet where we did the first time: SAC Bowles's office. Kaiser leads the way with a perfunctory knock, and though I hear voices, the office appears empty. Through the long window to my right, Lake Pontchartrain looks gray against the afternoon sky, dotted with a few lonely sails.

Walking farther in, I see Baxter, Lenz, and SAC Bowles

waiting in the private seating area in the deep leg of the L. Bill Granger, the violent-crimes supervisor, shakes Kaiser's hand on his way out and gives me an embarrassed nod. Clearly, he was in the loop that heard the transmission from Thalia Laveau's apartment. Wonderful.

Kaiser and I sit side by side on a sofa, facing Baxter and Lenz. SAC Bowles has a chair to himself on my right. No one looks happy, but neither do they look as dejected as I would have expected. They do look surprised to see me.

"You did a first-rate job today, Jordan," Baxter says in a chamber-of-commerce voice.

"Too bad I didn't shake anybody up."

He looks at Kaiser. "We've got forty minutes before the joint task force meets, and I want to go in there solid. As of now, we have two agents on separate planes escorting all the evidence the NOPD gathered today to the lab in Washington. Everything from paintings to DNA samples. The Director himself put an expedite on it, which means a twelve-hour turnaround on some tests, twenty-four to forty-eight on others. Three days on the DNA if we're insanely lucky."

"Three *days*?" says Kaiser. "I'd have been shocked at three weeks."

"Couple of the victims' families have a lot of stroke. And thank God for it." Baxter glances at me as though wondering whether to reassure me that the FBI works every case with equal fervor, but he doesn't. Everyone in this room knows that if the eleven missing women were crack whores, the evidence on those planes could languish in the lab for weeks.

"Before we decide where we're going," he says, "let's take stock of where we are. Today's interviews didn't produce the result we'd hoped for. Why not?"

"Two possibilities," says Lenz. "One, none of the four

suspects is the UNSUB/painter. This theory is unanimously supported by our art experts, who say the Sleeping Women weren't painted by any of the suspects. Two, one of the suspects *did* recognize Jordan, but fooled us by keeping his cool when she came in."

"Or her cool," Baxter reminds him.

"Nobody fooled us," says Kaiser. "Except maybe Frank Smith. He was startled by Jordan's face, but he explained it by saying he'd seen her at a party some time ago, a virtually uncheckable explanation."

Baxter looks at Lenz. "What did you think about Smith?"

"Brilliant, gifted, sure of himself. Of the four, he's the most capable of putting this thing together."

"What about the first possibility? None of the four is our UNSUB?"

"The brush hairs brought us to these four," says Kaiser. "I trust physical evidence more than I trust art experts."

"The evidence brought us to those four *and* the fifty undergraduates who could get access to the special brushes," Lenz points out. "How are we coming with them?"

"No student has been questioned directly," Baxter replies. "Because of their age, and because so few could be talented enough to have painted the Sleeping Women, they're a low-percentage shot. Also, the minute we start interrogating Tulane undergrads, the media's going to blow this case wide open. We've been lucky so far."

"Very lucky," I say quietly. "I wonder why."

"The New Orleans media's not that aggressive," says Bowles. "I don't know why. They could push a lot harder than they do."

"But once they get hold of it," says Kaiser, "it'll be a feeding frenzy. And with Roger Wheaton involved – not to mention rich, pissed-off parents and their lawyers – you'll get national press."

"Don't forget Jordan," says Bowles, with a nod in my direction. "She adds a little marquee value."

"Forget the media for now," says Baxter. "NOPD says none of the suspects seemed anxious about providing a DNA sample. If one of them had snatched the Dorignac's woman, he wouldn't have been cool about doing that."

"If the painter just paints," says Lenz, "and someone else does the snatches, the painter would have nothing to fear from a DNA test."

"Even if the UNSUB only does the painting," says Kaiser, "he should have been stunned by Jordan's face."

"True."

Kaiser looks at Baxter. "What's the new development you mentioned on the phone?"

I would have led with this question, but I guess these guys have their own rhythm.

"Even though the timing of Wingate's murder and the Dorignac's snatch were only two hours apart," says Baxter, "I've had a half-dozen agents working around the clock, checking flight manifests and interviewing passengers who traveled between New York and New Orleans in surrounding hours. It finally paid off."

"What do you have?"

"One hour after Wingate died, a lone man paid cash for a flight from JFK to Atlanta, then cash again for a flight to Baton Rouge on a different airline."

"Who was he?" I ask.

Dr. Lenz crosses his legs and answers in a pedantic voice. "A false name, of course. It could be that the UNSUB who killed Wingate was already in New York when you upset the applecart in Hong Kong. He silenced

Wingate, then flew straight – or almost straight – to New Orleans to warn his partner. If you study the timing, it could be that he arrived only six hours after the Dorignac's woman was taken. The plan may have been to paint her, but the New York UNSUB made the prudent decision. Do her and dump her."

Baxter gives the psychiatrist a sharp look. "That's possible. But no matter who the New York UNSUB is, or what he did *after* the Dorignac's victim was kidnapped, someone already in New Orleans had to kidnap her. Probably the painter."

A few moments of silence pass as this sinks in.

"You have a description of the New York UNSUB?" asks Kaiser.

"Very general. Mid-thirties to mid-forties, muscular, hard-looking face. Casual dress clothes. He's probably the guy who flipped Jordan the bird after the fire."

"Sock cap?" I ask, half jokingly.

"There's something else," says Baxter. "Linda Knapp – Gaines's girlfriend, the one who trashed his painting and left with you guys – turned back up at Gaines's place thirty minutes ago. NOPD wouldn't let her near Gaines, but she told them that whatever nights they needed alibis for, he was home with her, getting drunk or screwing her silly."

I recall how angry and desperate to get away from Gaines the woman had looked. Now she's back with him, protecting him from the police. This is a common mystery I've never understood and am not sure I want to.

"Has Knapp been with Gaines for the past eighteen months?"

"No," says Baxter. "Gaines named another girlfriend as his alibi for the murders that predate his relationship with Knapp. We're trying to locate her now. As far as the others' alibis, here's where we are. Based on credit-card activity, Roger Wheaton and Frank Smith were both in town for every murder. Leon Gaines and Thalia Laveau don't even *have* credit cards. Initial questioning by NOPD hasn't turned up any rock-solid alibis. It's not surprising, really. Almost all the kidnappings happened during the week, between ten p.m. and six a.m."

"What about Smith?" asks Lenz. "Surely he has some sleep-over lovers who could alibi him for at least one murder?"

"None he named today," Baxter replies. "Maybe he's protecting somebody."

"Someone in the closet," says SAC Bowles.

"What about Juan?" I ask. "The butler or whatever he was?"

"We didn't know about him till today," says Baxter. "NOPD's talking to him now. He tried to slip out, but they got him. Looks like an illegal. Salvadoran."

Now I realize why he looked familiar. I spent a good bit of time in El Salvador, seeing faces much like his.

"What else do we have?" asks Kaiser. "What about soldiers Wheaton served with? Convicts Gaines shared cells with?"

"I've got two lists," says Baxter. "I thought you might want to talk to the Vietnam vets."

As the men work out these details, a strange epiphany occurs at the dark center of my mind. The paradox of expert opinion versus physical evidence has been slowly working itself out there. "I've thought of a third possibility," I say quietly.

Kaiser waves his hand to silence the others, and they turn to me.

"What is it?" he asks.

"What if one of the four suspects we saw today is doing the murders, but doesn't *know* he's doing them?"

No one responds. Baxter and Kaiser look stunned by the suggestion, but Dr. Lenz is sanguine.

"How did you come up with that?" asks the psychiatrist.

"The old Sherlock Holmes theory. After you exclude all impossibilities, whatever you have left is the solution, however improbable it may seem."

"We haven't excluded the other possibilities," says Baxter. "Not by any means."

"We're not getting anywhere with them, either." Kaiser looks thoughtfully at Lenz. "What about that?"

The psychiatrist makes a noncommittal gesture with his hands, as though considering the idea for the first time. "You're talking about MPD. Multiple-personality disorder. It's extremely rare. Much rarer than films or novels would have the public believe."

"In all my time at Quantico, I never saw a proved case," Kaiser says.

"When it does happen," says Bowles, "what causes it?"

"Severe sexual or physical abuse during childhood," says Lenz. "Exclusively."

"What do we know about the childhoods of the three men?" I ask, recalling Thalia's confession of sexual abuse. "We know Laveau had that kind of problem."

"Not much," says Baxter. "Wheaton's childhood is pretty obscure. All we really have is the standard bio that appears in articles. Certainly nothing about abuse. We do know his mother left the home when he was thirteen or fourteen, which could be a sign of some kind of abuse, but we don't have details. And if the children were being abused, why not take the children with her?"

"We should ask Wheaton that," says Kaiser.

"What about Leon Gaines?" I ask. "I'll bet there was some abuse there."

"Undoubtedly," says Lenz. "He spent time in a juvenile reformatory, which is a high-percentage indicator for abuse. But the kind of radical psychological break I'm talking about has its roots much earlier in a child's life."

I look at Baxter. "Didn't you say his father did time for carnal knowledge of a minor? A fourteen-year-old girl?"

Baxter nods. "That's right. We'd better dig deeper on the father."

"Frank Smith," says Kaiser. "What do we know about his childhood?"

"Wealthy family," says Lenz. "Not the kind where abuse would be reported. I'll try to contact the family doctor."

As we ponder this angle in silence, the SAC's phone rings. Bowles goes to his desk, then motions Baxter to the phone. Baxter identifies himself, asks some questions I can't quite hear, then hangs up and returns to us, a tight smile on his lips.

"What is it?" asks Kaiser.

"Frank Smith's Salvadoran butler just told NOPD detectives that Roger Wheaton has visited Frank several times for extended periods at night. He's stayed over twice."

Kaiser whistles. "No kidding."

Baxter nods. "And get this. On those nights, he's heard them screaming at each other. Heard it through the walls."

This image is hard for me to reconcile with what I've seen of both men, but Dr. Lenz looks more excited than I've seen him to date.

"We've got to see both of them again," he says.

"No doubt," agrees Baxter. "How should we approach them?"

Lenz purses his lips but says nothing.

"I think I should talk to Frank Smith," I say firmly.

They all look at me. "Alone?" asks Baxter.

"He invited me back, didn't he? That's your best shot of finding out about those visits."

"She got Laveau to trust her," Kaiser reminds them. "I say let her do it."

Baxter looks uncomfortable, and turns to Lenz for an opinion.

The psychiatrist shrugs. "I know you'd prefer some other way, but Smith really responded to her. We have to go with the best odds."

Baxter sighs. "Okay. Jordan will talk to Smith."

"Arthur and I can see Wheaton," Kaiser says. "We should have the phone company fault their lines. We don't want any more warnings passing between them."

"Sounds like a plan," Baxter concludes. "How much of this do we give the task force?"

"All of it," says Kaiser. "They've proved trustworthy so far. If we hold out without reason, we're only screwing ourselves."

"The multiple-personality theory as well?" asks Lenz.

"No," says Baxter. "That's the kind of exotic speculation they rib us about, so let's play it down unless we have some reason to think it's the right track." He glances at me. "Something other than the Sherlock Holmes theory, at least."

A belated smile tells me he said this in fun.

"Any last questions?"

Kaiser flicks up his hand like a schoolkid. "This morning you said you had that Argus computer program chewing on digital photos of the abstract Sleeping Women. Has it turned up any recognizable faces?"

"They're looking more human," says Baxter. "But none

matches any murder victim or missing person in the New Orleans area over the past three years."

"Who's making those comparisons?"

"Couple of agents I borrowed from Counter-intelligence," answers the SAC. "Good men. Twenty years in, between them."

"I'd like to see whatever Argus spits out," says Kaiser. "I've studied a lot of victims' faces in the past few months."

"Will you see to that, Patrick?" says Baxter.

Bowles nods. "We'll get you copies of every image e-mailed from Washington, as we decrypt them. I hope you've got a lot of time on your hands."

Baxter looks at his watch. "We need to go." Turning to me, he says, "Jordan, more than ever, we need you to stay isolated from any friends from your former life here."

"No problem. I'm beat. I'm going back to my hotel, ordering room service, and racking out."

"Do you trust your brother-in-law to keep quiet?"

"No problems there."

His eyes linger on mine. "I've already gotten Wendy a room next door to yours. Just yell out if you need help."

I nod, preferring Wendy Travis to a stranger, though I sense potential complications from her presence.

Baxter slaps his thighs and stands, and the other men follow suit like football players rising from a huddle.

"Let's go talk to the boys in blue," says Baxter.

"Black and blue," says Kaiser. "The NOPD wears black and blue."

Baxter leads the way to the door, headed for the Emergency Operations Center, which I have yet to see. Bowles follows, and Lenz falls into line behind him. Only Kaiser hangs back, contriving to walk beside me as I move toward the door.

"So, you're going to bed early?" he says softly.

"Yes." I pause at the door and watch the others move down the hall. "But maybe not to sleep. Call me from the lobby."

Looking up the hallway, he touches my hand and squeezes slightly, then without a word follows Dr. Lenz. I give him a few seconds, then go around the corner to the elevators, where I find Wendy waiting for me.

18

I've been asleep for a while when the phone rings beside my bed. The TV is still on, set to HBO, but the sound is muted. I shut my eyes against its harsh light and pick up the phone.

"Hello?"

"It's me. I'm downstairs."

John Kaiser's face appears in my mind. "What time is it?"

"Well after midnight."

"God. The meeting went on that long?"

"The police questioned each suspect for hours, and we had to hear it all."

I rub my cheeks to get the blood moving. "Is it still raining?"

"It finally stopped. You were sleeping, weren't you?"

"Half sleeping."

"If you're too tired, that's all right."

Part of me wants to tell him I'm too tired, but a little tingle between my neck and my knees stops me. "No, come on up. You know the room number?"

"Yes."

"Will you get me a Coke or something on the way up? I need some caffeine."

"Regular Coke or Diet?"

"What would you guess?"

"Regular."

"Good guess."

"On the way."

I hang up and stumble into the bathroom, the fuzzy heaviness of fatigue telling me the last few days have been more stressful than I thought. Leaving the bathroom light off, I brush my teeth and wash my face. For a moment I wonder if I should put on some makeup, but it's not worth the trouble. If he doesn't like me as is, it wasn't meant to happen.

I am going to have to do something about the baby-doll nightgown, though. The short pink horror looks like something a 1950s sorority girl would have worn. When I first saw it, I wondered if the FBI agent who bought it for me was playing a joke on me, but she probably has one just like it in her closet at home. I slip off the gown and replace it with a white cotton T-shirt and the jeans I wore yesterday.

Kaiser knocks softly to keep from alerting Wendy next door. I check the peephole to make sure it's him, then quickly open the door. He steps inside, then smiles and sets two sweating Coke cans on the desk. He opens one and hands it to me.

"Thanks." I take a long sip that stings the back of my throat. "You tired?"

"Pretty tired."

"How do you feel about the case?"

He shrugs. "Not great."

"Do you think Wheaton and Frank Smith are lovers?"

"I don't know what else those visits would be."

"They could be anything. Discussions about art."

"That's not what my gut tells me."

"Mine either. What's the deal with Lenz? He doesn't want to say much in front of you, does he?"

"Since leaving the Bureau, he's found out how quickly you can be forgotten. He'd like to show that what Quantico has now is the second string."

"He wasn't surprised when I asked if one of the suspects could be killing people without knowing it."

"He didn't seem to be." Kaiser gives me a knowing look.

"Do you like that theory?"

"No. It's hard for me to picture someone that messed up pulling off eleven abductions and possibly painting like Rembrandt as well. But I'm going to research it anyway. Try to find out if any of the three males suffered sexual abuse." He opens his Coke and takes a sip. "Are we going to talk business all night?"

"I hope not."

I go to the far wall and open the sleep curtains, exposing a huge window that overlooks Lake Pontchartrain from fourteen floors up, a slightly different version of the view from the FBI field office to the east. The lake is a black sea now, but for the line of fluorescent lights marking the causeway as it recedes northward into the mist. I walk back and sit on the foot of the bed. Kaiser takes off his jacket and drapes it on the chair back, then sits opposite me, about two feet away, his gun still on his belt.

"What should we talk about?" he asks.

"Why don't you tell me what's on your mind?"

A hint of a smile. "You are."

"Why do you think that is?"

He shakes his head. "I wish I knew. You know how sometimes when you lose something, it's only when you're not looking for it anymore that you find it?"

"Yes. But sometimes by then you don't need whatever it was."

"This is something everybody needs."

"I think you're right." I feel warm inside, but a deeper hesitation keeps me from giving in completely to the moment. I take another sip of Coke. "I told you about some of my problems with men. With dating. Guys thinking they want me but finding they don't want the reality of my life."

"I remember."

"I want to know about you. You're no quitter. What really drove you and your wife apart?"

He sighs and sets down his drink can as though it has grown too heavy to hold up. "It wasn't that I let my work take over my life – though I certainly did that. If I'd been a doctor or an engineer, she wouldn't have minded. It was that the things I saw every day simply couldn't be communicated to someone normal. 'Conventional' is probably a better word. It got to where we had no common frame of reference. I'd come home after eighteen hours of looking at murdered children and she'd be upset that the new drapes for the living room didn't quite match the carpet. I tried more than once to explain it to her, but when I told the unvarnished truth, she didn't want to know. Who would, if they didn't have to? She had to shut all that out, and I got shut out with it."

"Do you blame her for that?"

"No. It showed she had good survival instincts. It's a lot healthier not to let those things into your head, because once they're in, you can't ever get them out. You know. You've probably seen more hell than I have."

"I don't think you can quantify hell. But I know what you mean about communicating it. I've spent my whole career trying to do it, and I sometimes wonder if I've succeeded even once. The pictures I've put on film don't convey a fraction of the horror of the pictures in my head."

Kaiser's eyes hold an empathy I haven't seen in a very long time. "So here we sit," he says. "Damaged goods."

What I feel for this man is not infatuation, or some neuro-chemical attraction that compels me to sleep with him. It's a simple intimacy that I've felt from the hour we first rode together in the rented Mustang. He has an easiness – and also a wariness – that draws me to him. John Kaiser has looked into the deep dark and is still basically all right, which is a rare thing. I don't look to men for protection, but I know I would feel as safe with this man as it is possible to feel.

"So, you want kids," he says, picking up last night's conversation from the Camellia Grill. I think of my niece and nephew, and curse their father for screwing up my time with them.

"Yes, I do."

"You're what, forty now?"

"Yep. Have to start pretty soon."

"You thinking about the Jodie Foster solution? Finding a donor you like?"

"Not my style. Do you want kids?"

He looks back at me, his eyes twinkling. He's clearly enjoying himself. "Yes."

"How many?"

"One a year for five or six years."

My stomach flips over. "I guess that lets me out of the race."

"I'm kidding. Two would be nice, though."

"I might be able to handle two."

After a few silent moments, he says, "What the hell are we talking about?"

"The stress, maybe. We're both under a lot of pressure. I've seen that start relationships before. They don't usually end well. You think that's what's happening here?"

"No. I've been under worse pressure than this without reaching for the nearest woman."

"That's good to know." I look him in the eye, hoping to read his instinctive response to what I'm about to say. "Maybe we should spend the night in this bed together. If we're still happy in the morning, you can pop the question."

He barks a laugh. "Jesus! Were you always like this?"

"No, but I'm getting too old to waste time." An absurd image of Agent Wendy Travis comes into my mind: she's crouching on her bed next door, her ear pressed to a drinking glass that she's pressed against my bedroom wall. "If you're just up here to get laid, I think you'll have better luck next door."

His smile vanishes. "I like this room just fine."

I prop my elbows on my knees and set my chin in my hands, which puts my eyes inches from his. "Are we nuts?"

"No. Sometimes you just know."

"I think so too." I let my right hand fall forward and touch his lower lip. "So, what are you thinking about?"

"What your hair smells like." He reaches out and touches my hair at the shoulder, and I suddenly wish it were longer for him. "What your mouth tastes like."

"I suspect you're wondering more than that."

"Yes. But it's hard to think about the conversation we just had as foreplay."

"We're both in strange businesses. You know what they say."

"What's that?" he asks.

"Embrace the weirdness."

"Who says that?"

"I don't know. Hunter Thompson, maybe. Just lean over here and kiss me."

Instead, he takes hold of my wrists and pulls me to my feet, which brings my face to the level of his chest. Then he slips his arms around my waist and looks down at me but does not kiss me. He peers into my eyes and pulls my waist to his, which leaves me in no doubt about his need for me. My skin feels hot and tight, itches for the flow of cool air or the touch of his skin. I'm thinking of taking his hand and placing it over my breast when it finds its way there on its own, as though moved by the impulse in my mind. He gives me a gentle squeeze, as if to say, *Here we are. We are real in this space, and aren't we lucky to be here?* Then he lowers his face and touches his lips to mine. My heart thumps against my sternum, as I knew it would, but it's nice to have my instinct confirmed.

"How long do we have?" I ask.

"All night."

"That's the right answer." I kiss him again, opening my mouth to his. Then I pull back. "Maybe I should start using your first name now."

His eyes shine with delight. "Whatever you want."

"We'll make the first occasion momentous. Ready?"

"Ready."

"Make love to me, John."

He smiles, then lifts me into his arms the way they do in old cowboy movies, and I sense the strength in his body. I expect to be lowered onto the bed, but instead he carries me into the bathroom.

"It's been a long day. You'd like me better after a shower."

"Or maybe during one," I reply, laughing.

He laughs and sets me on the counter, then turns the shower taps. Steam begins to fill the room as he takes off his shoes.

"Jesus, I forgot this."

There's a rip of Velcro, and then he's holding a small revolver in a ballistic nylon holster. The sight of the gun makes something inside me go cold.

313

"This is for you," he says. "It's a Smith and Wesson thirty-eight-caliber featherweight. You know how to use it?"

"Yes."

"Good. I'll put it out on the desk."

When he returns, I try to shake off the weight of dark memories. "You know what I like about American hotels?" I ask.

"What?" he asks, putting his hands on my knees.

"The unlimited supply of hot water. You can take a two-hour shower if you want to."

"Ever done it?"

"You better believe it. When I land in the U.S. after coming in from the Middle East or Africa, I open a cool bottle of white wine and just sit on the floor of the shower until I wrinkle into a prune."

"Well, then. I'd better take a quick look before you hit the prune stage." He takes the hem of my T-shirt in his hands and waits for me to lift my arms. I smile and oblige, and he slips off the shirt, then unbuttons his own and pulls my chest to his. This time I initiate the kiss, and he breaks it only to say, "I think the water's ready."

I wriggle out of my jeans, pleased by the fact that I feel no shyness in front of him, and step toward the curtain. As he slips off his trousers, his eyes take me in from head to toe.

"You're beautiful, Jordan."

The truth of his belief is plain in his face. "I feel beautiful right now."

He takes my hand, then pulls back the curtain and helps me into the tub. Even though I showered only hours ago, the shock of the hot water is wonderful, and having him under it with me even better. He soaps my back, and I soap his. Then we soap fronts, which is much more interesting.

I put my arms around his waist and pull him against me, which requires some adjustment on his part.

"It's been a pretty long time for me," I tell him.

"For me, too."

"That's what Wendy tells me."

"What?"

"She says all the women at the field office lust after you, but you haven't given in to one of them."

"You know what I like about showers in good hotels?" he asks with a teasing smile. "The nozzles are high enough for me to get my head under them."

"I see. Well. Are you too tall to put your head down here where it can do some good?"

He laughs, then leans down and gently kisses my breast, his tongue cool against my nipple in the steam. I reach down and run a fingernail along him.

"Are you in agony?"

"Mm-hmm," he moans.

"Good."

As the hot spray pours over my face and neck, one of his hands flattens in the small of my back, and the other searches lower. Then he is murmuring in his throat, passing the vibration into me. I lean back against one hand and settle upon the other, and in this exquisite embrace feel myself becoming as liquid as the water. His lips slide up my neck to my chin, then my mouth, and then a clamorous ringing shocks us motionless.

"Fire alarm?" he asks, but the sound dies.

"Bathroom phone."

"Who the hell is that?"

"Fifty bucks says it's Wendy."

It rings again, a maddening klaxon in the tiled cubicle. He sighs. "You'd better answer it."

I reach around the curtain and dry my hand, then pick up the phone.

"Hello?"

"Jordan, it's Daniel Baxter."

I mouth "Baxter" to John, who quickly turns off the water.

"What's going on?"

"Ah . . . is John up there with you?"

"Just a second, the TV's too loud." I press my hand over the transmitter. "He wants to talk to you."

"My cell phone battery must have died."

"Or you just didn't hear it. Which would mean Baxter knew to try my room second."

John shrugs. "He's not stupid."

"You want me to say you're not here?"

He shakes his head and takes the phone. "What's up, boss?"

As he listens, his eyes flick back and forth with growing intensity. "When?" he asks. Then he listens some more, and I see in his face that we won't be spending the night in each other's arms. Something terrible has happened. "I'll be right there," he says. "Right. I'll leave Wendy in the room with her." He hangs up, his eyes cloudy with confusion.

"What?" I ask, fighting my rising fears. "They found bodies? They found my sister?"

"No." He takes my hands in his. "Thalia Laveau has disappeared. Daniel thinks she's been taken by the UNSUB."

Nausea rolls through my stomach. "*Thalia?* But she was under surveillance."

"She purposefully evaded it."

"*What?*"

"He wouldn't give me the details over an unsecure

316

phone. I won't know anything more till I get there. Jesus, why her?"

Several answers come to me, but all I can think of is John's use of the singular pronoun. "Till *I* get there? What was that about leaving Wendy in the room with me?"

His eyes don't waver, and if he tells me I'm not going back to the office with him – that in essence I am good enough to sleep with but not to take into a meeting where I may not be wanted by some people – my mouth and breast are the only parts of me he will ever taste.

"Get your clothes on," he says. "You're coming."

I don't move, and neither does he. Standing naked in the tub with water dripping off us, Baxter's revelation doesn't seem quite real. But it is. And I have the strange sensation that once we step out of this tub, it may be a long time before we're this intimate again.

"You okay?" he asks, touching my cheek.

"I guess. What about you? Can you wait until whenever we get back here?"

He nods, but his heart is not in his answer.

"Do we have thirty seconds to spare?"

He nods again.

"Stay here."

On the counter by the sink is a sampler pack of soap, shampoo, conditioner, and hand lotion. I uncap the lotion and get back into the tub.

"I'm breaking one of my own rules," I tell him, "but you can pay me back later."

He groans as I close my moistened hands around him, but in the few seconds it takes him to lose consciousness, my head fills with images of the empathetic woman I met this afternoon, the semi-lesbian Sabine artist, Thalia Laveau, and my heart balloons with terror for her, a woman who fled her home and family to escape sexual abuse, who is now at the mercy of a man without mercy, a woman I am unlikely ever to see again.

The Emergency Operations Center, which has been kept from me until now, is the pounding heart of the NOKIDS investigation. It's huge – more than three thousand square feet – with long rows of tables marching toward the front of the room, like a high school science lab built to heroic scale. Behind each row of tables sit rows of men and women with banks of phones before them, the unused ones showing bright red decals reading "NOT SECURE!"

John posts Wendy at the door, then leads me into the EOC. Wendy was quiet during the ride over, and even when John tried to draw her into our conversation, her answers were clipped and professional. I felt for her, but there's more to worry about now than hurt feelings. As John and I reach the first table, at least twenty faces turn to mine, then look at each other with puzzlement. The unspoken question might as well be painted on the air: *What the hell is she doing in here?* But after a few seconds, they go back to their work.

At the front of the Operations Center, facing the tables, is an array of oversized computer monitors showing views of various buildings. The buildings are the residences of the four main suspects, plus the Woldenberg Art Center at Tulane. As I watch, a car drives past Frank Smith's cottage on Esplanade. I'm looking at live television surveillance of various parts of New Orleans. Beyond the monitors hangs a massive wall-mounted screen with lines of type scrolling down it a few clicks at a time. There are time notations beside each line. It's an unfolding timeline of the entire investigation-in-progress, reporting everything from the movements and phone calls of the suspects to the activities of the various law-enforcement agencies investigating Thalia Laveau's disappearance. I feel like I'm standing in the headquarters of Big Brother in Orwell's *1984*.

"So this is it," I say softly. "Where are Baxter and Lenz?"

"Baxter's right here," says a voice behind me.

"As is Lenz," says the psychiatrist.

"Joined at the hip," I say, turning to face them.

The ISU chief looks as though he hasn't slept for thirty-six hours. The dark circles under his eyes have become black bags, and his skin has a prison pallor. He gives John a reproving glance but voices no displeasure at my presence. Dr. Lenz appears to have changed suits and freshened up since this afternoon; he probably had an agent chauffeur him over to the Windsor Court for tea and scones and a midnight rubdown.

"How did she do it?" asks John.

"I'll show you," Baxter replies.

He walks up to a technician near the monitors and says something, then returns. One of the screens goes dark, and then we're looking at a frontal view of the Victorian house in which Thalia rented rooms. It's night, and sheets of rain cloud the view. As we watch, a woman wearing a floppy hat and carrying an umbrella runs out of the house and gets into a white Nissan Sentra parked on the puddled street.

"That's Jo Ann Diggs," says Baxter, "one of the women who rents a room on Laveau's floor."

The Sentra pulls quickly away from the curb, but a few yards down the street it skids to an abrupt stop, then backs up. Diggs gets out, runs back to the house, and disappears inside, looking for all the world like a woman who forgot her purse or the DVD she was supposed to return to Blockbuster. About twenty seconds later, she hurries back out of the house with a book in her hand, trots to her car, and drives away.

"That," says Baxter, "was Thalia Laveau."

"The roommate helped her," says John.

"Laveau was waiting just inside the door. She took the hat and umbrella and ran out to Diggs's car, while Diggs went back up to Laveau's apartment and watched television to cover."

"How did you figure it out?" I ask.

"Earlier today, Laveau called a woman friend from the campus and made an appointment to meet her at eleven tonight. The woman lives on Lake Avenue, on the Orleans–Jefferson Parish line. When Laveau didn't show by midnight, the friend called the NOPD. NOPD called us."

"The woman claimed Laveau was coming over for tea and sympathy," says Lenz, "but obviously it was more than that. She evaded our surveillance to protect her lover's identity."

"Maybe it wasn't sexuality she was hiding," says John. "Laveau could be involved strictly as the painter. Today's police interrogation could have scared her enough to make her bolt. By setting up a meeting with this other woman, then missing it, she leads us to conclude that she's become a victim."

Baxter starts to speak, but exasperation makes me jump in first. "You guys need a woman on your team around the clock."

"Why is that?" asks Lenz.

"To keep your heads out of your asses. I'm going back to my hotel. You don't have a prayer of finding Thalia with this kind of thinking."

"John," says Baxter. "Arthur wasn't guessing. Laveau did evade the surveillance to protect this woman. She's gay but very private. They had a long-standing relationship. Only her fear for Laveau made her tell us the truth. She can alibi Thalia not only for the Dorignac's snatch, but also for at least five of the other abductions."

I shake my head, fighting unexpected tears of helplessness.

"I'm sorry," John says. "I can't help thinking that way. It's a habit, working out the logic."

"It's not you," I tell him.

Neither Baxter nor Lenz speaks, and I'm not sure whether it's because of my tears or because they sense our new intimacy.

"I think I have to go."

I walk past them toward the wide door, but Baxter calls after me. "What would you do, Jordan? To find Thalia?"

I stop and turn, but I don't go back to them. "I'd assume the obvious. One of the male suspects has been lusting after Thalia from the start. Our questioning rattled him. He knows it's a matter of time before he's nailed. Faced with that, he decides he has nothing to lose by indulging himself with Thalia."

"All three were under round-the-clock surveillance," says Lenz.

"Thalia didn't have any trouble eluding it."

Baxter sighs and turns to John. "Frank Smith was in a restaurant at the time Laveau left her house, and afterward. It couldn't be him."

"Wheaton and Gaines?"

"Gaines was at his shotgun on Freret. By the way, forensics says his van was clean. No blood, hair, fibers, nothing. Like it was steam-cleaned in the last day or two."

John nods suspiciously, but his mind has already gone past this information. "What about Wheaton?"

"Wheaton was painting at the Woldenberg Center."

"What about Jordan's idea of natural light? Have we got aerial shots of all the courtyards or enclosed gardens in the city?"

"That's just not practical," says Baxter. "This city stretches over two hundred square miles, and that's being conservative. The killing house – or painting house, I guess – could be anywhere in that area, and owned under a name we can't possibly trace to one of the suspects."

"The painter wouldn't want to drive twenty miles every time he wanted to work on a painting. It's human nature. He wouldn't want to drive any farther than he absolutely has to."

"Granted," says Lenz.

"Wheaton and Gaines live within a mile of the university. Frank Smith lives at the edge of the French Quarter. Let's get aerial photos of every square block of those areas, and throw in the Garden District. Then we'll look for sheltered courtyards where the painter would have good natural light."

"The leaves are still on the goddamn trees," Baxter argues. "We could miss a hundred courtyards in the French Quarter alone."

"Then get architectural plans!" John snaps. "We should have agents at the courthouse doing title searches on every building in those two areas. We may find some connection to one of the suspects."

Baxter looks around the Operations Center, and two dozen shocked faces quickly turn back to their work.

"I guess that's all we've got," he says. "Other than Wheaton's nocturnal visits to Frank Smith."

"And we're on that in the morning," John says with a tone of finality.

322

I do believe the man wants to come back to the hotel with me. I just might forgive him his earlier fuzzy thinking about Thalia Laveau.

But Daniel Baxter has other ideas.

"John, you coordinate with the aerial surveillance unit. If you start making calls now, you can have the assets in the air at first light."

This is obviously a job someone else could do, but John has no trouble reading Baxter's intent. He nods wearily, then glances my way with a look of apology.

"What time are we talking to Smith and Wheaton?" I ask.

"Be here by eight a.m.," Baxter replies. "Agent Travis will drive you over."

The informality of "Wendy" has disappeared. Baxter obviously foresees potential conflicts developing out of the intimacy between John and me.

"Eight, then."

I feel a strangely proprietary urge to give John a kiss on the cheek, but he'd probably faint from embarrassment, so I spare him.

"If you want those pictures to be worth the trouble," I tell Baxter, "you should get your planes up tonight with thermal imaging cameras. Brick and stone will have enough temperature differential with trees and foliage to make plant cover irrelevant. You can shoot the same grids in the morning with infrared film for backup detail. By nine-twenty, you should have sunlight at thirty degrees on both horizons, but not much cloud cover. That's the best time."

While the three men stare in amazement, I say, "Good night, boys," and walk to the door where Wendy awaits.

19

New Orleans steams in the morning after rain. Even with a nip of fall in the air, the humidity wilts starched collars almost on contact. On this wet morning, Dr. Lenz has decided that he wants me in on the second Wheaton interview after all. I'm not sure why, and I didn't have time to question him about it. When I arrived at the field office, the building was besieged by camera crews. Sometime before the early news shows ran, the sheriff of Jefferson Parish announced to reporters that his office, working closely with the FBI, had developed strong suspects in the series of kidnappings that had plagued the city for over a year. Thalia Laveau's disappearance has already started a new wave of panic across the city.

This morning's interview will not happen at Tulane's Woldenberg Art Center, where we last met Wheaton. Today we're parked in front of the artist's temporary residence on Audubon Place, a private street adjoining the Tulane campus. Audubon Place has a massive iron gate complete with stone guardhouse in the tradition of World War II blockhouses, and the massive homes that line it stand out even compared to those on St. Charles Avenue, which Audubon Place intersects. The one Roger Wheaton occupies is owned by a wealthy Tulane alumnus who's been living abroad for two years. It's a palatial house that, combined with the lot and its location, looks like about two million dollars of real estate. But that's here. In San Francisco the place would cost nine million.

John, Lenz, and I approach the front door together. Before we reach it, Roger Wheaton walks onto his porch in blue pajama pants, a Tulane sweatshirt, his wire-rimmed bifocals, and his trademark white cotton gloves.

"I saw you through the window," he says as we mount the steps to the front gallery. "I saw a report on television about an hour ago. Has Thalia really disappeared?"

"I'm afraid so," says John. "May we come in?"

"Of course."

Wheaton leads us through a foyer into a magnificently appointed drawing room. With his long frame, pajamas, and too-long hair, he looks incongruous in the luxurious chair into which he folds himself. Only his white gloves fit the room, giving him the appearance of a newly wakened reveler sober enough to have removed his tux after a Mardi Gras ball, but too drunk to have remembered to remove his gloves. But the gloves are no accoutrements of style; they are soft armor for hands that cannot function in the slightest cold. John and I sit together on a sofa opposite the artist, and Lenz takes a chair to our right.

"Hello, again," Wheaton says as I sit, his long face conveying silent grief. "Are you taking more photographs today?"

"I wish I was. You're a wonderful subject."

"We just came from working another case," says Lenz. "Agent Travis was with us, and we didn't want to leave her in the car."

Agent Travis? Why am I really here? Is Lenz testing Wheaton's reaction to me yet again?

"Gentlemen," says the artist, "do you believe Thalia was taken by the same person who took the others?"

325

"Yes," says John. "We do."

Wheaton sighs and closes his eyes. "I was very angry yesterday, because of the invasion of my privacy. The police caused me considerable inconvenience, and they weren't even civil. All that seems a small thing now. What do you require of me?"

John looks at Lenz, who decides to lead with his chin.

"Mr. Wheaton, we're told you've made several lengthy visits to the private residence of one of your students, Frank Smith."

Wheaton's face tightens. This was clearly the last thing he expected to hear.

"Did Frank tell you that?"

Lenz does not respond directly. "We're also told that you argued vehemently with him on these occasions. We'd very much like to know the reason for these visits, and for the arguments."

Wheaton shakes his head and looks away, his desire to help apparently gone, or at least tempered by disgust. "I can't help you with that."

John and Lenz look at each other.

"All I can do is assure you that those visits have nothing whatever to do with the crimes you're investigating. You'll have to trust me that far."

I'm sure suspects must frequently refuse to answer FBI questions, but it's hard to imagine them doing it with such sincerity and gentility. I'd feel almost embarrassed to insist at this point. But Lenz doesn't.

"I'm afraid in these circumstances," he says, "your word as a gentleman will not be enough."

Wheaton gives Lenz a look hard enough to validate his history as a combat soldier. "I understand the urgency," he says quietly. "But I can't answer your question."

John glances at me as though seeking help, but I don't see any way to spur the artist into further revelations.

"Mr. Wheaton," says Lenz, "I personally dislike having to bother a man of your stature with intrusive questions. However, the situation is grave. And I can assure you that all answers you give will be held in the strictest confidence."

This, of course, is a bald-faced lie. Wheaton doesn't respond.

"I am a psychiatrist," Lenz says, with apparent faith that this assertion should win the day. "I also don't believe what you're hiding is anything to be ashamed of."

The artist looks at me with his clear eyes and says, "Why are *you* really here?"

"I am a photographer, Mr. Wheaton, but I don't work for the FBI. And my name isn't Travis. My sister was one of the victims of whoever is taking these women. She disappeared last year, and I've been hunting for her ever since."

Wheaton's lips part in amazement. "I'm so sorry. What is your name?"

"Jordan Glass."

"Jordan Glass. Well, let me assure you, Ms. Glass, before I ask these men to leave, that if I had information which could possibly help those women, I wouldn't hesitate to give it to you. I hope you believe that."

I do believe him, and I tell him so.

John gives me a dark look. "Mr. Wheaton," he says, "I appreciate your desire for privacy. But it might be that you have information you aren't qualified to judge the importance of."

Wheaton looks at the ceiling and lets his gloved hands fall beside the chair. "You're saying I might possess information that proves Frank Smith is behind these disappearances and not know it?"

"It's possible."

"It's *not* possible. Frank couldn't have anything to do with these crimes." Wheaton's face is red now, and he fixes John with his deep-set eyes. "However, because Ms. Glass has made me acutely aware of the stakes in this case, I will tell you something that's been bothering me since we last spoke. I hesitated before, because Leon makes such an easy target. He's often unpleasant, but I think he had a tough childhood, and sometimes that's the result."

Lenz is practically licking his chops.

"On the few occasions when I brought my graduate students together," says Wheaton, "both at the university and here at this house, I observed Leon making inappropriate remarks to Thalia. He also touches her without any sort of permission."

"What kind of remarks?" asks John.

"Overt sexual remarks. Things like, 'You look like you know your way around a Cajun hot link, Mama.' It sounds ridiculous, doesn't it? But that's the kind of thing Leon says. I've seen him say similar things to female undergrads. But with Thalia, it was something more. Once I saw him wait for her by her car. It was several weeks ago, around dusk."

"What happened?"

"She handled him with the firmness she always used. Thalia is a beautiful girl, and she seemed accustomed to putting off that kind of attention."

"She drove away alone on that occasion?"

"Yes. I think Leon kept at her because he knew she posed nude for a graduate painting class. He took this as some sort of sexual advertising."

He would, I think.

"Do you recall anything else between the two of them?" asks John. "Something odd or awkward?"

Wheaton looks reluctant to continue. "On a couple of occasions, as I left the art center, I saw Leon following Thalia across the quad."

"Closely, or from a distance?"

"From far enough back to avoid easy detection. As though he meant to follow her a long way. That could be an incorrect assumption on my part. They could both have simply been headed for the University Center."

"But that wasn't your impression," says Lenz.

"No."

"You were right to tell us," says John.

"I hope so. I strongly believe in the right to privacy, as I've already made plain." Wheaton leans slowly forward. Then, as though the simple act scrapes cartilage from his knee joints, he stands. "And now, gentlemen, unless you have *another* warrant up your sleeves, I must ask you to leave. I need to go to work."

The artist folds his arms, and the white gloves disappear behind his biceps.

"Again, I hate to intrude," says Lenz. "But we're unclear on some biographical points in your life."

Wheaton bunches his brows in consternation.

"Published interviews say very little about your background beyond a certain point, but we know, for example, that you were reared in a rural part of Vermont. Windham County. Your father was a farmer?"

Wheaton sighs with irritation. "And a trapper."

"What did he trap?"

"Beaver, fox. He raised some mink, unsuccessfully."

"Thalia Laveau's father was a trapper, I believe?"

"Yes. That's something we shared stories about."

"Could you share some with us?"

"Not today."

"We also know your mother left home when you were thirteen or fourteen."

Wheaton looks ready to throw Lenz bodily from the house.

"I realize this is painful," says the psychiatrist. "But we need to know. Why did she leave without taking her children with her?"

Wheaton swallows and looks at the floor. "I don't know. My father believed she met a man and ran away with him. I never did. It's certainly possible that she fell in love with another man – my father was unpleasant, to be frank, far too coarse for Mother – but she would never have left me – us – behind."

My throat feels tight; pressed mercilessly by Lenz, Roger Wheaton is articulating my own deepest fear and hope.

"I think she put herself into a vulnerable situation," he says, "and something bad happened to her. And either my father didn't tell us about it, or no one knew who she really was. If she were hiding her identity to be with someone else – in New York, for example – I can see how it would happen."

"Was your father 'unpleasant' to the degree that he abused your mother?" asks Lenz.

"By today's standards? Undoubtedly. But this was the 1950s, the middle of nowhere."

"Did he abuse you and your brothers?"

Wheaton shrugs. "Again, by today's standards, yes. He hit us with a razor strop, birch rods, anything close to hand."

"What about sexual abuse?"

The artist's deep sigh conveys utter contempt for the psychiatrist. "Nothing of the kind." Wheaton wipes his forehead with a gloved hand. "Now, I really must insist that you go."

330

Lenz fires a last shot as he gets to his feet.

"Mr. Wheaton, would you simply tell us whether you're homosexual or not? It would prevent a lot of further prying into your life, bothering of your friends, et cetera."

Wheaton seems to sag under the weight of the question. "The answer is academic, I'm afraid. My disease rendered me impotent over two years ago." He looks at Lenz. "Do you have your pound of flesh now?"

The artist glances at me, and the wounded pride in his face makes me look at the floor.

"Thank you for your time," I say before Lenz can press him further. I back toward the hallway. "I appreciate your honesty about Gaines. It really might help find Thalia and my sister."

Wheaton steps forward and takes my hand between his two white gloves. "I hope so. Is there really some hope that they're still alive?"

"Not much. But some."

He nods. "Maybe someday I'll find a way to explain why I couldn't answer the other question. So you'll know I did all I could. I care a great deal for Thalia. She's a wounded soul. You call me if you need to talk, or if you'd like to take more photographs. I'd like to paint you. We could do an exchange."

"I thought you only painted landscapes."

"I was quite a portraitist in the old days." He laughs. "It kept me in pea soup and ramen noodles."

"How is your painting coming? The final Clearing? It looked almost finished when I saw it."

"I'm very close. A day, maybe two. The president had to close the gallery. Word has leaked out that I'm nearly done, and all manner of people are showing up to gawk. Reporters, students, collectors. Soon I'll attach the final canvas panel to the circle, which means you'll have to climb scaffolding and descend a ladder to get inside. It'll be a relief to have it done."

"I would like you to paint me sometime. I'd like to see how you see me."

"Frank would do a more professional job, but I might see you more honestly than he."

John and Lenz watch Wheaton as though each word and gesture are fragments of some code.

"Well, thanks." I gently shake his hand.

"Thank you, my dear." Wheaton moves from the door so that John and Lenz can get into the hall. "Goodbye, gentlemen."

Dr. Lenz tries to shake the artist's hand, but Wheaton takes a step backward and gives him a tight smile. Then the three of us are outside again, walking toward the FBI sedan parked on the street.

"He just told us to go to hell," says John.

"Very smoothly," Lenz agrees. "But he certainly pointed his finger at Gaines."

"After saying nothing yesterday. I wonder why."

"He told you why," I say irritably. "He doesn't like talking about anybody's personal business. Even an asshole like Gaines. He knows the FBI will turn Gaines's life into a living hell because of what he just told you."

"Yes," Lenz says thoughtfully. "He does."

"What did you think about his answers about his mother?" asks John.

Lenz adopts his professorial tone. "He doesn't know why she left, but he can't let it be because she loved a paramour more than her children. As for childhood abuse . . . I don't know. Denial is classic adaptive behavior. Without more time with him . . . I'll have to think about that one."

John opens the front door of the car, holds it for me, and looks into my eyes. "I hope you have better luck with Frank Smith."

"I make my own luck."

He smiles. "I believe you. They faulted Smith's phones, both home and cell. No warning from Wheaton this time. You still want to go in alone?"

"Absolutely."

"Let's get to the Quarter, then."

The medical tape holding the T-4 transmitter at the small of my back chafes as I climb the steps of the Creole cottage on Esplanade and knock at Frank Smith's door. From the transmitter, a thin wire runs around my ribs and up to a microphone clipped to the V of my bra. This time the door isn't answered by Juan but by the owner himself. Frank Smith smiles broadly, revealing the gleaming white teeth of an affluent childhood, and leans against the doorjamb with languid grace.

"Is this visit social? Or government business?"

"I wish I could say the former, but it's not."

Smith arches his perfectly plucked eyebrows. "Well, then I don't think I'm at home."

His movie-star handsomeness is starting to irritate me. "Have you watched any TV this morning?"

"No."

"Read the *Times-Picayune*?"

"I took a long bath and had coffee in the garden. That's the sum of my morning. Why?"

"May I come in?"

His sea-green eyes narrow. "Don't tell me he's taken another one."

"Thalia Laveau."

333

Smith looks confused. "What about Thalia?"

"He took Thalia. Last night."

This is the first time I've seen Frank Smith lose his perfect control.

"May I please come in?"

He steps out of my way, and I walk inside. Instead of waiting for him to lead me to the salon, I walk through the house and make my way to the garden. The fountain that filled the courtyard with sound yesterday is switched off now, and a blackbird perches on the highest tier. There's a small wrought-iron table under the gnarled wisteria, and I take a seat there. Smith sits across the table from me. In his fine trousers and royal blue polo shirt, he looks less like an artist than a model, but there's no denying the quick intelligence in his eyes.

"How could Thalia be kidnapped when she was under surveillance?" he asks.

"Why do you think she was under surveillance?"

"Well, *I* am. Where are your FBI friends today?"

"Working."

"But they sent you here. To ask me something. Because I responded to you yesterday."

"I asked to come alone."

He mulls my answer. "So, I'm still a suspect. What is it you want to know?"

I quickly explain that the Bureau knows Roger Wheaton spent several evenings at this house, and also that he and Smith argued on some or all of those occasions.

"I wondered why Juan didn't show up this morning," Smith says. "I suppose they threatened to deport him?"

"I don't know what they did, Frank. I'm sorry. And I don't like butting into your personal business. But this is life

334

or death. Thalia could still be alive, and we have to try to help her."

"Do you really believe that?"

"That she could still be alive? Yes."

"I'm glad. But what you're asking has nothing to do with this case."

"That's what Wheaton said."

Smith turns up his palms as if to say, *Next subject.*

"Look, it seems to me there could only be a couple of innocent reasons for holding out. One, Wheaton is gay, and you guys have a relationship."

"And two?"

"I can't think of a second. Drugs, maybe. I think the first reason is it."

Smith is wearing a smug smile.

"And if it is, admitting it is the quicket way to get the FBI out of your life. They honestly don't care what you or Wheaton do for sex. What worries them is other possibilities."

"Like?"

"Like you being involved in a conspiracy to produce the Sleeping Women."

"Ridiculous."

"I think so too. But I don't run the FBI. Come on, Frank. What's the deal? Is Roger Wheaton gay?"

"Have you asked him?"

"He evaded the question."

"Well he would, wouldn't he?"

"Why would he?"

"Roger grew up in rural Vermont. He's fifty-eight years old, for God's sake. He's another generation altogether."

"You're saying he's gay?"

"Of course he is."

Of course he is. . . .

Smith runs a manicured fingernail along the wrought-iron scrollwork in the tabletop. "He's simply not comfortable with the kind of attention that comes with being gay and famous."

"Are you and he lovers?"

Smith shakes his head with what looks like regret. "No."

"Then how do you know he's gay? He told you?"

"Roger ran away to New York when he was seventeen or eighteen. How do you think he lived? Certainly not by selling his paintings."

"Are you saying he sold himself?"

"We all sell ourselves, in one way or another. Here was this talented, handsome kid schlepping his derivative paintings around to all the galleries. He got noticed, but not for the paintings. Before long, the old queens were fighting to give him a place to live and work. They took care of him until he joined the marines."

"You seem to know more about him than anyone else."

"Roger confided these things because he knew I would understand. And I'm telling you so that you'll do all you can to get the FBI off his back. His life is hard enough without that."

"I agree. And I will. But I'm not completely clear here. If the visits were about friendship, what were the arguments about? The yelling?"

Smith shakes his head again. "I can't answer that. The FBI can't know about that."

"Jesus, Frank. I won't give them details. I'll just tell them I'm satisfied that the arguments and visits mean nothing."

"I can't do it."

Filled with frustration, but also understanding Smith's

reluctance to violate Wheaton's privacy, I lean forward, pull the tail of my blouse out of my jeans, and rip the medical tape from the skin of my back. As the transmitter falls against the iron seat of my chair, I picture Daniel Baxter panicking in the surveillance van outside. I hope he has the sense not to come charging in with his gun drawn.

"I'm switching off," I say loudly. "Don't come in."

Smith gapes as I reach into my blouse and pull the tiny mike from my bra, unthread the wire, then drop the transmitter on the table between us and switch it off.

"We're no longer live, Frank. It's you and me."

He looks ready to throw me out of his house.

"Listen to me," I say with the conviction of my own pain. "My sister has two small children that she loves more than her life. She was yanked off the street by some predator, and she's probably rotting in the swamp somewhere right now. There are eleven other women just like her, one of them a friend you say you cared for and admired. The clock is ticking down on Thalia's life. Is it an invasion of privacy for the FBI to learn Roger Wheaton is gay? Yes. Is it a tragedy? No. If your arguments with Wheaton have nothing to do with this case, all the effort the FBI puts into investigating them is wasted. Do you want that wasted effort to cost Thalia her life?"

"I think you're exaggerating my importance."

"Bullshit! The FBI doesn't have much to work with, and they won't drop this angle until they understand it. Tell me the truth about the arguments, and if it's innocent, I'll tell them to leave you the hell alone."

Smith closes his eyes, takes a long breath, then expels it slowly and opens his eyes again. The look in them tells me this man does not easily grant trust. "You give me your word not to reveal this to the FBI if it's not relevant to the case?"

"Christ, you want me to pinky-swear? I'm not telling them anything they don't need to know to help my sister. I don't even like them. But they're the only hope those women and their families have."

Smith sighs and looks over at the old slave quarters that form one wall of his garden. A faint scent of lemon drifts into my nostrils.

"It's simple," he says. "Roger wants me to kill him."

A rush of heat passes over my face. "What?"

"His disease is steadily worsening. It's in his lungs now, and his other vital organs. The end will be . . . unpleasant. He wants my help when the time comes."

I feel like slinking away in shame. Suddenly everything is clear, Wheaton's reticence most of all. If the artist's wish to have Frank Smith help end his life became known to the NOPD, that might stop Smith from risking his freedom to comply, no matter where his sympathies lie.

"You get it now?" asks Smith.

"Part of it. But why the arguments? You refused to help him?"

"That's right. I thought Roger might be motivated by clinical depression. I thought he had a lot of great paintings left in him. I still think so." Smith gives me a weary look, as though concealing the truth is no longer worth the effort. "But he's wearing me down, honestly. He's shown me his medical records, not to mention his body, and I'm starting to understand how grave his situation is. Assisted suicide will get you ten years in this state, so it's not a decision I can make lightly."

"I understand."

Smith looks skeptical. "Do you?"

An awful flash of memory lights my mind. "I once saw an Afghan guerrilla ask his brother to kill him to keep him

338

from being captured. He'd been wounded during a raid on a Russian outpost. It was total confusion, people running around in the dark, Russian soldiers screaming, Afghans howling curses, and this poor half-starved guy shot in the hip. He couldn't walk, and they couldn't carry him through the mountains. He begged his brother to end it for him, but the brother couldn't do it. The others huddled beside the trail and talked; the Russians were getting closer; finally a cousin went back and cut the guy's throat while the others prayed. I heard the cousin sobbing as we climbed back into the mountains."

"What an encouraging story."

"I'm sorry. I'm just . . . I know it's a hard thing. How did he want you to help him? Did he have a method in mind?"

"How could it help you to know that?"

"I don't know. I'm curious, I guess."

"Insulin."

"Insulin?"

"It's a peaceful way to go, he says. He's researched it. Sleep, coma, then death. The problem is that sometimes you don't die. You just get brain damage."

"That's why he needed your help?"

"Yes. He wanted me to find some drug that would stop his heart after the coma. This was after I told him I wasn't putting a plastic bag over his head and watching him turn blue."

"Jesus. Okay. I'll tell the FBI they're barking up the wrong tree."

"Thank you." Smith forces a smile. "Would you like something to drink now? Coffee? A Bloody Mary?"

"I could use a drink, but I should go." I stand and gather up the transmitter, microphone, and sticky tape. "Look, the Jefferson Parish sheriff leaked to the media that we have suspects. He didn't name names, but you might want to get ready for that. Get a hotel room or something."

Smith shakes his head in exasperation. "I'll do that. Right after I call my lawyer and tell him to get ready to sue the shit out of the government."

He stands, takes my arm, then leads me back through the house. As we pass the dining room, I glance in at his nude portrait of Oscar Wilde.

"I really like that picture."

"Thanks."

Smith reaches for the doorknob, but I stop him by pulling my arm against my side. "Frank, tell me one thing. The brush hairs led the FBI to four suspects: you, Roger, Thalia, and Gaines. Thalia's out. If you had to pin it on Wheaton or Gaines, who would you pick?"

"Are you kidding? Was Leon under surveillance when Thalia was taken?"

"Yes."

"Hmm. Well. Roger too, of course?"

"Yes." A last, desperate thought pops into my head. "Has Wheaton ever told you he was abused as a child?"

Smith sighs angrily.

"I have a good reason for asking, I promise."

"He never told me anything like that. And if your next question is did I suffer anything like that, my answer is fuck you. All right?" He yanks open the door and stands clear of it. "Come again soon, now."

I walk out into the pale sunlight and damp yellow leaves of Esplanade, and the door closes behind me. It's been a long time since I felt this low. Probing private lives has never been my thing. All photojournalism is essentially exploitative, but in photography the act of invasion is mitigated by the wonderful speed of light, which lets you intrude from a distance. No messy questions or awkward silences; just click, click, click.

I turn toward the Mississippi River and start to walk, knowing that the FBI sedan bearing Baxter, Lenz, and John will come alongside at any moment. They'll be pissed that I pulled the wire, which is fine. I'm pissed that I've played the role of pawn in their dead-end investigation. I'd probably feel different if this morning's interviews had produced a lead, but they didn't.

The quiet hum of a motor announces my escorts. The sedan pulls up to the curb on my left and, when I don't stop, keeps pace as I walk. Baxter rolls down the passenger window, and I see Special Agent Wendy Travis driving the car. Her presence tells me John is tied up for the day, that I'm to be left under her watchful eyes yet again.

"Why did you kill the wire?" asks Baxter.

"You know why," I reply, looking straight ahead.

"What did he tell you?"

"He convinced me that Wheaton's visits there have nothing to do with the case."

Baxter glances into the backseat, where Lenz sits beside John. Then he looks back at me. "Do you think you're the best judge of that?"

"As good as any of you."

He turns to the backseat again, and I'm certain he's telling John to use his influence to get me to talk. Baxter may not like me being involved with his old profiler, but he doesn't mind exploiting the connection. I hope John knows better than to try.

The car stops, the back door opens, and John gets out. He walks to me, his eyes filled with concern.

"What do you want to do?" he asks softly. "Whatever you say, I'll make it happen."

"I want to walk."

"You want company?"

"No."

"You feel that Wheaton and Smith are both innocent, don't you?"

"Yes."

"Okay. I'm going to go back to the office and study the aerial photos of the courtyards. Call if you want to talk. Wendy has a cell phone."

I'm going to have company after all.

John squeezes my forearm, then motions to Wendy, who gets out wearing her usual Liz Claiborne skirt and jacket combo, the jacket there to hide her pistol. I resist the urge to say something smart; she's only doing her job as best she can. She falls into step a couple of yards behind me, and the sedan pulls forward and then passes us. As it recedes, I see John looking back at me over the rear seat, his eyes unreadable.

20

As I walk along the oak-shaded sidewalk of Esplanade, Agent Wendy trailing a few yards behind, my mind swirls with images I have no desire to ponder, and my stomach rolls with the low-level nausea I've felt since Dr. Lenz badgered Roger Wheaton into telling us his disease rendered him impotent years ago. Frank Smith's revelation of Wheaton's plea for euthanasia only made it worse. The impact of my shoes against the sidewalk offers a metronomic distraction from those thoughts, so I focus my mind on that.

From Esplanade I turn onto Royal Street, which farther on becomes the center of the antique trade in the Quarter, but here on the downriver end it's a peaceful lane of homes and shuttered warehouses. I spent a good deal of time walking this grid of streets when I moved here at seventeen, getting to know a world at once seamier and more exotic than the provincial one I left in north Mississippi. Two decades later the sights, smells, and sounds are the same. Ornate wrought-iron balconies laden with ferns and flags climb the faces of pastel buildings, not so bright as those in the Caribbean, but festive in their stately way; the aromas of baking bread and simmering gumbo drift from the direction of St. Philip Street; and shouted cries of the urban New Orleans patois collide with rapid precise French spoken by tourists standing on the corner of Ursulines.

Just three blocks to my left, beyond Decatur Street and the levee, rolls the Mississippi River, where great ships bob higher than the roofs of the buildings. I feel myself drawn toward it, but since the water is blocked by the wharf at the end of Ursulines, I stay on Royal, walking at a native's clip. My inner ear confirms what I have long known, that I am below sea level, walking in a world that exists only provisionally, that a hurricane making landfall here would spill the lake and the river into the Quarter like a great bowl and cover everything from the Lucky Dog men to the tourist traps of Bourbon Street, leaving only cathedral spires, Andy Jackson on his horse, and screeching gulls circling the electrical towers.

At St. Philip I break left, making for the river. Wendy's flats go staccato as she moves to keep pace with me. The sound of a slide guitar jangles from the doorway of the Babylon Club, and with every step the Quarter grows more commercial. There are restaurants and pubs now, lawyers' offices, small hotels. Yet still the odd doorway leads down a tunnel that opens onto a secluded courtyard, beckoning with the promise of midnight trysts and masked soirees. I shudder in sudden awareness that the Sleeping Women may have been painted in one of these courtyards. How strange to know that last night, while the people down here drank and laughed and loved and slept, government planes crisscrossed the sky above, shooting thermal images of the buildings, searching for a garden private enough in which to paint a dead woman without interruption.

Joan of Arc awaits me at the Place de France, a little concrete island in the traffic. She sits high on a golden horse, holding a golden flag against the gray clouds, an imperfect monument to a woman who overstepped what those in power saw as her place; an honest monument would show her burning at the stake. Wendy moves alongside me here, for suddenly we are awash in a sea of humanity, surging waves of tourists and cars and French Market merchants hawking vegetables, coffee, and strange souvenirs. I can smell the river now, a muddy, fetid scent on the cool air. Slipping between two fat cream-colored columns, I trot up some flagstone steps, and then I'm looking over a narrow parking lot at the levee and the booms of a freighter whose red-painted waterline floats at the level of my eyes.

"Where are we going?" asks Wendy.

"The river. There's a walkway on the levee, across the streetcar tracks."

"I know. The Moonwalk."

She stays at my shoulder as I march to the little streetcar stop at Dumaine, then cross over the tracks and climb to the brick walkway atop the levee. The river is wide here, and the water high for this time of year, a gray-brown flood separating New Orleans from Algiers. Pushboats and tugs churn across the water at surprising speed, gulls dipping and diving around them. We walk toward Jackson Square, and in the distance I see the hotels and department stores of Canal Place, the old Trade Mart building, the Aquarium of the Americas, and the twin bridges arching across to the west bank.

We're not alone on the walkway. There are tourists with cameras, joggers wearing headphones, buskers with open guitar cases full of change, and restless bums trying to catch the eyes of passersby, searching for likely marks. As we approach and pass each, I feel Wendy tense beside me, then slowly relax.

Below us on the right lie the streetcar tracks and the parking lot that runs the length of the Quarter; to our left the levee slopes twenty-five feet toward the water, an earthen wall lined with riprap, the heavy gray rocks the Corps of Engineers uses for erosion control. Driftwood clogs the riprap at water's edge, and every forty yards or so stands a fisherman with a cane pole or rod, hoping for a catfish or a gar.

"Wendy, do you remember the big scandal about FBI lab people giving false evidence testimony? Dummying up results to give prosecutors what they needed?"

"Yes," she says in an inquisitive tone.

"Wasn't it proved that a lot of the Bureau's high-tech forensic tests weren't half as accurate as claimed?"

"In some cases. But Louis Freeh made it a priority to correct all that. You're thinking about the sable brush hairs?"

"I'm wondering if the four people we've been badgering are tied to this case in any way at all."

"The lab wasn't aiming for some known result in this case, Jordan. They just came up with a rare type and lot of brush hair, and one of the few places that lot went was New Orleans."

Her answer is solid, and that reassures me a little. I can hear myself breathing harder from exertion, but Wendy speaks as though we're sitting across from each other at lunch.

"I've never worked a murder case," she says. "But I have total faith in John and Mr. Baxter."

I nod, but my faith is far from complete. Down at water's edge, a huge bearded man in an overcoat looks up the rocky slope as we walk past. He's far enough away that Wendy doesn't tense, but I sense that she could have her gun out in a second or less.

"What was Thalia Laveau like?" she asks.

"Really nice. She had a tough childhood. Her father and cousin sexually abused her."

"Yuck."

"Mm-hmm."

"She was gay?"

"She still is, I hope."

"God, yes." Wendy's face colors. "I didn't mean that to sound like it did."

"It's okay."

As we walk on, she seems to withdraw into her own thoughts. Then out of the blue she says, "I don't want to offend you or anything, but I heard during the interview with Laveau, you told her you got raped once. Is that true?"

I feel a flash of temper, knowing the story is probably making the rounds of the field office, but it's hard to be angry at Wendy, whose curiosity seems part of an eternal quest for self-improvement. "It's true."

"I really admire you for speaking up like that, knowing those guys could hear you on the wire."

"It was a long time ago."

"Does it feel like a long time ago?"

"No."

She nods. "That's what I figured."

"Have you ever had trouble like that?"

"Not that bad. A baseball player got really pushy with me in college once, in the backseat of his car. I waited until he exposed himself, and then I made him regret it."

"Good for you."

"Yeah. But something like this, where they snatch you off the street, someone who's all prepared with a rape kit—"

"We don't know the victims are being raped," I remind her.

347

"Well, right, except for the woman taken from Dorignac's."

A wave of heat comes into my cheeks.

"I shouldn't assume anything about the others from that," Wendy goes on. "We don't know for sure the UNSUB took her."

Her words stop me dead on the walkway. "The woman taken from Dorignac's grocery was raped?"

Wendy looks confused. "Well, they found semen inside her. She could have just had sex, of course, but I think the opinion of the pathologist was that she was raped."

As I stand speechless in the wind, a drop of rain touches my face. I had thought the police took DNA samples from the suspects to compare to skin found under the Dorignac's woman's fingernails. But they had more than that. And kept it from me. Turning left, I see a gray line of raindrops advancing across the river with the wind, dimpling the waves like soldiers marching over from the Algiers shore.

"I just put my foot in my mouth, didn't I?" says Wendy. "They didn't tell you."

"They didn't tell me."

"I guess they didn't want you to suffer any more than you had to, with your sister and all."

My rising anger is dwarfed by hurt at John's betrayal. How could he hold this back from me? But then come images of Jane suffering terror and rape –

"God, I'm in trouble," Wendy says. But instead of asking me to keep quiet, she says, "They should have told you."

I turn and continue along the levee despite the rain, which is light and will probably pass quickly, if my memories of New Orleans are accurate.

"You know it's raining," says Wendy.

"Yes."

The tourists and joggers are moving a little faster, but the fishermen stand their ground, knowing the odds favor a quick blowover.

A clattering racket behind us startles Wendy, but it's only the streetcar. In a few seconds it trundles past us and stops opposite Jackson Square. To our right is the burnt-orange roof of the Café du Monde, and the smell of coffee and frying beignets wafts over the levee, making my mouth water and my stomach ache.

"Pavlov's dog," I say quietly.

"Can we talk about something personal for a second?" Wendy asks in a hesitant voice.

"I thought we were."

"This is different."

I know what's coming. "Sure," I tell her, dreading the questions to follow.

"I think John has a thing for you."

"He does," I reply.

"And you have a thing for him?"

"Yes."

As a tall man in a sock cap approaches, she tenses and waits for him to pass. After he does, she looks back over her shoulder until he's well away.

"Well, I know you know I like him. John knows, too, I think. I mean, he'd have to be blind, I guess. When I feel something for somebody, I'm not very subtle about it."

"Nobody is, when they really feel something."

"I guess I'm just not what he's looking for," she says, her voice remarkably free of self-pity. "I mean, I know he likes me and everything, but . . . you know what I mean."

"I know what you mean. It's never easy."

She shrugs. "The weird thing is, I'm not jealous of you. If it was another woman from the office, I probably would

349

be." She kicks a small rock lying on the bricks. "Who am I kidding? I know I would be. I'd be comparing myself to her and asking why I fell short. But you're different."

Ahead on our right, there's a guitarist playing blues on a bench. A woman stands behind him, holding an umbrella over his head to protect the instrument from the rain. A knot of people listens with appreciation.

"Probably not as different as you think," I tell her. "I'm just a woman."

"No, you are. So many women I know – professional women – they're struggling for respect all the time. They're so conscious of how they're being treated, constantly looking for respect, that they're only using seventy percent of their brains for their job. Sometimes *I* feel like that. But you just go about your business like you never even think about it. You just expect respect, and you get it."

"I'm older than you are. Got a lot more miles on me."

"That's it," she says. "Not the age, but the miles. The fact that you've been all over the world, covered wars and stuff. Seen combat. I've never seen John or the SAC act the way they act around you – with another woman, I mean. Not even with female ASACs."

"You'll get there. It's not any great watershed moment, though. One day you just realize you're part of the game instead of a spectator. You're on the inside, and there's no getting back out again, even if you want to."

"I'll be glad when that day comes."

"Don't be in too much of a hurry."

"I think about Robin Ahrens sometimes. She was the first female FBI agent to be killed in the line of duty. It happened in eighty-five. They were trying to arrest an armored car thief, and things got confused. She was shot by a male agent who mistook her for a bad guy."

350

"You're curious about what action is like, aren't you?"

"I guess so. I mean, being on the SWAT team and all. You wonder about the real thing."

"Robin's story is a textbook lesson. Combat is total confusion from the first shot. Combat vets all say the same thing. Remember your training, and don't try to be a hero. That's pretty much the bible, right there."

"I just want to do my job," Wendy says. "Not mess up some stupid way and get someone hurt or killed."

"You won't. Your love life is more complicated than your job ever will be."

She laughs ruefully. "You're probably right about that. Well, anyway, I know why John is attracted to you, and it's okay. You guys don't have to hide from me or anything."

I wonder if I could ever summon the selfless goodness that seems to flow from this girl. Probably not. I touch her forearm. "Thanks, Wendy. And I haven't slept with him yet, if you're wondering."

"I wasn't asking that," she says quickly. Then she bites her lip. "Though maybe I was wondering. A little."

We both laugh, and suddenly the day does not seem quite so gray, or the rain so cold. I wave to the guitarist as we pass him, and then we're at the artillery park and Jackson Square. Just across Decatur wait the tourist carriages, their horses standing wearily in the rain, with a Lucky Dog man lifting wieners from his steaming cart nearby. On St. Ann, the card tables of tarot readers line the cement, and sidewalk artists advertise their services with portraits of Barbra, the Duke, the Beatles, and Jerry Garcia.

"The rain's not stopping," Wendy says. "Maybe we should call for a car."

"In a minute." I look to our left, where wide wooden

351

steps march right down into the swollen river. "Let's go down to the old Jax Brewery. Get some coffee."

Wendy nods, but I can see it goes against her instincts. I pick up the pace, fighting my anger at John for holding back on me. The rain has thinned out the walkway traffic, but two men are approaching, a young one with greasy jeans and an unkempt beard, and a few yards behind him a man wearing khakis and a teal Ralph Lauren button-down. Wendy tenses, watching the bearded man, then glances over her shoulder as he passes. While she watches him, the man in the Polo shirt brings up his right arm, and polished nickel gleams in the rain.

I shout a warning to Wendy, and before the sound fades she's in front of me, her hand flying under her jacket to the pistol holstered there.

A gunshot explodes over the levee, and something hot and wet stings my face. Wendy seems to stutter in place, then falls backward onto the bricks with a flat thump like a sack of sand. My white blouse is spattered with a fine red mist. Wendy's blood. Screams erupt from the parking lot, and I sense more than see people diving to the ground.

The man in the Polo charges me, his gun pointed at my chest, and grabs my arm with his free hand. *"Move your ass!"* he shouts, dragging me toward streetcar tracks. *"Move!"*

My eyes are locked on Wendy, who lies on her back, eyes open and fixed on the sky, a large bubble of blood on her lips. As I stare, my captor pulls up his gun and shoots her again, this time in the side. She doesn't make a sound.

I try to yank my arm free, but he swings the gun in a quick savage arc against my forehead, and the world blanks out for a moment.

"Move or I'll kill you right here!"

A jumble of thoughts: his tremendous strength; his lack of hesitation in shooting Wendy, as John predicted; the realization that this is no random attack, that he shot Wendy to get to me, that he wants me alive; that this is *him* – the kidnapper, the UNSUB, the motherfucker who took my sister. There's no hunting him anymore. He's hunting me. And he *has* me.

As he drags me toward the streetcar tracks, I notice one man in the parking lot who's not lying prone on the gravel. Both his arms are leveled in our direction, and I'm starting to duck when I recognize John Kaiser.

"Jordan!" he cries. "Drop!"

As I start to fall, my captor jerks me in front of him like a shield. John moves left, angling for a shot, but I'm in his way. The man holding me throws up his free arm and fires three times quickly in John's direction. John spins, trying to avoid the shots, but his spin continues to the ground and he does not get up.

"Dead cop," says the voice in my ear. The barrel of his pistol touches my temple. *"Move."*

He wants me in the parking lot. I can't let him get me into a car. My mind flashes onto the gun John gave me, but it's lying useless in its holster in my rented Mustang, parked at the FBI office. The only weapon I have is the knowledge that the man holding me doesn't want to kill me here. He has a much more exotic fate in mind.

I fire my elbow into his rib cage, earning a crack and a howl of agony. His arm goes limp for an instant, and in that instant I wrench myself loose and run back toward Wendy, an image of her gun in my head. But as I near her I realize she's lying on top of the still-holstered weapon. If I stop to turn her over, he'll catch me. There's no cover here but the river, so I lunge left, toward the wooden steps that lead down

353

to the water. As I reach the top step, a shot rings out behind me.

"Don't make me kill you!"

I'm silhouetted on the edge of the steps like a duck in an arcade, and I can't possibly reach the water in one leap. I'm going to have to wait for a better chance.

As I turn back, he marches up with the gun, his dark eyes blazing. He looks a little older than I am, with a shock of salt-and-pepper hair and a deeply lined face. I've never seen his face, but I recognize the dark light in his eyes, from places I prefer not to remember.

"We're going to my car," he says. "If you fight, I'll shoot you in the spine. You'll go limp as a rag doll, and I'll have to carry you, but you'll still be nice and warm between the legs and you'll still make a pretty picture for the man."

The icy conviction in his voice paralyzes me, wiping out every emotion but terror. Seizing my arm, he pulls me back across the walkway, his eyes full of purpose.

Thirty yards away, John lies on his stomach, struggling in vain to reach his knees. When we pass him, my attacker will fire a bullet into him, just as he did with Wendy. My limbs are heavy with the inevitability of nightmares –

"Jooordan!"

The scream stops me cold, and in some sliver of a second I know it came from Wendy Travis's throat. Twisting my neck, I see her lying on her stomach, propped on her elbows, her pistol clenched in both hands, her eyes shining brightly through the blood and rain. An arm whips around me to aim at her, but I bat it aside and throw myself as far away as I can.

Orange flame bursts from the barrel of Wendy's gun.

An explosive grunt sounds beside me. My attacker staggers, then pulls his gun back up. Wendy's gun spits again.

He bellows in rage and pain, then charges her with blind fury. Wendy fires again but misses, and he starts shooting, round after round. He misses four times, but then Wendy's head snaps back and I'm screaming in denial, knowing in my bones that she's gone.

He turns back to me, but he's wounded and can't move well. Blood has matted the teal Polo to his chest and shoulder. From twenty yards away, he raises his gun and points it at me. My eyes are full of tears, and I can see that he's abandoned his plan. He means to kill me now.

The gun wavers, steadies, then flies skyward as thunder booms behind me and ricochets back from the far shore. I whirl to find John kneeling at the edge of the levee, his .40-caliber automatic leveled with absolute stillness.

"Hit the bricks!" he yells.

I dive onto the walkway, and John empties his clip, blast after blast roaring across the river, the echoes of his first shots smashing into the reports of the later ones. When I look up, my attacker is gone.

As the last shot fades, I crawl across the bricks to Wendy, hoping it's not too late. The hair at the back of her head is a mass of blood and brain matter, and my heart knots against the truth. The first thing I learned in a military field hospital is that visible brain matter means the casualty won't make it.

"Get down!" John shouts. "Find cover!"

I kiss Wendy's hair, then get slowly to my feet and walk to the crest of the wooden steps and look down. The man in the Polo is doubled over near the bottom step, gasping for breath and trying to hang on to a wooden chain post. As I watch, my heart empty of pity, his hand slips off the post and he tumbles headfirst into the river.

After a moment he bobs to the surface, floating in place, his mouth opening and closing like that of a landed fish.

Then he slowly turns away as the current takes hold of him. I feel no urge to save him, but as the current pulls him along the bank, I realize that if the river takes him, we may never know who he was, never find Thalia, or Jane, or any of the others – or even learn what happened to them.

Hopping over the chain, I try to keep pace with him by running along the treacherous riprap. Navigating the gray rocks without breaking an ankle is difficult, and the high water carries him rapidly along, not only downriver but into the main channel. He's twenty feet from the bank and slipping farther away.

"Help!" he shouts, panic filling his dull eyes. "I can't breathe!"

His lungs are probably filling with blood. He could drown internally before the river gets him. I can't go in after him; he could drown me even without meaning to.

"Please!" he shouts. "I can't stay up!"

"Go to hell!" I yell, though I need to save him.

He's twenty-five feet into the channel now, turning in slow circles in the wake of a distant tug. Spinning away from me, he shouts something I can't hear. Then, as his face comes around, again he repeats it.

"Your sister's alive!"

A bolus of adrenaline flushes through my veins, and I have to fight every muscle to keep from leaping in after him. That's just what he wants, of course. He has to be lying.

"Where is she?" I cry.

"Save me!" he yells again. "I can save her! Please!"

"Tell me first!"

His head slips under the water, then bobs up again. I struggle down to the river's edge, where a big piece of driftwood lies wedged in the rock. It's a long branch, worn smooth by the water on its journey south.

"Jordan!" shouts a voice from miles away. It's John, back at the steps. "Bring him in with the branch!"

I pull at the limb with all my strength, but I can't free it from the rocks. Every second he slips farther downstream, my sister's fate going with him. I can't save the bastard without jumping in myself, and that would be insanity. Good swimmers drown in the Mississippi, even without someone trying to kill them.

Suddenly, without conscious thought, my hand flies to the zipper of my fanny pack, and my hand jerks out the Canon point-and-shoot I used at the gallery fire in New York.

I point the lens at the drowning man and shoot one exposure, then scrabble along the riprap, leaping from rock to rock with no regard for my bones, trying to get close enough for a clear shot. But the channel has him now. He's thirty-five feet out and spinning away. As his face comes around again, I shoot three quick shots, then sprint along the tops of the rocks, hoping for another turn. When he's forty feet out, I get off two more; then his head slips below the surface and does not return.

Panting with exhaustion, I turn away from the water and climb carefully to the top of the levee. John is sitting on top of the steps, fifty yards away, a cell phone in his hand. The sound of approaching sirens rolls over me from the direction of the Quarter. As I trot down to where John sits, he puts down the phone and tightens his belt, which he has tied around his thigh.

"You're hit in the leg?" I ask.

Clearly in great pain, he nods, then points down the steps. "Go down there and see if you can find his gun. He might have dropped it. Fingerprints."

I study every inch of weathered wood as I work my way

down the steps, but there's no gun. There is blood, and a lot of it.

"Look on the rocks just under the water," calls John.

They don't call the Mississippi the Big Muddy for nothing. You can't see through it. Dropping to my knees, I feel my way along the first submerged step, but a soft splinter is my only reward. The second is coated with funk. Moving sideways, I feel among the submerged rocks, and again find nothing. But as my hand comes out of the water, I freeze. Lying between two rocks in a rainbowed pool of oily water is a cellular telephone. Retrieving it from the water, I see blood on it.

"What have you got?" John shouts.

Holding the phone by its antenna, I climb back up the steps.

"Son of a bitch," John groans.

"It's still on," I tell him, looking at the water-filled LCD screen.

"Careful." He takes the phone by its antenna and holds it before his eyes. "Shit! It just shorted out. While I was looking at it!"

"You can still get prints, though, right?"

"Maybe. But what we really need is the memory chip. This phone's getting on a plane to Washington. Don't mention it to any beat cops. Wait for Homicide."

He points down the levee toward the French Market, where two white-helmeted mounted policemen are spurring their horses across the streetcar tracks.

I sit beside John, and in the first seconds of stillness, I start to shake. I wring my hands, trying to make them stop.

"Wendy's dead," I say softly.

He nods.

"She threw herself in front of me."

"I saw her. She did her job. She was a good kid."

"She wasn't a kid. She was a hero. And she worshiped the ground you walked on."

"I know. Goddamn it."

"She deserves a medal. For her family."

"Goes without saying."

"So what the hell were you doing here?"

John shakes his head but doesn't look at me. "I didn't feel good about you walking around the Quarter. I knew you'd gotten upset at Frank Smith's, and I've always felt you were in more danger than anyone realized. I also knew you didn't have your gun."

I squeeze his hand. "I'm glad you're paranoid."

"What did the guy say to you down there?"

"He said Jane was alive."

John looks at me, his eyes hard. "Did you believe him?"

"I don't know. What I do know is, he wasn't Roger Wheaton or Leon Gaines or Frank Smith."

"I know."

"He said something else, John."

"What?"

"If he had to shoot me in the spine, it would still be nice and warm between my legs, and I'd still make a pretty picture for the man."

John's face pales. "He said that? 'For the man'?"

"For the man."

"Jesus."

The clatter of hooves on brick is closer. John takes his wallet out of his pants and opens it to show his FBI credentials.

"You lied to me, John."

"What?"

"The Dorignac's victim was raped, and you knew it. They found semen in her."

He says nothing at first. Then: "The post was inconclusive as to rape."

"You must have asked the husband when he last had sex with her."

He sighs with resignation. "Okay, it was probably rape. I didn't want that weighing on you. Especially before the interviews. I didn't want you suffering needlessly, and nobody wanted you so mad at the suspects that you couldn't be professional."

"I understand all that, okay? But don't ever hold anything back again."

He nods. "Okay."

"Nothing, John."

"I got it."

The horses are upon us. Two cops – one black, one white – stare down with drawn guns.

"Get your hands up! Both of you!"

John holds up his credentials so that the cops can see them.

"Special Agent John Kaiser, FBI. This crime scene is to be secured for the joint task force. I've been shot and I can't walk, so you men get to it."

21

The wake of Wendy's death is a blur to me now, as I ride the elevator up to the fourth floor of the FBI fortress on Lake Pontchartrain. While John spent ninety minutes in the accident room at Charity Hospital downtown, I sat in a waiting room with enough armed special agents to make me feel like the First Lady. Daniel Baxter and SAC Bowles rushed out from the field office, but only to make their presence felt with John and the doctors. They sped off to manage the hunt for the UNSUB's body and a hundred other details, leaving me with images of Wendy fighting and dying to save me, her lifeblood spattered over my chest, and the UNSUB's voice hot in my ear: *If I shoot you in the spine, it'll still be nice and warm between your legs.* . . . I was lucky that one of my new protectors was a female agent. She brought me a new blouse from her car and bagged the bloodstained one I wore in case it was needed as evidence. But removing the blouse did nothing to erase my waking nightmare.

John came through surgery fine, but his doctor didn't want to release him for twenty-four hours. John thanked the man, picked up the cane a physical therapist had deposited in his room, and limped out of the hospital. Assuming I was his spouse – or at least a significant other – the surgeon gave me dire warnings about caring for the wounded leg. I promised to do all I could, then followed John out to a waiting FBI car.

"Where to, sir?" asked the young field agent driving the car. He and John were technically of equal rank, but in times of crisis, a natural hierarchy asserts itself.

"The field office," John replied. "Move it."

Baxter, Lenz, and SAC Bowles are waiting for us in Bowles's office. They've spent their last hours in the Emergency Operations Center, but Bowles's office has a leather chair with an ottoman on which John can prop his swollen leg.

"How is it, John?" Baxter asks as I help him sit down.

"Stiff, but fine."

Baxter nods in the way I've seen officers do when a needed noncom lies about a wound. Nobody's going to tell John Kaiser to take a medical leave.

"How are you doing, Jordan?"

"Holding it together."

"I know that wasn't easy, seeing what happened to Wendy."

I start to stay silent, but I feel I should say something. "You should know this. She did everything right. The first guy coming toward us looked much more suspicious, and he diverted her. When the well-dressed guy brought up his gun, she threw herself in front of me and was pulling out her gun as she jumped. Nobody could have done better. Nobody."

Baxter's jaw muscles clench as pain and pride fight for dominance in his eyes. "This is the first case where I've lost an agent to a serial offender," he says softly. "Now we've lost two. It doesn't need saying, but I'm going to anyway. We will not rest until every son of a bitch involved is rotting in maximum-security lockdown or dead."

"Amen," says SAC Bowles. "I've got a hundred agents downstairs ready to work twenty-fours a day. Wendy had a lot of friends."

362

"We still don't have his body?" John asks Baxter.

"No. The Coast Guard and contract divers are searching, but the Mississippi is unforgiving. Workers go off barges all the time without being found. We have to accept the possibility that we may never find his body."

"What about the cell phone?" John asks.

"No prints."

"No fingerprints on a cell phone? How is that possible?"

"It was wiped clean. He was carrying it wiped. This UNSUB was taking extreme precautions. He must have figured that if he dropped the phone during the abduction, prints would quickly lead to an ID. That's the good news. I think if we find the body, we'll get a name in no time."

"What about the memory chips inside it?"

"The Engineering Research Facility at Quantico just got the phone. They say if the short didn't fry the chips, we could get lucky. We should get a report anytime."

Baxter taps his fingertips together like a benched athlete waiting to get back into the game.

"What about my pictures?" I ask.

"That's the one bright spot. They were blurry but usable. The University of Arizona produced a decent enhancement of the best one, and it's been running on the local TV stations for two hours. Three calls so far, but they didn't pan out. The *Times-Picayune* will run the photo in the morning."

"Well," John half-groans. "We got what we wanted. We rattled the hell out of somebody. We just got a delayed reaction, and it was a lot tougher than we expected."

"Yep," Baxter agrees.

"What about the UNSUB's gun?"

Baxter shakes his head. "The river's high now, and the current fast. Also, the Mississippi has a sandy bottom in some places, and the water flows through it to some depth. Heavy objects sink into it in a matter of seconds. We're making extraordinary efforts, but again, no great hopes. We have to find that body. Then we can start checking for connections to Wheaton, Gaines, or Smith."

"Where were the three musketeers while this went down?" John asks.

"All present and accounted for. Wheaton was painting at the art center. Had been since you talked to him this morning. After Jordan left Smith's house, he lunched at Bayona, shopped at the Hurwitz-Mintz furniture store, then went back home. He's presently in the company of a handsome young gentleman we've yet to identify."

"And Gaines?"

"Gaines and his girlfriend woke up at ten a.m., started drinking, then arguing. They stopped long enough to have sex, then passed out. They've been sleeping ever since."

"Any of them make suspicious calls?" John asks in a frustrated voice. "Contacts?"

"Nothing."

"Screw this," mutters Bowles. "I say we have NOPD pull in all three and sweat them till somebody cracks."

"I'm worried they may do just that," says Baxter. "At this point, we have no more leverage to make them talk than we did yesterday. We have to ID the UNSUB and find a connection to one of the three."

The ISU chief expels air from his cheeks and looks from John to Lenz. "I want to hear thoughts. Anything. Gut feelings, twitches, psychic waves, whatever you've got. Now's the time. What are we dealing with here?"

Neither John nor Lenz seems inclined to speak first, so Baxter points to Lenz. "Arthur? Go out on a limb."

Silent until now, the psychiatrist leans forward on the

sofa. "I see a paradox. One of the UNSUB's remarks to Jordan could indicate that the previous victims have been raped by the UNSUB, then passed on to the artist to be painted. Yet our art experts say the Sleeping Women weren't painted by Wheaton, Smith, or Gaines. If you look at what the UNSUB said, it doesn't exclude the possibility that he himself was the painter."

I feel compelled to jump in. "I don't think a man capable of painting the Sleeping Women would refer to them as 'pretty pictures.' And when he told me, 'you'll still make a pretty picture for the man,' he could have been talking about a *buyer* rather than the painter."

"Marcel de Becque," says John. "The guy is deep into this thing. I'm not sure how. Maybe three or four guys share a similar paraphilia. I don't know."

Baxter's impatience crackles off him like static electricity. "I can't believe this is all we have!"

"What about Jordan's split-personality idea?" John asks. "We didn't get anything out of Wheaton or Smith on childhood abuse, but that concept has stuck with me. Is it possible that an artist with a split personality could paint in two completely different styles? Undetectably? I mean, how different can the personalities be?"

Lenz steeples his fingers and leans back. "They can be so different as to have different physical manifestations. There are cases of MPD on record where one personality required heart medication to survive, and another did not. One may require corrective lenses and the others not, or need different prescriptions. And there are many lesser manifestations."

"Come on," says Bowles.

"Documented fact." Lenz's voice has taken on a patronizing tone. "So – two completely different painters occupying the same body? It's technically possible. But given the scale of this case, the number of victims, the extraordinary lengths to which the dominant personality would have to go to conceal his acts from the others—"

"Wait," says John. "Not all the personalities know what the others are doing?"

"Correct. Generally one is dominant and knows everything, while the others remain partially in the dark."

"Jesus," says Baxter.

"It's a fascinating premise," says Lenz, "but it verges on pure fantasy. The image laypeople have of so-called 'split personality' comes from *The Strange Case of Dr. Jekyll and Mr. Hyde*. That construct appeals to our sense of evil masked behind a benign public face. But *clinically* that's not the way MPD manifests itself. You don't get a benign public person with a diabolical intelligence concealed behind it. You get pathetic fragments of personality, most of them manifesting as damaged children arrested in development at the age sexual abuse was visited upon them. The dominant personality is the one best able to adapt and cope under extreme stress. That's all."

John is nodding. "A lot of the serial offenders we've caught or interviewed have endured sexual abuse as children."

"But how many had multiple-personality disorder?" asks Lenz.

"None."

Lenz smiles like a chess master who has led an opponent into a trap. "Before we seriously consider this theory, we should fire our art experts and bring in a new group."

"Let's do that," John snaps. "We're not getting anywhere with the ones we've got. Goddamn it, everyone in this mess knows more than he's saying. The suspects, de Becque, even us."

"Wingate knew a lot too," I tell them. "I could feel it."

Baxter looks hard at me. "Have you changed your mind about telling us Frank Smith's explanation for his visits with Wheaton, or for their arguments?"

An image of Smith confiding Wheaton's desire for assisted suicide flashes through my mind. "No. You've just got to trust me on that."

"Does the reason reflect on their psychology?" asks Lenz. "That could be just as important."

"There's nothing unique about it. It's something normal people would argue about."

The phone on Bowles's desk rings. The SAC answers, then holds out the phone to Baxter. "ERF at Quantico."

The ISU chief gets up and takes the phone, his jaw braced for bad news. As he listens, his face gives away nothing.

"Got it," he says. "I understand."

"What?" asks John as he hangs up.

Baxter lays his hands flat on Bowles's desk. "It was a stolen cell phone, reprogrammed. No way to trace the UNSUB from that. But ERF salvaged the chips. They got the speed-dial numbers programmed into the phone. One belonged to Marcel de Becque."

As John pumps his fist in a victory sign, a memory of the old French expatriate standing before his great window comes into my mind, his cultured voice telling me about my father and the glory days in Vietnam.

Baxter presses a button on the phone. "EOC? This is Baxter. Tell me where Marcel de Becque is right now." We sit in silence as Baxter waits. Then his face goes ashen.

"When? . . . Call the FAA and the foreign legats. Then call me back."

He hangs up and rubs his hand hard across his chin. "Six hours ago, de Becque's jet left Grand Cayman. The pilot filed a flight plan for Rio de Janeiro, but he never arrived. De Becque could be anywhere."

"God*damn* it," says John.

Before anyone else can comment, Bowles's phone rings again. Baxter activates the speakerphone.

"Baxter here."

"We've got Chief Farrell on the phone for you."

"I'm ready."

"Daniel?" says a rich African-American voice.

"Afternoon, Henry. What's up?"

"We just got a call about the photo running on TV. A widow lady out in Kenner says she rents a room to the guy. She's dead sure. Says he goes by the name of Johnson, and he's hardly ever in town. Says he's a salesman. The address is Two-twenty-one Wisteria Drive. That's the south side of I-10, right by the airport. Jefferson Parish."

Even Baxter's poker face betrays excitement as he scrawls on a file folder. "Has the sheriff sent anyone out there yet?"

"He doesn't know about it yet. I thought I'd call you boys first."

Baxter looks heavenward with grateful eyes. "We've got the forensic unit ready to roll. We'll take care of the inter-departmental relations."

"Good luck, Daniel. The lady's name is Pitre."

"We owe you, Henry."

"I'll get plenty of chances to collect. Good luck."

Baxter hangs up and looks at SAC Bowles. "Five years ago, would we have got that call?"

368

"Not a chance in hell. Farrell's tough. He's fired or jailed hundreds of cops in the past five years."

Baxter punches a number into the speakerphone.

"Forensics," says a female voice.

"Two-twenty-one Wisteria Drive, Kenner. Take the whole unit."

"Sirens? Everything?"

"No, but step on it. We'll meet you there."

"We're gone."

Mrs. Pitre lives in a warren of streets just north of the runways of New Orleans' Moisant International Airport. As Baxter, Lenz, John, and I roll past cookie-cutter houses, an inbound jet floats down like a massive bird and passes over our Crown Victoria with a ground-shaking roar.

"Lovely neighborhood," remarks Baxter, who's driving. "You could shoot somebody in the head while one of those planes flew over and nobody would hear it."

"Something to think about," says Lenz, who's up front beside him.

Baxter looks over the seat at me. "Sorry, Jordan."

"Don't apologize for the truth."

John slides his hand across the backseat and covers mine.

"There it is," says Lenz, pointing. "Two-twenty-one."

It's a typical suburban tract house. When we pull into the driveway, I see the roof of a two-story garage behind it. The clapboard garage looks like it was added as an afterthought, and not by a master carpenter. The walls are out of plumb, and the roof overhung with branches from an elm that should have been cut before construction.

As Baxter kills the engine, a woman with a cigarette in her mouth walks out of the car port door, waving a set of keys in her hand. Though in her late fifties, she's wearing a pink spandex tube top and blue shorts that reveal legs shot with varicose veins.

John reaches for the door handle. "Here we go."

"Take your cane," advises Baxter. "There'll be stairs."

"Screw the cane," John replies, confirming my theory that male vanity is every bit as powerful as the female variety.

"You got here quick, I'll say that," Mrs. Pitre says in a smoke-parched voice pitched like a man's. "I've been worried he'd come back before you got here." She sticks out her right hand. "Carol Pitre, widowed four years since my husband got killed offshore."

"Special Agent John Kaiser." He shakes her hand. "Mr. Johnson won't be coming back, ma'am."

"How do you know? He gone on another business trip?"

"No."

She cocks her head at John. "What's he done, anyhow? Why you looking for him? The police said he was a federal fugitive, but that doesn't tell me anything."

"That's all we can say at this point, ma'am."

Mrs. Pitre bites her lip and takes John's measure again. She decides not to push it. "What happened to your leg there?"

"Skiing accident."

"Waterskiing?"

The forensic unit's Suburban pulls into the driveway with a roar and a squeal of brakes.

"Who's that?" asks Mrs. Pitre, craning her neck. "They part of your bunch?"

"They're evidence technicians, Mrs. Pitre."

"Like the O.J. trial?"

"That's right."

"I hope they're a damn sight better than the ones in Los Angeles."

"They are. Mrs. Pitre, we—"

"I guess you want to go up now."

As the doors of the Suburban slam, a second one pulls in behind it. The vehicles aren't marked with FBI decals, but if you look closely at the grilles, you can see blue lights and a siren.

"Mrs. Pitre, did Mr. Johnson show you any identification when he moved in?"

"Hell, yes. I asked for it, didn't I? Since Ray got killed in the mud tank, I can't be too careful. World's full of crazy people. Black or white don't matter these days."

John seems nonplussed by Mrs. Pitre's hyperactive style. "What did he show you?"

"Voter registration card, for one thing."

"A Louisiana card?"

"Nope. New York City. He had a New York driving license, too."

"He showed you that?"

"How else would I know he had it?"

"Of course. Did it have his picture on it?"

"What good is it without one? He wasn't a bad-lookin' man, either. A little hard in the face, but you live long enough, life makes you hard. Isn't that right?"

"We would like to go up now, Mrs. Pitre. Is it just one room over the garage?"

"Two rooms and a bathroom. Ray built it for Joey after we give him that set of drums. Couldn't stand having him in the house with that racket. I don't know if he was any good, but he could wake the dead with them."

"I see. Do you mind if we go up alone? We like to see things completely undisturbed."

Mrs. Pitre isn't overjoyed by this, but after a moment, she hands over the keys. "I want a receipt for anything you take."

371

"You'll get that." John turns to me and pulls me aside. "I'm going up with Daniel and Lenz for a quick look. I'd like to take you up, but it wouldn't fly with the forensic unit."

"I'm okay. Go on."

John confers with the head of the forensic unit, who hands him a sheaf of plastic evidence bags. Then he, Lenz, and Baxter climb the stairs inside the garage. Mrs. Pitre sidles my way as I watch, figuring a woman might give her more information, so I flee to the FBI sedan and lock myself in the front seat.

The roar of an outbound jet rattles the car and my bones, and I wonder why Mrs. Pitre isn't as crazy as a road lizard rather than slightly addled. As I settle in for a wait, John limps down the bottom four steps.

"Is it your leg?" I call, getting out and hurrying toward him.

"No." There's an evidence bag in his hand. He waves to the chief of the forensic unit, and a platoon of technicians hurry toward the garage with their cases and bags.

"What is it? What did you find?"

"The UNSUB knew we were coming. The place was wiped clean, like the cell phone. All we found was a stash of junk food: Pop-Tarts, potato chips, Hostess Twinkies, and beef jerky. He must have worn gloves when he bought them. But waiting for us on the kitchen counter was a perfect row of photographs."

A strange chill runs along my shoulders. "The victims?"

"Yes."

"How many?"

"Eleven. Not the woman from Dorignac's grocery, and not Thalia."

"So he didn't take the Dorignac's victim." I realize John

372

is still holding the evidence bag. "What's in that?" I ask, my chest tightening.

John sighs and touches my arm. "Jane's photo. If you're up to it, I'd like you to see if you can tell me where it was taken."

"Let's see it."

He hesitates, then opens the Ziploc and slides out the photo. It's a black-and-white print, shot with a telephoto lens. The depth of field is so poor that I can't distinguish the background, but Jane is clear. Wearing a sleeveless sweater and jeans, she's looking toward the camera but not into it. She looks more intense than usual, her eyes narrowed in the way people tell me mine do when I'm concentrating. As I study the image, searching for some telling detail, anything that might yield a clue to her fate, my heart clenches like a fist and my skin goes cold.

"Are you okay?" he asks, taking hold of my shoulders. "I shouldn't have showed that to you."

When he touches me, I realize he's shaking. His wounded leg is barely supporting his weight.

"Look at her arms, John."

"What about them?"

"No scars."

"What?"

A wave of vertigo throws me into a spin, though I know I'm standing still. "Jane was attacked by a dog when she was little."

"Dog?"

The photo begins to quiver in my hand as realizations clamor for attention. I've seen this photograph before. But the copy in my hand isn't a true photo print; it's an ink-jet facsimile printed on photo paper. Fighting tears, I press the picture to my chest and close my eyes.

"Careful," John warns. "There might be fingerprints."

"Look!" Dr. Lenz says over John's shoulder. "There's something written on the back."

John leans forward and studies the back of the print. "It's an address. Twenty-five-ninety St. Charles."

"That's Jane Lacour's address," says Lenz.

"There's a phone number, too."

"Seven-five-eight, one-nine-ninety-two?" I ask.

"No," John says softly. "It's a New York number. We need to trace this right away."

He reaches for the picture, but I push his hand away, turn over the photo, and read the number: *212-555-2999.*

"I know this number," I whisper.

"Whose is it?" John asks.

"Just a second." I try to think back through a haze of scotch and Xanax. "Oh my God . . . it's Wingate's gallery. Christopher Wingate. I dialed this number from the plane back from Hong Kong."

"Jesus," John says under his breath. "That's everybody tied in the same knot. Wingate, the UNSUB, and de Becque. They're all tied together now."

"Wingate's number on a victim's photo," muses Lenz. "That could mean Wingate selected Jane Lacour."

"How could he?" asks John. "He hasn't been in New Orleans for years."

"He didn't choose Jane," I whisper. "He chose me."

22

The causeway across Lake Pontchartrain is the longest bridge in the world built solely over water. The twenty-three miles of humming concrete and traffic push me inward like a mantra, toward the dark vortex of my fear and guilt. Somewhere on the other side of this shallow lake, amid the exploding construction caused by white flight from New Orleans, stands the house of John Kaiser. The man himself sits beside me in the passenger seat of my rented Mustang, the seat fully reclined so that he can stretch out his wounded leg.

Thirty seconds after he read Christopher Wingate's number off the back of my photograph, John's leg gave way and he collapsed in Mrs. Pitre's driveway. Baxter ordered him back to the hospital, but John argued that he was only tired, that he should have used the walking cane, and that he had to return to the field office to work the new connections between the UNSUB, Wingate, and Marcel de Becque. Baxter gave him two choices: go back to the hospital or go home and rest for the night. John chose the latter, but as we picked up my Mustang from the field office, he called upstairs and had an agent bring down a thick folder filled with the latest Argus-generated enhancements of the abstract Sleeping Women. He's like I used to be when I got my teeth into a war story – unstoppable.

The picture he pulled from the Ziploc bag floats in my

mind like a grayscale emblem of guilt. I've placed the photo now. It ran in several major newspapers two years ago, when I won the North American Press Association Award. Wingate must have accessed some database that contained that picture, printed it on photo-quality paper, and sent it to the UNSUB in New Orleans.

"Do you want to talk about it?" John reaches out and touches my knee.

"I don't know."

"I know what you're thinking, Jordan. A little survivor guilt is normal, but this is crazy. You're forcing everything to fit a predetermined result. And the result you're reaching for is that Jane died because of you. I don't know why you want to feel that guilt, but that's not what happened."

I squeeze the wheel, trying to control my temper. "I don't *want* that guilt."

"I'm glad. Because that would be really fucked up."

I grip the wheel still harder to bleed off my exasperation, but it does no good. "Will you call and see if they've compared the handwriting? If it's not Wingate's, I'll admit I'm being paranoid. But if it is, we'll know Wingate mailed or gave the UNSUB my picture."

John takes out his cell phone, calls the field office, and asks for the forensic unit. "Jenny, John Kaiser. Have you guys heard from New York on that handwriting yet? . . . What did they say? . . . I see. One hundred percent sure? . . . Right. Thanks." He presses End, then lets his head fall forward and sighs.

"What is it?"

"The phone number on your photo was in Wingate's handwriting."

My stomach goes hollow, and I slam the wheel with my open hand. "There it is. Somebody outside New

Orleans chose me as victim number five, and it got Jane killed."

He bites his lower lip and shakes his head. "If I had to pick someone, I'd pick Marcel de Becque."

"What if he *ordered* me, John? The way you'd commission any painting? He's known who I am for years. He tells Wingate he wants me in the next painting, but since I'm traveling all the time, Wingate finds an easy way to supply what de Becque wants. He takes Jane instead."

"There's one big hole in that theory."

"That de Becque didn't have Jane's painting? That's easy. Wingate sold it out from under him. That's the source of their bad blood."

"I was talking about coincidence. Every other victim lives in New Orleans. But for some unknown reason, de Becque chooses you – a world traveler based in San Francisco – as victim number five. To fill de Becque's order, Wingate decides to use your twin sister as a substitute. And that substitute just *happens* to live in the same city as all the other victims? That's a statistical impossibility."

A low pounding has started at the base of my skull. I reach down to the floor and unzip my fanny pack, looking for my pill bottle.

"What's that?" John asks as I bring it up.

"Xanax."

"Tranquilizers?

"It's no big deal."

"Xanax is a chemical cousin of Valium."

"I know that. Look, I need to calm down."

He looks out his window at the lake, but I know he's not going to let it drop. "Do you take them regularly?"

I pop off the lid, shake two pills into my hand, and swallow them dry. "This has been a bad day, okay? I watched Wendy die. I watched you get shot. A guy tried to kidnap me, and I just found out I'm responsible for my sister's death. You can put me in rehab tomorrow."

He looks back at me, his hazel eyes filled with concern. "You do what you have to do to get through this. I'm just worried about you. And me. We've got another fifteen minutes in the car. You're not going to fall asleep at the wheel, are you?"

I laugh. "Don't worry about that. Two of these would put you out, but they'll barely dent me."

He studies me for a long moment, then faces the causeway again. "Sooner or later, we're going to break through the wall, Jordan. We're going to find those women. All of them."

Sooner or later. It had better be sooner. Later is like the horizon; it recedes as you approach.

John lives in a suburban ranch house on a street with twenty others exactly like it. Homogenous Americana, enforced by neighborhood covenant. The lawns are well-tended, the houses freshly painted, the vehicles in the driveways clean and new. I park in the driveway, then help him out of the passenger side. With only me present, he uses the cane. It's slow going, but he grits his teeth and keeps walking.

Under the carport, he punches a security code into a wall box and opens the back door, which leads into a laundry room, then a spotless white kitchen.

"You obviously never cook," I remark.

"I cook sometimes."

"You have a maid, then."

"A woman comes in once a week. But I'm basically a neat guy."

378

"I've never met a neat guy I'd want to spend the night with."

He laughs, then winces. "The truth is, I've been sleeping on a cot at the office since Baxter called about your discovery in Hong Kong."

"Ah."

Beyond the kitchen counter is a dining area with a glass table, and a large arch leads on to a decently furnished den. Everything appears to be in its appointed place, with only a couple of magazines on a coffee table suggesting the presence of an occupant. The house feels like it's been cleaned up for sale, or is even a demo unit used to sell young marrieds on the neighborhood.

"Where's all your junk?" I ask, feeling a warm wave of Xanax wash against my headache.

"My junk?"

"You know. Books, videotapes? Old mail? The things you buy on impulse at Wal-Mart?"

He shrugs, then looks oddly wistful. "No wife, no kids, no junk."

"That rule doesn't apply to other bachelors I've known."

He starts to reply, but winces again instead.

"Your leg?"

"It's stiffening up fast. Let me just get on the couch there. I can go through the Argus photos there."

"I think you'd better rest before you start on those."

He limps to the sofa with his weight on the cane, but instead of helping him sit, I take his hand and pull him past the sofa toward the hall. "I don't want to sleep," he complains, pulling back against my hand.

"We're not going to sleep."

"Oh."

His resistance stops, and I lead him toward a half-open

379

door at the end of the hall, where a cherry footboard shows through. Like the rest of the house, the bedroom is clean; the bed is neatly made. With John's casual dress habits, I thought this inner sanctum might be the secret wreck of the house. Maybe that's just projection.

He starts to sit on the bed, but I stop him and pull back the covers first. Once he gets horizontal, the painkillers will kick in, and it will be a while before he feels like getting up again.

"I need to sit down," he says in a tight voice.

With me holding his upper arms, he eases back and sits on the edge of the bed, then lies back on the pillow with a groan.

"Bad?"

"Not good. I'm okay, though."

"Let's see if I can make it better."

I slip off my shoes, then climb onto the bed and carefully sit astride him. "Does that hurt?"

"No."

"Liar." Leaning forward, I brush his lips with mine and pull back, waiting for him to respond. His hands slide up my hips to my waist; then he kisses me back, gently, yet insistently enough to remind me of the passion I felt in the shower last night. A warm wave of desire rolls through me, which combined with the Xanax suppresses the shadowy images bubbling up from my subconscious.

"I want to forget," I whisper. "Just for an hour."

He nods and pulls my lips to his, kissing me deeply as his arms slip around my back. After a bit, he nibbles my neck, then my ear, and the warmth escalates into something urgent enough to make me squirm in discomfort. That's the way I am. I go a day or a week or a month without being aware of my body, and then suddenly it's *there*, making me uncomfortably aware of its needs. But my need runs much deeper than flesh. For the past year, I've lived with a growing emptiness that has threatened to swallow me whole.

"You have something?" I whisper.

"In the dresser."

I slide off him and move to the dresser.

"Top drawer."

When I get back to the bed, I stand looking down at him. He watches me with wide eyes, waiting to see what I'll do. The base of my skull is still throbbing, but not so badly now. I'd give a lot to have my shoulders rubbed, but he's in no shape to do that for me. Given what his doctor told us, he's not in shape to do anything I have in mind. But I suspect he feels differently.

"You okay?" he asks.

I smile at him and begin unbuttoning my blouse. The bra I put on this morning is sealed in an evidence bag in the belly of a plane on its way to Washington, and the agent who lent me a change of clothes didn't have an extra bra in her trunk. When the blouse slips off my shoulders, John's breath goes shallow.

I slide off my jeans and panties, then climb back to the spot I was in before. As he looks up at me, I see the pulse beating at the base of his throat. I touch his lips with my finger.

"Five minutes ago I felt as low as I ever have. I thought we were going to come in here and have violent sex that would exorcize our demons just long enough to let us sleep. But that's not what this is."

He nods. "I know."

"You make me happy, John."

"I'm glad. You make me happy too."

"God, we're a bad movie."

He laughs. "The real thing always sounds like a bad movie." He reaches up and touches my cheek. "I know you're torn to pieces inside, especially after seeing that picture. I don't—"

"Shh. This is how it is. Life happens in the middle of death. I feel lucky to have found you, and this is where we happen to be. You could have died today. So could I. And we'd never have known what this was like."

"You're right."

"Come on. We deserve it."

He reaches up and rubs my abdomen, and the warmth of his hand makes me shiver. He nods down toward his leg. "I'm not exactly in top form."

"You're still talking pretty well."

"And?"

"One critical part is still in working order."

He shakes his head and laughs. "You're not shy, are you?"

"I'm forty, John. I'm not a Girl Scout anymore. And you still owe me from the hotel."

"I wondered why you hadn't taken off my clothes."

I smile down at him. "First things first."

"How do we do this?"

"I'll make it easy for you."

Leaning forward, I take hold of the headboard and slide up his chest, then rise onto my knees. Without hesitation, he lays his hands on my hips and pulls me to him, kissing lightly. A thrill of heat races over my skin, and I settle against him.

"Is this okay?" he asks.

"Don't talk. Just keep doing that."

He does, and after less than a minute, I know this is not

going to take long. I learned long ago that the trick is not to concentrate on reaching a peak, but to be with someone with whom you feel totally at ease. Then you can close your eyes and let go of the world, and you'll be carried to the peak without ever taking a step. I've felt at ease with John from the first, and now is no different. He knows where I want to go and how to take me there, and I'm content to let him. I dig my fingers into his hair and pull him into me, and he groans with pleasure.

With a sudden tingle, a film of sweat covers my skin from my scalp to my toes. The tension builds steadily within me, and my thighs go taut and quiver with strain. As I hold myself still against his insistent kisses, his hands slide up my ribs and cover my breasts, and I feel him urging me toward completion, one flick no different from the last, the next a trigger that catapults me into another dimension, where every nerve ending sings with heat and every muscle trembles without command. For an instant all goes white; then the whiteness bends into waves that dissipate into soft color and the physical fallout of shivering and panting that let him know he has done well. He lifts his head and lightly kisses my belly, and I slide down his chest and hug him tightly.

"*Mmm.* I think I could actually sleep now."

"Hmm." The sound of consternation.

I reach back and tickle his stomach, then slide my hand farther down. "Feels like somebody needs some special attention before anyone goes to sleep."

He tries to look nonchalant, but he's not fooling anybody.

I reach back and undo his belt and trousers, then try to fit the condom on him with one hand. "This is like you learning to unhook a bra when you were a teenager, right?"

He laughs. "You're doing pretty well."

"There. Everything okay?"

He pulls my face down and kisses me again, gently despite his need. I playfully bite his bottom lip, waiting to see how desperate he is, but he just keeps kissing me. Before long I realize what he already seems to know: I want him inside me as badly as he wants to be there.

"You win," I tell him, sliding backward.

"Are you okay?" he asks.

"I will be in a minute. Go slow."

"I'm counting." His eyes twinkle. "Not easy to be still now."

He lays his hands on my thighs and slowly presses up into me, taking my breath away. Then he begins to move, sliding me forward and back with maddening regularity. The mere presence of him there is enough to scramble my thoughts. It's been almost a year since I made love with a man, and I feel as though I'm recovering from a sort of physical amnesia. To be so full and still need to be filled, to feel utterly vulnerable and yet primally complete, all of it comes back in the grip of his strong hands and the slow ebb and flow of him in my softest place.

I can tell he's happy, but I also sense that he's holding back. That at the core he sees me as fragile.

"I'm not a china vase, John."

"I know that."

"You're thinking about what I told Thalia."

He slows his movement, then stops. "You can't pretend that's not part of you. That you're completely over it."

"I'm not over it. But I am above it. Is it you that has a problem with it?"

"Absolutely not. I'm just worried about you. I want to take care of you."

384

"Then do that." I start to move against him, but he still looks uncertain. There's only one way to get past this awkwardness, and that's to rip him out of his preconceptions. It's a risk, but one I feel I have to take.

"Did Lenz tell you about my affair with my teacher?" I ask, watching his eyes as I move.

"No. But I saw something in his notes."

"Lenz showed you his notes?"

"They were on the table in the conference room." He looks troubled now. "I took a quick look."

"Only natural, right?"

"I'm an investigator. Nosy by nature."

"What did you think about what you read?"

"I don't judge anybody, as long as they don't hurt someone else."

"Good. Because I was really in love with him."

"I'm sorry about what happened."

I arch my back, and John closes his eyes and groans deep in his throat. "You know one thing I really liked in that relationship?"

"What?"

"When I went to school after being with him the night before, or that morning, nobody knew. But *I* knew. I could still feel him. I felt marked, you know? I belonged to him."

"That doesn't sound like you. Wanting to belong to somebody. Anybody."

"Shows how much you know. I'm as independent as they come, right?" I settle my weight and begin moving in slow circles. "But you know what?"

"What?" he asks hoarsely.

"After we've been together long enough for the CDC or whoever to clear us, you know what I want?"

"What?"

"I want you to fill me up. I want you to mark your territory every day, so I can always feel you."

"Jesus, Jordan—"

Tightening my muscles, I plant my palms on his chest and push. He moans with ineffable pleasure, and his eyes go wide, searching mine, trying to discover all that I am in a span of seconds. Foolish man. My neuroses alone would take years to plumb. He bites his lip against the pain of his leg and grasps my wrists in his hands.

"Now you see me," I whisper. "And I see *you*. I know what you want . . . how you want it. I'm all grown up, John. You can do what you want. Anything."

At last he snaps out of himself, out of the man who sees me as someone to be protected and into the one who wants me beyond restraint. His hands fly to my hips, pulling me down as he flails into me, not caring anymore about my feelings or his leg, nothing but getting as deep into me as physical limits will allow, making me his alone. The bed, which only squeaked before, hammers the wall. The lamp on the end table crashes to the floor. None of it matters. I grip the headboard with all my strength and hold him against the mattress until he screams and goes into spasms you'd think would kill a man but which in fact bring him gasping and sweating back to life. When he collapses onto the pillow, I fall beside him.

"Jesus," he says breathlessly.

"I know."

"You're amazing."

"Hardly."

"How do you feel?"

"The same way you feel about me. You think all the boys get this treatment?"

386

"I didn't know."

"Well, now you do."

He smiles with contentment. "I love you, Jordan."

"Take it easy. You're in shock."

"I think you're right. I haven't been – I mean, I haven't felt like that since . . ."

"When?"

He blinks and looks at the ceiling. "I was going to say Vietnam."

The mild euphoria I felt before slips away. "You slept with Vietnamese women over there?"

"Everybody did."

"They were beautiful?"

"Some."

"Different from other women?"

"How do you mean? In bed?"

"Yes . . . but not just that. I don't know. Like de Becque said. Like that Li, that woman we met on Cayman. Did they make you fall in love with them?"

He's looking in my direction, but his mind is focused thousands of miles away. "I saw it happen a lot. People over here think it's because Vietnamese women were more submissive than American women, but that's not it. They just – I'm not talking about the city girls, now, the bar girls, but regular Vietnamese women – they had a naturalness about them. They were very demure, yet open about certain things. It's seductive without trying to be. I knew a guy who deserted to be with one."

"And I just made you feel like they made you feel?"

"Not the same. Only the intensity." He touches my cheek. "You're thinking about your father, aren't you?"

"Yes."

"That he may have left you on purpose?"

387

I nod, unable to voice my fear.

"I'm not like your father, Jordan."

"I know. You're like the men he took pictures of."

"What do you mean?"

John's ceiling has a water stain. The house isn't perfect after all. "They were more real than he was. He seemed to make them real, to bring them into existence with his camera. And in a way he did. The way I do. We make certain things real to the rest of the world. But the rest of the world doesn't really matter. My father's photos didn't make soldiers eternal, the way someone wrote they did. What those *soldiers* did made them eternal. And whatever they did, I think, is still happening somewhere. All of it. All things, all the time. I probably sound nuts. That's what comes from living on the West Coast, right?"

"You don't sound nuts. The things I saw and did in Vietnam have never stopped for me. You know why I don't have post-traumatic stress disorder? Because there's nothing *post* about it. It's just something I live with. Sometimes nearer, sometimes farther away."

"Tell me something, John. The truth. Do you think my father is involved in this thing?"

"No." His eyes are steady and guileless.

"But you did before."

"I wondered, that's all. I still don't know what's happening. But if your father's involved, the only way I can see it is if he's in with de Becque somehow."

"But you don't think so."

"No."

"What do you base that on?"

"My gut."

I lay my hand on his flat stomach. "You don't have much of one."

"I'm glad you can still laugh."

"It's the same old choice. Laugh or cry." I rub my hand slowly over his abdomen. "Why don't you sleep for a while?"

He shakes his head. "I can't. Not with Thalia still out there. I can never sleep when things are breaking."

"You want me to make coffee or something?"

"Coffee would be good."

"What about food? You have anything in the fridge?"

"Can you cook?"

I laugh. "Mostly foreign dishes designed for campfires. But I don't think there's a Mississippi girl on the planet who can't do the basics."

"There are some chicken breasts in the freezer."

"Rice in the cabinets? Onions?"

"Probably."

"Jambalaya, then." I kiss him on the chin and climb out of the bed.

"Would you mind bringing those Argus photos in here?"

"I think they can wait, but I'll bring them."

I retrieve the thick manila envelope from the coffee table and toss it onto the bed. "How many of those have you looked at already?"

"I don't know. Until they adjusted the sensitivity of the program, I was looking at twenty different versions of the same face before it became recognizable as another one."

"Pace yourself. Jambalaya and biscuits, coming up."

I walk back to the kitchen and orient myself, but I've gotten no further than running water over the chicken breasts when John's voice echoes up the hallway. Something in the sound makes me freeze with my hand on the sink tap. I run for the bedroom, in my mind seeing him turning blue from a blood clot broken free by our strenuous lovemaking.

389

"I know this woman," he says, shaking a piece of paper at me as I come through the door.

"From where?" I ask, taking the picture from him. It's a facial shot of a young blond woman, maybe eighteen. She's like a template of an adult; her face has yet to develop the definition of personality. "Is she one of the missing persons you've been studying?"

"No. I saw her *years* ago. In Quantico."

"You mean you knew her? Personally?"

He shakes his head impatiently. "No. Every year we have city and state cops coming through Quantico. Our National Academy program. Most of them have a case that's dogged them for years, one they couldn't solve or get out of their minds. Sometimes it's a single murder. Usually it's two or three they think might be connected. A police detective showed me this woman at Quantico."

"A New Orleans detective?"

"That's the thing. I think he was from New York. This is a really old case."

My head is buzzing with a strange excitement. "How old?"

"Ten years? Remember at the Camellia Grill, when I told you I was working on something? I said if it panned out, I'd tell you? Well, maybe it has."

"How do you mean? What are you talking about?"

"The youngest of our four suspects is Frank Smith, who's thirty-five. Serial offenders don't just wake up one day and start killing people in middle age. Baxter's unit was checking all four suspects' past residences for similar unsolved crimes. Vermont, where Wheaton's from. Terrebonne Parish, where Laveau grew up. Those were easy. That left New York, for Smith and Gaines. Not to mention the possible accomplice. In fact, all four suspects have ties to New York. But when you're talking about missing persons – which is what this case is, because of the lack of corpses – you're talking about thousands of victims in New York, even if you only go back a few years. The VICAP computer is supposed to make those kinds of connections, but police compliance isn't always great, and it's worse the farther back you go. But I thought, What if there were unsolved homicides in New York that had only one or two similarities to this case?"

"Like . . . ?"

"Women taken from grocery stores, jogging paths, et cetera, snatched off the street without a trace, no witnesses, nothing. A professional feel to them, yet no obvious similarities between the victims."

"Did you check it out?"

"I called some New York cops I knew from the Academy program and asked them to poke around their old files. It was asking a lot, but I had to do it."

"Did you talk to the cop who showed you this woman?"

"No, that guy's retired now. And nobody's gotten back to me yet. But this woman . . ."

"You still remember her?"

"I told you before, I've got a knack for faces. This girl was pretty and young, and she stuck in my mind. That detective's, too. She was his informant, now that I think about it. Will you bring me the cordless phone?"

I get him the phone, and he rings the field office, asking for Baxter.

"It's John," he says. "I think we caught a break. . . . A big one. We need New York to liaise with NYPD in a big hurry. . . ."

I sit on the edge of the bed and look at the Argus-generated portrait again. It's a strangely nonhuman image, yet lifelike enough to pull a ten-year-old memory from John's brain. I say a silent thank-you to the photographer who confided the existence of Argus to me.

"Jordan?" says John, hanging up the phone. "Do you know what this means?"

"It means my sister wasn't victim number five. Whoever is behind this started taking women more than a decade ago. In New York."

He squeezes my arm. "We're close now. Really close."

23

I'm lying in John's tub, soaking in hot water up to my neck,
a pleasure I managed by jamming plastic wrap into the slits
in the side of the circular metal thing that operates the drain.
The glass bricks above me have slowly turned from black to
blue with the coming dawn, and while I don't feel rested, I
do feel less frazzled than I did yesterday.

Last night passed in a flurry of confusion, elation
mingled with depression, like sugar highs punctuated by
exhaustion. Prompted by John's recognition of the Argus
photo, Daniel Baxter rousted the midnight homicide shifts
at the NYPD. Using Argus-enhanced photos of the abstract
Sleeping Women paintings, New York detectives managed
to identify six of the eight unidentified victims in the
NOKIDS case.

Once the women were identified, the story came
together by itself. Between 1979 and 1984, a serial kidnap-
murderer was operating in New York City area without
anyone connecting more than three of his crimes. His
victims were prostitutes and hitchhikers – neither category
high on the NYPD's list of priorities. The significance of
this discovery was simple and devastating: the painter of
the Sleeping Women had not begun his work two years ago
in New Orleans, but more than twenty years ago in New
York.

The ramifications were more complex. First, our

youngest suspect, Frank Smith, had been only fifteen years old at the time. This alone did not exonerate him, but it shifted the focus of the investigation away from him. Second, not one Sleeping Woman had been sold at the time of the New York murders. Third, why would a serial killer murder eight women and then suddenly stop? In John's experience, only prison or death stopped serial murderers from pursuing their work. But most puzzling was why, having stopped, the murderer would resume his work fifteen years later. Had he been locked up for a decade and a half, only to emerge as hungry for victims as before?

John drank nonstop cups of coffee to fight the sedative effects of his painkillers, and sat on the sofa working out theory after theory in an attempt to fit the new parameters of the case. Too exhausted to be any use to him, I went into the bathroom, took three Xanax, and got into bed.

Sleep came quickly, but that was no blessing. With sleep came dreams. All the fantastic input of the past seven days had been brewing in my subconscious, and it finally burst free with a vengeance. Most of the images I can't remember, but one remains clear: I'm standing at the center of Roger Wheaton's room-sized masterpiece, a circular canvas that's no canvas at all, but a universe of forest and earth and stream and sky. Peering out at me from the twisted tree roots are shadowy grinning faces: Leon Gaines, his eyes blazing with lust; the murderous UNSUB on the levee; and capering through the trees like a beautiful demon, Frank Smith, naked, chasing Thalia Laveau, who struggles to keep a white robe from falling as she runs. The scene whirls around me like a Hieronymous Bosch nightmare while I stand trans-fixed, the floor under my feet flowing like a stream, and reflected in the stream, the face of my father.

That dream soon flowed into another, but I can't remember it. Sometime during the night, John began kissing me. Only half asleep, I started awake, but when I recognized his face, my heartbeat slowed and my fear abated. I made sure he was wearing something, then pulled him over and let him move slowly inside me until he shuddered and collapsed. I was asleep before he rolled off me, caught again in a spiraling descent into flashing darkness.

The phone rang ceaselessly for most of the night, and even in my sedated state, I stirred at every ring, fearing dreadful news. It finally stopped around four, and John fell into a deep sleep. Now, with the coming of dawn, it begins again. I'd like to let John rest, but I'm not getting out of this delicious water to talk to some homicide cop from Queens.

After three rings, the bedsprings groan and a hoarse voice says, "Kaiser." After a few moments, he says, "When? . . . Where? . . . Right. I'm on my way."

After ten seconds of thrashing in the bedcovers and grunting in pain, John limps into the bathroom, his hair a mess but his eyes alert. "A pushboat crew just fished the UNSUB's body out of the river, five miles downstream from where he went in."

Adrenaline flushes through me in a dizzying rush. I get to my feet and snatch a towel from the rack.

"Baxter choppered a forensic team down to the site to fingerprint the corpse. They'll be back at the office before we can get across the causeway."

"How's your leg?"

"It's still there. Get dressed. We're about to meet the man who tried to kidnap you."

Baxter and Lenz are standing in the main computer room with coffee cups in their hands when we arrive at the field office. Three technicians wearing headsets sit before a bank of computer terminals with continuously changing data, while above them large CRTs show live TV of every possible approach to the field office.

"You broke some speeding laws getting here," Baxter says to me, but he winks at John. "Chopper got the prints here five minutes ago. They're already in IAFIS."

IAFIS, as John explained on the way over, is the Integrated Automated Fingerprint System, a database of over two hundred million fingerprints.

"Our priority bumped everything in the queue," says Baxter. "If there's a match, we'll have it any second."

Dr. Lenz says, "When I started consulting, they did this job with note cards."

"Where's the body?" asks John.

"Going to the Orleans Parish morgue. Looked like four bullet wounds."

"Sir?" says a female technician, looking up at Baxter. "We have a match. One hundred percent."

The technician flicks her trackball and clicks a button. On her CRT, one large fingerprint superimposes upon another with near-perfect accuracy.

"Whose finger is that?" asks Baxter as we crowd around the screen.

The tech clicks again, and a criminal record pops onto the screen. In the top right-hand corner is a photograph, the face in it a younger version of the man who shot Wendy on the levee yesterday.

"Conrad Frederick Hoffman," reads the tech. "Convicted felon. Born Newark, New Jersey, 1952."

The three men tense around me.

"What was the crime?" asks Lenz.

"Murder."

"Where did he serve his time?" asks John.

"Sing Sing," says the tech. "New York State."

A more pregnant silence I've never heard. As if speaking with one voice, the three men say, "Leon Gaines."

"What years was Hoffman in Sing Sing?" asks Baxter. "Quick."

While the tech searches her screen, John taps the shoulder of the male tech next to her and says, "Call up Leon Isaac Gaines on NCIC. I need the exact years he was in Sing Sing."

"Hoffman served fourteen years for murder," says the woman, "1984 to 1998."

"Leon Isaac Gaines," says the male tech. "Two terms in Sing Sing, the first 1973 to 1978, the second 1985 to 1990."

"Son of a bitch," John breathes. "That's a five-year-intersect. They had to know each other. And both were free at the time of the New York murders."

"Sometimes the cards fall right," says Baxter. "Let's get back to the EOC."

"We need the warden of Sing Sing," says John, "and every convict we can get hold of who served during those years. Not just Gaines's known associates. And everybody who was involved in the art program in the prison."

John picks up a nearby phone. "Emergency Operations Center, please. Surveillance unit." He nods at Lenz, who can apparently read his mind. "John Kaiser here. Where's Leon Gaines right now? . . . What's he doing there? . . . You have him covered? . . . How many cars and men? . . . Get a chopper in the air. I want zero chance of losing him when he comes out. . . . Right. Where's his girlfriend? . . . Okay."

"Where's Gaines?" asks Baxter as he hangs up.

"He just pulled into the Kenner Wal-Mart. Isn't it a little early for shopping?"

Baxter shrugs. "He's a drunk and an addict, and he just woke up after sleeping twelve hours."

The ISU chief steps up behind the two techs and squeezes their shoulders. "Thanks a lot, people. This was big."

The gesture seems a little overdone, but both techs sit taller as we leave the room. Such is the gift of leadership.

Forty-five minutes later, we're grouped in SAC Bowles's office, and the mood is grim. An hour of phone calls to Sing Sing has not yielded the hoped-for results. No one has been able to establish a personal relationship between Conrad Hoffman and Leon Gaines, even though the two spent five years in the same prison at the same time.

"We have three options," says Baxter. "One, arrest Gaines now and interrogate him. Two, question him but don't arrest him. Three, wait until we have more information."

"You can't wait!" I cry in disbelief. "You've already wasted too much time. Thalia Laveau could be dying some-where right now!"

"I think Laveau is dead already," says Lenz, not even looking at me. "Even if she's not, Gaines may not know where she is. If he's merely the painter in the conspiracy, I mean."

"*You* think she's dead?" I ask, coming half out of my chair. "Who gives a goddamn what you think? How many times have you been right in the past week? Once?"

The four men gape at me in amazement, but I can't hold in my anger any longer. "Right now, Thalia is wherever all the

398

Sleeping Women were painted. In a killing house, like you talked about in the beginning. The house where the courtyard is. The house *you can't find*. And if that painter is Leon Gaines, Thalia is waiting for an artist who won't ever show up, because he knows we're watching him. She could be dying while Gaines strolls around Wal-Mart, dreaming about painting her and laughing at us!"

"That's true," John says quietly. "But Gaines can't help us with Thalia without admitting complicity in serial murder. And without knowing more, we can't offer him immunity. The victims' families would crucify us. The grim reality is that right now, we have no way to make Gaines talk. No legal way, anyhow."

A strange hush follows this statement, and Baxter hurries to break it. "Six hours," he says. "For six hours we work every possible lead, every snitch at Sing Sing. Go back over every fact of Gaines's past to see if we missed something. We rip his life apart. If we find something we can use against him, hallelujah. If not, we fall on him like a brick shithouse and try to scare him into talking."

"Bluff a streetwise ex-con?" mutters Lenz.

"We've got no other option!" Baxter shouts, in a rare breach of professionalism.

In the stunned silence that follows, I ask, "What about the girlfriend? Linda Knapp?"

"What about her?" asks Baxter.

"If you could talk to her away from him, she might recant her support for his alibis. She did it once."

"And then she went right back to him," says John. "Knowing he'd beat the crap out of her."

"She's alone in the house right now," Lenz says thoughtfully, his eyes on me. "Gaines is at Wal-Mart."

"Damn it," says Baxter, only now realizing what the

psychiatrist already has. "Jordan, you almost got killed yesterday. You haven't had enough?"

"Hoffman's dead. Gaines isn't home. Wire me up and send me in there with the girl. If Gaines starts home, knock on the door and I'll get the hell out of there."

Baxter is not convinced, but SAC Bowles looks like he has no objection, and John knows better than to get involved at this point.

"You know a woman has a better chance with her than any of you," I insist.

"We have plenty of female agents," says Baxter.

"Not one who knows this case like I do. Not one with something personal at stake. Knapp will feel that from me."

"She's right," says John. "We can't turn Gaines's woman against him with some bullshit come-on. And Knapp knows her already." His eyes lock onto Baxter's with dark intensity. "It's all we've got, Daniel."

"God*damn* it," mutters Baxter, throwing up his hands in surrender. "Let's get over there before Gaines fills up his shopping cart."

Baxter and Dr. Lenz are hunched in the surveillance van one block from Gaines's shotgun house on Freret Street. I'm parked behind the van in my Mustang, John's featherweight .38 strapped to my right ankle beneath my jeans. John leans into my window and points toward my foot.

"Everything secure?" he asks, knowing Baxter and Lenz can hear me over the wire.

"Good to go."

Seeing worry in his face, I slip my hand into my blouse and flatten the pad of my thumb over the microphone clipped there. "I'm not going to need it."

"That's just when you do need it," he whispers. "Like the camera in your fanny pack." He lays his hand on my upper arm. "I've never seen a female serial killer of the classic type, but we do get women who help men carry out vicious murders. Serials, even. And Linda Knapp fits the profile of that type of woman. Poor self-image, dominated by an abusive male—"

"I'm just going to talk to her, John. If she comes at me, I promise I'll shoot her. Now let me get going, before Gaines gets back."

He squeezes my arm, then backs away from the car. I wave and pull into the street.

Gaines's neighborhood is a sad sight in the early morning. I have a feeling that even the old people don't start stirring until well after daylight. Wheeling over to the broken curb in front of Gaines's shotgun, I kill the motor and sit for a moment. I don't want to appear too eager or rushed. Like an actress preparing for a scene, I let the worries of the present bleed away, and allow the emotions I keep buried in my heart to rise to the surface. My fears for Jane, my longing for my father, the humiliation of my rape – things I loathe, but which can be my allies now.

Gaines's stairs creak as I climb to the porch. The surveillance team says their thermal imaging camera shows Knapp still in the bed. I considered calling her first, but everyone agreed that would give her an easy chance to refuse to see me. Before doubt can assail me, I knock on the door. Three times, hard.

There's no answer, so I knock again, hard enough to bruise my knuckles.

"Come on," I say softly.

She doesn't come to the door.

"Maybe she overdosed in there," I say to the mike clipped to my bra.

Getting on tiptoe, I peer through the window set high in the door. Inside is the same dark and depressing cavern I wanted out of so badly the other day. Dirty clothes and pizza boxes litter the floor. The easel stands to my left, bare as a skeleton now. To my right is a blank wall that farther down becomes the wall of the hallway. Without warning, apprehension raises the hairs on my neck and arms.

Something is out of place.

What am I seeing? "Wrong question," I murmur, as apprehension escalates into anxiety. It's what I'm *not* seeing. The small abstract by Roger Wheaton, the one that hung on the wall to my right. It's no longer there. Why would Gaines take it down? In answer, Frank Smith's voice plays eerily in my head: *Pond scum . . . Roger gave him a matched pair of abstracts as a gift, small but very fine. Leon sold one of them two weeks later – for heroin, I'm sure.* Gaines took the painting with him because he's going to sell it. For what? Drugs? Or money to run?

I grasp the handle and try the door. It's locked, but the old wood panel rattles loosely in its frame. An eight-year-old could kick it open. Of course, if I do, Daniel Baxter will jerk me out of the house so fast I won't even reach the bedroom.

Gripping the handle firmly with both hands, I set my shoulder against the door and lean forward. Wood and metal creak, even under the marginal stress of my 130 pounds. Keeping my leg against the door, I lean back, then lunge forward with the pad of my shoulder. The door gives way with a soft crunch.

"Hello, Linda," I say for the benefit of the boys back in the van. "I wanted to talk to you if I could."

The smell of feces hits me in a wave. I recoil, sensing death, but my brain reassures me that for thermal imaging cameras to see Linda Knapp on the bed, she has to be alive. *Or very recently alive,* says a small voice. I could have the guys in the van busting in here with one word, but if I do, I'll lose any chance to question Linda Knapp alone. She may just be sleeping. The stink could be coming from an unflushed commode.

Bending over, I pull John's featherweight .38 from the ankle holster and move quickly through the front room, holding the gun in both hands. I keep my eyes forward, not focusing on specific objects, but staying alert to any movement, the way a British soldier once taught me.

The hall closes around me with a claustrophobic closeness. There's an open door ahead on my right. Crouching low, I ease my head past the frame. There's no bed, just a mattress lying on the floor, piled with blankets and surrounded by dirty clothes. The room looks empty, though a closet door stands partly open in the corner. It *looks* empty – but the thermal camera says it's not.

As I stand erect, the blankets piled on the bed suddenly coalesce into a recognizable shape. A human shape. With my eyes on the closet door, I dart to the mattress and jerk the blankets off the bed.

The stench nearly makes me vomit, but the sight is worse. Lying on the bed is a woman gagged with duct tape and wrapped in a blanket, the side of her head matted with blood, one eye open and staring sightless at the ceiling.

"*John?*" I whisper, but nothing audible comes out. "John, I need help. *Help!*"

The woman on the bed is Linda Knapp; the hard line of her jaw and the lank blond hair confirm it in my mind. Crouching over her, I put two fingertips beneath her jawbone and feel for a carotid pulse. There's a weak throb against my hand.

As carefully as I can, I pull the duct tape away from her mouth to free her airway. Then the little house begins shaking under the pounding of male feet, and a voice roars: *"Federal agents! Throw down your weapons!"*

John and Baxter crash into the room with guns drawn, but there's no one for them to shoot.

"She's alive!" I cry. "She needs an ambulance! Hurry!"

While Baxter issues orders over a radio and John checks the closet, Dr. Lenz rushes to the bed, bends over, and examines the beaten woman.

"Severe head trauma," he says. "He hit her with something heavy."

John points at a shadeless metal lamp lying on the floor with a shattered bulb. Its base is square and heavy and stained dark.

"Arrest Gaines right now," Baxter orders over the radio. "Presume him armed and extremely dangerous, but try not to shoot him. Confirm as soon as it's done."

"He wrapped her in an electric blanket," says Lenz. "Right around body temperature. Even if she died, we'd have been slow to notice anything." He pulls up Knapp's closed eyelid, then lets it close. "We'll be lucky if she can ever tell us anything."

"This is all wrong," says John. "You don't beat your girlfriend and leave her for dead, then go shopping at Wal-Mart."

"The painting's gone," I say dully.

"What painting?" asks Lenz.

"The one Wheaton gave him. He must have taken it to sell."

"He's pulling a rabbit," says John.

Baxter's radio crackles. "Sir, this is Agent Liebe. My agents inside lost visual with the suspect a couple of minutes ago. We're in the store in force now, but it's full of people. I think maybe—"

"Shut it down!" Baxter orders. "Nobody goes in or out."

24

The Kenner Wal-Mart is a riot waiting to happen. As we drove up, sirens blaring, I saw the parking lot half-filled with cars but empty of people, and though we entered the store through its rear loading dock, the low roar of an angry crowd rumbled through the service doors. In the twelve minutes it took us to get here, two agents sifting through the trapped customers and four searching the aisles and dressing rooms have turned up no sign of Leon Gaines, though his car still sits in the parking lot.

In the security room at the back of the store, a bank of video monitors displays feeds from three dozen video cameras mounted at various locations in the ceiling of the store. Baxter shows the head of security his FBI credentials, then asks the technician operating the VTRs to fast-forward from a point three minutes before Agent Liebe reported losing contact with Gaines to the point that he sealed the building.

"What's this guy done?" asks the security chief.

"He's a federal fugitive," says John. "That's all we can say."

"I don't think we can legally detain customers inside the store. The company could be liable."

Baxter turns away from the screens. "Your store was sealed by the federal government. You've got no worries."

"There's Gaines," says John, looking over the tech's shoulder.

On the screen, Leon Gaines pushes a grocery cart along the hardware aisle. He's wearing a dirty white T-shirt, black jeans, and has three days' growth of beard on his face. His curly black hair is a tangled mess, and he moves with a jerky sort of energy, like a man looking for a fix. His cart holds a gallon of milk, a pack of precut hamburger patties, some toiletries, and a copy of *Hot Rod* magazine. After ten seconds, he moves out of the frame.

Baxter's radio crackles. "Agent Liebe, sir. We just had to arrest an elderly gentleman at the main exit."

Dr. Lenz chuckles softly.

Baxter holds the radio to his mouth. "Keep the lid on."

"Give us the cameras covering the exits," says John.

"You don't want to try to follow him on other views?" asks the tech.

"Just the exits."

Two sets of automated glass doors appear on the screens, plus the large service exit at the rear.

"Run it normal speed."

We watch people stroll in and out of the store: male and female, young and old, black and white. Some customers stop beside the greeter and have a sticker affixed to a product they've come to return.

"Stop the tape!" says John.

"What is it?" asks the tech, stopping the tape.

John touches his fingertip to the figure of a brunette woman exiting through the automatic doors. "Look how tall she is compared to this other woman." His finger slides onto a blonde frozen in the entrance door; she looks almost a foot shorter than the brunette. Then his finger slides back. "I think this is Gaines."

Baxter crouches before the screen and squints. "Damn it. You're right. He shaved, put on a wig and coat, picked up a handbag, and walked right past our people."

"Probably brought a battery-powered shaver with him," says Lenz.

Baxter straightens up and turns to the security chief. "Let everybody go."

The man nods and hurries away to quell the incipient rebellion.

"He's been gone fifteen minutes, minimum," says John. "He could be anywhere."

"We're less than a mile from the international airport," Baxter thinks aloud. He lifts the radio to his mouth. "Liebe, your whole detail is going to the airport. Come back here first."

"Yes, sir."

Baxter touches Gaines's image on the screen and looks at the tech. "Can you give me a print of this 'woman'?"

"No problem."

"Print twenty. And twenty of him the way he looked in the hardware aisle. An Agent Liebe will be back here to get them." Baxter looks at John. "Back to the office?"

John walks over to the gray wall, then back, as though pacing will give him some insight into the situation. "We should leave somebody in the parking lot. In about a minute, a customer is going to start yelling that his car was stolen while he was trapped in here. Once we know the make, we can put everything we have in the air."

A muted ring sounds in the room. John pulls his cell phone from his jacket. "Kaiser here. . . . Just now? . . . Put him through." He looks at Baxter. "Roger Wheaton just called the office and asked them to page me. He said it was an emergency."

"Wheaton?" says Lenz.

"Hello?" John covers his open ear and turns away

from us to concentrate. "Yes, sir, John Kaiser. . . . Can you get out of the building? . . . I understand. Can you get them out? . . . Listen to me, Mr. Wheaton. If you can't get them out, get yourself out. They're not your responsibility. . . . We're on the way. Get to safety and wait for us to arrive."

John whirls to face us. "Gaines just sandbagged Roger Wheaton in his office at the Woldenberg Art Center. Gaines claimed he's being framed by the FBI and that he needs money to get out of the country."

"Is he armed?" asks Baxter.

John nods. "Wheaton told Gaines he would drive him to the bank and get him money, but that his wallet and keys were down in the gallery where he was painting. Gaines told Wheaton if he wasn't back in two minutes, he'd take students hostage and start killing them. There are fifty to seventy students spread through the building, and they have no idea what's happening. Wheaton ran down to another office and called us."

"Why not the police?" asks Lenz. "And why ask for you?"

"He said he didn't want Gaines shot out of hand. He's actually worried about that son of a bitch."

"I don't want him shot either," I say sharply. "He may be the only person in the world who knows where the women are."

Baxter takes out his cell phone and hits a speed-dial button. "This is Baxter. Give me SAC Bowles, right now." He looks at John. "We need a chopper out here – Patrick? Leon Gaines is at the art center at Tulane, and he probably has hostages. We need SWAT out there ASAP. . . . How many choppers do you have in the air? . . . Send them both to the Kenner Wal-Mart parking lot. And you'd better alert

409

the task force. Be sure they know who's running the scene at Tulane. . . . I'll keep you posted." Baxter waves away a sheaf of photo prints the tech holds up to him and looks at John. "We'll have two choppers outside in three minutes. Let's move."

Hurtling over New Orleans at a hundred knots, you can see why people call it the Crescent City. The older sections sit in a great bend in the Mississippi River, the main streets either fanning into the bend or running with it. Today the river flows the color of slate, thanks to a gray overcast, but a broad shaft of sunlight to the south shows a patch of familiar reddish brown.

John and Baxter ride the lead chopper, Dr. Lenz and I the one behind. Below us, Audubon Park stretches north from the river to St. Charles Avenue; north of St. Charles begins the rectangular garden that is Tulane University. As the lead chopper swings over a golf course and drops toward Tulane, an overwhelming sense of déjà vu brings sweat to my face and hands. I've descended into many cities this way, clinging to a spar with my cameras around my neck: Sarajevo, Maputo, Karachi, Baghdad, San Salvador, Managua, Panama City. The list is endless, but the city below me now is the one in which I began my career, and it strikes me that the symmetry of my ending it here might be quite a temptation for the fates. If so, I accept the risk. The placid green island below harbors a desperate situation, but in the resolution of it lies the answer to the mystery that has haunted me for more than a year.

The cockpit radio spits and crackles as a deskbound FBI agent with a university map guides the pilots toward their LZ. The helicopter drops fast enough to make my stomach roll, and I wonder if John and Baxter are flashing back to

Vietnam as we auger in. Parked at the center of one grassy quadrangle are two police cars with their lights flashing, while beside them an olive-drab Huey helicopter sits like a harbinger of battle, its main rotor slowly turning. I saw several Hueys on the National Guard base contiguous to the FBI field office lot; the FBI SWAT team has probably deployed from that chopper.

As I search the quad for armed men, we dip forward and bore in, at the last second flaring and coming to rest thirty yards from the lead chopper. John jumps out of his cockpit and runs toward us, while Baxter moves toward the waiting NOPD cops.

"It's not good!" John yells as I get out and run in a crouch beneath our rotor. "Gaines has a male hostage in a third-floor office. He's come to the window to show he has a gun to the guy's head. SWAT has set up a command post under the trees in front of the building."

Baxter runs over from the squad car. "Let's get over there, John!"

"Who's the negotiator?" Dr. Lenz asks, appearing suddenly.

"Ed Davis," John replies. "He's good."

"This isn't a normal situation," Lenz says, directing his words to Baxter. "This isn't a distraught husband or a suicidal cop. This is a probable serial murderer. You know—"

"I know what you want, Arthur," Baxter says brusquely. "We'll discuss it with the SWAT commander."

"Talk to Bowles," says Lenz. "It's his call."

Baxter starts running toward a large building on the north edge of the quad that I now recognize as the Woldenberg Art Center. John and I follow, with Lenz puffing after us. I should have recognized the building from the air, with its three massive skylights over the gallery where

Roger Wheaton's room-sized painting awaits its first public showing. From this angle, the building appears as two three-story brick boxes separated by a one-story section fronted with arches. If I remember correctly, the classical boxes house classrooms, studios, and offices, while the long section houses the art gallery. Gaines must be inside one of the two end sections.

The closer we get to the building, the harder it is to see. Massive spreading oaks line the road in front of it, obscuring most of the windows. Beneath one of the oaks, a knot of men in black body armor with "FBI" stenciled in yellow crouch around what looks like a map. John reaches them first, and immediately begins talking to one of the men on the ground. Baxter takes out his cell phone and dials a number, and Dr. Lenz hovers beside him. I edge in to listen to the SWAT leader briefing John. He's a tall man in his thirties with a black mustache, and a patch on his flak vest reads "Burnette."

"Gaines is still on the third floor," says Burnette. "He's keeping his gun to the hostage's head when we can see him, but most of the time, our view is obscured by venetian blinds. There's no high ground for snipers, so we're going to put a man up in the Huey and have the pilot hold a hover. That's not a good solution, but until we get some scaffolding out here, it's the only way to get a bead on that office. We also have two men on the roof with rappelling gear. They can drop and crash the window, but that's not my call. We've rescued about forty students and faculty so far, but there may be twenty or so still on the floor with Gaines, some in small private studios. He's barricaded the main access door. Those kids could be completely ignorant of the danger or completely under Gaines's control."

"Have you established contact with Gaines?" John asks.

"A secretary just gave Ed the number of the office. He's talking now."

As Burnette points across the lane, a man dressed in civilian clothes pockets a cell phone and runs toward us.

"He wants one of our helicopters to take him to the airport," says the negotiator. "He wants a plane waiting there to take him to Mexico. I tried opening a dialogue, but he hung up. The guy sounds like a hard case. Streetwise, prison-tempered. This could take a while."

Baxter steps up to Burnette and says, "SAC Bowles just designated Doctor Lenz the hostage negotiator for this event. He also put me in tactical command on the ground. I've got no problem if you want to verify that."

The SWAT leader shakes his head. "It's fine with me. You're from Quantico, right?"

"That's right."

Ed the negotiator looks like he wants to argue, but suddenly someone yells, *There he is!*

Three floors above us, wedged in front of some venetian blinds, stands Roger Wheaton. His long face is pressed flat against the windowpane, and there's a large pistol pressed against his ear.

"Goddamn it," John mutters. "I told him to get out."

"He's trying to be a hero," says Lenz. "Just like he did in Vietnam."

"Dial that office and give me your phone," Lenz tells the negotiator. Then he looks at Burnette. "Tell your snipers to stand down."

"Do it," says Baxter.

As the former negotiator makes his call, SWAT leader Burnette says, "Mr. Baxter, my sniper can shoot that pistol out of Gaines's hand. He can do it from here. I've seen him do it twice under pressure."

Baxter shakes his head. "That's not an option yet. We don't know how many weapons Gaines has up there."

"Yes, hello?" says Lenz. "Leon? . . . This is Dr. Arthur Lenz. . . . I was at your house the other day. . . . Yes. I'm here because I know you need to talk to someone who's not bound by the normal rules. . . . That's right. Some cases fall outside the lines, and this is one of them."

When I look back up at the window, Wheaton is gone.

Lenz lowers his voice. "A helicopter isn't out of the question, Leon. But everything has a price. You know that. That's the way the world works. . . . You may *seem* to hold all the cards. But you're assuming you know what our priorities are. There are twelve families who care a lot more about you getting a lethal injection than they do about a dying artist whose life you might shorten by a few months."

Ed the negotiator looks like he wants to snatch his phone from Lenz's grasp, but Baxter holds up a restraining hand.

"Leon," Lenz says irritably. "Listen to me. You—"

A dull pop slowly registers in my brain.

"Gunshot!" yells a SWAT agent.

Burnette's radio crackles. "Rooftop. We heard a gunshot. Please advise, over."

"Do nothing," says Baxter.

"Hold position," says Burnette. "But stay ready."

"Put a sniper up in the Huey," orders Baxter. "Get a thermal imaging scope up there with him. We need to see through those blinds."

As Burnette runs to the next oak tree, a woman screams from the direction of the art center. Then the front door of the studio wing crashes open and a dozen students pour through it like people running from a fire. Behind them, running with an awkward lope, is a tall man wearing white gloves.

414

"It's Wheaton!" I yell, starting toward him.

As SWAT agents race forward to help the students, John hobbles past me and takes Wheaton by the arm. The artist's mouth and nose are covered with blood.

"Are you all right?" John asks. "Were you hit?"

"No," Wheaton coughs. "We struggled, and Leon hit me with the gun. He could have shot me, but he didn't. I didn't think he would. That's why I tried it."

"We heard a gunshot," John says in a taut voice. "Was anyone hit?"

"His gun went off during our struggle, but he didn't shoot anybody."

"Is he alone up there now?"

Wheaton shakes his head. "He had two female students barricaded in an adjacent office. There's a sofa against the door. I knew I couldn't save them, but I thought I might be able to clear some of the grad students' studios on my way out." Wheaton suddenly recognizes me. "Oh – hello."

"I'm glad you're all right," I tell him.

"We'll get you an ambulance," says John, leading the artist back toward the command post. "But we need to know everything you can tell us."

"That's Sarah! Oh, my God!"

The sound of screaming college girls is more piercing than a siren. Looking up at the window, I see a petite brunette pressed to the pane, the gun barrel huge beside her head.

"Get those students out of here!" Baxter yells to the SWAT agents.

John sits Wheaton down beneath an oak tree, and an agent wearing rubber gloves begins wiping blood from the artist's face. Baxter, the SWAT leader, and I cluster around them.

415

"Did you see any other weapons besides the pistol?" John asks.

Wheaton takes the gauze pad from the agent and wipes the blood from his own lips. "No. But he has a bag with him."

"A bag." John looks back at me. "I didn't see a bag in his cart at the Wal-Mart."

"Under the magazine, maybe?"

A heavy beating sound ricochets off the face of the art center. The Huey on the quad is climbing into a hover fifty yards from the window behind which Gaines holds his hostage. Instant execution will soon be an option.

John raises his voice above the rotor noise. "Has Gaines said anything to you to indicate he's guilty of the abductions?"

"No." Wheaton's long gray hair flies as he shakes his head.

"Has he mentioned Thalia Laveau?"

"He claims he knows nothing about her. He says you're framing him. He said, 'Those assholes need a patsy, and I'm it.' He wanted cash. He has a painting I gave him as a gift, but he wants to get the most he can for that."

"Did he know you called the FBI?"

"Probably." Wheaton's gloved hands are shaking, but I sense that he's more frustrated than afraid. "But I had to go back up there. If I tried to get everyone out, he'd have heard me, and he might have panicked and done something crazy. Leon acts like he's in control, but deep down he's very unstable. The safest thing was to offer myself as a hostage."

"That took guts," John says, but the artist just shakes his head.

"Leon doesn't want to shoot anybody, Agent Kaiser.

He's scared to death. If you give him a way out of this, he'll take it."

John looks skeptical. "Mr. Wheaton, sometime last night or this morning, Leon beat his girlfriend into a coma. Then he gagged her and left her for dead."

A look of sadness comes over the artist's face. "Good God. I met that girl." The sadness is quickly replaced by a look of concern. "That's still no reason to shoot him. He's backed into a corner. Offer him a way out, then arrest him later."

"I don't know about that," I say. "But Gaines may be the only person in the world who knows where Thalia Laveau is, or my sister and the rest of them."

John looks over his shoulder at Lenz, who is angrily punching numbers into the commandeered cell phone. "Any luck?"

"He's not answering."

A look of puzzlement crosses John's face; then he pulls his cell phone from his jacket. He must have felt rather than heard it ringing.

"Hello?" he yells, cupping his free hand around the earpiece. "Thanks. I'll call you when we know more."

He puts the phone back in his pocket and turns to Baxter. "Linda Knapp regained consciousness at the hospital. She said she threatened to tell the truth about Gaines's alibis, and he went crazy. She has no idea where he went on any of the snatch nights."

"Could someone help me stand up, please?" Wheaton asks. "I may have to be sick."

Baxter pulls the artist to his feet. True to his word, Wheaton doubles over and vomits on the grass.

"I'm sorry," he apologizes, wiping his mouth on his sleeve.

"There's an ambulance on the way," says Baxter.

"I'm fine," says Wheaton. "Really. But I don't think I want to see what's going to happen next."

John grimaces and pulls out his cell phone again. "What is it? . . . What? . . . Put out a citywide APB. Hell, statewide. And keep me posted."

"What is it?" asks Baxter.

"Surveillance just lost Frank Smith."

"What?"

"He went into the antiques show down at the convention center and disappeared."

"Shit! What's going on, John?"

"I don't know. But we better get on top of it fast." He looks at Wheaton. "We'll have someone drive you home."

"I'm just going to walk a bit, clear my head."

Dr. Lenz appears and taps Baxter's arm. "Gaines told me that if we don't land one of our helicopters on the roof of the art center in five minutes, he'll kill that girl and drop her out the window. He says he's got another one up there."

John looks at Wheaton. "You said there were two girls, didn't you?"

Wheaton nods, then wobbles on his feet.

"I've got him," I tell John. "*Please* just remember that Gaines may be the only one who knows what we need to know."

John squeezes my arm, then leans down to me and says: "Stay in plain sight."

As I lead Wheaton away, John addresses a group of black-clad men who remember their SWAT teammate Wendy Travis much too fondly to be objective in this situation.

"We may be looking at explosive entry," he says. "I want every one of you to . . ."

I turn and catch up to Wheaton, who is walking aimlessly along the grass, parallel to the lane that runs in front of the Woldenberg Center.

"Leon really left that girl for dead?" he asks.

"I thought she was dead till I felt her pulse."

He stops and looks back toward the art studio wing. "They're not going to listen to us. They're going to kill him."

"They're not as gung ho as you think."

"Maybe not Kaiser. That's why I called him. But the rest . . . I saw it in Vietnam. You put enough guns and soldiers into a situation like this, somebody's going to fire."

"I hope not. But we said our piece. Let's find somewhere for you to sit down."

The sound of a bullhorn reverberates across the quad, and Dr. Lenz begins addressing Gaines through the window glass.

"I guess he quit answering the phone," I murmur.

"I don't want to see this," Wheaton says. "I'm going to go home."

"You're in no shape to drive. I'll get a cop to drive you."

"I'm really fine. But my keys are in the gallery with my bag, and I don't think that cop is going to let me get them."

He points to the low section of the building, where an FBI agent stands beneath the entrance arch. Wheaton's keys are far from Leon Gaines. This is the backwater of the hostage scene.

"I'll talk to him. You stay here."

"Thank you. They're on the floor in the center of the room. Right by my bag."

I trot across the grass and wave to the agent as I come under the arch. "I need to get some keys for one of the hostages. They're just inside the gallery."

"Nobody goes in," he says.

"You've got a radio. Call John Kaiser."

The agent lifts his walkie-talkie and makes the call.

"Where's Wheaton, Jordan?" asks John from his position forty yards away.

With exaggerated movements, I point out into the quad, where Wheaton has sat down on the grass.

"Go in with her," John tells the agent. "But don't let Wheaton go home yet. Bring him back to the command post. I'm sending an agent with him. We don't know where Frank Smith is, and I don't want anyone else kidnapped. No more surprises."

"Copy," says the agent. His face softens as he opens the door and holds it for me. "I'm Agent Aldridge, by the way."

I walk into the gallery, my eyes drawn to the Tiffany stained-glass windows I saw the first time we were here.

"Through here," I tell Aldridge, leading him through the makeshift plywood door that seals the gallery against nosy visitors. The access panel in the canvas circle is still open. I start to go through, but Aldridge pushes ahead of me.

"Wow," he says softly.

The electric lights are off in the gallery, but a flood of illumination pours through the skylights, bathing Wheaton's masterpiece in a bluish glow. As in my dream of last night, the forest clearing seems alive, its branches and roots seeming to grow as I watch them.

"This thing is massive," Aldridge marvels.

"There's the bag," I tell him, pointing to a leather tote lying in the middle of a huge drop cloth.

"Oh, shit," says the agent, looking at his shoes. "Look at this."

The drop cloth around his shoes is stained with wet paint.

"Is that oil paint?" he asks.

"I think it is."

"*Shit*. It'll take—"

A shattering gunshot echoes through the building, the echo fading over a span of seconds. Before it dies, Aldridge is moving toward me with his gun drawn.

"That was outside!" I tell him. "A rifle. Give me your radio!"

He passes me his walkie-talkie with his free hand.

"This is Jordan Glass calling John Kaiser. John! It's Jordan!"

There's a crackle of static, then John's voice jitters from the radio as though he's talking while running up stairs.

"They had to shoot him, Jordan. We don't know if he's dead. We're going up now. He can't get to where you are. Stay put for five minutes, then have the agent escort you to the CP."

"Okay. Be careful!"

John doesn't speak again.

"If Jimmy Reese took the shot," says Aldridge, "the tango's dead." The FBI man lifts one shoe and studies the bright blue paint on its sole. "I wonder what happened. The guy probably panicked and got wild with his gun."

I cannot reply. The knowledge that died with Gaines took part of me with it. Everything I hoped to learn has vanished with the impact of a sniper's bullet. My legs feel shaky, as though they might buckle. I fall to my knees and breathe as deeply as I can.

"Are you okay?"

"Just give me a minute."

"Sure. *Hey!*" Aldridge shouts, pointing his pistol at the opening in the painting.

Roger Wheaton stands just inside the canvas circle, his face a mask of anguish.

"They killed him," he says. "I heard Leon yell through the window, and I walked to where I could see. A sniper shot him in the head."

"Take it easy," I tell Aldridge. "It's his keys we came to get."

The FBI agent lowers his gun.

"John said Gaines might still be alive," I say without much conviction.

Wheaton shakes his head, reaches out with his blood-stained white glove, and touches the trunk of a tree on the canvas.

"Hey!" calls Agent Aldridge. "The guy who painted this might not like you touching it. It's still wet."

Wheaton smiles sadly. "I don't think he minds."

"He's the guy who painted it," I tell Aldridge.

"Oh. Hey, I like it."

"Thank you."

"But what's with the gloves?"

"They protect my hands."

"I thought the painting was done," I tell Wheaton, putting my palms flat on the floor to push myself to my feet.

"There are always last-minute additions. It's finished now."

My palms are wet. Turning them over, I see red and yellow paint on my skin, bright primary shades like the blue on Aldridge's feet. This much paint couldn't be the result of spills. Wheaton must have been painting on the floor. That's why the drop cloth is here. He wasn't satisfied with enveloping the viewer in a great wooded circle. He had to paint the forest floor too.

"Have I ruined anything?" I ask, holding up my palms so he can see them. "Are you going to do the ceiling, too?

Wheaton's face darkens as he realizes I've smeared the paint.

"Stand up and tiptoe to the edge," he says.

"I got some on my shoes," says Aldridge. "You shouldn't have sent us after the keys with it wet."

"Stay where you are," says Wheaton. "Both of you."

The artist tiptoes across the drop cloth in a complicated path, like a military engineer walking through a minefield he just laid. As he passes Aldridge, Wheaton takes the agent's hand and leads him toward me. When he reaches me, he escorts us both to the edge of the floor, then smiles at me.

"You've discovered my surprise. I thought it would be dry by now."

"May I look?"

"I suppose so."

Aldridge's walkie-talkie crackles loudly, and then John's voice sounds in the room. "Daniel? It was a CK. The hostage is unhurt and on her way down."

"Copy that," Baxter replies.

"What's a CK?" I ask.

"Clean kill," says Aldridge.

"I told you it was a head shot," says Wheaton, lifting the edge of the drop cloth. "Jordan, would you go down there and lift the other side? We'll walk it across. If you still want to see it."

In a haze of incipient depression, I walk down the edge of the cloth and lift the coarse material in my hands.

"Now, walk," says Wheaton. "Slowly and carefully."

As I walk forward, the cloth comes away from the floor like Saran wrap stuck to a birthday cake.

"Oh man, that's ruined," say Aldridge. "You put that cloth down too early."

"Thank you for stating the obvious," says Wheaton.

Halfway across the room, I stop, my eyes transfixed by the images on the floor. They look nothing like the painting on the canvas circle that surrounds us. They're bright, childlike human figures painted directly onto the hardwood. Wide curves of red, yellow, and blue, with mixed tones where the primary lines cross.

"That looks like finger painting," I say softly.

"It is. Think of what the critics will say!" Wheaton exults. "I can't wait to see their faces."

But I'm not thinking of the critics. I'm thinking that beside every figure is a large X, that all the figures have long hair, and that their mouths are open in huge wailing O's. I open my mouth to speak, but nothing comes out.

"That's freaky," says Aldridge. "You're the guy who painted this" – he points at a beautiful tree beside his shoulder, then back at the floor – "and you painted *that*?"

Wheaton touches Aldridge on the arm, and something crackles and flashes blue. The FBI agent falls to the floor, jerking like a man having an epileptic fit.

Then Wheaton turns to me, and the avuncular face is gone. A new intelligence stares out through his eyes: vulpine, knowing, cold, fearless.

"I'm *not* the man who painted that," he says, pointing at the Clearing. "The man who did is almost dead."

With the slowness of nightmares, I scrabble at the right cuff of my jeans, reaching for the pistol John gave me, but Wheaton jerks his end of the drop cloth and my right foot flies out from under me, spilling me onto the floor.

As my hand closes on the butt of the .38, a vicious wasp stings my neck, and my arms begin jerking spastically. The room blurs, fades, then returns. I feel myself rising toward the skylight, and I wonder if I'm dying until I begin moving laterally and realize Wheaton is carrying me.

He walks to the border of the canvas circle, away from the open panel, and I wonder if he thinks he can simply step into his own painting. But inches from the meticulously painted forest, he bends and sets me on the floor, then takes a knife from his pocket. With one great slash he lays open the canvas from top to bottom, then lifts me again and carries me through the crack like a ghost walking through a wall.

25

Consciousness returns before vision. I know I'm alive, because I'm cold, dreadfully cold and wet. Shivering. I try to touch my face, but my arms won't move properly. My legs either. With great effort I shift my hips, and pain shoots up my legs. The agony of circulation returning. I focus all my energy on opening my eyes, but they don't open. My sense of smell is working, though. Urine, pungent and ammoniac, floats all around me. Terror squirms in my chest like a rat trying to fight its way out of a bag.

Stop, says a voice in my mind, and I cling desperately to its echo. My father's voice. *Don't panic,* he says.

But I'm so afraid –

You're alive. Where there's life, there's hope.

Stay with me, Daddy.

Think of happy things, he says. *The light will come soon.*

My mind is a fog of confusion, but through the mist I see patches of light. I see a little girl, sitting at a desk in a room filled with desks. Beside her sits another girl, identical to her to the last detail. One of the little girls is me. I feel more like a boy than a girl. My favorite book is *The Mysterious Island.* I order my books from a flimsy catalog the teacher hands out to every student in the class. *Emil and the Detectives.* *White Fang.* Like that. Money is tight for us, but when it comes to books my mother is a spendthrift; I can order as many as I like. I sit here day after day, waiting for my books

426

to arrive. *My* books. It takes a month or more, but when they finally do, when the teacher opens the big box and passes out the orders to the kids, checking the books against a form taken from her desk, I glow with happiness. I've never had the newest dress, or the prettiest, but I always have the tallest stack of books. Little paperbacks that smell of wet ink. I lay my cheek against their cool covers, anticipating the stories inside, knowing all the other girls wonder what I could possibly want with those books.

That's how I discovered *The Mysterious Island*. It's about four men who try to escape from a Civil War prison camp in a hot-air balloon. A storm blows them out to sea, and they crash near an uninhabited island. Their task is survival, and they succeed mightily. One prisoner finds a kernel of corn in his pocket, and from this comes their first crop. A former engineer brings irrigation to their fields. The story is a fable of self-reliance, which makes it perfect for me. I have my mother and my twin sister, but my father is gone. Not dead, but away. Shooting pictures for the magazines.

There is a map in *The Mysterious Island*. A hand-drawn topographic sort of thing, showing the island as it would appear from the air. The beach. The cove. The volcano with its hidden caves. A forest of palms, streams running through it. I could almost see the men down there, doing their best to get by, using their common sense, their natural gifts. I began to draw maps of my own. In the margins of my textbooks, on the backs of the mimeographed drawings they handed out at Thanksgiving: the Pilgrim or the Indian, which we colored with crayons only after hungrily sniffing the solvent on the purple mimeograph paper, still wet from the machine. When we finished coloring, the teacher would collect the pictures and tape them above the chalkboard in a long line. Mine never got the star for being the best. There was always someone who stayed completely within the lines, or had some fancy shading, or outlined their picture in heavy black crayon that they scraped flat with their fingernail. But I knew – even if the teacher didn't notice – that on the back of my Pilgrim was a whole world, an island drawn with the finest detail a big red Eagle pencil could produce, a world I'd spent the last thirty minutes living in before hastily coloring in the lonely-looking Puritan with my Crayolas.

Without warning, my eyelids begin fluttering and my hands clench into fists. Something's happening to my muscles. A voice tells me to keep my eyes closed until I know more about my situation, but the hunger for light is too strong.

Vision returns as swirling clouds, wisps of white on gray. Slowly, the clouds part to reveal the face of Thalia Laveau. The beautiful Sabine artist is sitting across from me, immersed to her breasts in a pool of yellowish water. Her head lolls against a rim of white enamel. Her eyes are closed, her skin pale to the point of blueness, and she is naked. I am naked too. Between us just an old-fashioned faucet. We're in a bathtub.

I try to turn my head, but my neck muscles refuse to obey my brain. I must be content with what I can see from this position. The wall opposite me is made of glass. The roof above is also glass, long shining triangles of it, fanning out from a brace bolted to a redbrick wall above and to my left. Through the glass I see the sky, fading down to dusk. To my left, above the narrow ends of the fanning panes, the sky is blue; to my right, violet. I am facing north.

Moving only my eyes, I follow the glass down to within four feet of the ground, where it meets a brick wall. I'm in a conservatory of some type. A conservatory with a bathtub in it. Beyond the glass wall stand trees and tropical plants, beyond these a high brick wall. I'm almost convinced I'm dreaming when I hear the pad of feet.

"Welcome back," says a male voice. "Add some hot water if you're cold."

The voice sounds familiar, but I can't quite place it. It has the refinement of Frank Smith's voice, but it's pitched lower. With superhuman effort I turn my head to the left and find a scene so bizarre I am rendered speechless.

Roger Wheaton stands partly behind an artist's easel, a paintbrush in his white-gloved hand, working feverishly on a large canvas that I cannot see. He is naked but for a white cloth tied around his waist and between his legs, like those that Renaissance artists used to cover the genitals of Jesus in crucifixion paintings. Wheaton's body is surprisingly well muscled, but his torso is lined with bruises and hemorrhages, the kind I saw in Africa on pneumonia patients coughing themselves to death.

My first attempt to speak is only a rasp. But then saliva comes, and I get the words out. "Where am I?"

In one sense this is a rhetorical question. I'm in the place eleven other women occupied before me – twelve, including Thalia. I'm in the killing house. I am one of the Sleeping Women.

"You can't move, can you?"

When I don't answer, Wheaton walks over and turns the tap marked "H." At first I shiver more, but then blessed heat begins to roll against my hip and stomach. He walks back to the painting, leaving me to push myself away from the steaming rush of water.

"Where am I?" I repeat.

"Where do you think you are?" Wheaton's gaze moves from the canvas to me, then back again.

"The killing house," I reply, using John Kaiser's term.

He seems not to hear.

"Is Thalia dead?"

"Not clinically."

I fight to keep my fear in check. "What does that mean? Is she sedated?"

"Permanently."

"What?"

"Look at her."

The surreal sense of horror that suffused me when I saw Wheaton is ratcheting down to pure animal fear, but I force myself to look at Thalia. The bathwater comes halfway up her breasts, which because they float seem more alive than their owner. I see no obvious wounds on her body. One arm hangs limp in the water, the hand wrinkled like the skin of a prune. Her other arm hangs outside the tub. Peering over the rim, I discover that my fear has barely begun to ascend the scale of terror. A white venous catheter enters her arm at the wrist, held in place by medical tape. From the catheter, a clear IV tube runs in a serpentine loop around the base of an aluminum stand and up to a bag hanging from an IV tree. The bag is empty, drained flat.

"What was in the bag?" I ask, trying to control my voice.

Wheaton holds the brush poised motionless in the air, then strikes the canvas quickly and repeatedly.

"Insulin."

I shut my eyes, recalling Frank Smith's description of Wheaton's suicide plan: *Insulin is painless, but sometimes it doesn't bring death, just brain damage and coma....*

"She's in no pain," he says, as though this mitigates the situation.

I try in vain to lift my right hand to turn off the faucet. "What's wrong with my arms?"

Wheaton ignores me, flicking the brush over the canvas with remarkable speed. A belated impulse makes me turn over my own hand. The left one. It seems to take an eternity, but finally, on the outside of my wrist, I see a plastic tube running into one of my own veins. I try to yank it out but haven't enough muscular control.

Wheaton admonishes me with an upraised finger. "Your bag is Valium. And a muscle relaxant. But that can easily change. So please, don't bother the equipment."

Valium? My second-favorite drug . . .

"I expected you to be unconscious for at least another hour."

Wheaton suddenly straightens, then turns as though looking at himself in a mirror. Which is exactly what he is doing. To my right, propped between the bathtub and the wall, is a huge mirror like the ones used in ballet studios. Wheaton is not only painting Thalia and me – he's painting *himself.*

"What are you painting?"

"My masterpiece. I call it *Apotheosis.*"

"I thought the circular painting back at the Newcomb gallery was your masterpiece."

He laughs softly, as though at a private joke. "That was *his* masterpiece."

My mind flashes back to the primitive, childlike images finger-painted on the floor beneath the drop cloth at the gallery. Then Wheaton carrying me, stepping over the stunned FBI man's body. *I'm not the man who painted that. . . .*

"This is my last," he says.

"Last what?"

He gives me a sly look I could not have imagined on the Roger Wheaton I met a few days ago. "*You* know," he says in a singsong voice.

431

"The last Sleeping Woman?"

"Yes. But this one's different."

"Because you're in it?"

"Among other reasons."

"You're not wearing your bifocals," I think aloud.

"Those weren't mine."

"Whose were they?"

He gives me a look I translate as *Duh*. Then he says, "They belonged to Roger. The weakling. The *fag*."

My stomach turns a slow somersault. Jesus Christ. Two FBI profilers and a psychiatrist sit brainstorming around a table, and the photographer turns out to be right.

MPD, Dr. Lenz called it. Multiple-personality disorder. Fragments of the psychiatrist's patronizing lecture come back to me. *That's not how MPD works . . . that's Dr. Jekyll and Mr. Hyde.* Welcome to my nightmare, Dr. Lenz. What else did Lenz say? *Always caused by extreme sexual or physical abuse . . .*

"If you're not Roger Wheaton," I say carefully, "who are you?"

"I have no name."

"You must go by something."

An odd smile. "When I was a boy, I read *20,000 Leagues Under the Sea*. I loved Captain Nemo. Nemo means 'no one.' Did you know that?"

"Yes."

"Sailing beneath the oceans of the world, trying to cure man of his self-destructive obsessions. I've wandered some of those same oceans. But I learned the truth much earlier than Nemo did. Man can't be cured. He doesn't *want* to be cured. Only a child can express the purity in human nature, and already the world is bearing down on him with all its weight, its corruption and filth, its violence." Wheaton bites his lip, the gesture strangely childlike.

"I'm not sure I understand."

"Don't you? Remember when you were a little girl? Remember when you believed in fairy tales? And the shock you felt as each one crumbled in the face of reality? No Cinderella. No Santa Claus. Your father wasn't perfect. He wasn't even *good*. He wanted things for himself alone. He wanted your mother behind a locked door. He wanted . . . other things. And it hurt you."

Always caused by severe childhood sexual abuse. Always . . .

"There was no perfect prince waiting to carry you off to his castle, was there?" Wheaton's smoldering eyes never leave the canvas now. "All the little pretenders wanted the same thing, didn't they? They didn't care about *you*. Not the soft little you that lived in your secret heart. They wanted to spend themselves inside you, anything for that, to use you and then ignore you, throw you away like trash."

Wheaton's getting wound up, and I don't want him any more unstable than he already is. Time to change the subject. "I'm really hot now."

He frowns in exasperation, but after a moment, he walks over and turns off the faucet.

"How did I get here?" I ask as he walks back to the canvas. In the deep valley between his back muscles, the bones of his spine show through his skin like a ladder.

"You don't remember?" he asks, lifting his brush again. "You were conscious. Think back, while I finish your eye. And try not to move."

I do remember some things. Flashes of light, waves of vertigo. A gray sky, bubbles of glass, a bridge of white tubes, and a long fall. "The roof. You took me out on the roof."

Wheaton chuckles.

"But there were FBI agents up there."

"Not after Leon was shot. They all wanted to see the trophy. There's a catwalk of pipes running from the art center to the physical plant. It only runs over a narrow alley, but crawling over it with a woman on your back sure gets the heart pumping."

"But how did you manage that? You're ill."

Wheaton's lips curl in disdain. "That diagnosis is currently under review. Roger was weak. I am strong."

What is he telling me? He's not sick anymore? What did Lenz say about MPD? *There's a documented case of one personality needing heart medication to survive, and the other not. . . .*

"Why am I not like Thalia?"

Wheaton keeps painting. "Because I want to ask you something."

"What?"

"You're a twin. An identical twin."

"Yes."

"I painted your sister."

Oh, God. "I saw that painting," I say aloud.

"I've done some reading on twins. It's an interest of mine. And I find a consistent theme in their stories of childhood. Many twins share a closeness that borders on telepathy. They tell remarkable tales: precognitions of disaster, intimations of death, silent conversations when in the same room. Did you and your sister experience any of that as children?"

"Yes," I reply, since the answer he wants is so clear. "Some."

"You want to know if your sister is alive or dead, don't you?"

I close my eyes against tears, but they come anyway.

"Don't you already know?"

Through the tears I see Wheaton's eyes locked upon mine. This is a test. He wants to know if I know Jane's fate. He's testing my assertion of paranormal ability.

"Which is it?" he asks. "Alive or dead?"

Trying to read him, I'm suddenly thrown back to the street in Sarajevo, to the instant the world blacked out and I felt a part of me die. Despite all my subsequent hopes, despite the phone call from Thailand, I knew then that Jane was dead.

"Dead," I whisper.

Wheaton purses his lips and goes back to his painting.

"Am I right?"

He cocks his head as if to say, *Maybe yes, maybe no.*

"Why are you so interested in twins?"

"Isn't it obvious? Two personalities from the same genetic code? Twins are exactly like me in that way."

I don't know how to respond. He has clearly traveled far down this road, and I can only look for clues to what he needs to hear.

"When you first came into the gallery," he says. "With Kaiser. I knew it was a sign. Sent by whom, I have no idea. But a sign nevertheless."

"A sign of what?"

"That one half can survive without the other."

His words hit me like a stake through the heart. Even though I knew it to be true, this confirmation dissolves some essential fraction of my spirit. "She's dead?" I whisper.

"Yes," Wheaton says. "But you shouldn't be upset. She's far better off the way she is now."

"*What?*"

"You've seen my paintings. The Sleeping Women. Surely you understand?"

"Understand what?"

"The *point*. The purpose of the paintings."

435

"But I don't. I never have."

Wheaton lowers his brush and stares at me with incredulity. "The *release*. I've been painting the release."

"The release?" I echo. "From what?"

"From the plight." His face is like that of a monk trying to explain the Holy Trinity to a savage.

"The plight?"

"Femininity. The plight of being a woman."

A moment ago I felt only grief. Now something harder quickens my blood. A desire to know, to understand.

"I don't understand what you're telling me."

"Yes, you do. You've tried so hard to live as a man. You work relentlessly, obsessively. You haven't married, you've borne no children. But that's no escape. Not in the end. And you're learning that, aren't you? Every month, the little seed inside you cries out to be fertilized. Louder all the time. Your womb aches to be filled. You've let Kaiser use your body, haven't you? I saw it the morning you came back with him, to the house on Audubon Place."

So I'm not at Audubon Place. Of course I'm not. If I were, I would have heard the St. Charles streetcar bell by now.

"Do you mean that killing women somehow releases them from pain?"

"Of course. The life of woman is the life of a slave. Lennon said it: *Woman is the nigger of the world*. From childhood to the grave, she's used and used again, until she's but an exhausted shell, broken by childbirth and marriage and housekeeping and—" Wheaton shakes his head as if too angry to further explain the obvious, then dips his brush in paint and goes back to the canvas.

Different voices are speaking in my head. Marcel de Becque, telling me that westerners fight against death while the people of the East accept it: *This posture of acceptance is portrayed in the Sleeping Women.* John's voice: *All serial murder is sexual murder; that's axiomatic.* Dr. Lenz, saying Wheaton's mother left home when he was thirteen or fourteen, details unclear. Lenz badgering Wheaton about it at the second interview, Wheaton evading the question. *That's what all this is about – the paintings, the murders, everything – Wheaton's mother. But I'm not going to question him about her until I'm fairly sure I can survive the asking.*

"I do understand that," I tell him, my eyes settling on Thalia's inert body. "That's why I've lived the life I have." *How can this man possibly see the ruin Thalia is now as a release?* "But the painting you're doing now must have a different theme."

He nods, flicking his hand right, then left, his eye leading the strokes with lightning precision.

"It's my emergence," he says. "My freedom from the prison of duality."

"From Roger, you mean?"

"Yes." Again the strange smile. "Roger's dead now."

Roger's dead? "How did he die?"

"I shed him, like a snake sheds its skin. It took a surprising amount of effort, but it had to be done. He was trying to kill me."

Now Frank Smith speaks from my memory, confiding that Roger Wheaton wanted his help with suicide. "Roger went to Frank Smith for help, didn't he?"

Wheaton's eyes are on me now, trying to gauge the depth of my knowledge. "That's right."

"Why go to him? Why not to Conrad Hoffman? Your helper? Hoffman set this place up for you, didn't he?"

Wheaton looks at me like I'm three years old. "Roger didn't know Conrad. Except from that first show, which he quickly forgot. Don't you see?"

I can't digest the information fast enough. "Does – *did* – Roger, I mean – did he know about *you*?"

"Of course not."

"But how do you hide from him? How have you done all this work without him knowing?"

"It's not difficult. Conrad and I set up this special place, and this is where I do my work."

"Is that what you did in New York, too?"

Wheaton cuts his eyes at me, a wolfish look in them. "You know about New York?"

"Yes."

"How?"

"A computer program enhanced the faces in your earlier paintings, and an FBI man recognized one of the victims."

"Kaiser, I'll bet."

"Yes."

"He's a sly one, isn't he?"

I hope so. As Wheaton paints on, I ponder the chances of the FBI finding me here. They know what happened by now, of course. John and Baxter. Lenz. The NOPD. They know Gaines was not the killer. They've seen Wheaton's finger painting, found Agent Aldridge. But what could possibly lead John to this place? The infrared photos? FBI planes shot total coverage of the French Quarter and the Garden District; they have a definite number of houses with court-yards by now. Dozens of agents are probably at the New Orleans courthouse right now, wading through the deeds to those places, searching for any connection to Roger Wheaton or Conrad Frederick Hoffman. Will they include houses with conservatories? Yes. John will be thorough. We talked about houses with skylights; anything that lets in lots of light will be on the list.

How long have they been looking for me? Is this the

evening of the day Gaines was shot? Or the next day? Or the next? I suddenly realize that I'm terribly hungry. Thirsty, too.

"I'm starving. Do you have any food?"

Wheaton sighs and looks up at the glass roof, checking the diminishing light. Then he sets down his brush and walks to my left, out of my field of vision. Straining to turn my neck, I see him reach down into a brown grocery bag and bring out a flat narrow package about eight inches long. Beef jerky. Suddenly I'm standing in Mrs. Pitre's driveway, outside the garage apartment Conrad Hoffman rented, where John found Hoffman's stash of junk food. Beef jerky was part of it.

Beside the grocery bag stands something else that must have been Hoffman's. An Igloo ice chest. The standard three-foot-wide plastic model, big enough for two cases of beer. Or IV bags filled with saline and narcotics. It depends on the customer, I suppose.

Wheaton's gloved hands give him difficulty tearing open the yellow plastic wrapper of the jerky, but he knows I can't manage it in my present state. At last he pulls it apart and walks over to the tub. With tremendous effort, I raise my hand and take the brown strip from him.

"Very good," he says.

Ugh, I think as I slide the tacky stuff into my mouth. But when I grind the flat strip between my back teeth, my tongue savors the grease expressed from the meat like crème brûlée. If only I had some water to go with it. I could cup some bathwater and drink, but I don't fancy a mouthful of urine. If I regain my muscular control, I'll drink from the tap.

"How do you know Roger is dead?" I ask. If I have a potential ally in this room, his name is Roger Wheaton.

The artist laughs softly. "You remember the finger painting on the floor at the gallery?"

"Yes."

"That was his last gasp. His death throes. An infantile attempt at some sort of confession. Pathetic."

"And now you don't need your – *his* – eyeglasses anymore?"

"You see me painting without them, don't you?"

Yes, but you're still wearing your gloves. "What about your other symptoms?"

Wheaton glances at me, and his eyes flicker with confidence. "You're very close to it now. You see, Roger's efforts to kill me aren't anything new. He's been trying to kill me for a long time now. More than two years. Only I didn't know it."

"How?"

Wheaton pauses with his brush, then adds a few judicious strokes. "Autoimmune diseases are poorly understood. Multiple sclerosis. Scleroderma. Lupus. Oh, doctors understand the mechanics of how they kill you well enough. But the etiology? The cause? You might as well consult a witch doctor. Do you know what an autoimmune disease is? A phenomenon in which the body's immune system – which evolved to protect the body from outside invaders – actually malfunctions and *attacks the body itself.*" Wheaton gives me a triumphant look. "Isn't *that* food for thought? How did the weakling come upon it? Perhaps his guilt and self-disgust were so consuming, his desire to kill me so powerful, that they manifested themselves physically. My disease waxes and wanes in severity as it progresses, and I noticed that the waxing phases occurred when Roger had control. Then he began actively trying to murder me, with Frank Smith's help. With insulin. You know what *that* told me? There were chinks in the wall that separated us. He was beginning to see into my mind. That's when *you* walked into my life. A mirror

440

of a woman I'd already painted. A woman who was dead. Yet here was her double – her *other half* – perfectly healthy. I knew then. A new vision had come to me, and this painting was part of it. I had to save myself."

I stare speechless from the steaming tub. The complexity of his delusion is staggering. Born in the mind of an abused child, it blossomed and flowered in the crucible of a dying artist's fear of extinction.

"Are you – I mean, has it worked? Are you cured?"

"It's happening. I can feel it. I'm breathing more easily. My joints are less stiff."

"But you're still wearing your gloves."

A tight smile. "My hands are too delicate to take chances. And there's systemic damage. That will take time to heal." He glances up at the darkening sky. "I want you to be quiet now. My light's almost gone."

"I will. But there's one thing I don't understand."

He frowns, but I push on. "You say you killed the women you painted to release them from their plight. To spare them a life of pain and exploitation. Is that right?"

"Yes."

"Yet each Sleeping Woman was raped before she died. How can you stand there and tell me you're sparing them pain, when you're putting them through the worst thing a woman can experience short of death?"

Wheaton has stopped painting. His eyes glower with anger and confusion. "What are you talking about?"

"Conrad Hoffman. Before he died, he had a gun to my head. He told me he was going to rape me. He said that even if he had to shoot me in the spine, it would still be nice and warm between my legs."

Wheaton's eyes narrow to slits. "You're lying."

"No."

"Then he was trying to intimidate you, to get you into the car."

I shake my head. "I saw his eyes. Felt the way he touched me. I've been raped before. I know how rapists' eyes look."

A strange cast of compassion comes over the long face. "You were raped?"

"Yes. But that's not the point. The last woman taken before Thalia – the one taken from Dorignac's and dumped in the drainage canal – the pathologist found semen inside her."

His head jerks as if avoiding a blow.

"Was it yours?" I ask softly.

Wheaton throws down his brush and takes two steps toward me. "You're lying."

The prudent thing would be to stop, but my salvation may lie in the root of this paradox. "The FBI is sure you killed the Dorignac's woman. They worked out the timing of Wingate's death, and they know when Hoffman flew back from New York. Hoffman couldn't have taken her."

Wheaton is wheezing now, like a child with asthma. "I took her, but—" He stands with his mouth open, unable to continue.

He really does believe that by killing those women he was sparing them. But I can't spare him. Somewhere, buried behind those deranged eyes, is the gentle mind of the artist I met earlier in the week.

"Help me understand," I plead. "A man who saves a twelve-year-old girl from being raped in Vietnam turns around and helps some pervert rape the women he claims he's saving?"

Wheaton's chin is quivering.

"I guess it was Roger who saved that girl in Vietnam—"

"*No!*" A single, explosive syllable. "*I did that!*"

442

I say nothing. The fault line running through Wheaton's mind is torturing him more painfully than I possibly could. His face twitches, and his hands shiver at his sides. With a jerk of his head he looks up at the nearly dark sky. Then he walks to a table behind his easel, lifts a hypodermic syringe from it, and walks back toward me, his face devoid of emotion.

My newfound confidence vaporizes, leaving pure terror in its wake. If Wheaton wants to stick me with that needle, there's nothing I can do about it. That reality sends me hurtling back to Honduras, to the night my innocence died forever, when I learned the most terrible of life's lessons: you can shriek and fight and beg for someone to stop hurting you, but it won't make them stop; you can plead to God and your mother and father, and they will not hear you; your cries will not move to pity those who rend you.

When Wheaton steps behind my head, the skin of my neck crawls, awaiting the prick of the needle. Summoning all my strength, I twist my neck to look up and back. He is standing by my IV tree, injecting the contents of his syringe into my IV bag. I scream now, with all my power, but he tosses the empty syringe on the floor and walks back to his easel. My left arm begins to burn at the wrist, and tears of anger and helplessness flow from my eyes. Sucking in great gulps of air, I try to fight the unknown poison, but in a matter of seconds my eyelids fall as surely as shutters being pulled down by a man with a hook.

26

This time the world returns as stars in a black sky, a universe of stars slightly blurred by glass, and the sound of a man sobbing. The anguished sobs seem to echo all the way from a distant planet. The planet of childhood, I suspect.

I'm shivering again, which is not such a bad thing. It's when you stop shivering that you're in trouble. I can barely see Thalia across from me in the tub, so dark is the night. But I'm thankful for the darkness. I've been many places where my only light at night was the stars, and I know this: if I can see Polaris and the horizon, I can estimate my latitude. Not with enough accuracy to navigate a ship by – not without a sextant – but enough to guess my location in general terms. It's one of the practical tricks my father taught me. A good thing for a world traveler to know, he said, especially if you're ever hijacked on a boat or a plane, which he once was.

I don't know which star is Polaris yet, because I can't see either the Big or Little Dipper, which are the quickest guides. Polaris may not even lie within my field of vision. But I am facing north and surrounded on three sides – and overhead – by glass, my view only partly obscured by tree branches. If I can watch long enough, stay conscious long enough, all the stars will move around the sky but one: Polaris, which rotates in a two-degree circle above the north pole. The Pole Star. The North Star. That constant light has guided many a desperate traveler, and I am certainly that now.

My problem is the horizon. I can't see it, because of the high brick wall outside. *Not to worry,* says my father. *You can use an artificial horizon. The best is a bowl of mercury on the ground.* Mercury reflects stars remarkably well; you simply measure the angle between Polaris and its reflection, then divide by two. That's if you have a sextant, which I don't. In the absence of a mercury bowl, the surface of a pool of water can be substituted, and that I do have. But the conservatory glass distorts the starlight enough so that, combined with the movement of the bathwater caused by breathing and blood circulation, no clear reflection exists. *Not the end of the world,* my father assures me. *You can guess where the horizon is –*

The anguished sobbing has stopped.

I sense that Wheaton is lying on the floor somewhere, but I can't see him. As I try to make out objects in the room, an amazing new reality comes to me.

My muscles are under my control.

Leaning back, I look up at the silver line of my IV stand. The hanging bag is flat. Whatever was keeping my muscles in limbo has stopped flowing into me. But my mind is not yet clear. It seems unnaturally focused on the idea of the stars and where I am. But this information *is* important. New Orleans lies roughly on the thirtieth parallel. If I can verify that I'm on the thirtieth parallel, I can reasonably assume that I'm still in New Orleans, that Wheaton has not flown me to some distant killing house, where the other victims await me like the living sculpture Thalia has become. Of course, Polaris will not tell me my longitude; so the thirtieth parallel could put me in Bermuda, the Canary

Islands, or even Tibet. But these are outside possibilities. For me, thirty degrees latitude will mean a real chance of rescue by the FBI.

Control of my muscles brings to mind another possibility: that of saving myself. After flexing most of my cramped limbs, I decide I can probably get out of the tub. The problem is Wheaton. He's close by, even if I can't see him. Is he close enough to stop me from breaking out of this glass room? Surely he's thought of that. But do I really need to break out to save myself? I was wearing a pistol on my ankle when he overpowered me at the gallery. It must be here somewhere. But before I look for it – or do anything that entails risk – I must know how close he is, and what he will do when he hears noise. Reaching out with my right hand, I turn the hot-water tap and wait.

For twenty or thirty seconds the new water is cold. Then it begins to warm, and blissful heat flows under and around me, bringing blood to my bluish skin. The bathwater can't be that cold, I tell myself. No colder than the temperature of the air, which Wheaton must keep at close to seventy degrees because of his hands. *It doesn't have to be that cold,* my father reminds me. *You lose heat to water thirty times faster than you do to air. Sustained immersion can kill you.* Without regular infusions of hot water, Thalia might already have died of hypothermia.

The faucet continues to run, but Wheaton doesn't come to investigate. When the level approaches the rim of the tub, I shut it off. I want to get up, but a soft wave of whatever has kept my mind hazy resists my intention, and I lie back against the enamel. Sleep wants to enevelop me, but I force my eyes open and watch the slowly changing sky. The bathwater cools, then becomes cold. As I lie shivering in the dark, every star above me wheels slowly across the sky.

446

Except one. Bright and stationary, it hovers just above the treetops.

Polaris.

It's a matter of seconds to estimate where the horizon is, guess the angle between that imaginary line and Polaris, and subtract that number from ninety degrees. The answer sets my heart racing. *Thirty degrees.* I'm almost certainly still in New Orleans. If John Kaiser looks hard enough for me, he will find me. This possibility warms me more deeply than hot water could. And yet . . . I can't rely on rescue from outside.

Reaching up with a shaking hand, I turn the hot-water tap again, but this time I don't sit and wait to be warmed. This time I stand on shaky legs and climb out of the tub.

My muscles still aren't quite my own, but they do function. The IV tube in my hand presents a problem, but the IV stand has wheels, and the floor appears to be painted concrete. With careful steps, I drag the stand over to the glass wall of the conservatory. What I find is discouraging. The first four feet of glass above the brick wall supporting the conservatory is encased in a diamond-shaped metal mesh. Smashing the glass with something heavy will get me nowhere. There's a glass door leading outside, but it too has mesh between its metal struts, and a heavy padlock ensures that the door remains closed.

The space my body displaced in the tub is filling quickly. What options do I have? Creep into the house proper and try to slip past Wheaton? Surely he expects this. And the sobs I heard before came from close by, not far away. He may be lying on a sofa in the next room, my pistol in his hand. Or the gun may be nowhere in the house. He probably still has the taser he used on me at the gallery. He may have a dog. Is it worth the risk of looking? When I think of his eyes as he screamed denial of the rapes, that option strikes me as rather like sneaking into a dragon's lair. Do dragons really sleep? If they do, I fear, it's only lightly.

Think, says my father. *What do you know that he doesn't? What's near to hand that can help you?*

What do I know? That I'm more than half addicted to Xanax, which is a cousin of Valium. It's probably a cross-tolerance between those drugs that's made it possible for me to wake and tiptoe around while Wheaton believes me to be asleep. What is near to hand that can help me? I don't see any weapons. Not even paintbrushes. The table from which Wheaton took the hypodermic is bare. The room is as sterile and empty as a prison cell. Which it is. *Not quite empty,* I realize. On the floor behind my end of the tub sits the Igloo ice chest and the grocery bag. Conrad Hoffman's things.

I drag the IV stand toward them.

The bag is half filled with the same junk food John found at Hoffman's apartment. Pop-Tarts. Potato chips. Hostess Twinkies. Beef jerky. I stare at the boxes and bags, sensing important activity deep in my brain, but not quite understanding it. Slowly, the logic makes itself known to me. These aren't weapons. They are defenses.

Reaching into the bag, I quietly open the boxes and remove three shining foil packs of Pop-Tarts and a handful of cellophane-wrapped Twinkies. These I stash between the claw-foot tub and the mirror Wheaton uses to help paint himself into his picture. As I climb back into the tub, I realize I forgot to look at Wheaton's painting-in-progress. Understanding that image might help me. *But not as much as that ice chest,* I think. How long has it been sitting there? How long since I saw Hoffman swirling away in the Mississippi? Moving to the Igloo, I say a silent prayer, then pop open the white fastener and lift the lid. It's dark inside, so I blindly push my hands toward the bottom. They plunge into a rattling Arctic ocean of ice and water, with floating islands that feel like beer bottles. In seconds, pain radiates up my arms.

God bless you, you sick bastard, I say silently. My heart pounds with new hope, but I can't linger here. Warm water is lapping at my feet. The bathtub is overflowing, and not quietly. But this too is good. The spillover will wipe out the wet traces of my journey around the room, and perhaps convince Wheaton that I'm still in poor control of my faculties. Shutting the Igloo, I shove it a foot closer to the tub, then climb back into the near-scalding water.

I'm reaching for the tap when I hear a noise in the dark. I lay my head back and close my eyes. The water runs on.

"What are you doing?" bellows a groggy voice.

I reach out and take hold of Thalia's hand beneath the water. Footsteps approach the tub, stop.

Wheaton must be looking down at me.

"Beautiful," he says, sending a chill to my core despite the burning water. The tap squeaks, and the faucet stops running. Then something dips into the steaming water, and warm waves lap against my breasts. Wheaton's hand covers my left breast, gently, as though he's reliving some distant memory. I force myself to breathe with a regular rhythm. The hand slides over my heart, feeling the blood beating there, then slips beneath the water. It covers my navel, kneading the little pad of fat there, then slides down between my legs.

A sensation of falling nearly makes me scream, but numbness saves me. It spreads outward from my brain and heart, a numbness of self-preservation, born in the jungle of Honduras, neurochemical armor to help me endure anything in the cause of survival. Wheaton's fingers tremble as they explore, but I do not. I lie still and breathe, in and out, in and out. His hand is not the paw of a brute, but the inquisitive hand of a boy. The fingers entwine in my pubic hair and cling with childlike tenacity. In the silence of the dripping faucet, a long, keening moan of grief cuts me to the quick. Like the cry of an orphaned animal beside its mother, it reverberates through the glass room, terminating in a sob. Then the fingers uncurl, and the hand vanishes.

Footsteps move away, and I hear a clatter in the other room. Then the footsteps return, this time behind my head. My IV bag rattles in the stand. He's changing it.

"Soon," he hisses. "Tomorrow."

As he walks away, my wrist begins to burn. *Valium,* I tell myself, even as my eyes try to close. *Not insulin. Insulin doesn't burn.* But just in case, I reach between the tub and the mirror, strip the wrapper from a Twinkie, and gobble it in two bites, dumping protective sugar into my blood as fast as possible. Then I eat another. My dry throat makes it hard to swallow, but after a look at Thalia, I force down a third.

Should I pull the IV catheter out of my vein? If I do, I'll bleed into the tub, maybe for some time. And tomorrow Wheaton will see what I did. I could always say it was an accident. Beneath the water, I squeeze Thalia's hand, wishing with all my heart that she could squeeze back. "We're going to make it, girl," I whisper. "You wait and see."

Pull out the tube, says my father. *Lift your hand out of the water. The vein will clot in the air. . . .*

"I can't feel my hand," I tell him. "I—"

I'm reaching for the IV catheter when my eyes go black.

I awaken in full daylight, but I don't open my eyes. Wheaton will expect me to be unconscious longer. For an hour I lie with my eyes closed, reconstructing my environment from sound alone. Just as yesterday, Wheaton stands behind his easel, painting with sure, rapid strokes. Now and then the easel creaks, and the soft sibilants of his breathing alter with his stance. There's a new urgency to his movements. How long will it take him to finish this painting? How long before he turns me into another Thalia?

I have to slow him down. The longer I lie here alive, the more time John will have to find me. But I must also prepare for the possibility that he may not find me. That Wheaton will finish his work. *First things first*, says my father. *Get him talking*.

When the sun shines noticeably brighter through my eyelids, I make a show of coming awake. "How does it look?" I ask.

"As it should," Wheaton answers in a clipped voice. He clearly doesn't recall last night's conversation with fondness.

Rather than push him, I lie quietly and try not to look at Thalia, who seems several shades paler than she did yesterday.

At length, Wheaton says, "I saw a report on television this morning. If the local anchors aren't lying for the FBI, you told me the truth last night. About the rapes."

I say nothing.

A quick glance at me as he paints. "Conrad was raping my subjects."

"Yes."

"I'd do anything to change that. But I can't. I should have known, I suppose. Conrad always had poor impulse control. That's why he went to prison. But rape is just a symptom of what I told you about yesterday. The plight. If Conrad hadn't done it, someone else would have. In a different way, perhaps. The husband's way. But still. They're all much better off now, your sister included."

Wheaton steps away from the canvas and studies himself in the mirror. "It's worse for *you* that she's dead, of course, but for *her,* there's no more pain. No more helpless wishing, no more subservience."

If I think about Jane now, I won't be able to keep it together. "I understand about the plight. I understand the Sleeping Women. But I don't think you're telling me everything."

His eyes flick to me, then back to the canvas as he resumes painting. "What do you mean?"

"Your feelings about women didn't just come to you out of the blue. They must have been shaped by women you knew." I have to be careful here. "Maybe the woman you knew best of all."

Wheaton's brush pauses in midair, then returns to the canvas.

"I know your mother disappeared when you were thirteen or fourteen."

He stops painting altogether.

"I know what that's like. My father disappeared when I was twelve. In Cambodia. Everyone said he was dead, but I never believed it."

He's watching me now. He knows I'm telling the truth, and he can't fight the compulsion to know more. "What did you think had happened?" he asks.

"At first I created all sorts of scenarios. He'd been wounded and had amnesia. He was crippled and couldn't get back to me. He was held prisoner by Asian warlords. But as I got older, I realized that probably none of that was true."

"You accepted that he was dead?"

"No. I came to believe something even more terrible.

452

That he hadn't come back because he didn't *want* to come back. He'd abandoned us. Maybe to be with another woman. Another family. Another little girl that he loved more than me."

Wheaton is nodding.

"It almost killed me, thinking that. I racked my brain, trying to figure out what I'd done to make him angry enough to stop loving me."

"It wasn't your fault. He was a man."

"I know, but last night, I was thinking – dreaming, really – about you. And I saw a woman. I thought she must be your mother. She was holding a boy and trying to explain why she had to go. I tried to ask her why she would leave you—"

Red blotches have appeared on Wheaton's face and neck, the way they used to on my sister's face. He jabs his paintbrush at me like a knife. "She never left me! I was the *only thing that kept her alive.*"

"What do you mean?"

His face goes through tortured contractions, as though he's reliving some horrible moment. Then he dips his brush in the paint and goes back to his canvas, almost as if no conversation ever took place.

And then he begins talking.

27

"I was born during the war," Wheaton says, painting with absolute assurance. "Nineteen forty-three. My father was in the Marine Corps. He came home on leave after basic training, and that's when he fathered me. That's what he thought, anyway. He was a hard man, merciless and cold. Mother couldn't explain to me why she married him. She only said, 'Things look different when you're young.'"

"My mother said the same thing more than once," I tell him.

"When my father was drafted, she was left alone for the first time since she'd been married. She had two sons, but they were only four and five. It was a liberation. She was free of the cutting voice, the brutal hand, the ruthless insistence of the nights when she protested in vain to the ceiling and the walls, begging God for some reprieve. God had finally answered her prayers. He had sent her the war."

Wheaton smiles with irony. "A month after my father shipped out for the Pacific, a stranger came to the door asking for water. He had a limp. Some injury or disease had crippled him, and the army wouldn't take him. He worked for the government, one of the WPA artists' projects. He was a painter. Mother fell in love with him the first day. She worshiped art. Her prize possession was a book a dead aunt had given her. A big color-plate thing called *Masterpieces of Western Art*. Anyway, the painter camped nearby for two weeks, and when he left, Mother was pregnant. She never knew where he went, but he said was from New Orleans. He told her that much."

My God, I say silently.

"I was born two weeks premature." Wheaton twirls the tip of his brush on his palette. "That made the timing almost work out. It meant Mother could lie about my paternity and get away with it. At least for a while.

"When my father came back from the war, he was different. He'd been captured by the Japanese, and they had done something to him. He rarely talked. He became a sort of religious fanatic. But he was just as brutal – with her and with us.

"He saw immediately that Mother treated me differently from my brothers. She told him it was because I was premature, that I was fragile. He tried to force me to be like the others, but she resisted him. After a time, they came to an arrangement. She bought me a sheltered childhood with subservience. Anything he wanted, he got. His word was law. In daily life. In his bed. Only where I was concerned did her word count.

"My brothers worked the farm and helped him trap when they weren't in school. My life was different. Mother taught me things. Read to me. Pinched pennies to buy me paint and canvas. She encouraged me to imitate the paintings in her book. My brothers made fun of me, but secretly they were jealous. They beat me when they could get away with it, but that was a small thing. In the summers, Mother and I spent our days in an old barn in the woods. We escaped."

A look of transcendence comes over Wheaton's face.

"It stood in a small clearing, surrounded by ancient trees, with a stream flowing beside. Part of the roof had fallen in, but we didn't mind. The sun fell through the hole in

455

great yellow shafts, the way it does in Gothic cathedrals."

"What did you paint there?" I ask, even as the answer comes to me. "Did you paint your mother?"

"Who else could I paint? After I outgrew copying from the book, she would bring different clothes from the house, or things she'd bought on a rare trip into town. Things she never showed my father. Gauzy gowns, robes like those the women wore in the classical paintings. Hour after hour I would paint, and we would talk, and laugh, until the shafts of light began to fade, and we began to whisper, putting off until the last second our walk back to the dark little house of rage."

"What happened? What ended all that?"

Wheaton's body freezes like a tape being stopped. His jaw moves, but no sound emerges. Then, slowly, his right hand extends the paintbrush to the canvas. "When I was thirteen, I became . . . curious about certain things. Many of the pictures in Mother's book were nudes, and I wanted to paint like that. She understood the necessity, but we had to be careful. Sometimes my father took work at the mill in the town. My brothers would do his trapping then. That's when she posed nude for me."

Though the bathwater is cold, my face feels hot. I sense that we're heading into the unmapped territory of incest.

"Did you become . . . intimate?"

"Intimate?" His voice is an echo from a cave. "We were like the same person."

"I meant—"

"You meant *sex*." He lifts his brush, his face showing disgust. "It wasn't like that. I touched her sometimes, of course. To pose her. And she told me things. About the way love was supposed to be, how somewhere in the world she hoped it really was. But mostly we made plans. She said I

456

had a gift that would make me famous one day. I swore a thousand times that if I ever got away, I would succeed and come back for her."

A frightening vision comes to me. "Did someone catch you with her like that?"

Wheaton closes his eyes. "One spring afternoon, instead of trapping, my brothers spied on us. They watched until Mother disrobed. Then they ran all the way to town and got my father. When he burst into the barn and saw her naked, he went crazy. Screaming gibberish about harlots and God-knows-what-else from the Bible. My mother shrieked at him to get out, but he had murder in his eyes. He told my brothers to hold me down, and he – he started to beat her. But instead of taking it, as she usually did, she fought back. She clawed his face, drew blood. When he saw that, he picked up an old scythe handle. . . ."

Wheaton squints as though staring at a distant object. "I can still hear the whistle it made. And the impact, like the sound of an eggshell. The way she fell. She was dead before she hit the floor."

His voice sounds the way mine does when I speak of my father's "death" – higher in pitch, tremulous. "Why isn't there any record of this?"

"There was no one around for miles. She had no family left."

"Did your father bury her?"

"No."

No? "What happened?"

Wheaton looks at the floor, and his voice drops to a barely audible whisper. "He came over to where my brothers were holding me down and leaned over my face. He told me to bury her and go home. His breath *stank*. He said if I told anyone what had happened, he and my brothers

457

would swear they'd caught me raping her in the barn, after she was dead. I'd never even heard of such a thing. It paralyzed me with fear. No one would believe me, he said. I'd be sent to a reform school in the city, where boys would beat me every day and sodomize me in the night. Then they left me with her."

"I'm so sorry," I murmur, but Wheaton doesn't hear me.

"I couldn't bury her." His voice is almost a whine. "I couldn't even look at her. The side of her head was broken. Her skin was like blue marble. I cried until my eyes were like sandpaper. Then I dragged her down to the stream. I fetched her gown and washed her from head to toe, cleaning away the blood and straightening her hair as best I could. The way I knew she'd want it. I knew they might come back at any moment, but I didn't care. I'd realized something. Her agony was finally over. All her life was pain, and now it had ended. She was better off dead." Wheaton lays down his brush and drives his fingers through his tangled hair. "*I* wasn't better off. I couldn't even imagine life without her. But *she* was. You see?"

I do. I see how a shattered child made the mental journey to a state that allows him to kill women and believe he is doing a good thing.

"I went back to the barn and painted over what I'd been doing. Then, in the dying light of the clearing, I painted Mother in her peace. It was the first time I'd seen her face completely relaxed. It was an epiphany for me. My birth as an artist. When I was finished, I took a shovel from the barn and buried her beside the stream. I didn't mark the spot. I didn't want them to know where she was. Only I knew."

"What happened when you went home?"

My question seems to suck the humanity out of Wheaton's face. "For four years, I lived like an animal. My

458

father told the few people who asked that my mother had run away to New York. Then he began poking into her past. He became convinced that I was illegitimate. He talked to her doctor, studied the records at the courthouse. He was right, but he couldn't prove it. He just *knew*. There was nothing in me of him – *nothing* – and I thank God for it. But after that, they did things to Roger that you simply can't imagine. They starved him. Beat him. Worked him like a slave. The father gave the older brothers permission to do as they liked with him. They burned him. Cut him. Shoved things inside him. The father used him sexually, to punish him." Wheaton shakes his head dismissively. "If it weren't for me, he'd never have survived."

Severe sexual or physical abuse during childhood, Dr. Lenz told us. *The kind of radical psychological break I'm talking about* . . . "How did you protect Roger?"

"I listened. I *watched*. My hearing grew frighteningly acute. I could hear them breathing in their sleep. If their breathing changed, I knew it. If they got out of bed, I knew Roger was in danger. I told him when to hide, when to run. When to hoard food. When to give in, and when to resist. After a while, it got where I could hear them *thinking*. I saw the morbid desire in their minds, pictures forming into intent, intent traveling from their brains down their sluggish nerves, moving their heavy limbs to action. That's how Roger survived."

"Did you tell him to run away to New York?"

Wheaton resumes painting, the brush moving quickly again. "Yes. But the city wasn't how I thought it would be. Roger tried to paint, but he couldn't make a go of it. People offered help, but they didn't want to help him. They were helping themselves. They gave him food, a place to sleep, space to paint. But in exchange they wanted their pound of flesh. They wanted *him*. And he gave himself to them. What did it matter? They were so much gentler than his father and brothers. For four years he moved among them – soft, greedy, gray old men – painting derivative work, doing anything they asked of him. Things had to change."

An almost cruel smile touches Wheaton's lips. "One day, walking down the street, I saw my opening. I darted into a recruiting office and joined the marine corps. One quick irrevocable act. There was nothing he could do. The war in Vietnam was heating up, and almost before Roger knew what had happened, he was on his way there."

Pride flashes like diamonds in the artist's eyes. "That's where I came into my own. Vietnam. He couldn't make it without me. During the days he would poke along, joking and cursing and slapping backs, trying to fit in. But at night he made room for me. On patrol. On point. I could smell things he couldn't even *see*. I could hear bare feet bending grass at fifty meters. I kept him alive. The others, too. They gave me medals for it."

"What about after?" I ask, a fraction of my mind still wondering how far John and Baxter and Lenz have come down the investigative trail to this house.

"I went back to New York, didn't I? I was a different man. I took my GI Bill money, went to NYU, and painted for four years. When I got out, I did portraits to keep myself in groceries. I was searching for my destiny. And it found me. My surviving brother died in the merchant marine, and the farm went up for sale. I decided to buy it. I thought of burning the place down, but I didn't. Every day was a sweet revenge. Those rooms had witnessed all Mother's pain, and Roger filled them with color and light. It was then that he began to paint the Clearing."

"When did *you* start painting? The Sleeping Women?"

Wheaton purses his lips, like a man trying to recall the year he got married or joined the service. "Seventy-eight, I think. I was driving out of New York, and I saw a girl beside a bridge, hitchhiking north. She was young and pretty, and looked like a student. A waif, you know? A leftover hippie. I asked where she was going, and she said, 'Anyplace warm, man.'" Wheaton smiles at the memory. "I knew exactly how she felt. I'd been there too.

"I drove her back to the farm. On the way, she got high. She had pills with her, and they made her talkative. Her story was like others I'd heard from women. A father like mine. A mother who couldn't protect her. Men who used her. At the farm, I fed her. She got sleepy. I asked if I could paint her, and she said yes. When I asked if I could paint her nude, she hesitated, but only a moment. 'You wouldn't do anything freaky,' she said. 'You're too nice.' And then she took off her clothes. I posed her in the tub."

Lulled into a trance by his story, I feel a sudden nausea as his last words sink in.

"I painted as Roger never had. I was in control, you see? *I* had the brush. It worked under *my* will."

"But something happened," I say hesitantly.

Wheaton puts down his brush and vigorously massages his left hand. "Yes. Before I finished the painting, she woke up. I was naked. I'm not sure how I got that way, and what does it matter? I only know I was naked and painting, and I was aroused. The girl panicked."

"What did you do?"

"I panicked too. She knew where she was. If she told people the way things had happened, it could cause trouble for Roger. I tried to calm her down, but she took it wrong. She fought. She gave me no choice. I pushed her under the water and held her there until she stopped fighting."

Jesus. . . . "What did you do then?"

"I finished the painting." Wheaton picks up his brush, dips it, and goes back to his work. "She looked so peaceful. Much happier than she had when I picked her up. She was the first Sleeping Woman."

Nineteen seventy-eight. The year I left high school, Roger Wheaton drowned a waif junkie in New England and started down a road that led ultimately to my sister.

"What did you do with her body?"

"I buried her in the clearing."

Of course he did.

"I waited a year before I picked up another one. She was a runaway. She made it so *easy*. And I knew what I wanted by then."

"What about Conrad Hoffman?"

"That was 1980. Roger had a one-man show in New York, and Conrad showed up for that. He saw something in The Clearing paintings that no one else did. He saw *me*. The germ of me. He was charismatic, young, dangerous. He hung around after the show, and we went for coffee. He didn't fawn over Roger, as some did. He sensed the power hidden in the paintings. The darkness. And I did something I never thought I would do."

"You showed him your Sleeping Women."

Wheaton nods cagily. "There were only two then. You should have seen his face when he saw them. He knew immediately that the women were dead. He knew because he'd seen women that way. And when he looked back at me from the paintings, I let him see my true face. I dropped the mask."

As you did with me, after tasing the FBI agent in the gallery.
"What did Hoffman do?"

"He reveled in it. When I saw that he understood, I felt

462

some irresistible power well up within me. And I ravished him."

"*What?*"

"I wasn't like Roger – facedown and taking it in pain. *I* was the one in control. Conrad saw my genius, and he wanted to experience its totality. He was a vessel for my power." Seeing shock in my face, Wheaton says, "Conrad was bisexual. He'd told me in the car. He picked it up in jail."

"And after that, he started helping you?"

Wheaton is painting with almost mechanical speed now. "Conrad procured my subjects, mixed the drug cocktails, worked out what was best to keep them sedated while I worked. The insulin. He carried many burdens for me."

"And he raped the women as a reward."

Wheaton's brush hardly stutters. "I suppose he did. I doubt they were conscious while it happened."

I pray they weren't. "What made you stop? In New York, I mean?"

"Conrad killed someone in an argument. He was sentenced to fifteen years. He told me not to take any more, but I . . . I couldn't stop. I tried to pick up a girl in New York. She sensed something wrong, and she fought. Screamed. I barely escaped the police. *That's* what made me stop. Conrad had told me about prison. I couldn't go there. It would have been like being back in my father's house."

"So you channeled your desires into the Clearing paintings. Didn't you? That's why they became more abstract."

"Yes. And the more I put into them, the more famous Roger got. I wanted the world to see *my* work – *purely* – not through the distorted mirror of Roger's abstracts."

"Is that why you started killing again, fifteen years later?"

463

"No." He gives me a simple, clear gaze. "I was dying. I had to do what good I could, while I could."

"Hoffman was out of prison by then? He helped you?"

"Six months after my diagnosis, he was released to make room for new inmates. I'd already moved to New Orleans. I had a juvenile fantasy of finding my biological father. Or his grave. Something tangible. But I never did. But yes, Conrad helped me begin my work again."

"Why did you *sell* the paintings? Why take the risk? You already had money. Fame. Respect."

"*Roger* had those things." Wheaton's brush pecks the palette, then flies to the canvas. "In his bourgeois way. But when collectors saw my Sleeping Women, they recognized an entirely different level of truth."

"Like Marcel de Becque?"

"He was one."

"Do you know him well?"

"I know he buys my work. Nothing more."

Strangely, I believe him. So what explains the connections between de Becque, Wingate, and Hoffman? Were they all exploiting this tortured artist and his twisted vision?

"What do you intend to do now?"

"I'm going away. To live as myself. Openly. Money's not a problem, and Conrad established new identities for us long ago. Just in case."

"Will you paint?"

"If I feel the need. After this one, I don't suspect I will."

"What do you plan to do with me?"

"I'm going to give you what you most want. I'm going to reunite you with your sister."

My eyes close. "Where is my sister?"

"Very close."

"Driving distance? Walking distance?"

464

Wheaton sniffs. "Closer than that."

John's voice sounds in my head, an echo of the first day I met him. Lakeshore Drive. *The water table has fallen considerably in recent years. He could be burying them under a house, and they would stay buried. And dry. Toss in a little lime every now and then, they wouldn't even stink.*

"Is she buried here? Under this house?"

There's not even a hitch in Wheaton's brush stroke as he nods. It's almost more than I can bear.

"The other women too?"

"Yes. Your sister was a bit different from the rest. She tried to escape. I'm not sure how she managed it, but she made it out to the garden. Conrad caught her, but she fought, and he had to end it there. He buried her immediately. I finished painting her using only a photograph."

For the first time in many hours, anger boils to the surface. Reaching out to the tap, I turn it as I have twice before – only this time I open the cold valve. Wheaton doesn't seem to notice.

As I fight the tortured images called into being by his words, he puts down his brush, massages his hands again, then lifts a watch from the table behind him and looks at it. With a soft grunt, he turns and walks into the main house. There's a soft clatter followed by the low murmur of a voice. He's making a phone call.

I roll over, get to my knees, lean out, and drag the Igloo cooler up to the tub. Praying the running water will cover the noise, I take several panting breaths, then lift the cooler to the edge of the tub and dump the contents inside.

The icy shock sucks the breath right out of my lungs. Even my thoughts seem to stutter, so cold is the water, but I haven't time to waste. Three bottles of Michelob have fallen into the tub. I put them back into the empty cooler, then slide it back to its place. A droning voice floats through the doorway to my left. I hear the word "ticket" several times. Possibly the word "departure."

God, it's cold. I won't be able to stand much of this. My sluggish brain has already forgotten something critical. My insulin defense. Reaching down between the tub and mirror, I bring up a pack of Pop-Tarts and tear open the foil with stiff fingers. I break the hard pastries into pieces, shove them into my mouth, and chew them just enough to get them down my throat.

Wheaton is still talking. I rip open another foil pack and gobble two more Pop-Tarts.

Footsteps.

"Come to me," I say softly, trying to keep my teeth from chattering. *"Said the spider to the fly."*

When Wheaton reappears, I suddenly realize how strange he looks in his white linen cloth. After two days of painting, I've gotten used to it. But after hearing him talk on the phone like a normal person, it's a shock. He looks like a man who believes he's Jesus. A sixty-year-old Jesus. He stands before the easel, examining the canvas with a critical eye.

The ice water feels like it's draining the life out of me, and the pain is greater than I anticipated. The line between ice and fire quickly vanishes.

"Is the painting done?" I ask.

"What?" Wheaton says in a distant voice. "Oh. Almost. I—"

The ringing telephone cuts him off. He looks confused. It rings again, faint but insistent. With a quick glance at me, he goes back into the house.

I have an almost irresistible compulsion to leap out of the tub. *Turn on the hot water,* says a voice in my head. *A little won't hurt —*

466

This time the footsteps return at a run. Wheaton rushes into the room, his face blotched red again, only this time there's a gun in his hand. A Smith & Wesson featherweight .38. The gun John gave me.

"What's the matter? What happened?"

"They hung up." His voice is a ragged whisper.

"That happens all the time."

"Not here. And it wasn't dead when I got there. They listened for a few seconds before they hung up."

I try to keep my eyes flat as hope blossoms in my chest, "It was probably a kid. Or some pervert."

Wheaton shakes his head. The animal awareness shining in his eyes is a fearsome thing to see: survival instinct honed to a gleaming edge.

"Why are you making explanations?" he asks. "Why do you care?"

"I don't. I just—"

"Shut up!" He turns and looks at his unfinished painting, then back at me. "I have to go."

"Go where? Why?"

"Sometimes I know things. And I never second-guess that feeling. This place isn't safe anymore."

I feel a sudden urge to leap out of the freezing tub, but before I can act, Wheaton says, "I know you can move."

My heart stutters.

"Don't pretend you can't. I ran out of muscle relaxant. I have to get ready to leave. I'm going to walk over there and put some more Valium into your IV. Enough to knock you out for a while, but not enough to kill you."

His face looks sincere, but I know who I'm talking to. "You're lying. You already said you're going to kill me."

"Jordan. I could shoot you right now if I wanted to kill you."

"Maybe we're too close to other houses. Or maybe you can't stand to kill that way. Using insulin gives you the illusion of euthanasia."

A strange smile touches his lips and eyes. "I shot a lot of people in Vietnam. That's not a problem."

He crouches four feet from the tub and looks me in the eye. "Why doesn't Valium work on you, Jordan? Do you have a little *habit*? Is that it?"

"Maybe a little one."

He laughs appreciatively. "You're a sly one, aren't you? A survivor, like me."

"So far."

He stands and goes into the other room, then returns with a syringe. "Stay right where you are. If you try anything, I'll have no choice but to shoot you. Same thing if you pull out the IV."

Wheaton walks out of my field of vision, and though I can't see him, I know what he's doing: leaning in from as far away as possible and injecting the contents of the syringe into my IV bag. Could he be telling the truth about the Valium? Would he really let me live? He hasn't let anyone else. They're all buried somewhere under this house.

My wrist should start burning, but it doesn't. Wheaton reappears on my left side and crouches again, three feet away. He doesn't say anything. He just watches.

"You're shivering," he says at length. "How do you feel?"

"Scared."

"There's nothing to fear. Don't fight it."

"Fight what?"

"The Valium."

"It's not Valium." A wave of nausea rolls through me. "Is it?"

468

"Why do you say that?"

"Because my wrist isn't burning."

He sighs, then smiles with something like compassion. "You're right. Trust a junkie to know her drugs. It's insulin. Soon you won't have a care in the world. No pain at all."

Four feet opposite me, Thalia Laveau looks like exactly what she is: a living corpse. I cannot end my life like that. I only pray that Conrad Hoffman didn't rape her before she went into a coma.

"Sleepy yet?" asks Wheaton, cradling the gun in his left hand.

The sugar that the Pop-Tarts flushed into my blood will give only limited immunity to the insulin, depending on the dose he gave me. If he comes no closer than he is now, I'll pass out before I can do anything to save myself. Unless I pull out the IV. And then he'll shoot me.

"I . . . I am," I say in a slurred voice. "Am. Sleepy."

"That's right," he half-whispers, glancing past me, through the glass wall of the conservatory. He looks as if he expects to see armed men crossing his garden at any moment.

The bathwater doesn't feel as cold as it did before, and for a second I'm thankful. Then I understand: the insulin is affecting my perception. Near panic, I shake myself, then kick my legs up out of the tub, which sends me sliding down into the water. My behind skids between Thalia's thighs, and my head slips beneath the surface.

It takes a supreme act of will to hold my head under the water, but this is the only path to survival. I make a show of fighting to get my head above the water.

A shadow appears above the tub, then coalesces into a definable shape. A head. Shoulders. Wheaton is looking down into the tub. What does he see? A replay of the first woman he ever killed? The waif? With a macabre sense of dislocation, I watch my last moments on earth through his eyes. He wants to pull my head clear of the water; I can feel it. To give me a more humane death.

Starved for oxygen and stunned by the cold, my lungs burn to reach the surface. I can't wait for Wheaton to reach in. With a scream of desperation I explode out of the water, hands extended like claws. His eyes bulge in terror, and he tries to wheel backward, but I have him by the wrists. He roars and tries to fight, but his feet haven't enough purchase on the wet floor to allow him to use his weight against me. With all my weight, I jerk both his hands down into the icy tub.

His eyes go wide with the incomprehension of a child being tortured for reasons it cannot guess, and his feet go out from under him.

Still I hold on.

New faces come alive in his eyes: the abused boy who could read his father's lustful thoughts; the soldier who heard the enemy's bare feet from fifty meters. As I struggle to keep his hands pinned, one of his wrists jerks in my hand, and a muted explosion hammers my ears. Blood swirls through the bathtub. His wrist jerks again, and my ears ring like cymbals.

He's firing the gun under the water.

I don't feel hurt, but sometimes you don't know. Amplified by the tub, the blast alone stuns me, but I don't let go. Bright red blood sprays through the icewater as though from a hose.

Thalia. A hole in her thigh is spurting blood with every beat of her heart. She's still alive enough to die badly. Screaming in rage, I cling to Wheaton's wrists as the gun kicks my freezing hand across the bottom of the tub.

When silence returns, it shocks us both. Wheaton's face is bone white, and his arms have stopped struggling. The icy water has done its work. Before I know what I'm doing, I've let go of his wrists and scrambled out of the tub. The IV stand crashes to the floor beside me, and the catheter pops out of my wrist, sending a warm rush of blood down my hand.

Wheaton straightens slowly, and for a moment I think he's been shot. But he's not holding himself anywhere; he's struggling to remove the soaked gloves from his shaking hands. He looks like a burn victim trying to remove melted clothing. One glove drops to the wet floor, then the other, and then he's holding his hands up before him, fingers splayed and quivering. The fingers are blue. Not a pleasant blue, but the morbid blue-black that signals tissue death. As I stare, Wheaton's mouth forms an O and he roars in agony.

The scream snaps my trance. Backpedaling away from the tub, I turn toward the door of the main house. It seems a short distance away, but when I try to run, my legs go watery. I have to stop, bend, and grip my knees to stay on my feet. Panic balloons in my chest, cutting off my air. Is that the insulin too?

I need sugar. Rather than try to reach my stash by the mirror, I fall backward onto my rump and throw my hand toward the grocery bag. Wheaton plods toward me, his eyes blazing, but he doesn't look like much of a threat. It's like being attacked by a man without hands. Scrabbling in the grocery bag, I rip open a Twinkie and stuff it into my mouth, swallowing the spongy cake almost without chewing.

Wheaton suddenly veers away, back toward the tub. He's looking down into it like a monk ordered to retrieve some relic from a kettle of fire. The gun. He's trying to summon the courage to plunge his dying hands back into the ice.

I rake my fingernails down my left forearm, drawing blood. The pain momentarily sharpens my senses, and in that window of clarity I force myself to my feet.

Wheaton bends over the tub and plunges one arm in up to the elbow. Then he pops erect like a jack-in-the-box, his gun arm trembling, and whirls to face me.

The pistol is rising when I charge him, arms oustretched. The gun bellows as my hands strike center mass, driving him backward over the tub and into the mirror propped against the wall. The mirror snaps five feet from the floor, and the top half crashes over us, bursting into lethal shards as big as china plates.

Wheaton falls across the tub, stunned but still conscious, straining to hold himself above the icy water. As I struggle to get off him, his eyes flash with life and he jams the gun barrel into my throat.

"Don't," I plead, hating myself for begging. *"Please."*

He smiles with odd regret, then pulls the trigger.

There's a hollow click.

Wild-eyed, he jerks back the gun to bludgeon me, but his flexing shoulder slips off the rim of the tub and sends him down into the water. He doesn't even scream. He sucks in a massive gulp of air, and one dark hand flies to his chest as though to massage his heart. Before pity can gain a foothold in mine, I put both hands on his head and shove it beneath the icy surface.

He struggles, but his strength has left him. I want to hold him down, if only to end his torture, but I can't afford to. The sugar in my blood could be metabolized by insulin before I get ten paces from the tub. If it is, I'll leave this place feet first with a tag around my toe.

I raise myself from the tub and stagger to the door behind

472

the easel. The door leads to an oblong room containing a television, a sofa, and a telephone table. Stumbling through it, I find myself in a wide hall that runs forty feet to a great wooden door, much like the one in Jane's house on St. Charles Avenue. I start toward the door, focusing on my balance, but two-thirds of the way there my legs give way and I fall headlong into a white baseboard.

There's a strange fog loose in my head. I want to lie on the soft wood and let it enfold me. But from the midst of the fog rises an image so indelible that my heart begins pounding under the force of it: shallow graves, eleven in a line, low mounds of dirt moldering in the dark beneath a house. *This house.* Beneath my feet wait the remains of eleven women whose husbands and parents and children pray each night to know their fates. My sister waits with them. And there is no question whom she's waiting for. My duty is not yet done.

Struggling to my knees, I crawl the last few yards to the door, then reach up with my right hand and turn the knob.

It doesn't move.

A few still-active brain cells paint the image of a window behind my closed eyes, but I've no hope of reaching one. I can go no farther.

"Please," I hear myself sob, and again the indignity of begging embarrasses me. *"Open."*

The door remains closed. A pathetic end for a decently lived life. Naked. Alone. Lost in a white fog that blows with insidious silence, deadening the sound of my sobs, then the rasp of my breathing. Soon all will be whiteness.

As my ears chase the last hissing echo of my respiration, an inhuman screech splits my fading consciousness like an ax. There's a pounding of drums, then a shattering cacophony like the mirror breaking in the conservatory.

Black insectile figures swarm over me, their metallic voices ringing against my eardrums. One is trying to ask me something, his goggle eyes wide and earnest, but I can't understand him.

A scream of utter desolation cleaves the air, stretching toward infinity. It punches through my heart like a bullet of pure misery, fusing with the grief that has festered there so long. My hands fly up to cover my ears, but the scream smashes into a black wall, leaving only a ringing vibration in the air. The goggle eyes above me go wide, then vanish, and a human face appears in their place.

John Kaiser's face.

He thinks I'm dead. I see it in his eyes. The fog has almost swallowed me. I have to tell him I'm alive. If I don't, he might bury me. Deep in my mind, a spark winks to life. A lone pinpoint of white in a black sky. And from that star comes a voice. Not my father's voice. A woman's voice.

My sister's voice.

Speak, Jordan! Say something, damn you!

Two syllables fall from my lips with eerie clarity, and they trigger a burst of frantic activity. The word I say is "Sugar." Then I slap my wrist. *"Sugar!"* I say again, slapping the bloody IV hole like a monkey on amphetamines. *"Sugar, sugar, sugar . . ."*

A white-clad angel bends over me. "I think she wants us to check her glucose level."

Then the star winks out, and John's face vanishes.

28

"Jordan? Jordan?"

White light spears my retinas, but I endure the pain. I don't want the dark. Anything but that.

"Jordan? Wake up."

A shadow floats over my eyes, shielding them. A hand. After a moment, the hand pulls back and a face leans in.

John's face. It's creased with worry, and his eyes are red with fatigue.

"Do you know me?" he asks.

"Agent Kaiser. Right?"

The worry doesn't leave his face.

"I told you, John, I'm not a china vase."

"Thank God."

"Wheaton?"

John shakes his head. "He ran screaming into the hall when you were down. He had a gun. It was turned around in his hand, like a club. I shouted for SWAT not to fire, but by then someone had. He was killed instantly."

"CK," I whisper.

"What?"

"Clean kill."

"Oh."

Turning my head, I see that I'm lying on a table in what looks like an ER treatment room. There's an IV running into my arm. I have to fight the urge to rip it out.

"Where are we?"

"Charity Hospital. Your blood sugar's back to normal. The doctors say you're dehydrated, but they're fixing that now. Their main worry was your brain."

"That's always been my worry, too."

"Jordan."

"I feel like I have a bad hangover. That's all, really."

"Physically. But what about inside?"

Inside. I pick at the bandage over the wrist where Wheaton's IV was. "A couple of times this past week, I got my hopes up for Jane. But deep down I knew she was gone. But Thalia . . . After Hoffman died in the river, I thought we might find her alive and all right. Waiting for the ax, you know?"

John's eyes are steady but somber. "She was probably in that coma within an hour or two after being taken. Once she evaded surveillance and Hoffman got her, there was nothing we could have done."

I nod. "Where was I?"

"Four blocks from Wheaton's house on Audubon Place. Five blocks from St. Charles Avenue. One block from Tulane."

"Jesus, they had some nerve. What's happening there now?"

He gives me a hard look. "Are you sure you want to know?"

"Yes."

"They've taken two corpses from shallow graves under a crawl space."

"Jane's?"

"No IDs yet. We're in the process of gathering all the victims' families at a hotel. We're going to proceed very slowly on the exhumations. We don't want any mistakes."

"I understand. Wheaton told me the New York victims are buried in a clearing on the family farm in Vermont."

John nods as though not surprised. "We're already working on paperwork up there. That farm is mostly a commercial district now. Big deal to start poking random holes in search of bodies."

"I don't want to stay here tonight."

"The doctors want to keep you."

"I don't care. You're the FBI. Do something about it."

He takes a deep breath, then lays his hand on my arm. "Listen, there's something you're going to want to know."

"What?" I ask, my throat tight with fear.

"We just got a message from Marcel de Becque."

"What?"

"An invitation, really."

"What do you mean?"

"He wants to talk to you. In person."

"De Becque's here? In the U.S.?"

"No. He wants to see you at his house. In the Caymans. He says he'll send his jet if you need it."

"Do I need it?"

"No. There are still serious questions in this case, and only de Becque can answer them now. Baxter says we can take the Bureau jet."

"When?"

"When you're strong enough."

"For a two-hour flight? Tell them to get the plane ready. And go handle the doctors. I don't want to deal with that."

John looks at me like a parent who knows his child will not take no for an answer. Then he squeezes my shoulder, bends, and kisses me on the forehead.

"I guess we're taking a trip."

★

Grand Cayman lies like an emerald on the Caribbean, smooth and flat after the mountains of Cuba. Our pilot lands the Lear at the airport near Georgetown, but this time there's no pair of escorts waiting with a Range Rover. At the FBI Director's request, the governor of the islands has provided state transportation, a black limousine flying the Caymanian flag from its fenders. Our native driver speaks with a crisp British accent, and he loses no time shepherding us to de Becque's colonial estate on North Bay.

The door is answered by Li, who stands with the same self-possession I noticed the first time we were here.

"Mademoiselle," she says with a slight inclination of her head. "Monsieur. This way, please."

This time there will be no body search. John is carrying two service pistols, and the governor knows it. De Becque knows it too, and he's made no objection.

Li leads us to the great hall at the back of the mansion, where the massive window looks out onto the harbor. Just as before, the tanned, silver-haired French expatriate stands framed in the lower corner of his window, staring out to sea like a man with an unquenchable yearning.

"Mademoiselle Glass," Li announces, and then she backs soundlessly down the hall.

De Becque turns and nods with courtly grace. "I'm glad you came, *chérie*. I'm sorry to bring you so far, but alas, my legal situation does not allow me to travel to you." He takes a step toward us, then hesitates. "I have things to tell you that you must know. For my sake, and for yours." He motions us deeper into the room. "*S'il vous plaît* – come in. Please."

John and I walk over to the sofa we sat on less than a week ago and sit side by side. De Becque remains standing. He seems ill at ease, and he paces as he speaks.

"First, the matter of the Sleeping Women. I want to assure you that I never knew the identity of the painter, or of his associate. I did know Christopher Wingate, the art dealer, and it's him that what I have to say concerns. As you know, I bought the first five Sleeping Women he offered for sale. The sixth painting was also promised to me, and I paid a deposit on it. Then Wingate 'stiffed' me, as they say. He sold the painting to Hodai Takagi, a Japanese collector, though he knew I would match any price Takagi paid."

"Why would he do that?" I ask.

"To open new markets," John replies. "Right?"

"Quite so," says de Becque. "It's a business, after all. But this painting had been promised to me, and I was angry. I'm not a man to brood over an injustice. I'm not what the psychiatrists call 'passive' – I'm sorry, what is the term?"

"Passive aggressive?" I suggest.

"*Oui*. I happened to know that Wingate was heavily invested in a development project in the Virgin Islands. I made a few phone calls, and very shortly, Monsieur Wingate discovered he had made a very bad investment. His principal was wiped out. Am I boring you, Agent Kaiser?"

"I'm riveted, actually."

The Frenchman nods, his sea-blue eyes flickering. "Wingate was infuriated by what I had done, and he sought revenge. Now, you should be aware that Wingate had visited my estate here on three previous occasions. I'd entertained him over a period of days. He learned a bit about my life. He sat in this room. He saw many of my things, among them certain photographs." De Becque waves his hand toward the wall where his collection of Vietnam photos hangs. "You have seen these photos. Some, anyway."

He walks over to the wall and takes down two black-and-white photos, then comes back to us, studying the pictures all the way. "These were not hanging here during your last visit. Perhaps you'd like to see them?"

With a strange sense of foreboding, I take the frames from his hand. The first picture is of me, my standard publicity head shot. The second is of Jane, her graduation photo from Ole Miss. My heart begins to pound.

"What are you doing with these?"

At last de Becque sits on the sofa opposite us. "Listen to me, Jordan." Again the soft "J." "Because of the circumstances when we last met, there were certain things I could not tell you. Now things have changed. You should know that I knew your father much better than I led you to believe. I think perhaps you suspected this."

"Yes."

"He was a good friend to me, and I to him. I did what I could for his career, and for his life."

"What did he do for you?"

"He enriched my days. That's a great gift. But what you really want to know is this. Did your father die on the Cambodian border? Today I tell you – he did not."

"Oh, God."

"He was shot there by the Khmer Rouge, yes. But he was found alive later by others. There are many angles in an Asian war. Business, always business. Even with the Communists, until they win. Jonathan Glass was my friend, and when I heard what had happened to him, I exerted considerable effort to learn his fate. Over a period of months, I managed to negotiate an exchange for him, for certain considerations that need not be mentioned here."

"How badly was he hurt?"

"Very seriously. He had a head wound. There had been infection."

John takes my hand and squeezes tightly.

"He was not the same man he had been before the wound," says de Becque.

"Did he know who he was?"

"He knew his name. He remembered certain things. Other things, no. His vision was impaired as well. Photography as a career was over for him. Though I don't think he much cared at that point. His frame of reference had been reduced to fundamental things. Food, shelter, wine—"

"Love?" I cut in. "Is that where this is going? Did he have someone here? Someone like Li?"

De Becque raises his eyebrows in a way that says, *We are all adults here, no?* "There was a woman."

"She was with him before he was shot?"

"Oui."

I take a deep breath, then plunge on to the almost unspeakable question. "Did he have children by her?"

De Becque's eyes tell me he understands my pain. *"Non.* No children."

Relief washes through my soul, but new fear follows. "Did he remember us at all? My mother? My sister?"

The Frenchman holds up his flattened hand and tilts it from side to side. "Sometimes yes, sometimes no. But let me speak plainly. If your anxiety is that Jon simply decided to abandon you, to not go back to America – this should not be a concern. He was in no condition to do such a thing. I had a plantation in Thailand, and he lived out his days there in a simple way. He did simple work, he knew simple joys."

John squeezes my hand again, and I'm grateful for his presence. The emotions pouring through me now are too intense to bear alone. Amazement that my secret hope turned out to be true. Sadness that my father was not himself afterward, that perhaps he did not remember me in any meaningful sense. But deeper than any of these wells a relief that even tears cannot express. My father did not abandon his family. He did not choose others over us. He did not voluntarily stop loving us. Though I do not voice it, a child's simple cry of joy bursts from my heart: *My daddy didn't leave me.*

There is no sight quite like gentlemen in the presence of a lady reduced to tears. John blushes and reaches for a Kleenex he doesn't have, while de Becque, the Old World man, pulls a silk handkerchief from his trouser pocket.

"Take a moment, *ma chérie,*" he says in a soothing voice. "Family matters . . . always difficult."

"Thank you." I wipe my eyes and blow my nose, and neither man seems to mind much. "Tell me the rest, please."

"I anticipate your next question. Your father lived until 1979. Seven years past the wound that probably should have killed him. He was lucky to have those years."

Seven years. My father died during Jane's sophomore year at Ole Miss, the year I became a photographer at the *Times-Picayune.* Before I can think of what to ask next, John speaks.

"Monsieur, your story began with the daughters, not the father. With the photographs. And a point about Christopher Wingate?"

De Becque looks at me. "If you are now composed?"

"Yes. Please go on."

"You understand the situation? Wingate had offended me. Cheated me. I then taught him a lesson about the consequences of breaking promises."

"We understand."

"Wingate was not content to learn this lesson. Perhaps he could not afford the loss he sustained in the Caribbean. In any case, he wished to revenge himself upon me. And he wished certain people to know he had taken that revenge.

482

To this end, he set about trying to hurt me as deeply as possible. This is not so easy as it might sound. I have no family in the ordinary sense. No hostages to fortune. I'm a businessman, a citizen of the world. Not a vulnerable man. So Wingate had to look hard for a weakness."

"I think I know where this is going," John says.

"You wish me to continue?"

"Please," I tell him, giving John a look that tells him not to interrupt again.

"Wingate knew about more than painting. He knew photography. When he was here, he naturally noticed my Vietnam photos. He encouraged me to tell stories. I confess, I am fond of doing so, especially after a few bottles of wine. I know when to keep my mouth shut, but some stories seem harmless enough."

He sighs with regret. "I always kept pictures of you and your sister, for Jonathan's sake. I showed them to him sometimes. I had a newer picture of you because you are famous. Anyway, Wingate knew your story. He knew who your father was, and that I cared about you."

"Cared about us?"

"On one of your father's better days, he asked me to look after you. This was near the end of his life. You were almost grown then, and I didn't know you were in financial difficulty. Had I known . . . well, what are words worth now? After Jonathan's death I learned that you were doing all right but that Jane needed money for university. I made sure she got it."

I shake my head in wonder. "I never knew how she stopped depending on me. I thought she had scholarships or something. Pell grants."

"She did, I'm sure." De Becque smiles. "But she also had help from Uncle Marcel."

"You're telling us Wingate chose Jane Lacour as a victim to hurt you," John says, unable to contain himself. "Right?"

"I believe it happened this way. Wingate never knew Roger Wheaton's identity, but I think he knew where the victims were coming from. I believe he had close ties with an associate of Wheaton's."

"Conrad Hoffman," says John.

"Perhaps," says the Frenchman. "In any case, by this time, I too had surmised that the girls in the paintings were being taken in New Orleans."

"You told us you had no idea—"

"No *proof*," says de Becque. "Merely the conjecture of an old man. But I was interested enough to watch the New Orleans newspapers, and keep an ear to the ground through contacts I have there. I suspected that if another victim were kidnapped there, a new Sleeping Woman might soon come on the market."

"Jane was victim number five," John says in a cold voice. "You suspected all the way back then?"

De Becque suddenly looks very serious. "Do you wish to waste time with another useless philosophical debate? I assure you, a Frenchman likes nothing better."

"No," I cut in. "Just tell us what you know."

"All right. I think it happened this way. Wingate was casting about for a way to revenge himself upon me. One day, as he searched his memory, he remembered the story I'd told him of the famous Jonathan Glass, and of the lovely twin girls I watched from a distance: the world traveler, and the southern belle of St. Charles Avenue."

My mouth falls open.

"A simple matter of mental association. In any case, once he hit upon it, the mechanics were simple. He sent a photograph and an address to Wheaton's associate, made a request, possibly promised a bounty, and the thing was done."

John and I sit in stunned silence.

"So," says de Becque. "Jane Lacour, née Glass, became the only Sleeping Woman chosen by someone other than Wheaton or his associate. At least that is my guess."

"It's a good guess," John says. "Jane Lacour died because she knew you. How did that make you feel? No big deal, I suppose?"

De Becque's lips flatten to a thin line. "You are near to offending me, young man. I do not advise it." A tight smile now. "Because I was watching New Orleans for other disappearances, I learned very quickly of Jane's disappearance. I owed my dead friend. I could not let this thing pass without taking steps."

"What did you do?" I ask.

"I sent an emissary to discuss the matter with Wingate."

"Who did you send?" asks John.

"A retired military man. A friend from my Indochina days. Perhaps you've met the sort of man I mean."

"A persuasive man?"

De Becque gives a single firm nod. "Just so. He made clear to Wingate that the death of Jane Lacour would mean not only the death of Christopher Wingate, but the death of his line. His women, children, parents—"

"Stop," I plead. "I don't think I want to know this."

De Becque makes a gesture of apology. "I merely wished you to be aware that I spared no effort."

"But you didn't do much good, did you?" says John.

De Becque sighs. "Some things, once set in motion, are difficult to stop. Wingate understood the stakes, and he used all his influence to get Wheaton's associate to release Jane. The associate agreed to try."

"He may have tried," I tell them, recalling what Wheaton told me of Jane's death. "Wheaton said Jane tried to escape and almost succeeded. Hoffman only caught her in the yard, and he – he ended it there. Wheaton finished painting Jane from a photograph."

"I know that upset you very much."

John is staring at de Becque with open hostility, but de Becque ignores him. The Frenchman reaches out and takes my hand.

"Prepare yourself, *chérie*. I have news for you."

"What?"

"Your sister lives."

My hand jerks out of his as though of its own accord. *"What?"*

"Jane Glass is alive."

"What the hell is this?" asks John. "You're saying Hoffman didn't kill her?"

"*Oui*. Considering what Jordan just told me, I would guess this Hoffman released Jane, then lied to Wheaton to protect himself."

"If Jane Lacour is alive," says John, "where has she been for the past eighteen months?"

"Thailand." De Becque shrugs. "I still have a plantation there."

"You're lying. Even you wouldn't—"

"Save your indignation," scoffs de Becque. "I found myself in a very difficult position. A woman had been kidnapped. Several women, to be exact. I knew more than I should about those events, in a legal sense. Normally, I would not have interfered. But this woman was special. I had no choice."

"If this is true, you could have solved the case! You could have saved—"

486

"I don't care!" I shout. "I don't care what he did! All I want to know is if he's telling the truth."

De Becque nods. "I am."

"The phone call?" I say softly. "The phone call from Thailand?"

"That was your sister. She was drinking at the time, a bit confused. She had recently learned the truth about your father, and it upset her."

"I want to go to Thailand," I tell him. "Right now."

The Frenchman stands and claps his hands twice. Li appears in the far doorway like a brown-skinned princess conjured from thin air. De Becque nods once, and she vanishes.

"Will you take me?" I ask. "I won't believe she's alive until I see her."

"There are other things you must know first."

"Oh God," I whisper, an image of Thalia Laveau in my mind. "Don't tell me she's brain damaged or—"

"No, no. But she endured a traumatic experience at the hands of this Hoffman. He was a man of peculiar tastes."

Now I understand my precognition of Jane's death in Sarajevo: perhaps she did not physically die; perhaps what I felt was the death of innocence that is every rape, the murder of part of the spirit.

"She has largely recovered now," says de Becque, "but she is fragile in some ways. At first she required much care. Later, quite naturally, she desired to return home. I was unable to allow that. For legal reasons, as I mentioned, but also because I did not wish to stop the painter of the Sleeping Women. I make no apologies to anyone but you, but to you I apologize."

"Please, take me to her!"

"You are on your way, *ma chérie*."

"Jordan," John says in a low voice. "Don't let this guy get your hopes up. He's a—"

John comes out of his chair and stands with his mouth open, as if struck dumb.

In the doorway at the far end of the great room stands a mirror image of the woman he claims he loves. Jane is wearing a white robe like Li's, and the French-Vietnamese woman stands behind her like an attendant. My hands begin to shake, my palms go clammy, and my bladder feels weak. Never in my life have I felt such emotions, and how could I? I have never witnessed a resurrection.

"You son of a bitch," John says softly to de Becque. "How long would you have kept her?"

Jane is walking toward me, her cheeks red, her eyes glittering with tears. Li follows one step behind, as though ready to catch her if she falls. Jane looks more beautiful than she ever did, thinner perhaps, but with a self-awareness in her face and bearing that wasn't there before. De Becque's voice rises in argument with John, but I don't hear their words – only blood pounding in my ears. When Jane is halfway across the room, I find the strength to take a step – and then to run. As I fly to her, a fleeting image passes through my mind: a tall man with a camera walks down a Mississippi road, a little girl on either side of him; one clings tightly to his hand, the other skips ahead, her eyes on the horizon. That man is gone now, but not the little girls.

488

29

It is dusk, and the house on St. Charles Avenue looks just as it did the day Jane walked out of it in her jogging suit, eighteen months ago. But the people inside are different. The lights glow warm and yellow through the windows, hinting to passersby of an idyllic life beyond the wrought-iron rail and polished door, but this is a false impression. A woman once told me that good homes have hearts. This house had a heart once. Now it has a great emptiness.

Jane and I mount the steps together, hand in hand. After much discussion, we agreed it would be better this way. Not to call first. Not to try to explain. Why put Marc or the children through an hour or even a minute of confusion? And why let Marc see her first, when it is undoubtedly the children who miss her most terribly?

Behind us, at the curb, John waits in the car. Not my rented Mustang, but an FBI sedan that let us all be comfortable. I look back at him, then raise my hand to knock on the door, but Jane stops me with a touch on my shoulder.

"What is it?" I ask. "Are you all right?"

She's crying. "I never thought I would stand here again. I can't believe my babies are inside."

"They are." I know this because an FBI agent posted on the street outside notified us when Marc got home. Marc is here, and the children, and Annabelle the maid, too. I take

Jane's hand. "Don't think too much. Enjoy every second of it. You're blessed beyond belief."

I start to say more, but I don't. To remind her that eleven other women won't be going back to their homes would only trigger the survivor's guilt that I know so well. Instead, I hug her to my side and hold her there.

"Here we go."

I knock loudly on the door and wait.

After a moment, footsteps pad up the cavernous hallway and stop before the door. Then the knob turns and the great door opens, revealing Annabelle in her black-and-white uniform.

The old black woman starts to greet me, then freezes, her mouth open. Her hand flies halfway to her mouth, then stops and begins to shake. "Is it . . . ?"

"It's me, Annabelle," Jane says in a quavering voice.

"Lord *Jesus*. Come here, missy."

She pulls Jane into her arms and squeezes tight. "Mr. Lacour don't know anything?"

"No. I thought it would be better if they saw Jordan and me together. Then they would know they could believe it."

Annabelle nods with exaggerated amazement. "I wouldn't believe it myself if I wasn't seeing it right now."

Jane slowly disengages herself. "Where are the children, Annabelle?"

"In the kitchen, waiting for me to fix supper."

"How are they doing?"

The old woman starts to reply, but instead shuts her eyes against tears. "Not good. But everything gonna be all right now. Yes, Lord. What you want me to do?"

"Where's Marc?"

"He's in his study."

"Let's go in the kitchen."

Annabelle takes Jane by the hand and leads her down the hall. The long, wide corridor throws me back to Wheaton's killing house, just blocks away, and I quicken my steps to stay up with them. Jane looks back and hurries me along with her hand, knowing the children need to see us both to understand.

At the kitchen door we pause, and Jane whispers something to Annabelle. The maid nods and goes in ahead of us. Henry's high-pitched voice asks her who was at the door, and Annabelle answers in a voice laced with excitement.

"You chil'ren close you eyes now."

"Why?" they ask in unison.

"Your Aunt Jordan brought you a special present."

"Aunt Jordan's here?" asks Lyn, the hope in her voice breaking my heart.

"You shut your eyes!" says Annabelle. "You never gonna get a present like this again in your whole life. Neither one of you."

"They're shut!" cry the little voices. "Aunt Jordan?"

As Jane takes my hand, I feel hers quivering. I look into her eyes, she nods, and we step through the door.

Henry and Lyn are standing side by side, facing the doorway, their hands pressed hard over their eyes.

"Aunt Jordan?" asks Lyn, parting her fingers in an attempt to see.

"You can look now," I tell them.

When the hands slip down, the children's mouths drop, and their eyes flick back and forth between Jane and me. Then their eyes flash with a light I haven't seen in twenty years of traveling the world. The light of those who witness a resurrection.

"*Mama?*" Lyn asks in a hollow voice, her eyes on Jane.

Jane falls to her knees and holds out her arms, and Henry

and Lyn rush to her breast. She enfolds them in a shuddering embrace, and in seconds her eyes are pouring tears. When the children find their voices, they begin jabbering questions, but Jane can only cradle their faces in her hands and shake her head.

"What's going on?" comes a deep voice from the hall. "Annabelle? What's all the racket—"

Marc Lacour, wearing a pretentious seersucker suit, looks from me to the back of the woman holding his children, his face clouded with confusion. He can't see Jane's face, but something about her shape and manner has told him much already. She embraces the children once again, then stands and turns to face him.

Marc takes one step backward, unwilling to trust his eyes.

"It's me," Jane says. "I'm home."

Marc steps tentatively forward, then jerks her into his arms and hugs her tight enough to break her back.

"My God," he whispers. "My *God,* it's a miracle."

"It is," Jane says, reaching backward with one hand.

I clasp that hand and squeeze it, and then I slip around them and through the kitchen door.

"Where are you going?" Jane asks.

I nod at the door. "I need to talk to someone."

She reaches out again. When I take her hand, she silently mouths two words.

Thank you.

She lets my hand slip free, and then I'm walking down the long hall alone. For eighteen months Jane has lived in suspended animation, imprisoned by a man who saved her life, a desolate bird in a gilded cage. All that time, I trudged alone through a dark tunnel, burdened by guilt, haunted by loss, feeling hope die. A metaphor for my life, really: a lone woman lost in a tunnel with a camera, bearing witness to

492

what happens in the dark, even as the darkness seeps into her. But today . . .

Today I emerge into the light.

John is leaning against the passenger door of the FBI sedan, watching me for clues to what happened. I walk down the steps, take both his hands in mine, and kiss him lightly on the lips.

"Are we going in?" he asks.

"No. They need time alone."

"Where are we going?"

"We need time alone, too."

He takes me in his arms and squeezes me tight.

"It's time to start living again, John."

"That it is," he says, reaching back to open the door. "That it is."